I0594104

ALL OR NONE

CLIVE FLEURY

coffeetownpress

KENMORE, WA

coffeetownpress

A Coffeetown Press book published by Epicenter Press

Epicenter Press
6524 NE 181st St.
Suite 2
Kenmore, WA 98028

For more information go to:
www.Camelpress.com
www.Coffeetownpress.com
www.Epicenterpress.com
www.clivefleurywriter.com

Cover design by Scott Book
Design by Melissa Vail Coffman

All or None
Copyright © 2025 by Clive Fleury

Library of Congress Control Number: 2025938056

ISBN: 978-1-68492-266-6 (Trade Paper)
ISBN: 978-1-68492-267-3 (eBook)

I want to thank my wife, Rose, for all her support, which has helped me develop my ideas and kept me sane.

ACKNOWLEDGMENTS

THANKS TO EVERYONE ON THE COFFEETOWN PRESS publishing team. A special shoutout to Jennifer McCord for championing the Detective Ryan Mystery series and providing invaluable insights into this latest book, All or None, and to Edwina Searle for her brilliant editing help.

ONE

WINTER

There were eleven of them squashed into the red Ford Transit van. All were in high spirits—except, that was, for the driver, Tommy Clarke. He wasn't happy.

Tommy had thought long and hard about offering his services locally as a driver and wouldn't have if it hadn't been for Anne, his wife. She had heard that people were looking for transport into the city for a protest march and saw it as the perfect opportunity for them to earn some money—even though it was scheduled for Saturday, which would mean Tommy missing the big match: the Swans versus the Eagles.

He had tried to argue, but it was a waste of time. Anne Clarke was an unstoppable force of nature and opposing her was an exercise in futility. Still, it was that same determination and persistence that had attracted him in the first place—that and a body that could stop traffic.

Before meeting his wife, Tommy had drifted like a ship without an anchor. But Anne had plans—lots of them—and the principal one was to buy a house. Of course, properties cost money, and Tommy had no idea where they would get that. Luckily, Anne did.

She stuck a big whiteboard up in the kitchen, taping it to the wall. Using a black marker, she split the board vertically into three columns: incomings, outgoings, and savings. Then, she crossed the lines with dates. Every week, she filled the boxes with numbers—money they earned, spent, and saved together. The savings column had gotten larger and larger, but they still needed every cent they could get, which was why Saturday's driving job had to go ahead.

Tommy picked the passengers up outside Absolute Muffin, Church Point's only bakery. He stashed their banners and signs in the back of the Transit and then set off to Sydney Town Hall, where they would join the others for the Future Is in Your Hands march. After they returned, Tommy would drive them back. He would get three hundred dollars cash for the job.

It was the first demonstration Tommy had attended. He thought protests and marches were a waste of time and was surprised at the eclectic mix of people he had picked up for the protest. There was old Mrs. Deans, who was almost eighty and could hardly walk; a farming family, the Morinas—father Antonio, mother Lucia, and their eight-year-old son, Sasha; Claire Nichol, who owned the local ladies' fashion boutique, and her husband Noel, a teacher; a couple of hippies whom Tommy had never met before; and the Coopers, newlyweds who were older than Tommy and Anne but had gotten married at almost the same time and in the same church. Theresa Cooper worked as a dental hygienist and was bubbly and outgoing. Irwin was more intense, an academic who worked as a chemistry lecturer at the local college.

"So, what's this all about?" Tommy had asked Theresa Cooper after they'd set off.

"It's about justice and fair play," Irwin Cooper said before his wife could answer. "Unless we do something now, The Man will destroy the world. And by The Man, I mean those blood-sucking vampire developers and money-grubbing capitalists who'll do anything and everything to line their own pockets."

Tommy nodded, regretting that he had started the conversation.

"This protest is all about drawing a line in the sand," Irwin added.

"What Irwin is trying to say is that this march is about protecting the environment and making sure that our views are taken as seriously as the developers," Theresa clarified.

"Exactly," Irwin said. He pointed behind him. "Take the Morinas back there. They used to own a small farm in Spain before they emigrated to Australia. They bought a plot of land here and began farming. Now, they have a son and what could be a thriving business. They're well on their way, but some property group has bought everything around them. They want to buy out the Morinas, too, and build a hotel and golf course, but the family doesn't want to sell."

"They shouldn't, then." Tommy gripped the wheel tight as the Transit hit a pothole and bounced up and down.

"The problem is, if they don't, those people will make their life hell," Theresa said. "They've already made threats. And they've bought their way into the local council."

"Yep, see, it's all about fighting The Man," Irwin added.

"Oh, right," Tommy said, switching on the wipers as rain started to fall.

Theresa held her husband's hand. "Irwin, we should let Tommy concentrate on driving, don't you think?"

And that was the end of that conversation.

ARRIVING IN SYDNEY'S CITY CENTER, TOMMY parked. "Come back here when you're finished," he instructed the passengers before they disembarked to join the other protestors.

After everyone left, the reluctant driver ate the chicken and avocado sandwich his wife had made, lay across the back seat, and closed his eyes for a nap.

When he awoke, the march was ending. The crowd was dispersing, and people were heading home.

Tommy picked up his camera. Anne had reminded him to take a picture, which she would use to advertise the Transit van's services. He attached it to a tripod and then joined the passengers lined up along the side of the truck for a group photo.

After that, Tommy set off at high speed, ignoring the rain that was now hurtling down. He was desperate to get back to see the end of the match, so it was only twenty minutes later that the van reached the top of Clifton Hill and began its descent.

The van picked up too much speed; Tommy tried to brake as the vehicle skidded on the wet, greasy bitumen. Passengers' screams rent the air as the Transit spun around and out of control. It finally left the road, gliding across silky grass before plunging over the cliff into the angry, foaming ocean waters below.

TWO

20 YEARS LATER—FALL

THE SOUND OF A VEHICLE SKIDDING to a halt brought Detective Ramesh Ryan to his apartment window. Peering out, he saw a silver SUV and a small sedan facing each other like two boxers readying to rumble. The four-by-four was the skidder. It had sped around the corner and braked as the road narrowed to one lane, desperately trying to avoid crashing into the little silver Kia Soul. Now, both vehicles sat nose-to-nose, neither moving.

This happened regularly, no matter that there were slow-down warning signs on both roads. Of course, the problem could easily be fixed. The council needed to make the street one-way, but that required making a decision, something bureaucrats were never very good at.

The Kia began to reverse slowly, pulling in close to the sidewalk. The big Jeep advanced, revving hard as it brushed past the smaller car. From his vantage point on the third floor, Detective Ryan couldn't see inside the SUV but knew that by about now, the driver would be giving a cheery wave to the other motorist while mouthing a string of abuse that could have made a Marine blush.

Turning away, the detective moved to the kitchen countertop. Grabbing the handle of the coffee press, he poured the brew into a mug. The dark brown fluid lightened as it mixed with the milk at the bottom of the cup. Ryan took a sip. It was his first coffee, and he felt the hit immediately.

Detective Ryan had long ago accepted that he was a coffee addict, but an addict who cared what he drank. He ground his beans, choosing Ethiopian when available, and had recently weaned himself off sugar to enjoy the coffee taste even more. Unfortunately, he still needed to add milk, though today, for a change, he had put this into the cup first. It was a bold move that proved to be a mistake. Too much milk had diluted the coffee.

The detective went into the living room and was about to sit down when there was a knock at the door. He placed the mug on the side table next to a small, rectangular, candy-striped wrapped package and then moved to look through the peephole, which gave him a narrow view of the corridor outside. Letting out a small sigh, he opened the door.

"Detective Ryan . . . Good. You're in. Do you have a minute?" The question came from a middle-aged woman with a plump face and spiky, dyed orange hair. She wore Coke-bottle glasses and a floral maxi dress.

"Morning, Maude," Ryan said. "You're up early."

Maude Adams stiffened. "Is that a criticism?" she said.

"No. It was just an observation," Ryan backpedaled.

Maude stared at him and then smiled. "Well, if you say so. We must trust our policemen are telling us the truth, right?"

Ryan forced himself to smile back. He liked to spend the few minutes before leaving for work drinking his coffee slowly and contemplating the world. Instead, this morning, his routine had been interrupted, first by those cars outside his window and now by the arrival of his neighbor and her notoriously prickly personality.

"How can I help you, Maude?"

"Help?"

"I assume you need something?" Detective Ryan said.

"Well, yes, in a way. It's regarding something we all could do without." Maude paused for effect. "Rats," she finally hissed.

The force of her utterance took Ryan by surprise. "What?"

"Haven't you noticed, Detective Ryan? We have an infestation of vermin around the garbage bins at the back of the property. I've only just seen one of the foul creatures scuttling around out there." The woman shuddered. "It scared the living daylights out of me."

"Rats? Really?" Ryan sounded surprised. "Have to say I hadn't noticed."

Maude sniffed. "And you call yourself a detective."

"I've been a bit busy recently," Detective Ryan said, barely managing to hide the weary tone in his voice.

"Well, I want you to clear your calendar for tomorrow night. And before you say it, I know it's short notice, but rats wait for no man." Maude chuckled. "See how I did that. Changing the word 'time' for 'rats'?"

The detective looked at her blankly. Maude barreled on.

"As you know, I am president of the strata and have called tomorrow's emergency meeting to deal with the rodent problem."

"But . . ." Ryan stopped. He was desperate to make an excuse, but having recently bought the apartment, he also knew that strata meetings were part of the deal, and he was not a man to shirk responsibility.

"Yes, of course," the detective said. "Where is the meeting?"

In my unit. Eight o'clock." Maude paused. "So, I can count on you being there?"

"I will do my best."

"I'll mark you down as a definite then, Detective Ryan," Maude said, ignoring his answer. "I will see you tomorrow evening."

The detective slowly closed the door. Picking up his coffee, he sat back on the sofa and took a long gulp before pulling his cell from his suit pocket. Pressing the keypad, he waited. The call went through to voicemail. "If you need me, please leave a message." The woman's voice was low and breathy, with just a hint of an Indian accent.

"Happy birthday, Mom. Have a great day. I'll be around to give you your present this evening. Love you." Ryan ended the call.

After taking another slug of coffee, the detective clipped down the leather holster flap over his Glock 40 and buttoned up his suit jacket. Then he grabbed the wrapped birthday present, slipped it into his briefcase, and headed for the door.

RYAN HURRIED DOWN THE SMALL ART deco block's narrow, winding stone stairs and crossed the courtyard to the main gates. Exiting to the street, he hurried across to his parked car. The large silver Hyundai Sonata allocated to him with his new position in the Homicide Squad was a step up from the small Ford Focus he previously drove.

Detective Ryan pressed the fob, opened the door, and got in, putting the briefcase on the passenger seat. Strangely, his mom still hadn't rung back. He had expected her to call, unsolicited, at daybreak, on the pretext that she wanted to wish him luck on the first day of his new job. He would, of course, have teased her by waiting as long as he could to wish her a happy birthday—the real reason for her call. It was a game they'd played many times before.

Before setting off, Ryan tried calling her once more but was again put through to voicemail. He didn't leave a second message but instead pressed a different number into the keypad.

"Hello," a woman said after a few moments.

"Hi, Agnes," Ryan said. Agnes Gray, his mom's Irish cleaner. It had taken Ramesh an age to persuade his mother to get someone in to help with the cleaning, but she'd finally agreed. This, being a Monday, was Agnes's cleaning day.

"Is that you, Mr. Ryan?" the woman said in her broad Irish brogue.

"Yes. Is Mom there?"

"Don't you think Mumta should chuck out this antiquated piece of junk? Who uses a landline now anyway?" Agnes said, ignoring the detective's question.

Ryan frowned. From his few conversations with the cleaner, he knew Agnes had a habit of talking in non sequiturs, but even for her, this was an odd way to steer the conversation.

"Well, when your mother isn't answering her cell, I'd say a landline is a handy backup," Ryan suggested.

There was a sucking intake of breath on the other end of the line. "You may have a point there, Mr. Ryan . . . an excellent point. Maybe I should rethink my stand on landlines."

"Maybe, yes. So, can you get my mother, please?"

Silence.

"Agnes . . ."

"I know. I heard you." There was a long pause. "It's your mom's birthday, you know."

"Yes, that's why I'm calling—to wish her a happy birthday." Ryan waited, but Agnes was silent. "Agnes, could you get her for me, please?"

"I could do that, I suppose." She paused. "Normally, that is."

"Normally?" Ryan repeated.

Silence.

"Agnes, you still there?" the detective asked, becoming irritated.

"The problem is, she told me not to tell you," the cleaner said after a moment.

This was like getting blood from a stone. "Tell me what?" Ryan asked.

"Okay, I'm just going to come out and say it, and damn the consequences, if you'll excuse my French. . ... Your mom's at the hospital."

"She's where?" Ryan asked.

"Now, no need to worry, Mr. Ryan. She's at the hospital having a small procedure. At least that's what she told me. But she didn't want to tell you because she doesn't want you to worry."

"It's a bit late for that, Agnes," Ryan said, concerned. "What kind of small procedure?"

"It's a woman's problem. . ... That's it. A woman's problem. But she said it was nothing to worry about and that she'll be out and about by the end of the morning right as rain."

Ryan jabbed the push-button ignition and started the engine. He knew his mother was stoic to a fault and might have given the same prediction had she gone in for an amputation. "Which hospital, Agnes?"

"St. Vincent's on Darlinghurst Road."

"Thanks."

Ryan hung up, pressed the cell screen again, and waited. A woman answered. "Yes," she said.

"Hi. This is Detective Ryan. Please message homicide that I have been delayed and will be in later."

"Will do, Detective Ryan," the woman said.

Ryan put down the cell and jammed his foot hard on the accelerator pedal.

THREE

DETECTIVE RYAN SPED DOWN MANNING STREET before pulling up at the junction to Macleay Street, the main thoroughfare that dissected the suburb of Potts Point.Ramesh was not a man given to panic, nor was his mother a hypochondriac. If she was in hospital having tests, there would have been a good reason; this was precisely why he was worried. Mumta Ryan avoided doctors like the plague. The detective's mind started to race. What if she had been ignoring symptoms? What if she had left things too late?

Ryan's car accelerated, turning right and heading north. He drove past the El Alamein Fountain and the police station, praying that some overzealous cop wouldn't pull him over for speeding. Continuing, he braked at the light next to the giant illuminated Coca-Cola sign—a well-known landmark.

After a few moments, the signal changed, and Ryan's Hyundai shot across the highway onto Darlinghurst Road. Like Potts Point, Darlinghurst, once a haven for the down and out, had become gentrified and was now crisscrossed with coffee shops, restaurants, and upmarket bars. St. Vincent's was less than a quarter of a mile away, and the detective could make out the hospital's tall gray roof that jutted out above the smaller two- and three-story Victorian properties.

Detective Ryan was a history buff and had researched the Darlinghurst area, so he knew a little about St. Vincent's. The facility was started over a hundred and fifty years ago by the Sisters of Charity as a free hospital for all, but especially for the poor. The founding nurses had come from Ireland, with a number having been trained in France, and they brought their knowledge to the new colony. Since then, it had been massively expanded and was now one of the city's principal medical facilities.

"Shit," Ryan shouted and slammed his foot down on the brake. A skinny, disheveled, toothless man, his hair wrapped in a dirty red and yellow bandana, had just stepped out in front of the Hyundai.

The man peered at the detective and raised his finger in the sign of the bird. "Fuck you, mate, watch where you're going," the man spat before continuing across the street.

Ryan shook his head. People like him were everywhere in Darlinghurst. Mentally ill, drunk, or drugged out of their minds—take your pick. Darlinghurst may have had a makeover, but some things would never change. They were part of the scene and a constant traffic hazard.

The detective drove off and looked for somewhere to park. Being a cop, he could have driven straight onto the hospital grounds, but his car was unmarked, and he had no sign to put out to announce who he was.

Ahead, the detective saw a white Audi drive out of a space. He pulled in quickly and jumped out of his vehicle. Hurrying through the gates and passing the parked ambulances, the cop reached the glass-fronted main entrance and hesitated. He hated hospitals. As a kid, Ryan had spent almost a year in London's Middlesex Hospital, where medics fought to keep him alive by pumping him full of drugs and antibiotics, killing off the tuberculosis that was racking his body. Since then, there had been no sign of a reoccurrence of the disease, but the events had scarred him for life.

The doors slid open. Detective Ryan took a deep breath and stepped inside. The building was a monument to seventies architecture—high ceilings and an overabundance of concrete and glass. A bank of elevators stood to the right. A long reception desk ran along the other side. He headed over.

"Good morning," said the receptionist. "How can I help you?"

"This is going to seem like a strange question. I'm looking for my mother, but I have no idea where she would be," Ryan said.

"What's your mother's name?" the receptionist began as the detective felt a tap on his shoulder. "Your mom's over there," he heard a voice say.

Ryan turned to face a gray-bearded man. He was pointing toward the café, where a familiar figure could be seen frantically waving.

"I'm Harry King," the man said as they set off to meet the detective's mother. "And you must be Mumta's son, Ramesh."

"Yes," Ryan agreed, looking a little confused. He had no idea who this man was to his mother. He'd never seen him before.

"Mom, are you all right?" the detective said as they arrived.

Mumta Ryan looked up at her anxious son. "All right? Of course, I'm all right. But what are you doing here?"

"You weren't answering your phone. Agnes told me where you were."

Mumta sighed and signaled at an empty chair. "Take a seat, Ramesh."

As the detective sat down, Harry lightly touched Mumta's shoulder.

"I think I had best be going. It was lovely meeting you." As he said it, he reached into his pocket and pulled out a card, handing it to her. "This is my number. Perhaps I could take you out to dinner sometime?"

Mumta hesitated before accepting the card. Glancing down, she read the inscription out loud.

"Chief executive officer. That's impressive."

"It's only a small construction company," Harry said in an attempt at modesty.

"Still impressive. Size has never been important to me, Harry," Mumta said, trying to disguise a smile.

Ryan rocked back in his chair. His mother was flirting with the man and using double entendres. If Harry had picked up on it, he wasn't giving anything away.

"As I said, it was lovely meeting you, and hopefully, we can make dinner work."

"I'll let you know," Mumta replied, smiling.

"Right. . . Nice to meet you too, Ramesh," Harry said before leaving.

The pair watched him go.

"Mom . . ." Ryan began as Mumta turned back.

"Before you ask, Harry King's a lovely man I just met here. His moon boot was taken off this morning."

"Moon boot?"

"Those big plastic things they stick on people's legs when they fall. It happens constantly . . . falling, that is . . . and then you have to have one of those things strapped on for a few months."

"Oh," said Detective Ryan. "Mom, what are you doing here?"

"Didn't Agnes tell you?"

"She said something about a woman's problem. But why didn't *you* tell me you were coming here today? You knew I'd be calling . . .. Oh, and happy birthday, by the way." He frowned. "Damn."

"What's wrong?"

"I left your present in the car."

Mumta smiled. "That's nice. I appreciate presents. When you get to my age, you are grateful for anything."

"Your age. You're fifty-nine. Sorry, sixty today, and hardly . . ." Detective Ryan began.

"Shh." Mumta put her finger to her lips. "Don't go around telling everyone my age."

"Oh . . . okay." Ramesh peered at his mother. Her black hair framed an attractive, symmetrical face and bright, shining brown eyes. "You know you look good for your age."

"Must you, Ramesh. I'm not too fond of that expression. It makes me feel like a horse about to be put down."

Ryan shook his head. This always happened with his mother. She had a habit of taking the conversation completely off-base. It was time to return to the slopes.

"So, Mom, my question was, what are you doing here?"

Mumta leaned forward and whispered. "I came for a biopsy on my br—" She hesitated. "I don't like talking about this with you. That's why I never mentioned it."

"Your breast? You just had a breast biopsy?" The detective's face registered his concern.

Mumta picked up a cup from the table and sipped tea. "Yes. But it's nothing to worry about. I'll get my results in a few days, and I'm sure everything will be fine."

Ryan studied his mother. He was trained to spot deceit, and what his mom had just said was a blatant lie. She *was* worried. If she was concerned, so too should he be.

"What exactly did they say?" Ryan asked.

"If you had become what I wanted you to become, a doctor, you would know." Mumta waved her hands around. "They're all here."

"Who?" asked Ryan, confused.

"Doctors, of course. And you could have been one of them if you hadn't decided to become a policeman." Mumta spat the word out like a piece of dirt from her mouth.

Ryan began to say something, but his mother raised her hand. "I know you love your job," she said. "And apparently, you are very good at it, and it's why you got this new position. Head of the New South Wales Homicide Squad."

"I'm a detective in the New South Wales Homicide Squad, Mom, not *head* of anything."

"Well, you will be soon. But being a doctor is a better career, Ramesh. And there are lots of Indian doctors here." She pointed at a man entering an elevator. "See, there's one there."

"Mom, I've told you a thousand times. I'm not Indian. You know I've only been to India once, and that was years ago and only for a few weeks. I'm Australian."

"Well, *I'm* Indian," Mumta said, sounding a little hurt.

"I know that," Ryan pleaded. "This isn't Delhi. If you'd wanted an Indian son, maybe you should have agreed to that arranged marriage like your parents wanted you to instead of marrying a Brit and coming here. Like it or not, Mom, this is my home. And it's your home now, as well."

Mumta screwed up her face as Ryan put his hand on her arm. "Let's not fight about this. It's your birthday, after all," he said gently. "Now tell me why they asked you to come in for a biopsy."

"Well," she proceeded slowly. "I had my regular mammogram . . . .." Mumta stopped as he saw her son's expression. "I didn't tell you about that, but why would I? I have one every year."

"And . . .?" the detective pressed.

"Well, this time, they found a lump." She took in his look of dismay. "A small one . . . nothing serious, I'm sure. Nothing that they won't find an innocent explanation for." She watched her son as he let her words sink in. It broke her heart to see him so worried. She stood up. "Anyway, enough about me. Shouldn't you be at work, Ramesh?"

The detective glanced at his watch. He was going to be late. "Yes, maybe. But . . ."

"Well, you should love me and leave me," Mumta said, signaling for him to stand.

"I can't just abandon you now," the detective said as he followed his mother across the hospital lobby.

"Abandon me? What am I? Some incapable child?" She stopped and stared at him. "I'm not *that* old. Not yet."

"No, of course not."

"I'll get a taxi, and you must go to work. They'll need you to fight the crime wave that is apparently sweeping Sydney."

"Are you sure, Mom?"

"Of course. I tell you what, why don't you come to see me tonight?" She waited.

Detective Ryan took a deep breath. His mom did seem all right, and he really should get going. "Okay," the detective said, leaning across to kiss her on the cheek. "And happy birthday once more."

"Thank you. Now, off you go.. . . . And don't forget that present, will you?" Mumta shouted as her son headed out.

FOUR

DETECTIVE RYAN CHECKED HIS WATCH AS the elevator juddered to a halt. He was forty minutes late—hardly a glowing endorsement for his first day with the Homicide Squad—but he'd had to see his mother, so consequences be damned.

Ryan knew little about a breast biopsy—Dr. Google, whom he'd consulted quickly after parking the car, said it was a routine procedure carried out to determine whether a lump in the breast was cancerous or not. Apparently, the vast majority of biopsy results came back negative, so Ryan reassured himself there was nothing to be concerned about. He repeated this mantra in his head as, clutching his briefcase tightly, he stepped out of the lift and headed down the corridor.

Reaching the Homicide Squad office, the detective opened the door and entered. There was little reaction to his appearance—just a few nods and grunts as the detective walked to his allocated desk. Wanting to be ahead of the game, he had moved his stuff up from the Organized Crime Department over the weekend. He lowered himself into his seat, but before he could settle, a voice yelled out: "Ryan. Here. Now!"

Detective Ryan turned to see the imposing figure of Detective Superintendent Dan Dudley standing by his office door in the far corner of the room. Six feet four and weighing in at around two hundred pounds with cauliflower ears, a pug nose, squinty eyes, and a large head, Dan Dudley looked more like a prizefighter than a man chosen to run one of the most powerful police units in Australia.

"Hurry up. I haven't got all day," Dudley yelled as the detective hurried to join his boss.

"Come in," Dudley said, waving and lowering his considerable bulk into the chair behind his oak desk.

Detective Ryan went to take a seat and did a double take. A pretty Asian woman in her midtwenties, conservatively dressed in black trousers, jacket, and white shirt, sat opposite the superintendent.

"Ryan, I believe you know Detective Yang," Dudley said.

"Hi, Ryan. Good to see you again," Detective Yang said, swiveling around and smiling.

Ryan was surprised. "Detective?" he queried.

"Yes," the woman said. "For over a year now."

Dudley cut in. "Okay, enough of the pleasantries. First things first. You're late, Ryan."

"Yes, sir. I called in that I would be late. I had to go . . ."

"I don't care," Dudley said, interrupting. "It will not happen again. Understood?"

"Yes, sir."

"Good. Now, you missed my stirring motivational speech this morning, but I'll give you the gist. I explained that, like everyone else in the force, I was shocked by the sudden death of Superintendent Green and that I would do my best to match the excellence of his leadership. I then introduced Detective Yang and gave you a name check . . . even though you weren't there."

"Sir, like I said, I'm sorry . . ." Detective Ryan began.

"Yes, yes . . . we've already been through all that," the superintendent said. "Now, I want you and Detective Yang to work together."

"As a team?" Ryan said doubtfully.

"Yes, of course," Dudley said. "A case has just come in, and I've already given Yang the details."

"A homicide, sir?" Ryan asked.

Dudley stared at him. "This *is* the Homicide Squad, Detective."

"But sir . . ." Ryan started.

Dudley sighed. "I know. You have questions, so here are the answers.

I have assigned Detective Yang to the squad. She will be your subordinate and assist you on this case." He stopped as Detective Ryan frowned. "Is there a problem?"

"Sir, if I could have a word?" Ryan said. "In private," he added, glancing over at Detective Yang.

Superintendent Dudley stood up, strode across the office, and yanked open the door. "Burke, in here, now," he shouted.

Moments later, a rotund, scruffily dressed man in his midforties appeared at the office door—Detective Terry Burke, one of the leading lights in the Homicide Squad.

"Sir?" Detective Burke asked, entering.

"Burke, I want you to meet Detective Ryan," Dudley said. "Due to unforeseen circumstances, he missed this morning's address and introductions."

Detective Burke glanced over at Ryan. "We've already met," he said.

"At the weekend," Ryan concurred. The detective had bumped into Detective Burke when moving his belongings into the Homicide Squad office.

"Really," Dudley said. "That's good. Consider this an *official* introduction."

Detective Burke nodded but didn't move.

"That's all, Detective. You can go," Dudley said.

Burke turned and left.

"What do you think of Detective Burke, then, Ryan?" Dudley asked.

"Think? I haven't had enough time with him to form an opinion, sir."

"Bull poo. Of course you have. And I think I know what you think. But here's the thing. I know what the 'private talk' you want with me is about. I thought I'd short-circuit that conversation and let you meet the alternative."

"Detective Burke?" Ryan asked, though he already knew the answer.

"Yes," the superintendent confirmed. "Do you still want to have that talk?"

"No, sir," Ryan said quickly.

"And I take it you are now happy to partner with Detective Yang?"

"Yes, sir."

"And you with Ryan, Yang?"

"Yes, sir," Detective Yang replied.

"Wonderful. That's all sorted, then. Chop, chop. Off you go." Dudley waved them off.

Rising, the two cops moved to the door.

"And Detectives," Dudley said.

Ryan stopped.

"I want a quick result on this one."

"I'll do my best, sir," Detective Ryan said, opening the door and stepping into the main office. Detective Yang followed.

THE TWO DETECTIVES HEADED DOWN THE corridor to the elevators. Detective Ryan pressed the button.

Silence. Then: "When did you know?" Ryan asked.

"About coming down to Sydney?" Detective Yang asked.

Detective Ryan nodded.

"A few days ago."

"Oh. So, it was sudden?"

"Very sudden," Yang began, "You see . . ."

Ryan waved his hands, brushing her off. "That's okay. I don't want to pry. What I do want to know is what Dudley's told you about the case."

There was a beep as the elevator door slid open.

"We have to go to Ku-ring-gai Chase National Park," Yang began as she entered the empty elevator. "A man's body was found in a holiday rental cabin. I have the location. That's all the information he gave me," she said as the door closed and the elevator descended.

Detective Ryan snorted. "That's Dudley for you. He gives you the bare minimum."

The elevator came to a halt. The door opened, and the detectives entered the underground car park. "You coming with me or taking your car?" Ryan asked.

"I haven't got a pool vehicle yet," Yang said. She looked at Ryan and smiled broadly. "I know this wasn't what you expected, but I want you to know I'm very pleased to be working with you again."

The detective shot her an awkward glance.

"It's still early days. Let's see how you feel by the end of the week," he said grimly before pointing toward his Hyundai. "My car's over there."

FIVE

"So, you've been a detective for over a year?" Ryan said as their car exited the car park and turned into the busy Parramatta High Street. "In Gosford?"

"Yep." She paused. "I'm sorry I couldn't tell you I was coming down."

"And why is that, exactly?"

"Dudley wanted to surprise you." Detective Yang paused. "Were you? Surprised?"

"Yes and no," Ryan said, glancing at the GPS screen. "I always thought you had potential. I hope he hasn't thrown you in the deep end too soon."

Detective Yang's smile was thin-lipped. "Well, thanks for your vote of confidence."

Ryan took a breath. He liked Zoe and didn't want to undermine her confidence. The pair had worked together two years earlier when Zoe Yang was a senior constable in Barton. The pleasant Central Coast town had been relatively crime-free, but soon after Ryan was dispatched there, it became a criminal hotspot. Despite initial reservations, however, Detective Ryan grew to like the place and the people he worked with . . . including Zoe Yang.

After he'd wrapped up the case of a missing boy and returned to Sydney, he hadn't kept in touch—that wasn't in his nature. Ryan had gotten a few emails from Zoe enquiring how he was getting on, but he had kept his replies short and to the point. Soon, the missives stopped coming.

"Superintendent Dudley fought like hell to get me down here and into the squad. It's a fantastic honor. I mean, a detective being transferred into the Sydney Homicide Squad . . . the cream of the crop, and . . ."

"So, why did Dudley do it?" Ryan interrupted, letting his irritation show.

Zoe Yang glanced at him. "The superintendent thought that the old guard in homicide, cops like Terry Burke, would resent working with you."

"Really? And why would he think that?" Detective Ryan asked.

Zoe paused, deciding whether to proceed.

"Well, apparently, you're considered a bit of a prima donna." She watched him for his reaction. It was subtle, but Detective Yang noted the slight stiffening of his posture.

"Is that right?" Ryan replied.

"You didn't know?"

He did, but he wanted to hear what Zoe had to say. Did she also think he was a prima donna?

"Any other reason they wouldn't like me?" Detective Ryan asked.

Zoe took a deep breath before heading into unchartered territory.

"Well, look at you. Look what you're wearing. You dress like you're on a fashion shoot." Detective Yang reached across to touch his lapel. "Boss? Tailored wool, right?"

Ryan nodded. "Very good."

"Old school detectives like Burke prefer polyester jackets and matching trousers. The kind of stuff that makes them look like refugees from the nineties." Zoe paused. "Then there's your liking for gourmet food and fine dining."

"When I can afford it," Ryan qualified.

"Of course. But it's not something they'd ever want to splash their cash on. They think you're . . ." Zoe hesitated, searching for a word that wasn't too insulting. "Well, they think you're odd."

Ryan snorted. "Thank you for that, Detective."

"Sorry, but I know you prefer people to be honest." She paused. "However, you are a brilliant detective, and that's why the superintendent desperately needed you to join him in homicide."

"He told you that?"

"Not as such . . . .. But it's obvious. Those prancing ponies aren't bringing home the bacon, if you'll excuse the mixed metaphors. But you can." Zoe stopped. "I mean, *we* can. Together."

"And you don't mind that I'm a prima donna?" Detective Ryan asked.

"It's not the way *I* think of you. And anyway, do you really care?" She paused. "Look, you've got to have a partner. That's the department's rules. And Dudley knew you would tolerate me." Zoe Yang stared at him. "That's right, isn't it, Ryan? You will tolerate me, won't you?"

Silence. Then: "We'll see."

"Thanks," Yang said wryly. "Not exactly a ringing endorsement."

"I'm just being truthful, Zoe." He stopped. "You do know how difficult it will be for you here?"

"Because I'm a woman?" Detective Yang asked.

"Yeah, there's that. You'll be the first one in the Homicide Squad ever. It's always been a boys' club. But that's not all," Ryan said and hesitated.

"What?" Yang said.

"You and I . . . we're both . . . different."

For a moment, Yang looked confused. Then she realized what he was saying.

"Culturally, you mean? Because my father is Chinese? It's the twenty-first century!" Yang said incredulously.

"Not in the Homicide Squad," Detective Ryan said. "There, it's still the nineteen seventies."

Zoe stared at him, slightly stunned, as his words sank in. She turned her gaze to the road ahead and wondered just what she had let herself in for.

THE MAN WATCHED IT UNFOLD *while stretched out in the park's dense undergrowth. It started when the ranger arrived. She jumped out of her car, strode up the steps, checked the open lockbox, and, finding nothing, rapped hard on the hut's wooden door. There was no reply.*

After waiting a few more moments, the woman turned the handle and tentatively pushed open the door.

"Hello?" she shouted. Nothing. She entered the hut. Moments later, he heard her piercing screams.

The ranger ran out, almost tripping down the stairs. Running back to her SUV, she locked herself in the vehicle.

Then the cops arrived. The fat one was first, his marked car skidding to a halt beside the ranger's car. He had a swagger about him, that one. A small-town cop who thought he had seen it all. But he knew nothing.

The cop spoke to the ranger before hurrying up the stairs and into the hut. There were no screams this time, but when the policeman came out, the color had drained from his chubby face.

The man lay back, relaxing for a few minutes, listening to the rustle of the leaves, the creaking of the branches, the birds singing, the insects humming—the forest sounds he knew so well. Then, he returned to watching the scene below.

The fat policeman was unfurling blue and white tape, marking off the crime scene as the others arrived . . . another police car with two young, uniformed cops, then a Ford SUV and two white vans. The trucks had the words Crime Scene Services stenciled in large black letters across their sides.

Next came a rusty Holden sedan. It parked across from the crime scene vehicles, and the medical officer got out. He began suiting up while two forensic assistants, already in protective clothing—blue coveralls, gloves, and masks—unloaded equipment from the open back doors of the CSS trucks. Two other assistants, wearing blue coveralls and carrying steel boxes, climbed up the stairs and entered the hut.

But the man hadn't been waiting for any of these arrivals. They were the monkeys. He wanted to see the organ grinders . . . the ones in charge . . . and it looked like they were arriving.

SIX

RYAN PARKED HIS HYUNDAI SEDAN BESIDE the blue and white plastic crime scene tape that ran across and around the trunk of a large eucalyptus tree. It formed a barrier in front of a green BMW sedan and a small hut perched on stilts a short distance from the river.

The detective felt the usual adrenaline rush on arriving at a new crime scene. Seventeen years on the force, and he still wasn't jaded. It was the only thing he had ever wanted to do. As a boy, Ryan had spent hours alone in his room reading novels about the fictional detective greats—Sherlock Holmes, Inspector Poirot, and Miss Marple—as well as researching true-life sleuthing heroes like Joseph Kenna, a US detective lieutenant who had investigated 387 homicide cases over his twenty-three-year career.

That skinny, shy child had grown into a tall, good-looking man. Helped by a photographic memory and with skills developed to hunt out clues, Ryan had risen through the police ranks to become an admired detective. But despite his success, some things remained the same. Detective Ryan was still a loner and awkward socially. Yet, he knew being a detective was the best job in the world, and today, embarking on a new case was exactly what he needed to stop him worrying about his mother's health.

The two detectives exited the Hyundai and walked to the back of the vehicle. Ryan popped the trunk. The cops' briefcases were inside. From them, the detectives pulled out blue boot covers and white latex protective gloves and put them on.

"Who are *you*?" a voice demanded from behind them.

Detective Ryan turned to face a heavy set, uniformed cop with reddened, pockmarked skin and cropped brown hair.

"Well?" the cop asked.

Detective Ryan flashed his ID. The policeman peered at it. "Homicide?" Ryan nodded.

"Hers too," the policeman said, indicating Detective Yang. Ryan saw a flash of anger in his partner's eyes as she took out her ID. The cop studied it for longer than was necessary. "Okay," he said finally.

"Your turn," Ryan said, putting away his wallet. "What's *your* name?"

"Sergeant Roger Baldwin." The cop looked the detectives up and down. "So, you're working on this together?" The question sounded harmless enough, but something was niggling the uniformed cop.

Now in his midforties, Sergeant Baldwin had planned to be a detective someday, but for whatever reason had still not made it . . . and never would. Today, he was confronted with two detectives, both younger than him: one brown-skinned, the other Asian. It reinforced all his prejudices about the way the world was going.

Detective Ryan couldn't care less about all that. He had been polite—overly polite, if anything. Now, it was time to exert some authority.

"Okay, Sergeant, where's the body?"

"In the hut. The ranger found it," he said, pointing across at a young woman in a brown park ranger uniform sitting alone in the front seat of an SUV.

"She came by to check that it was clean and tidy after the rental, found the dead man, and called us."

"You're from the local station? From Hornsby?" Detective Ryan asked.

Sergeant Baldwin nodded. "I was out on patrol, got the call, and came to check it out."

Ryan looked at Detective Yang. "Can you talk to . . ." He stopped. "The ranger's name?" he asked the sergeant.

"Susan Collins," the cop said, producing a notebook and peering down at it. "Your partner doesn't need to do that." He held the notepad up. "I've already been through everything with her myself."

Detective Ryan ignored Baldwin. "Yang, can you do that?"

"Will do," Detective Yang said, heading to the ranger's vehicle.

"Okay, I can take it from here, Sergeant," Ryan said.

"Don't you want to hear my report?" Baldwin asked.

"Detective Yang can take the details from you after she's finished talking with Ranger Collins."

"You sure?" Sergeant Baldwin asked.

"Completely. There is one thing, though. When you went into the cabin, did you put gloves on?"

Baldwin hesitated.

"I'll take that as a no. That's unfortunate . . .. Now forensics will need to fingerprint you *and* your men if they, too, went gloveless," Detective Ryan said.

Baldwin opened his mouth to object and then decided against it. "Right," he said.

SEVEN

D ETECTIVE RYAN BENT DOWN TO THE small black combination lock-box. The box was screwed into planks at the side of the hut. He peered in. Empty. He stood up and entered the building.

Inside, it was already crowded. Two forensic assistants were laying out yellow number markers around a body, which lay sprawled out on the wood floor beside a two-seater couch. The pathologist was bent over the dead man as a videographer and a stills photographer moved around recording details of the crime.

Detective Ryan glanced around and sniffed. There was a strong smell of bleach in the room.

"It's hard to miss that, isn't it, Detective Ryan?"

Ryan turned his attention to Noah Bellman. The detective was pleased to see the fifty-year-old pathologist there. Although Noah had a reputation for being a bit of a character, the detective had known him for a long time and was confident about the medical examiner's abilities.

"All that bleach will not help the investigation, Noah," Ryan said.

"Yep. Guessing we won't find much in the way of DNA. Whoever did this was thorough, I'll give them that." He stopped. "Does the OCS have an interest in the case, then?"

Ryan shook his head. "Not that I know of. I'm in homicide now."

"Really? The glamor squad?" Noah said, impressed.

The detective didn't answer. Nicknaming homicide a glamor squad seemed to Ryan to be inappropriate. In his opinion, murder was never glamorous.

Ryan squatted down next to the pathologist and studied the dead man. He looked to be in his late fifties and expensively dressed. Shoeless and sockless, he wore sharply pressed cotton chinos and a pale green linen shirt, its cuffs undone, sleeves pushed up to the elbows. The man's hands lay outstretched on the floor, showing off a thick gold wedding band on his ring finger.

Noah slipped his hand around the back of the man's bald head and turned it to face Ryan. Brown eyes stared out of a gray face. The man's mouth was open wide as if silently screaming.

"He didn't go peacefully," the detective said. It was a statement, not a question.

"Yes, he looks like he was in agony right until the moment he took his last breath," Noah said.

"Which was?"

"Your guess is as good as mine at this stage. You know that."

"Just try to narrow it down for me. Six hours? Seven?"

Noah looked back down at the body. "Rigor mortis has set in on the muscles of his face." The pathologist lifted the man's right hand. "It has progressed to the limbs, but that process hasn't yet been completed. So, I would guesstimate he's been dead around four or five hours, but don't hold me to that."

"So, what do you think killed him?" the detective asked.

Noah gave the detective a wry smile. Ryan—always trying to get ahead of the game.

"I'd value your expert opinion *before* the official autopsy," Ryan pushed.

"Okay, well, at first glance, there's no sign of strangulation, no knife or gunshot wounds. No blood, either."

"Suffocation, maybe?"

The pathologist shook his head.

"I don't think so. No blotches on the skin or in the eyes."

"So, what then?" Detective Ryan asked.

"Poison, maybe, but don't hold me to that either." Noah paused. "Not natural causes. That's my gut instinct."

"Murder?" Ryan asked.

Noah nodded: "Yes, but I'll confirm the exact cause of death after I do a full autopsy."

Ryan stood up and looked around the room again. In its center, a round wooden table with four chairs pushed under it. On the far side, a made-up double bed with a bedside table and a small white closet next to it. A narrow Formica kitchen counter ran along the back wall. Two electric hob rings were cut into the counter with a bar fridge pushed under.

The detective walked over to the table. Here, the smell of bleach was strongest. Ryan studied the seats. They were substantial—heavy, rustic wishbone dining chairs. He bent down to examine the one closest to him. He touched a tiny remnant of duct tape stuck to the chair seat. The killer or killers had done a thorough job of cleaning up, but not quite thorough enough. They had missed this trace.

"Over here," Ryan said, gesturing to a tall, skinny woman dressed in gloves, booties, and blue coveralls working nearby. She came over.

"Could you bag this, please?" the detective asked, pointing at the duct tape remnant.

"Sure," the woman said. "I'm Sophie Flores, by the way, Detective Ryan."

"We've met before?" Ryan asked. He had no memory of the woman.

"No . . . but I've seen you around, and everyone in forensics knows your reputation," she said, smiling.

"Well, good to meet you, Sophie," Ryan said, blushing as he walked away. The detective was always embarrassed by compliments, particularly from pretty women.

Reaching the other side of the room, the detective walked through the open door into a pocket-sized, tiled bathroom. A shower compartment stood at the back, and close to the door was a sink with a mirror and single shelf above it and a small vanity below.

The detective peered into the shower. Shampoo, conditioner, and body gel bottles were lined up in the caddy that hung from the showerhead. He returned to the sink. A toothbrush and razor sat in a glass on the shelf above the washbasin, next to a tube of toothpaste and a can of shaving gel. A single bar of soap rested in a cheap, plastic soap dish.

Detective Ryan opened the wooden cupboard below the sink. Inside was a black nylon wash bag. He unzipped the bag and peered in. It was empty except for a large pack of condoms.

Leaving the bathroom to re-enter the main room, Detective Ryan headed to the closet. He slid open the door. The four shelves were empty except for five black socks and four pairs of Calvin Klein boxer shorts. A metal rail ran from one side of the closet to the other. Two polo shirts, one black, one blue, a pair of neatly ironed jeans, black slacks, and a black jacket hung down from the rail.

Ryan carefully patted the jacket with his gloved hand and retrieved a leather wallet from its inside pocket. He stared at the driver's license visible through the clear plastic sleeve. A headshot of the man whose body lay a few yards away stared back at him. Gary Young, date of birth April 20, 1967. Address: 14 Stewart Street, Church Point, Sydney 2015.

The detective reached for his cell and took a photo of the license before examining the wallet's contents. There were two credit cards—an Amex and a Visa—and a Westpac debit card. Ryan counted the notes: five twenty-dollar bills. Robbery clearly wasn't a motive.

The detective replaced the wallet. He would leave it for the forensic team to take prints. He felt around the jacket again, removing a set of keys from the right-hand pocket—house keys, he guessed, and a key fob for the green BMW outside.

Taking a clear plastic ziplock bag from his pocket, Ryan dropped the keys and fob inside, sealed it, and put it into his pocket.

Looking down, Ryan studied the black holdall on the closet floor. It was unzipped and empty. A smart black leather briefcase and two pairs of immaculate white sneakers sat beside it.

Detective Ryan turned the briefcase onto its back and pushed open the latches. He levered the lip ajar to reveal a gray Apple Mac computer and a cell phone.

Ryan picked up the iPhone and stared at the screen. On it was a photo of the dead man, his arm around an attractive younger woman. Returning the phone to the briefcase, the detective closed the lid and clipped the latches shut.

The detective grasped the case. He would take it with him, and the IT nerds back at the base could open the devices.

Ryan heard the front door and turned to see Detective Yang standing in the doorway. She had stopped to peer at the body.

"Let me introduce you to Detective Yang, Noah," Ryan said, walking over as the pathologist looked up from what he was doing.

"Good to meet you, Detective. Noah Bellman," the medical examiner said, standing.

"Likewise," Yang replied.

"You're new?" Noah asked.

Detective Yang nodded. "Yep, just arrived from the Central Coast."

"Well, you drew the short straw getting Ryan as a partner," the pathologist said, smiling. "Now, a few words of warning about . . ."

"Detective Yang and I worked together when I was with organized crime," Ryan said, "so she is well aware of my idiosyncrasies." Noah shot Zoe an amused look as Ryan continued. "When will you have the autopsy report, do you think?"

"One of your new partner's many endearing qualities is that he's a demanding son of a bitch," Noah joked before turning back to Ryan.

"There's a bit of a backlog at the moment, staff shortages, etc. Strangely enough, few people are keen to do this sort of work. However, I'll try and get an initial report completed ASAP."

EIGHT

"Is this how it's going to be?" Yang said as she and Ryan exited the hut.

"What do you mean?" Detective Ryan asked.

"What's the point of me being here if you don't give me time to look around the crime scene?" Detective Yang said.

"That's a problem for you?" Ryan asked as the cops began walking single file down the stairs.

"Damn right, it is."

Detective Ryan smiled to himself. Yang undoubtedly had a lot to learn, but she was feisty, and he liked that.

"I am the senior officer, Detective Yang," Ryan said, reaching the bottom of the steps.

"And that means I simply tag along and do nothing?" Yang said, her temper rising.

"You interviewed the ranger. I wouldn't call that 'nothing.'" Detective Ryan stopped and met her gaze head-on. "I appreciate that you want to be more involved, but before that can happen, I want to know that you can handle the nuts and bolts of detective work—the boring stuff like interviewing witnesses who, nine times out of ten, can't tell you more than you already know."

Zoe Yang looked at her shoes. She knew he was right but was reluctant to admit it.

Ryan continued: "You were in the cabin for a good two minutes. Tell me what you gleaned in that time."

Detective Yang was silent for a moment, thinking.

"Well . . . the place reeked of bleach, so whoever murdered him was determined to leave no trace." She paused. "And there was no sign of blood on the body, and no bruising that I could see, so possibly . . . someone put a plastic bag over his head, or . . . poisoned him, maybe?" She looked to Ryan for his reaction.

"Not bad," Ryan said, nodding. "And what did you find out from the ranger?"

Zoe consulted the small notebook she still held in her hands.

"She told me that the National Parks and Wildlife Service rents out this hut. The deceased's name is Gary Young, and he booked it online with a credit card. He'd reserved the place twice before and always on weekends. His check-out time was nine this morning. The ranger arrived at ten for a routine inspection to ensure there was no damage to the property. She wasn't expecting any. The previous times, Young had left the property immaculate. The lockbox was empty, which was unusual, but Ranger Collins assumed Young had either left the key inside or was still there. She knocked and got no answer. She tried the door, and it was open. Entering, she saw the body." Yang looked up from her notes. "She was pretty shaken up."

"That's everything?" Ryan asked.

"Yep."

"You've got all of the ranger's details?"

"Of course."

"Okay, well, you can tell her she can go. There is no point in her hanging around. You can write up the interview when we get back." Ryan lifted Gary Young's briefcase. "Put this in my trunk, too. It's the victim's computer and phone. It goes to IT when we get back."

Detective Yang took the case and paused. "Look, I'm sorry about being a little testy just now. I know that working with you is a fantastic opportunity."

Detective Ryan nodded. "Understood," he said, dropping his car keys into Detective Yang's hand before heading for the green BMW.

Reaching it, Detective Ryan, still wearing his latex gloves, ran his hand over the hood. It was cold. He took the ziplock bag out of his pocket and pressed the fob through the plastic. The car horn beeped twice quickly, confirming that this was Gary Young's vehicle.

The detective moved to check out the trunk. It was empty. Closing it, he pulled open the driver's door and peered inside. Pristine. Nothing had been left on the seats or in the center console. Opening the glove box, Ryan examined the insurance documents. They confirmed what he already knew, that the vehicle belonged to the man who was murdered, and the details of his home address matched the one on his driver's license.

Detective Ryan dropped the bag of keys and the fob on the driver's seat. Forensics could take the bag with them when they examined the car.

Closing the car door, he turned to study the hut. It was in a beautiful spot—on the forest's edge and bounded by the river—ideal for a romantic weekend getaway or a few days of "me time." On the downside, its solitary location meant that the killer or killers could have carried out the murder confident that they wouldn't be disturbed. But how had they gotten in? There had been no sign of forced entry, so had Young let them in? Or had he left the door unlocked, and they had entered when he was asleep?

Detective Ryan walked along the side of the hut, studying the ground. The grass was thick and lush. Anyone stepping through it would leave no permanent trace. He reached the tree that marked the taped boundary of the crime scene. There had been a heavy rain shower last night, and a patch of freshly wet mud was visible around the base of the trunk.

"Sergeant!" the detective shouted, waving at the uniformed cop, who was smoking while leaning against the side of his car.

Sergeant Baldwin threw down his cigarette and headed over to Ryan. "Yeah?" he said, arriving.

"What size are your shoes?"

"Nine. Why?"

Ryan didn't answer. Instead, he looked across at his car. "Over here," he shouted to Detective Yang. She hurried across.

"The sergeant says he wears a size nine shoe," he said. "And you're around five foot nine or ten, right?"

"Yes," Baldwin confirmed.

Ryan pointed down into the mud. "That shoe print there would be yours?"

"Yes, probably," Sergeant Baldwin said.

"But that one," Ryan said, indicating a much bigger print right on the edge of the soft soil, "that's someone else's." He paused. "Sergeant Baldwin, how tall would you say your two colleagues are?"

Baldwin peered over at the two uniformed cops who stood next to their car. "Tommo . . . Constable Bill Clark . . . he's about my height. And Pook . . . Constable Harry O'Henry . . . he's a short-ass."

"It's unlikely that either made that print?" Detective Ryan said, indicating the large footprint. "The size of the print suggests someone taller."

"Yes, there's that. Plus, I put out the tape. Neither of them has been anywhere near here."

"You think that could be the killer's shoe print?" Detective Yang asked Ryan.

"It's possible," the detective said, pausing. "Detective Yang, can you get someone from forensics? They should take a mold of the print. And Sergeant Baldwin, make sure neither you nor your men come anywhere near here until that's done. Forensics will want to take your shoe print to confirm that one is yours, too," Ryan pointed at the smaller print. "Now, who else has regular access to this area?"

NINE

*T*HE MAN WATCHED AS THE MALE *detective walked back to the hut. He hadn't intended to stay this long, but a lot was happening, and he was enjoying himself.*

Hearing a vehicle approaching, he watched as a golf buggy appeared. Two young, uniformed cops hurried over, one raising his hand while the other blocked the vehicle's path.

The buggy stopped, and two men got out. They were both dressed in gray security uniforms. One was shorter, under six feet and around two hundred and fifty pounds, and the other was around six feet two and younger.

The detective and the sergeant spotted the new arrivals and walked over.

The man pushed up from the thick undergrowth. It was time to go.

"WE WERE TOLD TO COME DOWN here?" the security guard said as he approached the policemen.

"That's the man you want." One of the uniforms pointed to Detective Ryan as he approached with the sergeant.

"Hi, Steve," Sergeant Baldwin said, interrupting and looking at the shorter of the two security guards.

"Morning, Sarge," the man replied. He was bald, with a chubby face and large brown eyes.

"Detective Ryan, meet Steve Prince. He worked with me before he went over to the dark side," Sergeant Baldwin said.

"Really?" Steve grinned. "The dark side now, is it?"

Baldwin grinned back as Steve indicated the guard next to him. "This is my offsider, Alex Riva."

"Hi," Alex said. In his late twenties, the tall, muscular man had a triangular-shaped face, bright blue eyes, and thinning black hair.

"You work for Parks and Wildlife?" Detective Ryan asked.

"No. We work over there, Detective," Steve said, pointing back through the trees. "At The Palms Hotel."

"What's going on?" the other guard, Alex, asked.

Detective Ryan didn't reply. Instead, he turned and watched as Detective Yang approached. "Done?" he asked.

"Yeah, forensics are dealing with it," Yang said.

Detective Ryan nodded and turned back to the security guards. "Were the both of you on duty last night?"

"I was," Steve said.

"I started my shift at six this morning," Alex offered.

Did either of you see or hear anything unusual?" Ryan asked.

Alex shook his head. "Nope."

"Me neither," Steve said. "But if you tell us what's going down, it may jog our memories."

"I'm afraid it's too early to say, Steve," Ryan said, being deliberately evasive. "Detective Yang, can you note these two men's details?"

Detective Ryan pulled out a business card and offered it to Steve Prince. "Just in case something does come to mind." He looked across at Sergeant Baldwin. "A word?"

The pair walked away, stopping by the detective's car. "This place will soon be awash with journalists and general busybodies, and I want to ensure we're on the same page. Everyone is to be kept back from the crime scene, and neither you nor your colleagues should supply them with any information."

Sergeant Baldwin glared at Ryan. "You've got a fucking cheek, Detective," he said. "We may not be in your flash Homicide Squad, but we're not idiots."

"No offense intended, Sergeant." Ryan pulled open the car door. "I never assume, that's all." He turned to his colleague. "Detective Yang?" He motioned for her to get in.

The next task was one Detective Ryan hated most—informing the family.

PIETRO GUFFINI, AKA THE OWL, WAS well acquainted with death, though you wouldn't know that at first blush. He was someone you could pass on the street without a second glance—stocky, with the neck of an ox, his balding pate sitting atop a square, bespectacled face. Mr. Ordinary. This persona had served him well when, back in the day, he had worked as a driver for Oscar Bruno, then the head of one of the largest and most violent organized crime gangs in Australia. Underneath The Owl's subservient, everyman demeanor beat the heart of a burningly ambitious man, a cold-blooded killer prepared to do anything to achieve his ultimate goal—to replace Oscar Bruno and head up the crime gang himself.

The Owl's chance came when Bruno was murdered, killed by a sniper's bullet. His number two and three had died around the same time, so suddenly, everything was up for grabs. One by one, would-be successors had been eliminated. After all of the blood and mayhem, The Owl was the only man left standing.

After removing all the opposition, he had started going through the accounts and discovered, to his horror, that they were in complete disarray.

Pietro Guffini could have left cleaning the books to a professional bean counter. But anyone examining them would have a complete blueprint of all the gang's illegal activities. He decided to do it himself.

"Boss," a baritone voice said, interrupting his work.

A man placed a cup of tea on the desk before him.

The Owl nodded his thanks, and Jacky Orologio, his job done, stepped back to join his brother, Joey.

Anyone seeing the two men for the first time always did a double take. They were identical. Thirty years old, big, strong men with crude, cartoonish faces—pug noses and squinty pig eyes—and black hair razor cut to a stubble. Both wore black suits with open-neck white shirts.

The brothers Orologio had been The Owl's secret weapon in his rise and rise. He had taken a week off immediately after Oscar Bruno's death. No one cared. They were too busy fighting among each other to question where the dead boss's driver had gone. If anyone had enquired, The Owl had an excuse: his mother had died, and he had to attend her funeral in Italy. It was a lie. Not the bit about her dying, but the timing of her death. That had happened fifteen years ago.

Unlike the other gang members, The Owl didn't come from Sicily, the traditional home of the Mafia, but from Calabria, a region on the boot of Italy, best known for its landscape of dramatic cliffs, sprawling beaches, and dense forests; its delicious food; and the 'Ndrangheta, which, though less well known than the Mafia, was much more powerful than its sister organization. It was because of the 'Ndrangheta that The Owl had chosen to return.

The Owl had put feelers out and heard good things about his second cousins Jacky and Joey Orologio—stone-cold killers currently freelancing for the 'Ndrangheta. The twins lived in Spilinga, a medieval seaside town whose main claim to fame was as the home of 'Nduja, a fiery, salty pork salami adored throughout Italy.

The twins had honed their murder expertise as teenagers when they discovered they could make a living as guns for hire. They freelanced for various gangs in the region, never willing to commit to anyone. At first, the brothers took all the work offered, but they became more discerning as time passed. Like most people who spent too long in the same profession, though, they got restless. The killing had become mundane. The brothers made a decision. They would only take on work that offered a challenge. The men found that by doing fewer killings, they earned much more. Being exclusive meant people would pay whatever they asked.

The twins had settled into a comfortable routine. They lived high on the hog, murdering only when they deemed there was some challenge involved, and yet, they were becoming bored. After much discussion, they decided that this feeling came not from the job or the money but from the place. They were tired of living in Calabria in particular and Italy in general. The brothers started to read travel brochures, and Australia caught their fancy. The more they studied the country, the more videos they watched on YouTube, and the more they concluded that it could fit them well. At just about this time, Pietro Guffini, aka The Owl, came calling. When he offered them entry into the top echelons of one of the biggest crime gangs in Australia, they were only too eager to accept.

Before closing the deal, The Owl explained that one problem remained. They needed a nom de guerre, or an alias. It was impossible to join the gang without a snappy name for each of them, something people would remember them by.

The men huffed and puffed, protesting that they only needed a couple of Glocks to make their mark, but The Owl had insisted. He offered up the names Tik and Tok because, as he explained, their surname, Orologio, was the word for clock in Italian. Jacky, the oldest by five minutes, insisted on taking Tik, leaving Tok for younger brother Joey.

On their arrival in Sydney, it had taken The Owl and the twins just a few weeks to clean things up. Then, Pietro Guffini was installed as the organization's new head, with Tik and Tok as joint second-in-command.

THE OWL PICKED UP THE CUP of tea, took a sip, and frowned as he stared at the screen.

"Problem, Boss?" one of the brothers asked.

"Nothing that can't be dealt with, Tik, but thanks for asking," The Owl said.

"Tok," the brother said.

The Owl looked up. "What?"

"I'm Joey. Tok. Jacky's Tik, right? That's what we agreed?"

"Yes . . . yes . . ." The Owl said. He was going to have to do something about that. Maybe one of the brothers could have a small tattoo inked on his neck—but that would have to wait. There was something much more important that needed to be dealt with. Something was going on with these accounts. The figures didn't add up. It looked like someone was cheating him.

TEN

NOT THAT FAR AWAY, DETECTIVE RYAN stopped in front of a large, modern, three-story house. The property was about fifteen minutes from the murder site and sat in splendid isolation at the top of a hill, surrounded by a thick copse of pine trees. It looked down on the sparkling blue of Pittwater Bay.

Ryan did a quick calculation. He reckoned he could fit at least fifteen of his apartments into this building.

"What do you think?" the detective asked, looking at Yang.

She paused, taking in the scale of the home. "I think some people have far too much money."

"My thoughts exactly." Ryan nodded. He took a deep breath. "Let's do this, then, shall we?"

The cops exited the car and climbed steep stone steps to the front door. Ryan rang the bell and waited.

Nothing.

Ryan rang again.

"Hello, can I help you?" a voice shouted from behind them.

The detectives turned. An attractive woman in her midthirties with tied-back blond hair stood below at an open gate framed by high walls. She wore a short white skirt showcasing tanned, muscular legs and a white polo shirt. It was the woman on Gary Young's iPhone screen.

"Mrs. Young?" Detective Ryan asked.

"And you are?" the woman said, climbing the steps to join the detectives.

Ryan produced his identity card. The woman squinted at it, looking puzzled. "Police?"

"I'm Detective Ryan, and this is Detective Yang," the detective said, indicating Zoe.

There was a shout: "Abi, are we going to finish this game?"

The cops turned to view the man who had appeared at the gate below. In his midtwenties and ruggedly handsome, he, too, was dressed in white sportswear and carried a tennis racket.

"I think we'll call it a day, Rob," the woman shouted.

"Oh, all right," the man said, disappointed. "Same time tomorrow, then?"

"Yes. Definitely," the woman said.

"Good. Your service is coming along, but we need to keep up the practice."

"Ooh, you are such a hard taskmaster," the woman answered, smiling. She watched momentarily as the man headed to an SUV, then returned her attention to Detective Ryan. "Police?" she repeated.

"Yes, ma'am," Ryan said.

The woman held out her hand. "Abi Young." Ryan shook it. "What's this about?" Abi asked.

"I think it's best to speak inside," Detective Ryan said.

"Come in, then." Abi stepped past the detectives and pushed the door open.

The cops followed her in. "This way," Abi said, leading them down a high-ceilinged hallway. Stopping, she opened a door and ushered them into the living room.

"Please, take a seat." She indicated a plush sofa. As she did, Ryan turned to face her, eager to get this challenging task over and done with, but Abi was already heading back out to the corridor.

"I'll make a quick change if you don't mind. I'll only be a moment," she said, bounding up the metal stairs that led to the first floor.

Ryan shot Detective Yang a look of frustration. This was becoming far more drawn out than he was comfortable with.

While they waited for Abi to return, the detectives looked around. The room was expensively furnished. Two leather-clad sofas and two armchairs were arranged in a rectangle with a coffee table in the center. A long oak table with a set of six white Eames chairs was at the far end of the space. Full-length French doors opened onto a terrace that overlooked the bay.

Ryan walked over to an impressively large chest of drawers pushed against the wall. Framed photos sat on its top: pictures of Abi, close-ups and full-length. Mostly, she was dressed in expensive-looking skirts, blouses, and trousers, but a couple showcased her curvy figure in a bikini. There were two framed photos of a sullen-looking, suited man and a few more of the same grim-faced man and Abi posing together.

Walking up behind Ryan, Detective Yang picked up one of the photos. "That's Gary Young, isn't it?" she asked.

Before Ryan could answer, the mistress of the house breezed back into the room.

"That's better," she said, smiling broadly. She had brushed out her hair, which now spilled casually over the top of a blue and white striped shirt tucked into a pair of designer jeans. She gestured to a sofa before continuing.

"Look. I think I know what this is about, and—"

"I don't think you do," Ryan interrupted, but Abi wasn't listening.

"I had nothing to do with the demise of that tree." Abi was defiant as Ryan and Yang exchanged looks of confusion.

"Tree?" Ryan queried.

"Yes, the tree," Abi said impatiently. "The one that used to block our view of the bay. The one that busybody environmentalist accused us of poisoning."

"Mrs. Young, that's not why we're here," Detective Ryan explained, but Abi Young wasn't finished.

"I'll admit we weren't happy about the council refusing our application to have the tree removed, but we did *not* take matters into our own hands, as she seems to think . . . ."

"Mrs. Young!" Ryan cut in forcefully. "Please," he implored. "That is not why we're here."

Noting the look on Detective Ryan's face, Abi pulled up short.

"Well, then . . . why *are* you here?" she asked, looking concerned.

Ryan took a breath in. "We have some bad news." He stopped. He hated this.

"It's about your husband," Detective Yang said, seeing Ryan's unease.

"What about him?" Abi asked.

"This morning, at approximately 11a.m., Detective Yang and I attended the scene of an apparent homicide," Detective Ryan said slowly as Abi's face drained of color. "We have identified the deceased as Gary Young. Your husband."

Abi leaned back in the chair, her face ashen.

"Are you sure?" she asked.

Ryan nodded and waited a moment to give the woman time to process the news.

Abi stood up, shaking her head in disbelief. "Homicide? Who would do that? Are you sure it wasn't his heart? He wasn't a healthy man! I mean, look at him!" Sounding distraught, she picked up one of the framed photographs the detectives had looked at earlier and brandished it in front of them.

"Does that look like a healthy man to you?" she asked, clearly in shock.

Ryan took the photograph before gently guiding her back to her chair.

"We can't be certain until we have the autopsy results," Detective Yang said gently. "But we believe his death is probably down to foul play."

"I don't understand," the woman said quietly before looking up at Detective Yang with a sudden thought. "Will I have to go to Melbourne to identify his body?"

"Melbourne?" Ryan queried.

"Isn't that where . . . where you found him? He was in Melbourne for a work conference." She paused. "He was due back today."

Detective Ryan shook his head. "No. He was discovered here," he said.

"In Sydney?" Abi asked, confused.

"Yes," Ryan confirmed. "In a rented cabin in Ku-ring-gai Chase National Park."

ELEVEN

"TOMORROW, FOR THE AUTOPSY RESULTS?" ABI said solemnly as she opened the front door to usher the detectives out.

"Yes. But we will contact you later today to give you an exact time and place so you can officially identify your husband," Detective Ryan confirmed.

Abi nodded slowly. "Thank you."

As she began to close the door, Ryan raised his hand. "One more question, if that's okay. Do you know the codes for your husband's computer and iPhone?"

"What?"

"The passwords?"

"No. No." She paused. "There might be someone at his work who would know. Gary is . . . Abi stopped. "Was . . . an accountant . . . and a partner in the Faith Company. They own The Palms Hotel and Golf Club out by Ku-ring-gai Chase. His office was at the hotel."

"The one at the southern edge of the park?" Ryan asked.

The woman nodded. "Yes," she said, wiping away the tears that were forming.

"And are you certain Mr. Young said he was going to Melbourne for a conference?" Ryan said.

"Absolutely." Abi paused. "He went to those things quite regularly."

She slowly closed the door as Detective Ryan and Detective Yang headed back down the stone steps

LIKE ABI YOUNG, SIMON FAITH WAS having a lousy morning. After review-
ing a depressing report from Gary Young on the hotel's escalating refurbishment costs, he read an email outlining the unofficial council feedback
on the Faith Company's plan to build two twenty-story tower blocks adjacent to the hotel and golf course.

Simon and his partners had been fighting for planning permission for
the project, arguing that it would dramatically increase available housing
in the area. But this was not a view held by all. A protest group—rabid
lefties, in Simon's view—argued that the proposed development shouldn't
be given the go-ahead because the apartments were intended only for
the wealthy. What's more, the development would encroach on national
park land. It also seemed from the email that the council was taking these
objections seriously.

The hotel boss shook his head in disgust. Idiots! What was it about
bureaucrats that they couldn't write in plain English? He peered at the
computer screen: "The development needs to take a more sympathetic
approach to its plan and incorporate more design flexibility in its posi-
tioning and application."

Exasperated, Simon shouted, "Yvonne, come in here, will you?"

After a few moments, a dumpy, plain woman in her late twenties
entered the office.

"Yes, Mr. Faith?" she said.

"I thought I asked you to get Gary over," Simon snapped.

"He isn't in yet," Yvonne Lewis replied.

"Are you sure?"

"Yes," the PA said quietly.

Simon stared at her. She was just like all the others: useless! What she
had just said didn't make sense. Gary had many irritating traits, but turning up late to work wasn't one of them.

"He's never late. Check again," Simon instructed dismissively.

"I did check only five minutes ago," she said.

"Okay, well, in that case, the moment he arrives, tell him I need to see
him."

"Will do," Yvonne said. She waited, knowing there was more to come.

"Can you also ask Luke to join me?" Simon Faith said.

"Luke Saker? Or Robinson?"

"Saker."

"Right." She nodded her understanding, still not moving.

"Is there something else?" Simon asked.

"There is. One of the security guards is outside. Alex Riva. He wanted a word. And a Detective Ryan called. He and his partner are on their way over."

Simon frowned. "Did the cop say why?"

Yvonne shook her head. "No, Mr. Faith, but apparently, police cars have been seen down by the cabin. I imagine it has something to do with that."

"Police cars? Why am I only finding out about this now, Yvonne?" Simon demanded.

Right on cue, a police siren could be heard as it sped along the adjacent highway. Simon shook his head in annoyance and silently hoped that whatever was going on in the park did not have the potential to affect The Palms Hotel's reopening.

"Should I send Alex Riva in?" the PA asked.

"Go ahead," Simon said.

Yvonne Lewis opened the door. "Alex," she said. "Mr. Faith will see you now."

The security guard entered but waited to speak until after the young woman had left the room. Then: "Steve and I have just been down to the cabin. It's swarming with cops."

"So, I believe. *And*?" he spat, irritated.

"They wouldn't tell us a thing." He shrugged.

"And why are *you* telling me this?" Simon enquired. "Steve Prince is my head of security. Why isn't *he* here?"

"He was busy dealing with another matter downstairs," Alex said.

"How convenient," Simon Faith said, peering at Alex. He hadn't been happy with Prince's recent performance. This guard could be a possible replacement. He was a new addition to the company but had already impressed Simon as a conscientious worker.

There was a knock on the door.

"Yes," Simon said. The office was getting busier than a palm tree in a hurricane.

Luke Saker entered.

Luke and Simon were a study in contrasts. Although both were in their midfifties, Simon Faith looked at least ten years older. Overweight, with short, thinning gray hair, the hotel boss had a face that was blotchy and wrinkled from too much time in the Australian sun. Unlike Luke, Simon's taste in clothing was dire, too . . . ill-fitting black suits, white shirts, and dull-colored ties. On the other hand, Luke was taut, muscular, and always dressed to impress. Today's attire was an expensive blue suit, a sky-blue shirt, a striped, yellow silk tie, and black loafers.

"Morning, Simon. You wanted to see me?" Luke said.

"Yes, it's about the tower plans," Simon informed him.

"I'll be off then?" Alex said, interrupting.

"Yes, all right." His boss waved him away dismissively.

"Can you ask Yvonne to bring me up a Diet Coke?" Luke asked as the security guard reached the door.

"Sure," Riva replied, heading out.

Luke flopped down on the couch in the corner. "So, what about the towers?"

"I've just got the unofficial council report through. They're siding with the troublemakers," Simon said.

"I wouldn't worry." Luke shrugged. "I'm sure we can fix it. We'll sweeten the deal to bring more councilors on side."

"Good idea," Simon said. "Not so good, though, is that Gary has sent over the latest hotel refurbishment breakdowns. The work has gone way over."

Luke shrugged. "We can afford it, can't we? We'll get it all back in spades when the hotel reopens."

Before Simon could answer, Yvonne entered.

"There you go," she said, handing Luke a Diet Coke.

"Thanks," Luke said, pulling on the tab.

"And the two detectives are outside, Mr. Faith. Should I bring them in?" the PA asked.

"Hi," Ryan said, appearing in the doorway before Simon could answer. He offered up his ID. "Detective Ryan."

"Detective Yang," Zoe said, walking in behind and showing her ID, too.

"We've come about a confidential matter, Mr. Faith," Detective Ryan said, glancing across at Yvonne and Luke.

"Yvonne, you can go," Simon said. "Luke, you can stay, though," the hotel boss said as the PA closed the door behind her. "Luke is one of my partners and the company lawyer. Whatever you have to say to me, you can say to him, too."

Simon Faith signaled over at the chairs across from his desk. "Please take a seat, detectives."

As the cops sat, Simon Faith leaned back. "Now, how can I help?"

"We have been led to believe that Gary Young is an employee here," Detective Ryan said. Simon looked at him, surprised.

"Not just an employee. Gary is the third partner in this enterprise," Simonsaid as the penny started to drop. "What is this about, Detective?"

"I'm sorry to have to tell you this," Ryan began slowly, "But Mr. Young's body was discovered approximately three hours ago in the hut that borders hotel property."

Simon and Luke stared at the detectives in disbelief.

"What?" Simon shook his head. "I think you've made a mistake. Why would Gary be in the cabin?"

"That's what we will be endeavoring to find out," Ryan continued. "We have made a positive ID of the body, Mr. Faith. We are in no doubt." Ryan looked from Luke back to Simon. "When did you last see Mr. Young?"

"Friday," Simon said as he stared into the middle distance. "Shit. I can't believe it. We are the founding fathers . . . the Three Musketeers, as we like to call ourselves."

"How did it happen? Heart attack?" Luke asked, still trying to process the news.

"We don't like to speculate. The autopsy report should be ready tomorrow," Ryan confirmed.

"But . . . you're homicide, right?" Simon questioned, putting two and two together. "So, it's suspicious?"

Detective Ryan gave a tight smile. He didn't answer the question.

"Does his wife know yet?" Luke asked quietly.

"Yes," Detective Ryan confirmed.

Simon shook his head. "She must be devastated."

"Yes, she seemed shocked," Ryan said soberly.

"Seemed? What does that mean?" Simon said, narrowing his eyes.

"Just a turn of phrase," Ryan explained, expressionless. "I don't like to assume that I know what anyone might feel in such a situation."

"It means they think Abi could have had something to do with Gary's death," Luke said.

"What?" Simon looked from Ryan to Yang, shocked at the suggestion.

"I'd say you're drawing rather a long bow, Mr. Saker," Ryan suggested, his interest piquing.

"You haven't denied it, though. The spouse is always the number one suspect when someone dies suddenly. Isn't that right, Detectives?" Luke said.

"I think we're getting ahead of ourselves." Ryan's expression became more serious as he attempted to steer the conversation back on course. "We will be following several lines of inquiry. But we would like to start here." Detective Ryan looked to his partner, who took a small notebook and pen from her pocket.

"Mr. Faith, you said you last saw Gary Young on Friday?"

"Yes. He left as usual bang-on five," Simon said. "Gary is . . ." The hotel boss stopped. "*Was* a very strict timekeeper. He always arrived at precisely eight in the morning." He paused. "Except this morning, of course. And now I know why."

"And this weekend?" Detective Ryan asked. "Was he working then, too?"

Simon shook his head. "Gary considered his weekends to be sacrosanct."

"He didn't ever go to, say, a weekend work conference?" Ryan asked.

"No. Never," Faith said, frowning. "Why?"

"His wife believed he was at a conference this weekend," Detective Yang interjected.

"What?" Simon said, surprised.

"How did he and his wife get on?" Detective Ryan asked quickly.

"Well, wouldn't you say, Luke?" Simon asked, glancing across at the lawyer.

"Yes," Luke confirmed. "There didn't seem to be any problems, if that's what you're suggesting."

"Quite an age difference, though?" Detective Yang mused.

"So? What are you insinuating?" Simon asked defensively.

"My colleague is not implying anything," Detective Ryan said. "It was just a statement of fact. He was fifty-something, and she's in her midthirties."

"Fifty-six . . . my age," Simon Faith said. "And Abi is what, Luke, thirty-eight?"

"Yep," Luke said.

"Married long?" Detective Yang asked.

"About five years. We thought Gary was a confirmed bachelor, and then Abi came along and swept him off his feet." He paused and looked across to Luke for help. "Wouldn't you agree?"

"That's accurate," Luke said.

"Right," Detective Ryan said slowly. "Do you know Gary Young's laptop and iPhone passcodes?"

"What?" Simon was surprised by the non sequitur.

"His wife didn't know the codes and said you might have them."

"And you need these codes because . . .?" Simon asked.

"Because it would be good to get access to those devices as part of our inquiries," Detective Ryan responded.

Silence as Simon Faith appeared to consider the request. Then: "I'm sorry, Detective, but we don't have them. Gary was very security-conscious and kept those to himself."

"He used the devices personally and for business?" Detective Ryan asked.

"I believe so," Simon confirmed.

"You have them?" Luke asked.

"Yes," Ryan replied.

"Okay. Well, now I have a question for you. What do you intend to do with the material you find if you break into those devices?"

"Yes, some of that information will be about our company, which is highly confidential," Simon asserted.

"We will only be considering material relevant to our investigation," Detective Ryan said carefully.

"Good," said Simon, "because Luke here can be a real pit bull when it comes to the police overstepping their mark."

Detective Ryan stood up, noting the threat. Detective Yang followed suit.

"Thank you, gentlemen. We'll bear that in mind," Ryan said, taking his wallet out and handing cards to Simon Faith and Luke Saker. "Don't hesitate to call if you think of anything else."

"No problem," Simon said, forcing a smile as he stood. "And you'll have to excuse us if we've seemed abrupt. We're both shocked about the news of Gary's death. He's been our friend and business partner for many years."

"Of course. We understand." Yang nodded with restrained sympathy.

Simon Faith pulled open the door. "Yvonne, the detectives are finished. Please show them out."

TWELVE

FOUR MILES AWAY, HEIDI MILLER WAS readying to show out Dimitri Bodyak. They were the last remaining poker players at the table. Like him, the four others Heidi had dispatched had all been men. No surprise there, though. Good women poker players were as rare as hens' teeth . . . not that that worried Heidi. She used it to her advantage.

This was the first year the poker competition had been held in Sydney. Moving the event from its previous home in Melbourne had been a gamble. The Sun Casino feared that international players wouldn't bother to attend even with the winnings jacked up to seven million dollars.

Taking the risk, though, had proved to be an excellent gamble. Six hundred had applied, including all the big card sharps. Seventy-five tables, with between six and eight per table, all ready to pay expensive buy-ins to the tournament. Over fifty percent of them were international players, the rest Australians, some of whom, like Heidi, had good reputations.

Today, though, being the start of the competition, there were more than a fair number of chancers—though they usually didn't last long. Over the last four hours, the other players at Heidi's table had collapsed like flans in a cupboard. Moving on to the next round was now down to the result of the matchup between her and the twenty-four-year-old Russian man.

Heidi was stunning. In her late thirties, with long blond hair, bright blue eyes, and a heart-shaped face, she knew combining her looks with the right clothes gave her a not-so-subtle advantage . . . the means to distract male players.

Today, the first day of the five-day Australian All-Comers Poker Tournament, Heidi had opted for cowboy boots, white pants, and a blue silk camisole under a well-fitted black blazer. Powerful but feminine.

She had already chosen outfits for each of the remaining days of the tournament, a mix of pants and vintage jeans, vests and blouses, and silver and gold jewelry. She had also brought a range of accessories—scarves, eyewear, and expensive handbags; whether and when she used these would depend on how she felt on the day.

Bodyak stood up from the table and peered at the dealer. He was waiting to see the last card. He believed he could still win, take the pot, and wipe out the woman. But Heidi knew that was unlikely. She had played well, and the odds were in her favor.

The woman flicked the edges of the two cards, their faces hidden. It was a nervous habit, and one Heidi tried not to do. She knew perfectly well what the cards were: two kings. There were two kings, a seven, and a nine on show, too, so she had four of a kind. The hand could only be beaten by a straight or royal flush.

The dealer turned the final card over—an ace.

Bodyak could have folded, but he chose not to. He pushed his chips onto the table. "One hundred and fifty thousand," he said.

Heidi matched his bid before revealing her two concealed cards.

Bodyak grimaced. "Lucky," he muttered, flicking over his cards. He turned and hurried away.

Heidi watched the Russian go. They all had felt the sting of losing and were usually gracious in defeat. Not this young Russian, though. Heidi was confident that with his kind of attitude, he wouldn't be around for long.

She pushed up from the chair. She had made it through another day . . . one step closer to paying off her sponsor, one step closer to getting away from Pietro Guffini. Partnering up with that mean son of a bitch had been the worst decision of her life.

DETECTIVE ZOE YANG WAS THINKING ABOUT bad decisions, too, considering whether moving down to Sydney to work with Ramesh Ryan had been such a great move. As the detective's partner, she had anticipated sharing thoughts and ideas, but that didn't seem to be high on Ryan's agenda.

Zoe intended to broach the subject as they drove back from The Palms Hotel to police headquarters. "Can we talk?" she asked.

"Sorry, Zoe, not now. I need some quiet time," the detective said. He was busy playing back his conversation with Simon Faith and Luke Saker. Both had seemed genuinely shocked by the news of the death of their business partner. And yet . . .

"Okay, well, for what it's worth, I wouldn't trust those two men farther than I can spit . . . and I'm a very bad spitter," Detective Yang said, ignoring Ryan's reply.

"What?" Detective Ryan said, coming out of his reverie.

"I said I'm not a very good spitter."

"Me neither," said Ryan. He glanced over at her. "Look, Zoe, how would you like to help me with something?"

"That's what I'm here for. At least that's what I was led to believe," Detective Yang said pointedly.

Ryan ignored his partner's tone. "The thing is, I'm not very good at paperwork, so I was thinking maybe you could help complete daily reports and be a first point of contact, too."

The offer had been made to kill two birds with one stone. Detective Ryan had handed over a task he hated while making a peace offering to Zoe by getting her more involved, something he knew she wanted. However, his definition of being involved and Zoe's were very different.

"That's what you want me to do? Paperwork?" Detective Yang asked, trying to keep the disappointment out of her voice.

"I would appreciate it, yes."

Detective Yang hesitated. She didn't have much choice. Ryan was the senior officer, and at least it meant she was doing something constructive.

"Okay," she said finally.

"Good." Ryan paused. "By the way, you're going to love Elina. She's quite a character."

THIRTEEN

ELINA BENNETT, THE THIRTY-YEAR-OLD INSPECTOR WHO headed up the police IT department, was nothing less than striking. Standing just short of six feet, she towered over most women. Moreover, piling her long purple-dyed hair into a bun and wearing wedge platform sandals boosted her height considerably. Add to this the policewoman's choice of garish jackets and bold-colored blouses and pants, and it was apparent that Inspector Bennett was no shrinking violet.

Prewarned, when Detective Yang entered the small, windowless IT room, she tried not to react.

"Told you," Detective Ryan whispered as Inspector Bennett walked over.

"Good to see you, Ryan," the inspector said. "And I see you've brought me a newbie."

"Zoe's my new partner."

The woman detective reached out her hand. "Zoe Yang," she offered.

The inspector shook it. "Bennett, Elina." She looked Zoe up and down. "So, they finally added a woman to the team. It's about time. Way too much testosterone here for my liking."

Ryan coughed.

"Not that I include Detective Ryan in that category," the inspector added.

"No?" Yang asked. "Is that a compliment or an insult?"

The inspector glanced from Detective Yang to Ryan. Things were prickly between the pair.

"I know Ryan can be a major pain in the ass sometimes, but bear with him. He'll teach you a lot," Elina said diplomatically.

Detective Ryan smiled, quietly pleased with the endorsement. Elina smiled back. The two cops liked each other and had much in common. With his brown skin, snappy suits, and love of good food, Ryan had always felt like a fish out of water in the all-male police club where lousy taste and machismo seemed to be de rigueur. He had survived because of his stand-out abilities as a detective; Elina Bennet had risen to head the IT division despite her youth and somewhat unusual appearance because, like Ryan, she was gifted at what she did.

"That for me?" Elina asked, pointing at the briefcase Detective Ryan was clutching.

"Yes," the detective said, carefully placing the case on Elina's desk. He flipped open the clasps and took out Gary Young's computer and iPhone, placing them down.

"I take it you want me to open those things up, Ryan," Elina said.

"That's the general idea."

"I'm guessing you don't have the passcodes?"

"Nope."

The inspector walked to the end of the desk and picked up a silver and black box. Returning, she put it down and reached into her jacket pocket to retrieve two leads and a power cord.

"Okay, Detective Yang, you can help me with this. I'll plug the leads into the back of the box, and you connect the other ends to the iPhone and computer inputs."

Zoe did as asked while Elina pushed the plug into a socket to turn the apparatus on.

"What *is* that?" Detective Yang queried as the box lit up.

"It's a Cellubrite UFED Touch3 Ruggedized Tablet and has comprehensive data extraction collection capabilities."

Ryan felt himself drifting. Zoe, though, seemed fascinated.

"It runs through all the various possibilities and eventually cracks the passcode," Detective Yang mused, impressed.

Elina stared at the newbie. "Very good. I don't often come across a cop with any interest in my work. Yes, this device runs through countless combinations until it finds the right one. A simple code can take one to three hours. A more complicated setup, when the owner has thought about security, well, that can be a day or two or even more." The inspector paused. "Was the person who owned these devices security conscious?"

"So we've been told," Detective Ryan said.

"Okay, leave it with me, and I'll get back to the OCS as soon as I have a result."

Ryan shook his head. "I'm not in organized crime anymore. I've moved to homicide."

"I joined him there today," Detective Yang said, offering the inspector her pristine white business card. "And it's best to use me as a point of contact rather than Detective Ryan, as I will be handling . . ." She paused, looking for the right word. "The nuts and bolts of the investigation," she said, parroting the term that Ryan had used earlier.

Elina studied the card before pocketing it. "Seems like you've got your prayers answered, Detective," the inspector said, looking at Ryan. "Someone to do your donkey work." She paused. "Now, with your permission, I'd like to give Detective Yang a tour of the department and our *extremely* expensive software. It's the same tour I gave you some time back. Hopefully, she'll find it more interesting than you did!"

A FEW MILES AWAY, THE MAN GRASPED the knife in his gloved hand and carefully slid the blade along the edge of the Diet Coke pack. Then, after lifting the cardboard flap, he reached into the box and removed the contents. He lined up the ten cans of soda on the wooden desk next to ten disposable plastic syringes, each filled with clear liquid.

As a kid, the man had liked Coca-Cola—the Classic, though, not the chemical-filled diet stuff. But as he got older, he had given up drinking soda. He knew how addictive it could be, and addictions were for weaklings. The recipient of these cans was one such person.

Reaching for the first can, the man gently pulled up the tab and pushed down the metal lid into the brown liquid. He turned the tab to the five o'clock position. Then, he picked up a syringe and held its needle over the opening. He pushed the plunger down. Liquid dropped into the dark bubbles of Coke, disappearing immediately. Removing the syringe, the man checked it was empty. Satisfied, he put the hypodermic back down. Next, he slowly and gently began to pull the lid up until the small piece of tin inside began to surface. Once the tab was visible, he ran his fingers around it and pressed so it filled the top.

Stages one and two were now complete. It was time for stage three. Holding the can's tab between his thumb and index finger, he twisted it back to its original position while pushing it down. The first can of Coke was ready to go.

As the man repeated the operation, he got quicker. He only made a few mistakes, where the tabs had proved impossible to replace. But he had anticipated this and had bought spares.

When all the cans had been removed, the man placed them back into their original packaging one by one. Then, it was time for the final stage . . . gluing the box flap back.

The man knew that certain materials called for certain types of glue. The best adhesive for corrugated cardboard may be different from that for cardstock. After extensive research, he opted for polyvinyl acetate glue. It dried to a transparent finish, virtually invisible to the eye. And it worked well on cardboard.

He picked up the glue bottle from the table and squeezed it along one edge of the flap before repeating the operation along the other side. After waiting for the glue to become tacky, he pushed the two pieces of cardboard closed to form a bond. The box lid containing the tampered Coke cans was now back in place. After thirty more minutes, the glue would be completely dry, and there would be no sign that the package had ever been opened. Perfect.

There was a knock on the door. The man checked his watch. Right on time.

"Come in," he shouted, "the door's open."

FOURTEEN

T HE FRONT DOOR OPENED, AND RYAN leaned over to kiss his mother.
"Happy birthday," he said.

"When you get to my age, no birthday is happy. But thank you anyway,
Ramesh," Mumta said.

After instructing Detective Yang to complete the daily report, Ramesh
Ryan had driven to his mother's large Federation house in Double Bay, a
ritzy suburb on Sydney's east side. He had felt guilty about leaving work
early but knew Mumta's "Why don't you come over tonight?" comment
this morning was no casual take-it-or-leave-it invitation. His mother was
generally forgiving about seeing her son less than she'd like. However,
birthdays were important, and there was one strict rule about the celebra-
tions—they were not to be missed.

"So, who else is coming?" the detective asked as he walked with Mumta
down the hallway.

"Just you."

"Oh, right."

Ramesh hadn't needed to ask. He was just being polite. If his mother had
invited her friends—a group of expensively coiffured ladies who lunched—
she would be wearing jewelry and a bright-colored sari. Instead, Mumta
was dressed in casual loungewear—baggy gray trousers and a matching
gray sweatshirt.

"Something smells good," Ryan said, following his mother into the living room.

"It's your favorite—fish curry. Now sit down," Mumta said, indicating the dining table. It was set for two, with plates of naan, popadams, and dishes of chutney and pickles already laid out on the pristine white tablecloth.

"I'll just finish up," Mumta said, heading for the kitchen.

"You sure you don't want a hand?" Ramesh asked, smiling to himself. It was the same rhetorical question that he asked every time he came to his mother's house for a meal.

His mother swiveled back around. "Help from you with cooking? That'll be the day."

"If you're sure?"

"Yes, I am. Now sit," Mumta said.

Ramesh sat at the table as his mother disappeared into the kitchen. He glanced around the room at the old, high-backed yellow sofa, the two large, beige armchairs on either side of the fireplace, and the wooden dresser lined with photos—pictures of him, his mom, and his dead father—but something was different. There had been changes. The couch had been moved farther down the wall and cozied up with piles of multicolored pillows; more photos had been placed above the mantel, a large new silver-framed mirror positioned above it; and multicolored glass vases and other knickknacks had been added to the bookshelf next to the fireplace. What was going on?

Mumta walked back into the room carrying two steaming curry bowls and noted her son's interest in the room. "What do you think, Ramesh?"

"You've made some adjustments," the detective said tactfully.

"Yes." Mumta paused. "I did say that I've been taking interior design classes, didn't I?"

"You did," the detective agreed.

"What do you think?" his mother said as she placed one of the curry dishes in front of him.

The new look wasn't really to Ramesh's taste, but there was no way he would say that to his mother. "It looks much better," he complimented.

Mumta beamed. "Thanks. Now, come on. Eat up."

Ramesh dug a fork into the food. His mom always expected him to taste her cooking before she began.

"As usual, it's delicious," he said.

Mumta sat down and tried the curry herself. "Yes. Not bad."

"It's perfect, Mom."

"If you say so," Mumta said, spooning chutney onto the rice.

"You should teach me how to cook," Ramesh suggested, taking another mouthful.

"Why would I do that?"

"So that I could make *you* something one day."

Mumta put down her fork. "Are you trying to put me out of a job?"

"No, it's not that . . . ."

"Well then, let's not talk about it anymore."

Mother and son ate in silence for a few moments. Then Ramesh asked, "You're enjoying the classes?"

"They're wonderful . . . an inspiration. You know, redecorating a house doesn't require all new furniture and paint. There are easy tricks to refresh and zhoosh up a room. That's what Tristram says, anyway."

"Tristram?" Ryan queried.

"Tristram De Vries." She paused. "Surely you've heard of him, Ramesh?"

The detective shook his head. "Nope. Sorry."

"That's surprising. He is a very well-known interior designer."

"And he talks about 'zhooshing,' does he?"

"Yes, he does." Mumta stopped. "You're not making fun of me, are you?"

The detective smiled. "No, of course not."

"Good," she said.

Silence as they continued to eat, and Ramesh readied himself. He had put off broaching the subject, but it had to be done. "Mom, about this morning? Why didn't you tell me?"

Mumta put down her fork. "Because it's nothing. I've had these lumps and bumps before. They've never proved to be anything." She paused. "Anyway, how was your first day?"

"You remembered?" Ramesh asked.

"I'm not senile, you know."

"I'm just surprised that with everything going on, you hadn't forgotten."

"What? That my only child was beginning work today in that murder place?"

Ramesh's spoon was halfway to his mouth when he paused, looking at his mother. He let out a small sigh before proceeding patiently. "It's called the Homicide Squad, Mom."

"Whatever. Just answer the question. How was it?"

Ramesh peered at Mumta. In another life, she would have made a very good police interrogator.

"It was . . . good. I met my new partner, too. Zoe Yang."

"Zoe Yang?" Mumta frowned. "Why do I know that name?" She clicked her fingers. "Got it. Isn't she the woman you worked with on the Central Coast?"

"Yes. You remembered that, too?"

"For goodness' sake, Ramesh, do I have to repeat that I'm not completely doolally?" She shook her head with seeming disappointment before continuing. "But I thought she was a *uniformed* policewoman."

"Zoe's a detective now, Mom," he said, looking down at his plate so his mother would not detect his irritation. "Superintendent Dudley has decided to team us up."

"I see." Mumta paused. "Why did it take you so long to tell me?"

"I only found out myself today." Ramesh looked at his mother, surprised by the question. "And I didn't think you'd have the slightest interest."

"What? In knowing who you were working with . . . a woman?" She put down her fork. "And there's something else you haven't mentioned."

"What?"

"Not a what. A who. Harry."

"Harry?"

"You know exactly who I'm talking about, Ramesh. Don't pretend otherwise."

"Oh, you mean the man you were chatting with at the hospital, who invited you to dinner."

"Yes, him," Mumta said and stopped. "Slow down, Ramesh. You eat far too fast."

She watched impatiently as he chewed. Then: "Well?"

"He was a nice guy."

"That's it?" Mumta peered at him suspiciously. "You're not upset, are you, Ramesh? You know I'll always love your dad."

"I know, Mom. I'd be happy if you found someone else. Honestly." He paused. "Now, if I could change the subject for a moment, I've got something for you." Ramesh reached into his pocket, took out a small package wrapped in red and gold striped paper, and offered it to Mumta.

"Is that for me?" his mother said, feigning surprise.

"I don't see anyone else around, do you?"

Mumta took the gift, undoing the wrapping and opening the box to reveal a stunning gold necklace.

"What do you think?" Ramesh asked.

"You shouldn't have," Mumta said, leaning over to kiss her son before carefully clipping the jewelry around her neck.

Ramesh smiled. "Are you saying I can't buy my mother anything for her birthday?"

"Of course not, though I'm not sure your job pays you enough to buy an expensive present like this."

"I earn more than enough, Mom," Ramesh said.

Mumta snorted. "Not half as much as you would if you had a decent job . . . like being a doctor or a lawyer."

Ramesh's shoulders slumped a little. He wasn't surprised by the comment, but he had been hoping for a reprieve from his mother's ongoing disappointment.

"Mom . . ."

"All right. I know you like your work." She stood up and walked over to peer at the necklace in the mirror hanging over the mantle. "This is beautiful," she said as Ramesh came to join her. "I would have preferred it if you'd bought it for your girlfriend."

"I haven't got one of those, Mom. You know that."

"Yes. And that's unfortunate."

"So you keep reminding me."

"If you had a girlfriend, you could marry and have children. It's not nice for a woman to leave the world without grandchildren."

Ramesh tilted his head at her, suddenly concerned. Was this his mother's usual melodrama or something else?

"What do you mean, 'leave the world'? Is there something you aren't telling me?"

Mumta smiled. "Not a thing."

"This comment has nothing to do with your hospital visit," Ramesh pressed.

"No. Of course not."

"You're sure?"

"Yes, yes. Stop being a worrywart."

"Mom . . ." he began with a slightly scolding tone.

"I know. I know. You're too busy for all that girlfriend business, but I don't understand why finding one is so difficult. I mean, even your mother has suitors." She smiled. "And it would be nice, wouldn't it? Grandchildren?"

FIFTEEN

*T*HE SUN HAD TORN THROUGH THE *morning's thin cover of wispy-white cloud, its rays beating down on the man's shirtless, tanned body as he dug his shovel into the large pack of Richgro. After filling the spade with the ammonia nitrate fertilizer, he walked across the freshly mowed lawn, sprinkling the powder.*

The man was still buzzing from last night's work. He was proud of what he had done. Solving the Coca-Cola problem had reawakened memories of what he used to do.

"It's looking good, isn't it?" a voice asked, interrupting his thoughts.

The question came from a bikini-clad woman who stood at the back door of her large two-story house.

"Yep, you have a great lawn here, Mrs. Saker," the man said.

"Thanks to you," she said and stepped onto the grass.

The man raised his hand. "I wouldn't, ma'am. Not just yet. Not barefoot."

"Oh," McKenzie Saker said, taking a step back. "How long, then?"

"Give the fertilizer a couple of hours to sink into the soil. Then you'll be right."

"So, what's good for the garden isn't good for me?" McKenzie Saker smiled.

"No, not at the moment."

"Okay, well, when you're finished, knock, and I'll pay you."

"Will do, Mrs. Saker," he said.

The woman went back into the house and closed the door.

Happy to be alone again, the man reached for his backpack. Opening it, he lifted out a blue metal bottle, clamped his fingers around the cap loop of the bottle, and pulled the top open. He took a large gulp of water. In all the years he'd worked as a gardener, none of his wealthy clients had ever offered him a drink. They seldom even allowed him into their homes.

He closed the bottle and returned it to the backpack. There was no point in getting upset. He loved gardening. It provided a seamless link between his life in the forest and what people called "the real world." He was alone in both, and that was the way he liked it.

Wiping the sweat from his face, he peered over at the pool, its blue water sparkling in the sunlight. He didn't have much time for pools. He preferred rivers, where the water flowed freely and wasn't filled with toxic chemicals. He didn't like lawns much, either, though most of his clients loved them. At first, he had tried to persuade them to grow vegetables instead. But they wouldn't, so eventually, he gave up. There was no point in trying. Their lives had nothing to do with his . . .. Until now, that was.

SEVERAL MILES AWAY, DETECTIVE RYAN PARKED in front of the ugly new modernist building that housed Sydney's forensic medicine department; he was still mulling over what his mother had said last night. Grandchildren! Not just one, but several!

It was the only time Ryan could remember Mumta being so direct about her desire for grandkids. Usually, she was content to lecture him about the importance of finding a girlfriend. This time, though, she had jumped that stage and, based on zero evidence, assumed he would soon find a suitable long-term marriage prospect—not just any woman, either, but someone who would be happy to have the squadron of children his mother so longed for. Did this have something to do with her health, he wondered? Something she wasn't telling him?

Ryan grabbed his briefcase, exited the vehicle, and headed for the entrance. He tried to refocus as he waited for the door to slide open. He must concentrate on the case.

AT THE FRONT DESK, RYAN SHOWED his ID to the receptionist. She checked on the computer. Yes, Noah Bellman had rung through to confirm Detective Ryan's visit.

The woman handed the detective a white visitor's label. Ryan hated stickers. They always left marks on his suit, but as the receptionist watched, he had no choice but to slap the label on his lapel.

"A woman named Abi Young is coming in about half an hour, so please ring pathology when she arrives," Ryan said.

"Will do. And Mr. Bellman's room is . . ."

"Thank you, I know," Ryan said, turning and setting off.

Detective Ryan followed the curve of the brightly lit corridor, walking past closed doors before arriving in front of one marked Pathology Three. He knocked, turned the handle, and entered a small empty anteroom. Every visitor had to go through it to reach the morgue. He mused that it appeared to serve as a barrier between the living and the dead.

Ryan walked across the room and opened the door on the opposite side. Inside, Noah Bellman was stooped over a steel table in the center of the space. White tiles covered the walls from floor to ceiling. Noah wore a long lab coat, jeans, and rubber boots. A hairnet checked his messy brown hair.

"Morning, Ryan," the pathologist greeted him, twisting around to face the detective. "You made good time."

"Traffic was light," Ryan said. "You sounded excited on the phone. It's not an emotion I usually associate with you."

"That's harsh, Ryan." Noah grinned. "Just because I deal with death doesn't mean *I'm* emotionally dead."

"Wasn't suggesting you were," the detective replied with no hint of irony.

Noah had called Ryan just as the detective was about to leave home, requesting that he come over immediately. The pathologist had been tight-lipped about the results of his work except to confirm that Gary Young had, as suspected, been murdered.

After Noah called him, Ryan rang Detective Yang to tell her of the pathologist's news. She had news, too. Elina Bennett from IT had cracked the passcodes on Gary Young's computer and iPhone. Did Ryan want her to search through the devices now?

Detective Ryan had reluctantly agreed. He liked to be hands-on with every part of the investigation, but given that the first few days of any homicide inquiry were critical and Zoe had been desperate to do more, he had consented.

"What have you got for me?" the detective said, bending down to peer at Gary Young's naked body, which lay sprawled out on the metal table. Signs of the autopsy were visible—the crude stitching that showed Young had been cut open and his organs examined.

"Poison," Noah said. He pointed at the dead man's left arm. "Take a look."

Ryan stared at the cluster of tiny pinpricks Bellman was indicating.

"The toxin entered there," the pathologist said. "And this wasn't just *any* poison. Let me show you."

Noah motioned the detective to follow him to a steel desk, where a thick book lay open. "I brought this in for you to see. It's—" the pathologist began, but Ryan cut him off.

"*Illustrated Toxicology* by P.K. Gupta is an excellent read. And I'm guessing that you believe this nettle, the gympie-gympie, killed him," the detective said, pointing at a photo of a green heart-shaped leaf. He looked at the pathologist and nodded. "I had a feeling," he said.

Noah stared at the detective, incredulous. "A 'feeling'? You never cease to amaze me, Ryan. How did you know?"

"I didn't. That's to say, it was only one of the possible poisons I suspected."He explained further. "I researched 'the local vegetation—specifically, plants toxic to humans."

Noah shook his head, impressed, as Ryan continued. "What have you estimated as the time of death?"

"About two to three hours before he was discovered. The process of poisoning, though, would have begun at least a day earlier. And he would have been in agony for quite some time before he died. Whoever did this wanted to make him suffer," Noah said as he walked back to the body. He pointed again at the pinpricks on Gary Young's arm. "As you know, every part of the gympie-gympie plant is covered in silica hairs which act like hypodermic needles, so this was definitely the poison's point of entry."

Ryan leaned down. "Someone must have attached a leaf or leaves to his arm and then watched him die."

"Yeah, and they must have had a reasonable knowledge of the park's flora in order to obtain the plant."

The pathologist's cell rang. Answering it, he listened. "Yes. Yes . . . I'll pass it on," he said. He ended the call. "That was the reception. Mr. Young's wife has arrived."

THERE'S A SMORGASBORD OF EMOTIONS CONNECTED to the identification of a body. Fear and anxiety as people come face to face with death; relief that there can be some closure; and anger that a life has been cut short, a family destroyed.

But Abi Young showed none of these. She was subdued. The woman had dressed down for the identification, wearing a black T-shirt and jeans. She had yet to speak as she walked with Detective Ryan from the reception, down the corridor, and through to the anteroom. Ryan had done all the talking, explaining that she needn't stay long. All they required was for her to confirm it was her husband.

Entering the morgue, Abi hesitated, apparently unwilling to take the few steps to the table where the body lay. Seeing the woman's reluctance, Noah came over.

"Mrs. Young, this is the pathologist, Noah Bellman," Detective Ryan said, introducing them. "If you want, I can stay here, and he can take you over."

"No, no . . . that's fine." She took a deep breath. "I can do this," she said, sounding unsure.

With Noah leading, the group headed for the table. A white sheet had been placed on top of Gary Young's corpse. "Are you ready?" the pathologist asked gently.

"Yes," Abi said, her voice low, tears welling in her eyes.

Noah pulled back the sheet.

Abi gasped, putting a hand to her mouth. "Yes. Yes. That's Gary."

"You're formally identifying your husband, Gary Young?" Detective Ryan asked, watching her carefully.

"Yes." She nodded.

Ryan looked to Noah, who drew the sheet back over the body in response.

Abi began to shake before bursting into a torrent of tears. "Poor, poor Gary," she sobbed.

Ryan watched the woman intently as Noah put a comforting arm around her shoulders. Ryan had been here many times before; had witnessed the grief of bereaved husbands, wives, parents. He had never questioned the authenticity of their reactions. But something about Abi gave him pause for thought.

SIXTEEN

WHEN HE RETURNED TO POLICE HEADQUARTERS, Detective Ryan had been summoned into Superintendent Dudley's office.

"Sit down," Dudley ordered, indicating the empty chair next to Detective Yang. Ryan did as he was told, shooting a questioning look to Yang as Dudley stood at the window, appearing to study the street below.

Yang shrugged. Like Ryan, she had no idea why they'd been called in.

After a moment, Dudley spoke. "Right, detectives. Would you like to tell me what you've both been doing for the last twenty-four hours?" he asked, his back still turned.

Ryan frowned, still confused. "Investigating a murder, sir."

"And?" Dudley watched as cars moved along the busy thoroughfare below.

"Well, it's very early days, but we're making progress," Yang answered. "We've identified the deceased as Gary Young, a fifty-six-year-old male who was found, as you know, in a rental cabin in Ku-ring-gai Chase National Park. We've spoken to the wife, and it appears her husband lied to her about his whereabouts over the weekend," Yang continued. "We don't yet know why, but we are pursuing leads."

"And cause of death?" Dudley turned to face the detectives.

"We only just got the results from pathology. He was poisoned by a toxic plant native to the area. Whoever did it had local knowledge."

"Poisoned? What else wasn't in the report?"

"Sir? I'm sorry, but I'm not sure I follow," Yang said uncertainly.

"I want to know more about your conversation with his business partners. There wasn't much in the report about *that*." He looked squarely at Detective Yang as he said it.

"Sir?" she began uncertainly. "I think I included everything of relevance."

"I'll be the judge of that, thank you, Detective," he said, his voice rising. "I asked for comprehensive reports, which is *not* what I've been given."

Detective Yang looked slightly exasperated as Dudley walked from behind his desk to stand in front of his seated subordinates—a favorite tactic designed to intimidate. Meanwhile, Ryan had been trying to figure out where all this was going. Dudley's disinterest in daily reports was well known, and the fact that he'd bothered to read one was surprising in itself, but that he'd found Zoe's report lacking was . . . intriguing.

"I read her report myself, and I'm quite certain it covered all the salient points," Ryan protested.

Dudley was irritated. He was also sweating. He took a handkerchief out of his trouser pocket and wiped his face. "And why was he there? On a fishing trip? Entertaining prostitutes?"

"We don't yet know the answer to that," Ryan replied, "but we know he rented the cabin regularly. As far as anyone else being present apart from the killer, we are yet to determine this, as the crime scene had been bleach-cleaned of all traces of DNA."

Dudley nodded thoughtfully as Ryan continued. "But again, that was all in the report, sir."

Dudley turned his attention back to Yang. "What about Mr. Young's involvement in the Faith Company? Was *that* in the report?"

The detectives looked a little nonplussed.

"We interviewed the other two partners," Yang said. "We will be looking at them more closely, of course, but at this stage, there's nothing to suggest that either of them was involved."

Dudley looked from Yang to Ryan.

"Had either of you heard of the Faith Company before this investigation?"

Detective Yang shook her head.

"I did some research late yesterday . . .." Ryan paused momentarily as the pieces started to fall into place. That's why they'd been called in for this meeting. It was all about public relations, he thought.

"I remember reading something about the Faith Company sponsoring a yacht . . . ." Ryan began.

Dudley snapped his fingers.

"An eighteen-footer, to be exact," Dudley said. "One of ours."

"I still don't . . ." Yang looked at Ryan, confused.

"The Faith Company sponsors a skiff that is part of the Eighteen-Footers Club and crewed by children whose parents have been killed or injured in the line of duty," Ryan explained.

"In other words, the Faith Company's relationship with New South Wales Police is highly valued by my superiors," Dudley added. "So, while I want no stone left unturned in this investigation, turn them carefully. Understood?"

"Understood, sir," Ryan said.

"Yes, got that, sir," Detective Yang concurred.

"Good. Meeting over. You can both go."

The detectives stood up and walked to the door.

"One more thing," Dudley said.

They turned.

"How well are you two getting on together?"

"No complaints," Ryan answered.

"And you, Yang?" Dudley asked.

"Yeah, great," Zoe agreed.

"Good. And remember what I said about the Faith Company. Caution is the watchword!"

SEVENTEEN

SIMON FAITH YAWNED. HE WAS BORED. The eighteen-footer sailing race would soon be over, and the result didn't look to be in any doubt. Their boat wouldn't win the race. The Fisher & Paykel yacht was way ahead. Some distance back, the Kitchen Maker and Faith Company vessels vied for second place.

Sailing had never held much appeal for Simon, nor indeed for Luke Saker, the man standing next to him swigging from a can of Diet Coke. It had been Gary Young who, years ago, had persuaded both partners to sponsor one of the eighteen-footers.

Sailing was Gary Young's passion—one of the few things that had made him happy. Even though the accountant was usually tighter than a duck's ass when it came to spending money, he'd been all in for sponsoring one of the skiffs and had written a detailed outline explaining why it would be a mistake for the company not to do it.

Back then, Simon had idly perused the document, confident he would turn down the plan, but he'd had a change of heart after reading that children of New South Wales police officers were involved in the sailing club. Suddenly, sponsorship was a no-brainer. Having the police on their side was a must.

Today, sixteen-year-old Terry Graham had been assigned to the Faith Company boat. The boy was the son of a high-ranking policeman killed in a horrific shooting. There had been an outpouring of public and media grief following the top cop's death.

Simon signaled Luke to follow him to the spectator ferry's bow. The men could talk freely there, away from others.

"I don't know how Gary did it," Simon said as they arrived.

"What do you mean?" Luke queried.

Simon stared at his business partner. "I don't know how he survived two hours of this every month. I'm bored out of my brain."

"Yeah, well, better get used to it. Without Gary, it's up to us to keep the company flag flying."

Simon scowled, but he knew his business partner had a point.

There was silence as they watched the race some more. Then, Simon said: "Has anyone asked you where he is yet?"

"Yeah, one guy. I gave him the 'he's sick with the flu' line."

"Did it work?" Simon asked.

"Yes."

"Astonishing," he said before starting to clap.

Luke peered at him. "What are you doing?"

"That's our boat, there." Simon pointed into the distance. "Show some enthusiasm."

"Woohoo!" Luke shouted. "Come on. You can catch them. You're doing great."

Simon leaned close to his partner. "Okay. That's enough. Now you're being too enthusiastic."

Silence. Then: "When do you think the cops will release news of Gary's death?" Luke asked.

"Soon, I think."

"Right."

"You know his dying could be a blessing in disguise. It'll focus the media on the hotel's reopening. Give them a good hook," Simon added.

"You think?"

"Sure."

"Won't it put off people coming to the hotel?"

"I wouldn't think so. It'll add a bit of spice," Simon said, smiling. "People love drama."

Luke studied Simon for a moment, his eyes narrowing.

"No such thing as bad publicity? Right?"

"Exactly," Simon replied.

There was silence. Simon felt Luke's eye on him. He turned to look at him.

"What?"

"Nothing."

The hotel boss peered at his business partner. "Liar. Come on, tell me."

"Okay, well, you were always complaining that three is a problematic number for decision-making, and recently, there have been more arguments than usual."

"So?"

"So, nothing," Luke said evasively.

Simon stared at him. "Fucking hell, Luke, do you really believe that I had something to do with Gary's death?"

"Of course not." Luke backtracked. "But it *is* a mystery, isn't it?" He paused. "Do you think he really was murdered?"

"I don't think homicide would get involved if he weren't," Simon replied sarcastically.

"But who would want to kill Gary?" Luke asked.

Simon thought. "I guess there is one possibility."

Luke stared at the hotel boss. "You're not thinking of . . .?" He shook his head. "No way. Out of the question."

"You're saying he's not capable of it?" Simon Faith laughed.

"No, of course he is. But why would he?"

Simon considered the question for a moment before responding.

"Yeah, you're right. Ridiculous thought," he said, staring at the Faith Company boat now sailing closer to them. "Wow. Come on, guys, you can do it!"

"Yeah, go, guys!" Luke shouted.

They followed the race for a few more moments before Simon looked down at his watch, a prized possession he never took off.

"Lunch?" he queried.

"You're on," Luke replied.

EIGHTEEN

Detective Ryan sat with Detective Yang in the far corner of the deserted police cafeteria.

The detectives had gone to the café on Dudley's suggestion after their debriefing with the superintendent. In the interest of collegiality, Ryan had agreed. Now, though, he was having second thoughts.

"What do you think?" Detective Yang said, studying Ryan as he swallowed a mouthful of a limp cheese sandwich.

"Sometimes it's nice to eat food this bad. That way, you can really appreciate the next good meal," Detective Ryan replied.

"You're such a snob," Detective Yang said, jabbing a fork into her Greek salad bowl. "We haven't got time to go to one of your fancy restaurants. Never mind the expense."

Deliberately ignoring the comment, Detective Ryan changed the subject.

"Tell me, what did you find on Gary Young's computer and iPhone?"

"That he's not a great social media user. He only posted intermittently—pictures of him and his wife and their perfect marriage."

Ryan scowled. He hated social media with a passion. "And was there anything particularly sensitive on there? To do with the Faith Company?"

"Nothing that stood out."

"Interesting that Simon Faith and the lawyer made such a fuss about confidentiality, then."

"Probably just paranoid and covering their butts. You know what these business types are like—everything's a trade secret." Zoe paused. "There were, though, a couple of interesting personal items."

"Like?"

"The payout on the Youngs' life insurance coverage had recently been increased," Zoe said.

"How recently?"

"Three months ago."

"Always a red flag," Ryan said. "Not necessarily surprising, though, seeing as how Gary Young is . . . was . . . no spring chicken," Ryan said, pushing his plate away.

"Are you going to eat that?" Detective Yang asked.

"Unlikely."

"You should," Zoe admonished. "I bet you haven't eaten anything all day."

Detective Ryan grunted and picked up the bready triangle without enthusiasm. "What exactly was on the policy?"

"Abi Young was the sole beneficiary," Detective Yang said.

"Goes to motive." Detective Ryan paused. "Especially when you consider the . . ."

"Tennis coach?" Detective Yang said, finishing the sentence.

"You saw that, too?" Ryan asked.

"Hard not to. They're obviously having an affair. The only thing surprising was the time you took to bring it up." Detective Yang peered at Ryan. "Were you waiting to see if I'd mention it?"

Ryan said nothing as Zoe took a sip of tea and pulled a face. "You may have a point about this place," she said after a moment.

"Not good?"

"I've had better . . . much better." She pointed at his cup. "And yours?"

"If I were marooned on a desert island and had a choice between drinking from a polluted lake or downing this coffee, the lake would be my first choice." He paused. "Is that it?"

"Not entirely. There was one strange item. A copy of an invoice to Gary Young from City Reports, a private investigation company. It was dated last Tuesday."

"And what was it that Gary wanted investigated?" Detective Ryan asked.

"It didn't say. It was just a request for a payment of two thousand bucks for services rendered."

Silence as Ryan discarded a dry sandwich crust.

"Are we going back to see the wife? Ask her about the life insurance?" Detective Yang asked.

Ryan stroked his chin. "Yes, but not just yet." The detective stood up.

"Not eating your crusts?" Zoe grinned. "I heard it makes your hair curly."

"I suggest you check your sources, Detective. A white-bread myth, if ever I've heard one." He grabbed his jacket from the back of the chair, smiling at his own joke.

"Where to now?" Detective Yang asked as she followed him out the door.

NINETEEN

THE DETECTIVES TOOK THE ELEVATOR TO the tenth floor of the tall CBD office building and walked down a brightly lit corridor to a door embossed with the company name City Reports in bold type.

The waiting room was large and luxuriously furnished, with two white sofas arranged in an L shape and facing a reception desk that looked like it had come straight from the control deck of the Starship Enterprise—a block of nine-foot-long warm oak with black German Hueck textured surfaces. Ryan could hear typing coming from behind a massive, curved Samsung computer screen.

Detective Yang closed the door as Ryan walked over. "Hello," he said.

A young woman slid into view from behind the screen. The name Angela Stevens was printed on a small card pinned to her black jacket.

"Yes?" she asked.

"I'm looking for the private investigator who did work for Mr. Gary Young," Detective Ryan said, offering his ID.

Angela peered at it for a moment. "Just one moment, Detective."

She disappeared behind the screen again—more typing. Then, the woman reappeared.

"That would be Mr. Scallini," she said. "Take a seat, and I'll let him know you're here."

The two detectives perched on one of the expensive leather sofas. It was as hard as a rock, proving how style and comfort rarely married.

After a moment, a man in his early thirties appeared—square-faced, with dark, piercing brown eyes and neatly groomed shoulder-length hair. He was dressed in an expensive-looking black suit with a blue shirt and a striped yellow and black tie.

"Detective?" he said, pausing in the doorway and peering at Ryan.

"Detectives," Yang corrected.

"Yes, of course. Detectives," he said, walking over. "Guy Scallini. It's a pleasure to meet you."

"Detective Ryan."

"Detective Yang."

The detectives shook his hand before following Scallini out of the reception area.

"My office is at the end," the private detective said, pointing down the narrow corridor.

They passed two closed doors before reaching one with the inscription GUY SCALLINI on it. The PI opened the door and motioned them inside.

The room had the same aesthetic vibe as the reception area—a similar desk, screen, and phone—but it had the addition of a spectacular view of the Sydney Opera House.

"Please, take a seat," Scallini said, pointing at two metal chairs that looked like a member of the Spanish Inquisition had designed them.

"You told my receptionist that this has something to do with Gary Young?" Scallini said as he took a seat behind his desk.

"Yes. I believe he was a client of yours?" Ryan said.

"That's correct." Scallini looked intrigued.

"What exactly did he hire you to do?" Detective Ryan asked.

Scallini didn't answer immediately. "You know, you're rather well-dressed for a police detective."

"I don't see the two as mutually exclusive," Ryan replied.

Scallini smiled. "I don't think the rest of the Homicide Squad got that memo, if you don't mind me saying." He glanced quickly at Yang without comment. Detective Yang frowned, looking down at her own attire.

"I'm sorry, but you didn't answer the question," Ryan reminded him.

Scallini smiled. "What was it, again?" he said, appearing to stall.

"What did Gary Young pay you to do?" Detective Ryan repeated.

Scallini hesitated as the door opened and Angela the reception-ist, appeared. She carried a glass of water and carefully placed it on Guy Scallini's desk.

"Is that all, Mr. Scallini?" the woman said, taking a step back.

"Perhaps the detectives would like something to drink? Coffee? Tea? Something stronger?" the PI asked and smiled, revealing a set of glistening white teeth.

The detectives shook their heads.

"That's all then, Angela," Guy Scallini said

The detectives waited a moment for the woman to exit. Ryan had seen this ploy play out before. Angela was the distraction, someone who could break up the flow of conversation and give Scallini time to work out what he was and wasn't prepared to say.

"Sorry, where were we?" Scallini asked.

"Asking about Gary Young and why he hired you," Ryan said.

Scallini shook his head. "Of course."

Silence.

"And the answer is?" Detective Ryan said after a long moment.

"As you know, licensed private investigators have strict rules, so I'm afraid I can't give you that information . . . not without the client's permis-sion." He stood up. "Now, if that's all . . ."

Neither Ryan nor Yang moved.

"I'm afraid that won't be possible," Ryan informed him.

Scallini detected the gravity in the detective's voice. He resumed his seat. "What do you mean?" he asked, already suspecting the answer.

"Your client was found dead, days ago. And we suspect he was murdered."

"I see," Scallini said quietly.

Ryan continued. "Now, can you tell us what you were doing for Gary Young?"

TWENTY

IN THE CASINO, HEIDI MILLER HAD survived two so-so hands, three of a kind and a flush, before dealing a death blow to Danny Ivey, the only other remaining player at her table. Hailing from the US of A, Ivey was a cowboy-hat-wearing misogynist who ranked just above Heidi. He hadn't taken kindly to the loss and had stormed off.

As Heidi swept up his chips, she tugged at her jacket sleeves. It was a tell, a nervous celebration of victory while wearing her lucky red blazer.

Heidi had first donned the jacket five tournaments back. She'd won the event and had attributed her success to the blazer. Heidi knew she looked good in it, and accentuating her curves distracted her male opponents. After that win, she always wore the jacket at some point in a tournament—usually on the last day. But this event was proving tricky. It had already produced lots of surprises. Several high-ranking players had been unceremoniously dispatched by unknowns who had previously been considered long shots. So, the blazer had come out early.

After the game, Heidi retreated to the bar. A Hendrick's gin and tonic was part of her routine. Only one was allowed, and only if she had triumphed. It helped slow her down and stopped her from replaying bad hands in her head.

Casino bars tended to be tucked away, the establishment preferring to serve drinks on the floor so gamblers didn't move from the tables. This bar was no different. The Sun Casino in Sydney had hidden it behind a shimmering curtain some distance from the cards and machines. It was almost empty.

"There you go," the barman said, putting the glass of liquor down.

"Thanks," Heidi said while peering at the barman's name tag. "Put it on the room, please, Fred. Number . . ."

"No need. It's covered." Fred pointed to a man in his thirties seated at the counter's far end. He was dressed in a crumpled brown suit and had the kind of face that wasn't exactly ugly, but it wasn't handsome, either—the sort of person you'd never remember in a crowd.

Heidi turned back to the barman and shook her head. "I can't accept that."

"Are you sure?" a voice said.

Heidi swiveled around to see the man in the crumpled suit approaching.

"It's strictly a no-strings-attached offer," he said.

"You're paying for my drink out of the goodness of your heart? Sorry, but that doesn't pass the smell test." Heidi turned back to the barman. "I'll pay for the drink, Fred. Put it on my room."

The barman nodded. "Will do." He moved away as the man took the seat next to Heidi.

"Okay, look, you got me. I do have an ulterior motive. I want to congratulate you on your game today. You were on fire."

"You were watching?"

"Three rows back . . . I'm Dave Jupiter, by the way."

Heidi sighed. This was getting tedious. "Look, Mr. Jupiter, I prefer to be left alone after a match," Heidi said, ignoring Jupiter's outstretched hand.

"I understand . . . of course." He made as if to get up but then stopped and sat back down. "The thing is, I was hoping you could help me. You're a great source of inspiration, overcoming so many obstacles to get to where you are."

Heidi stared at him. "You're a journalist? That's what this is all about?"

Jupiter shook his head vigorously. "No." He paused. "Until a few months ago, I was in the navy . . . .. Fifteen years in the service."

"Well done," Heidi said and meant it.

"Thanks," he said. "The thing is, when I left, I had no idea what came next. I wanted to do something completely different."

Heidi smiled. Now she had it. "And you're thinking of a career as a poker player."

Jupiter smiled back. "Right in one."

Heidi had met a few Dave Jupiters before—men, and it was always men, who fantasized about taking up poker professionally. Most would never do it.

"So, you're looking for advice," Heidi said, gulping her drink.

"Exactly."

She put the glass down. "My advice is . . . don't. It's a hard life. Few earn a decent living."

"But you have?"

"Yes, but I've thought about giving up many times."

"I'd be surprised if most hadn't," Jupiter said. "The thing is. I believe I have the talent to do it. And I don't give up easily. But, and this is why I wanted to talk to you, I need backing, certainly for the first few years . . ."

"Let me stop you there. If this is some shakedown, you're speaking to the wrong person. I can't back you."

Jupiter smiled. "No. No. That's not it. I need to be pointed in the right direction." He paused. "You do have a sponsor, don't you?"

Heidi said nothing.

"It's a tricky area, sponsorship. I'm just interested in who yours is and what you're expected to do for them. What are the obligations?"

"Obligations?" Heid said, repeating the word.

"You know, is there anything that's . . . demanded of you?"

The conversation was starting to make Heidi more than uncomfortable.

"Mr. Jupiter, there's only one obligation my sponsor expects me to meet, and that's winning," Heidi said, swigging back the remains of her drink and standing. "Good luck with your career choice."

Jupiter watched Heidi go. The conversation hadn't reaped the rewards he had hoped for, but the meeting had been worth it. Jupiter was old school and believed in getting close to your mark. Then, it was just a matter of time before he reeled them in.

TWENTY-ONE

DETECTIVE RYAN AND DETECTIVE YANG WAITED outside Abi Young's front door. After a few moments, it opened. Abi was dressed in a very different outfit from the one she had been wearing at the morgue. She wore an elegant, flowing silk cocktail dress and wedge sandals; her hair was up, and her lips were stained with bright red lipstick.

Abi's mouth dropped open as she stared at the two detectives. "I wasn't expecting you."

"We were in the area, so we thought we'd drop by and fill you in on where we are with the investigation," Detective Ryan said.

"Oh, right," the woman said, flustered. "You'd best come in, then."

The detectives followed Abi down the hallway into the living room.

"Please take a seat," she said, pointing to the sofa. "I hope this won't take long, detectives. I have a drinks rendezvous with some friends. You just caught me in time."

Abi looked from one detective to the other, clearly uncomfortable. "I know what you're thinking, but it's not like that."

"Like what?" Detective Ryan asked.

"Me, all dressed up and going out just after Gary's death, but . . ." She searched for the right words. "Gary wouldn't have wanted me to sit at home crying, and . . . this little soiree, well, it's just close friends who want to . . . to support me . . . ." She broke off nervously. The detectives, meanwhile, remained straight-faced.

"How you grieve is none of our business," Detective Ryan offered.

Abi smiled uncertainly and sat down opposite the cops. "You said something about an update?"

"We have news about the cause of your husband's death." Detective Ryan took a deep breath. "It appears that he was poisoned."

"What?" Abi said, the color draining from her face.

The front doorbell rang.

"Poisoned?" Abi repeated.

The bell rang again.

"Would you like me to get that?" Detective Yang offered.

Abi stared at her for a moment before answering.

"No . . . thank you. I'll go," she said, before slowly standing and heading for the front door.

When Abi returned, it was with a man the two detectives recognized immediately, though instead of tennis whites, he wore a smart, bright blue jacket and beige chinos.

"Detectives, good to see you both again," the man said.

"You remember Rob McMillan? He's my tennis coach," Abi said, looking uncomfortable again. "And tonight he's also my plus one."

"Mrs. Young asked me to accompany her to the drinks party," Rob said, appearing a little too eager to explain.

"I wanted the company . . . with the trauma of this morning, and now even more so after what you've just told me," Abi said.

Rob looked over at her, concerned. "Has something else happened?" he asked.

"Take a seat, please." Detective Ryan motioned to a chair.

"Gary was poisoned," Abi said quickly as the coach sat down.

"Poisoned?" Rob repeated, shocked.

"Yes, the police have just told me that was the cause of Gary's death," Abi said, sitting next to the coach.

"In light of the new information, there are a few questions we'd like to ask both of you," Detective Ryan said.

"Both of us?" Rob queried. "But I'm just Abi's tennis coach."

"Nevertheless, I need to speak to you, too," Detective Ryan said.

The pair glanced at each other. "Do I need a lawyer?" Abi asked.

It was the one question Ryan hated so early in an investigation, and he was surprised that Abi thought she might need one. That didn't usually happen unless the person was concerned that they might be a suspect. Ryan had deliberately gone to the house to avoid that by keeping things informal. The presence of a lawyer would change everything.

"That's up to you, Abi, but if you insist on a lawyer, we will have to adjourn and set up a formal interview for you both at the station."

"Abi?" Rob said, looking over at her. "I would prefer to do this here, now. I've got nothing to hide."

Abi considered this for a moment, then nodded. "Me neither."

"If we can begin," Detective Ryan said, hiding his relief as Detective Yang took out her iPhone and pressed record. "Interview with Abi Young and Rob McMillan," she said, adding the time, day, location, and usual cautions.

Detective Ryan opened his briefcase and removed a small stack of A4-sized color photos. He spread them out on the table.

"I'd like you both to look at these." Ryan sat back. The images showed the pair making love on the living room floor.

The couple peered at the pictures.

"What the fuck!" Rob exclaimed.

"Who took these?" Abi demanded.

"A private investigator," Detective Ryan said.

Rob slumped back. "Jesus, Abi . . ."

Abi leaned forward, angry. "Who hired him?"

"You don't know?" Detective Ryan asked.

Abi met his gaze head-on. Her demeanor had changed to one of defiance. She knew exactly who was responsible. "Well, Gary, I suppose."

She spun around to look at Rob. "I told you he knew, but you wouldn't believe me."

Detective Ryan glanced over at Detective Yang before continuing. "The two of you were having an affair?"

Abi looked down at her hands, which were tightly clenched in her lap. She momentarily thought about making up a lie, but considering the photos, there didn't seem to be much point.

"Gary and I weren't exactly compatible. He was set in his ways. Didn't want to go anywhere. Didn't want to do anything."

"You found him dull?" Detective Ryan asked.

Abi hesitated, knowing how her answer might make her look.

"As ditch water," Abi said firmly.

"But you married him?" Detective Yang said.

"Yes." She stared at Zoe. "Gary wanted a wife, and I wanted . . . a nice life," she said unapologetically. "Gary was twenty years older than me. He was overweight, had a bad heart, and loved fast food. I figured he only had about five years left, and I was prepared to suck it up." She looked at the view outside the French doors before continuing. "But then I met Rob." She shrugged. "And I thought, why not? I couldn't see anything wrong with having a bit of fun on the side."

The tennis coach stared at her. "Did you say 'a bit of fun'? Is that all you think I am?" he said. "I thought . . ."

"You thought we would get married and have kids?" Abi interrupted, incredulous. "And live happily ever after?"

"I thought you were in love with me."

"God. You are something else," she said in disbelief.

"You never considered hurrying things along?" Ryan asked, interrupting.

Abi stared at the cop. "I may be many things, but I am not a murderer, Detective."

"What about the life insurance policy and payout increase?" Detective Ryan asked.

Abi hesitated. "You know about that?"

"If you could answer the question, please, Abi," Ryan prompted.

Silence. Then, "That was Gary's decision, though we both discussed it. He said he wanted to make sure that in the event of either of us dying, we were more than well covered."

"'Set for life' is the expression, isn't it?" Ryan asked.

"Certainly better than a divorce settlement," Yang added.

Abi stared at them and then shook her head. "Oh, you don't that think . . ." she began, her voice trailing off.

"Don't think what?" Rob said, looking confused.

"For Christ's sake, Rob, don't you get it? They think we poisoned Gary for the insurance money." Abi pointed at Rob. "Look at him, detectives. He's hardly MENSA material. He couldn't plan a piss-up in a brewery!"

"Hey, Abi, that's insulting," the coach said, glaring at her.

"You are saying neither of you had anything to do with the murder of your husband?" Ryan said.

"No!" Abi Young said emphatically.

"Absolutely not," Rob McMillan confirmed.

TWENTY-TWO

"DID ABI YOUNG MURDER HER HUSBAND?" Detective Ryan asked as he drove the car out of the driveway and onto the main road.

"No. But you knew that anyway, didn't you?" Detective Yang answered.

"I did?" Ryan asked.

Yang peered at him. "Both of us knew she had an alibi. That sleazy PI, Scallini, told us he was taking photos at the house the night when Gary Young was being murdered. Abi Young and Rob McMillan were there all night and never came out. Neither of them could have killed him." She paused. "I don't understand why we had to drive out here to discover something we already knew."

Ryan twisted the wheel, guiding the car around a bend in the road. "Isn't it possible that one or both of them hired someone else to do the job?" he asked.

Detective Yang thought about this for a moment. "Good point, I suppose." She smiled grudgingly before turning her gaze to the road ahead. Ryan was silent as he allowed her to mull over what they knew. Then she turned, struck by a thought.

"What if they knew they were being watched?" she said. "What if they put on a little show for that PI, knowing it would give them an airtight alibi?" Yang looked at Ryan, pleased with herself.

"Nicely deduced." Ryan nodded, looking impressed. "If only that were true, we could have this case sewn up by the end of the week."

"What do you mean, 'if only'?" Zoe asked, frowning. "What do you know that I don't?"

Ryan eased the car to a stop as he reached a set of lights. He smiled. "Abi Young didn't kill her husband. But I only knew that for certain after we questioned her, which is why we went to the house. I was hoping you'd reached the same conclusion."

Detective Yang looked at him, unimpressed. He really could be a supercilious bastard sometimes. Ryan continued. "You want me to tell you how I know that?"

"Please. Enlighten me," she replied sarcastically.

The light changed to green, and Ryan accelerated. "At the morgue, when Abi identified the body, she gave a teary performance."

"Performance?" Yang repeated, surprised.

"I never doubted that she felt *some* sadness over her husband's death. But the flood of tears at the morgue just seemed a little . . . rehearsed. Then, as she was leaving, I noticed that she checked her lipstick in the little mirror above the sink. Almost imperceptible, but I saw it."

Zoe narrowed her eyes, not yet understanding where this was going. "If you think she was faking, wouldn't that strengthen the theory that she arranged to have Gary killed?"

"It might have done had she given a similar performance in the house. But when I told her about her husband being poisoned, I'm certain she was genuinely surprised. And she made no pretense about why she had married him, either—for the money. If Abi Young had been involved in Gary's killing, she would never have admitted that. Moreover, her exclamation that she was happy with the marriage made perfect sense."

"What? That she was okay with having affairs while enjoying spending her husband's cash and waiting for him to die?"

"Exactly," Detective Ryan said. "That seems a reasonable explanation to me. But Abi underestimated her husband. She didn't think he knew what she was doing."

"What if Abi wanted to speed things along?"

"If she had decided to do that, would she arrange her husband's murder while the tennis coach was around?" Ryan asked. "I mean, why complicate matters? Dump him first."

"How about if Gary intended to kill Abi, then? That would explain the increased insurance arrangement," Detective Yang proffered.

"That's a possibility and something that we'll never know for certain. But we do know that Abi was happy to increase their life insurance because she believed her husband could keel over at any moment," Detective Ryan said.

The detective's phone rang. Ryan looked at the cell screen before holding it to his ear.

"Yes," Ryan said and listened. "We're on our way."

DANNY IVEY WAS ON HIS WAY, too, after being knocked out from the poker tournament prematurely by the woman player, Heidi Miller. Finished packing, he wheeled his carry-on to the hotel door, stopping to check around. His bed was unmade, he had left some of his clothes in the closet, and his toiletries were still in the bathroom. He was satisfied. Anyone looking for him would assume he was still staying there.

Danny knew he should have planned his escape but hadn't because, being an optimist, he had always believed he could win the tournament. Truth be told, he couldn't afford not to believe—his financial situation was grim, and the prize money would have gone a long way to keeping the wolf from the door. Things hadn't gone well. Now it was time to go, though he still had to figure out what to do next.

DETECTIVE RYAN PARKED IN FRONT OF a small, run-down hotel just off the main Kings Cross drag. The area was only half a mile from Detective Ryan's home, but it was a very different suburb from Potts Point. Bordered by William Street, Victoria Road, and Darlinghurst Road, The Cross had been the center of Sydney's red-light district since the forties. It was home to an eclectic bunch of residents—artists, writers, performers, and many of the city's down and out. The area remained quiet in the day, but as darkness set in and the clubs and bars opened, it came to life, and the partying began.

"You made good time," the security guard said as Detective Ryan and Detective Yang climbed out of their car. He held out his hand. "Alex Riva. We met before."

"I remember," Ryan said, ignoring the hand. "So, where's your boss, Steve Prince? He said he was coming down."

"Steve had a last-minute engagement. He sent me instead."

"You know why we're here, then?" Ryan confirmed.

"Sure. Because Steve phoned you to tell you about the full details of the argument we heard between Gary Young and Jimmy Webb."

"And Jimmy Webb is a receptionist at The Palms?" Detective Yang asked.

"*Was*," Riva corrected as he stubbed out a cigarette. "Turned up late for work one time too many."

"Back to the argument . . ." Ryan cut in. "How is it that you and Steve Prince came to hear this row?"

"We'd just stepped out for a smoke," Alex explained, "and we were standing under Gary Young's open window. It's one of the few places where the hotel guests can't see us."

"What were they arguing about?" Detective Yang asked. "Just for the record."

Before Alex could answer, Ryan cut him off. "We'll get to that later. Is Jimmy inside?" He cocked his head in the direction of the hotel while Detective Yang silently fumed at being sidelined once more.

"He's not answering his phone, and I haven't been inside yet. Steve said to wait for you before I did anything."

"Okay, well, let's go find him," Detective Ryan said, setting off for the hotel's entrance.

Entering, the detectives and the guard climbed a creaky set of stairs to reach the carpeted landing on the first floor. A young man sporting a bad case of acne sat at the reception desk, peering at a magazine. His lips moved as he read.

Detective Ryan coughed.

The man looked up, shoving the magazine under the desk. He pasted on a smile. "Welcome to the Ritz Hotel. How can I help?"

"The sign outside says The Windsor," Detective Yang said, curious.

"Yes. We've recently changed names and haven't updated the signage yet. The boss thought the new name was more high-end . . . .. So, again, how can I help?"

"We're looking for a Jimmy Webb. Is he here?" Detective Ryan asked.

"He may or may not be. Who wants to know?" Spotty Face replied.

Ryan produced his ID.

Spotty straightened in his chair. "Detective?"

"Yes," Ryan said.

"Number nineteen. Third floor."

"And he's in?" Detective Yang asked.

"No idea," Spotty said, standing. "We can check. I'll take you up."

They headed for the elevator. "Is Jimmy in trouble or something?" Spotty asked as they stopped at the elevator and he pressed the button.

"We just need a few words," Ryan responded.

"All three of you?"

"Yes," Ryan said.

Spotty stared at Yang. "You a detective, too, then?"

"That's right," Zoe said.

"I wouldn't have picked you for that . . . or him, for that matter," Spotty said, pointing at Detective Ryan.

"Why's that then, Mr. . . ." Zoe peered at his name tag.

"Candy . . . on account of . . ." the man said.

"You being sweeter than honey," Alex said.

"No. Because Candy's my name." He glanced across at the detectives. "Who's this guy? He a detective, too?" He looked at Alex doubtfully.

"He's assisting us with our inquiries," Detective Ryan said as the elevator arrived and the door slid open.

Detective Yang entered the small space first, followed by Alex, Detective Ryan, and Spotty. It was a tight squeeze.

"All aboard," Spotty said, pressing the third-floor button.

"Has Jimmy lived here long?" Ryan asked as the elevator slowly climbed.

"Around six months. He's one of our longer-term residents. Most are only here for a month or so."

The elevator came to a juddering halt, and the door inched open.

"Nineteen is to your right," Spotty offered.

The lights flickered as they followed the receptionist down the dank-smelling corridor, passing four doors, two on each side, before reaching Jimmy Webb's room.

Spotty knocked on the door. "Jimmy, you there?"

Nothing.

Detective Ryan leaned past Spotty and banged harder on the door. "Mr. Webb, police."

There was still no answer.

"Some of our residents are heavy sleepers," Spotty said, reaching into his pocket to produce a bunch of keys. He flicked through them and chose one. "Let's take a look."

"Ryan? We can't be doing this. We don't have a warrant," Detective Yang said.

"You don't need one," Spotty said. "The residents' rental agreements state that the hotel has access to all rooms at any time, and this is 'at any time.'"

Spotty pushed the key into the lock, twisted it, and pushed open the door. "Jimmy," he shouted as he entered.

TWENTY-THREE

Jimmy Webb's small studio was a mess. The bed was unmade, and clothes were strewn across the floor.

"God, it stinks in here," Alex said, screwing up his nose.

"You should go into a few of the other rooms." Spotty chuckled, watching Detective Ryan as he peered into a rickety closet.

"That's his work clothes," Alex said, peering over Detective Ryan's shoulder at a gray suit hung on a rail.

Ryan closed the closet door and turned his attention to an ugly brown wooden chest of drawers. A bottle of water, a plastic tumbler, and a '50s-style lamp sat atop it. Pairs of white sneakers and black loafers were pushed under the dresser.

"Ryan, we really shouldn't be doing this," Detective Yang cautioned, coming out of the bathroom. Ryan ignored her and bent down to examine a few shards of glass on the floor close to the cabinet. He reached under the drawers and carefully pulled out a small, framed photo, its glass shattered.

Ryan held the picture up for Alex to see. "Is that Jimmy Webb?" he asked, pointing at one of the two men in the picture—a smiling, handsome guy in his midtwenties. He had his arm around a much older, bald man—accountant Gary Young.

The guard peered at the photo. "Yeah, that's him," he said.

Detective Ryan reached for his phone and took a shot of the framed photo before placing it back underneath the dresser.

"Any idea where Jimmy could be now?" the detective asked, turning to Alex.

"*I* do," Spotty offered, grinning.

DANNY IVEY GLANCED AROUND. THE LOBBY of the inner-city Hyatt hotel looked reassuringly familiar . . . a world of marble, glass, and brass, ornate lamps, and modernist tables and chairs.

It was busy. People were hurrying past, arriving, departing. Corporate managers took up one table, strategizing how to make their first million. A group of well-dressed ladies who lunched gossiped together in another corner. A smattering of suited men sat alone, working on their computers or murmuring on phones. No one paid any attention to Danny; no one cared. They had better, more important things to do.

He sat down and pressed his phone's keypad.

"All Nippon Airways, how can I help?" a voice said on the other end.

"Hi. I want to book a one-way ticket in premier class for today's flight to Tokyo," Danny said.

"Just a minute, sir. I'll see if there's anything still available," the woman said.

Danny had decided to fly to Japan for several reasons. Going direct to the States was a no-go. Too obvious. A stopover was better. And he had been to Tokyo twice before and liked the place. As for the travel class, business was too expensive. He needed to conserve his remaining cash. But economy? That was just a bridge too far. A premier economy ticket would allow comfort and access to the ANA airport lounge while he waited for the plane.

"Good news, there is a free seat," the woman said. "How would you like to pay?"

Danny took a credit card from his wallet. He knew it could be traced, but with any luck, he'd be well away before they thought to check for it. "Amex," he said.

After making the payment, the woman confirmed that his flight departed in six hours.

"I'll send the ticket now," the woman said.

She was as good as her word. It arrived in Danny's inbox a moment later.

The booking complete, Danny headed to the bathroom. Closing the stall door, he smashed his phone against the top of the porcelain tank and flushed the pieces down the bowl. Life without a cell would be difficult, but it was better than someone tracking him. He would pick up a new phone in Japan.

Danny's next destination was the barbershop on the hotel's ground floor. Here, he opted for a new haircut—a Caesar—which, the chatty barber informed him, was a style named after the Roman Emperor Tiberius Julius Caesar Augustus and "very in." Then, what remained of his hair was dyed from blond to dark brown. Finally, Danny reluctantly decided to shave off his beard. He'd had it for years, but needs must.

Danny examined his appearance in the mirror. He looked like a different man without his tell-tale cowboy hat, long blond hair, and shaggy beard—just what the doctor ordered.

With time to kill, Danny headed to the hotel bar. He knew it would be quiet at this time of day.

"There you go, sir," the waiter said, putting a burger on the table. "Enjoy."

As he ate, Danny pondered what to do next. Continuing life as a professional poker player was out of the question—at least for now. But he would need money, so what were the alternatives? He could always return to his old job waiting tables if desperate enough. Danny shuddered at the thought. Still, thousands of people spent their lives working in hospitality, so he shouldn't be such a diva—and it would only be for a short time. Better, anyway, than being buried in the woods . . . or worse.

TWENTY-FOUR

B ACK IN THE CROSS, THE DETECTIVES entered Baxter's Bar. It was low-ceilinged and dark, with wooden tables and intimate booths lit by wall lights and freestanding lamps.

The venue was packed with men, their conversations fighting to be heard over the booming disco music.

Spotty had told the cops they would probably find Jimmy Webb here. The bar was a stone's throw from the Ritz Hotel.

While Alex had left for home, the detectives had headed for the bar.

"I can't see him, can you?" Detective Yang shouted, weaving past tables and checking out the customers.

"Nope," said Detective Ryan as he reached the long bar at the back of the room. Here, a handsome, fit-looking barman dressed in a white, close-fitting tee and tight black shorts was frantically serving customers.

"Hey," Detective Ryan shouted.

The barman ignored him.

"Hey, you," the cop repeated.

"Wait your turn," the barman shouted back as he handed a green cocktail to a man with bright pink shoulder-length hair.

Detective Ryan held up his ID. "Police," he said.

The barman stepped over and examined the card. "You should have said, mate. How can I help?"

Ryan took out his cell phone and selected the photo he had just taken of Jimmy Webb and Gary Young.

"Have you seen this man tonight?" the detective asked, pointing at Jimmy Webb.

The barman peered at the picture and shook his head. "I don't think so."

"You sure?" Detective Yang asked, arriving.

"Mate. You going to serve us or what?" A man dressed in a black tee and leotards yelled.

"I told you. I don't think so," the barman said. "Excuse me." He moved away to serve the customer.

Detective Yang leaned over to Ryan. "I don't think he's here."

Detective Ryan nodded. "Me neither," he said. "Let's go."

The detectives pushed back through the crowd and headed for the exit. As they neared, a door opened to their right, and a man emerged. He stopped to stare at the detectives before spinning around and hurrying back the way he'd come.

"Wasn't that . . .?" Detective Yang asked.

"Yeah, Jimmy Webb," Ryan said, reaching the door. Pushing it open, he sprinted down the corridor. Detective Yang followed. They didn't get far. A fat man stepped out from the restroom, blocking the pathway. Ryan smashed into him, bounced, and fell back into Zoe.

"Look where you're going, mate," the fat man said, striding past the downed detectives.

Ryan was first up and saw Jimmy Webb exiting through the fire door at the end of the corridor. Running to catch him, Ryan pushed open the exit and entered a dark alleyway.

He looked around. The alley was empty. Jimmy had vanished.

DANNY IVEY'S PLAN TO DISAPPEAR WAS, for the most part, going smoothly. Arriving at Sydney airport, he quickly found the ANA counter, where a desk clerk checked his passport and gave him his boarding card.

Boarding would begin in an hour—plenty of time to go through security and passport control.

On the way over, there had been a few minor hitches. After leaving the Hyatt, he tried to drop off his rented Toyota, but Hertz had moved to a temporary shack miles from the airport. Arriving, Danny had waited while a smiling receptionist spent forever organizing the checkout.

Then he had to wait half an hour for the free shuttle bus, which only had drop-offs at the domestic terminal, so Danny had to catch another shuttle to the international terminal. Through it all, he had remained calm, which was entirely in character. His self-control and refusal to reveal his true feelings had made him a competent poker player.

He had bluffed all his life . . . since school, anyway. His friends had no idea about his home life. No idea that his father would come home drunk and slap his mom around. No idea that Danny was *this close* to running off.

"It's just the booze," his mother had said as she traced her fingers around the bruises on her face. "Your dad's a good man."

Danny was unconvinced. He knew his father was a piece of shit, but his mom's lack of self-esteem and fear of being left alone meant she always made excuses for his behavior.

Danny pulled his carry-on over the terminal's tiled floor on his way to the security area. It brought back memories of how, all those years ago, he had dragged another suitcase out of his house in the dead of night. After he'd finally given up trying to convince his mother to leave, he knew what he had to do—get the hell out. And that was precisely what he had to do now.

A heavy hand came to rest on his shoulders. "Danny," a deep voice rumbled.

He twisted around to face a giant.

"Hi, Tik," Danny said, his heart sinking and his mind racing. Could he get away if he kicked this humongous ape in the balls?

"Not Tik. Tok," the man corrected and pointed to another monster watching only yards away. He's Tik."

Danny shrugged. "Sorry," he said, realizing that the odds of getting away had just dropped to zero.

He smiled. "How can I help?"

TWENTY-FIVE

DETECTIVE RYAN DECIDED THAT LOSING JIMMY at Baxter's, although not helpful, was not necessarily a game-changer. True, they had lost the element of surprise, but Jimmy was probably flat broke and sooner or later would have to return to his humble lodgings. After checking with Spotty that the man hadn't returned to his room, Detective Ryan and Detective Yang sat outside the ambitiously named Ritz Hotel in the car, prepared for what could be a long wait.

After three hours stuck in a confined space with a man who practiced the economy of language with the devotion of a Buddhist monk, Detective Yang started to get restless.

"Ryan . . ." she began.

"Nope," he said.

"You don't even know what I was going to say."

"Sure I do. You think we're wasting our time."

"He knows we're looking for him. Why would he come back here?" she argued.

"Where else is he going to go?" Detective Ryan asked, not expecting an answer.

Yang sighed. She knew that trying to reason with her partner wasn't productive. Stubbornness was a necessary trait for a detective, and Ryan had it in spades. Maybe, though, too much of it was counterproductive.

Detective Yang took a small white and green metal box from her pocket. Opening it, she offered the container to Detective Ryan. "Mint?" she asked.

"Sure," Ryan said, taking out one of the small, white, oval candies before popping it into his mouth and sucking on it.

"Fisherman's Friend?" he asked.

Zoe nodded. "Yep. The original and the best."

She took one, too, and put it in her mouth before closing the box.

"Did you know I was living with my aunt?" she asked as she sucked on the sweet.

"Of course."

"Of course," Yang repeated and turned to face Ryan, looking doubtful. "I don't think that's true. I don't think you have *any* idea where I'm living."

"You're calling your senior partner a liar, Detective Yang?"

He said it with a straight face, and Yang reddened.

"I didn't mean it like that," she said quickly. "It's just . . ."

"You don't think I'd want to know where you're staying?" Ryan said, interrupting.

Yang was dubious. "No . . . why would you? Unless you're a stalker?"

She smiled uncertainly, trying to lighten the mood.

"I like to know as much about a partner as possible," he explained.

"Could've fooled me," she joked.

Ryan gave her a small smile before flicking his gaze back to the hotel's entrance.

"You may think that because I don't ask personal questions, I'm not interested. But the truth is, I like to draw my own conclusions. And in our line of work, knowing things about your partner can be the difference between life and death."

Detective Yang frowned, and Ryan could see she wasn't buying it.

He continued. "A person's home life will necessarily affect their work performance. And the fact that you're living with your aunt worries me."

Zoe looked confused. "What? Why?"

Ryan straightened in the car seat. "Hold on. Someone's coming."

The detectives peered out, watching as a young woman, clutching tight to a scruffily dressed older man, walked toward the Ritz Hotel. He guided her through the open door.

"Not him," Detective Yang said.

"Agreed. That's not the kind of company I would expect Jimmy Webb to keep," Ryan said.

They lapsed back into silence. Then, "So go on. What worries you about me living with my aunt, Ryan?"

"Well, you have a girlfriend," he said.

"So?"

"She didn't come down with you." It was a statement, not a question.

"I see," Zoe said. "Well, for starters, Louise is my partner, not my girlfriend."

"I'm sorry," Ryan said, sounding contrite. "I shouldn't have said that. It's an important distinction," he admitted. "But it only strengthens my point."

"You're right," Zoe said as she opened the box of mints again and offered it to Ryan. He took another candy.

"Am I right?" he said, looking surprised.

"A partner would have come to Sydney with me. Louise knows how important this is."

"And why didn't she come?" Ryan queried.

Yang studied Ryan's face for a moment. The tone of his voice had almost suggested that he cared. Still, who could tell with him?

Yang avoided the question, not quite ready to share the nitty-gritty of her private life. Instead: "Wanting to know more about me . . . and all that 'life and death' stuff . . ." Zoe stopped. "Does that mean you think we have a future? As partners, I mean?" she quickly clarified.

"My mother will tell you I'm a commitment-phobe." He smiled wryly. "But . . . I think we can make this work."

"Would you like to know what *I* think?" Yang asked, feeling brave.

"Not really," Ryan replied, only half joking.

"I think we *do* have a future. Providing we can iron out a few wrinkles."

"Do those winkles include my not being the sharing type?" Ryan asked.

Zoe's smile faded, and she became more serious. "You haven't told me yet exactly what Jimmy Webb and Gary Young argued about when Alex Riva and Steve Prince overheard them. And I don't understand why you're keeping it from me," she said.

Ryan paused, considering his explanation. "I have found it useful in the past when partners, in the early stages of an investigation, can come at it from different angles." He turned to watch the entrance of the Ritz as he spoke. "New information can distract us from pursuing certain avenues, and I wanted you to have fewer distractions. I wanted *you* to keep *me* on the straight and narrow."

Detective Yang stared at him in surprise. So, keeping her in the dark was an investigative tactic rather than just an indication of some power trip that Ryan was on.

"In any case, I think it's probably time I did fill you in," Ryan continued.

"I'm all ears," Yang replied, feeling a tad more respect for her partner than she had done five minutes before.

Detective Ryan paused. "Okay, in his phone call Steve Prince told me Gary Young and Jimmy Webb argued about their relationship in the accountant's office. Webb wanted money, and he was upset that Gary Young wouldn't give it to him. Steve Prince and Alex Riva overheard everything when they were smoking outside."

"Did they hear how much cash Jimmy Webb was asking for?"

"Yes. Twenty thousand," Ryan said.

Zoe whistled. "That's twenty thousand reasons for murder." She paused. "What was the money for?" Zoe raised an eyebrow. "Services rendered?" She offered a sly smile.

"*That* is just one of the reasons we need to talk to Jimmy," Ryan replied.

Zoe nodded, thinking. She turned the small tin of mints over in her hand.

"Did you know Fishermen's Friend was invented nearly *two hundred* years ago?"

"I didn't. But you'd be forgiven for thinking I might," he said in a slightly self-deprecating way.

Zoe continued. "By a pharmacist called James Lofthouse. The sweet's shape was based on the buttons of his daughter's dress."

"Interesting," Detective Ryan said, and meant it. He collected trivia in the same way that magpies swept up shiny objects.

Zoe offered the open box to the detective.

He shook his head. "You know you're starting to sound like me. Offering up nuggets of useless information."

Although Detective Yang didn't respond, she took this as a compliment. She shifted in her seat to alleviate the discomfort of sitting in the same place for too long. As she did, she leaned forward to peer through the windshield. "Do you honestly think he's going to return?"

"Like I said, he's probably short on cash and options," Ryan said.

They continued to watch in silence.

"There!" Detective Ryan pointed across the street.

Zoe squinted at a man, hunched up and walking slowly toward the hotel entrance. "Yep, that's him," she confirmed.

"We'll let him go inside first, and then we'll grab him," Ryan said. "That way, we can keep the fuss to a minimum."

TWENTY-SIX

DANNY IVEY OPENED HIS EYES AND squinted at a bright white light that pointed directly at him. He tried raising his hands to block the beam but couldn't. His arms were bound behind him, roped to a chair.

"Hello?" Danny shouted. "Mr. Guffini, you there?"

Nothing.

"Could you turn the light off, please?"

Silence.

Danny went to stand, but his legs, too, were roped to the chair. He tried to rock it to move out of the beam, but the seat was clamped to the floor.

"Mr. Guffini, I need your help on this," Danny said. "That light is driving me crazy."

Silence.

Danny closed his eyes tight.

"Tik . . . Tok, you there?" he shouted.

No answer.

Where was everyone?

Danny took a deep breath. Now he had another problem—a shooting pain in his head. It was like a migraine, only worse. A result of Tik, or possibly Tok, punching him. Why had they done that? He'd been cooperating. He'd gotten into the back of the car, and the punch had come out of nowhere.

"Mr. Guffini, I feel like a dozen possums are duking it out inside my head."

Silence.

"Just an Advil or a Tylenol would help. Even an aspirin. Please!"

More silence.

Danny was getting nowhere. A new approach was necessary.

"I'm not sure what's going on, Mr. Guffini, but I'm certain we can work this out. I did offer to help."

He waited.

"Which one would you like?" an amplified voice finally said.

"That you, Mr. Guffini?"

"I asked you a question, Danny."

He shrugged. "I don't know. Either."

"Okay. Tik will get you an Advil. That's what I take if I have a bad headache."

"I think this is more than a headache, Mr. Guffini. It feels like a tsunami is swirling around inside my brain," Danny pleaded.

"So, do you want it?" Guffini said.

"The Advil? Sure. I'm happy to take up that offer . . . and the light. If you could move it away or turn it off, that would help."

Danny waited.

The beam playing on his closed eyelids disappeared.

Danny opened his eyes. The room was now black.

He heard a door opening. Twisting his head, he saw daylight spilling through the entrance. Moments later, a giant stepped through, closing the door firmly behind him.

There was a click, and the overhead fluorescents came on.

Danny saw he was in a cavernous space, empty except for a single black leather armchair positioned opposite him and a floor-to-ceiling mirror that hung on the wall by the door.

Danny looked down at his chair. It was clamped to the concrete floor by two large metal bolts.

The giant approached. He carried a plastic cup, which looked tiny in his massive hand.

He raised the cup to Danny's lips and, with his free hand, pulled back the poker player's head.

"Open," he said.

Danny gulped down the water and what appeared to be two Advil. He hoped it wasn't poison, but only time would tell.

The door opened again, and Mr. Guffini, aka The Owl, entered.

"Thank you, Tik," The Owl said as he walked over to the leather armchair and sat.

Tik, carrying the empty cup, walked to the back of the room. He joined another huge man—Tok.

"You've changed your look, Danny. Gone from bearded Texas cowboy to blond Roman emperor," The Owl said, looking the poker player over.

"You've gone casual, too, Mr. Guffini," Danny said, staring at the man in beige sweatpants, a top, and white sneakers.

"Not that casual, Danny boy. The sweats are Balenciaga, and the shoes are by Louis Vuitton. They cost me a fortune."

"Oh, right," Danny said. He'd heard of Louis Vuitton but had no clue who the other designer was. "You look good, anyway."

"Thanks," The Owl said and waved his hands. "Okay, enough small talk; I need answers."

Danny nodded. "Ask away."

"First, what do you think of the room?" The Owl said.

"This room?" Danny replied, nonplussed.

"Don't make me repeat myself, Danny."

Danny looked around, uncertain of what to say. The room's designer had taken minimalism to a new level. Too far for Danny's taste, but should he tell The Owl that?

Danny opted for a more diplomatic approach. "I'm not sure. It's difficult to decide."

The Owl nodded. "Good answer. That was my opinion, too, so I put you in it to better understand whether it worked." He waved his hands around. "My predecessor, Oscar Bruno, built the space. The walls are soundproofed." He twisted around and pointed. "The one-way mirror is top of the line. The light . . ."

"The fluorescents?" Danny queried.

"No, not those lights. Those are run-of-the-mill standard. I'm talking about the non-scanning correlation interrogation device." He pointed above the one-way mirror to a black box with a lens poking out. "That one there. The light that was shining in your eyes."

"Gotcha," Danny said.

"Then there's this chair, too." The Owl stroked the arms of his leather seat. "It's a copy of the one they use on *Mastermind*." He paused. "So, what do you think? Does everything work?"

Danny again was stuck for an answer. Work? What did the Owl mean by "work"?

"Oh, for Christ's sake," The Owl said, seeing Danny's confusion. "Did the setup disorient you? Did it make you feel afraid? Do I have to explain everything?"

What the fuck was up with all these bizarre questions, Danny wondered. He stared at the man in the chair. He'd realized when he signed up with Guffini that the guy was mad as a hatter but, in his defense, he had desperately needed the sponsorship cash, so Danny had chosen to overlook the mob boss's questionable sanity.

"The light, the darkness, the voice . . . it was all just very confusing, if you want the truth, Mr. Guffini," Danny said.

"Were you confused enough to spill your guts?" The Owl asked.

"I don't have any guts to spill, Mr. Guffini."

"Oh, right. If you say so," The Owl said, standing and looking to the back of the room. "Didn't I tell you boys this room's fucking garbage? A waste of time! We should just take them out to the woods, kill the fuckers, and then bury them. We don't need all this shit."

There were grunts of agreement from Tik and Tok.

The Owl sat down again. "You know . . . we have a lot in common, Danny boy," he said. "Like our families. We're better off without them, am I right?"

"Exactly," Danny agreed nervously.

"And that makes *you* trying to run off so much more disappointing." The Owl stopped. "When we met two years ago, what did I say to you?"

"You thought I was a winner and knew we'd make a great team," Danny said.

"A team, Danny. That's right. And teams have rules. I agreed to loan you four hundred K, and in exchange, you'd pay back all that money *plus* a sizeable share of your winnings."

The crime boss stared at Danny. "The money's peanuts to me. I do this sponsorship lark because I like poker. But what I don't like is someone taking the piss." He paused. "Two years, and I ain't got a cent back!"

"Yeah, I know, Mr. Guffini, but that's just part of the ebb and flow of the game," Danny explained nervously.

The Owl shook his head. "No. In your case, there was no flow, just ebb." He tapped his fingers on the chair. "And then you ran away."

Danny said nothing.

The Owl stood up and walked over to Danny. He stared down at him. "You do know I sponsor others?"

Danny shook his head. "I wasn't aware of that, Mr. Guffini."

"No, you weren't, because Danny thinks only of Danny."

"Look, Mr. Guffini, I apologize for the misunderstanding, okay? Because that's all this is, a misunderstanding." He looked at the crime boss pleadingly. "I'm sure we can sort something out."

The Owl ignored him. "You know the woman who beat you?"

"Heidi Miller?" Danny asked.

"That's the one."

"Yeah."

"She's another one of my protégés. And I must set an example for her and all the others I support. I need to show them why they must stick to the rules and what happens if they don't."

Danny shivered. He felt sick. "Mr. Guffini . . ." he began.

"I have a question for you," The Owl interrupted. "It's about ethics. See, you chose to run away instead of staying and being honest. Was that the ethical thing to do?"

"Not exactly 'running,' Mr. Guffini. More like leaving to regroup."

The Owl slammed his hand hard down on the arm of his chair.

"Quit the semantics, Danny. You wanted to disappear. Paying me back was the furthest thing from your mind."

Danny sighed. "Okay, you're right, that's what I was going to do." He paused. "But I'm truly sorry. You have my word that it will never happen again."

"Good. Now we're getting somewhere."

The Owl stood up.

"Tik, Tok, untie Danny, will you?"

The two giants ambled over.

"You're probably wondering how we found you," The Owl said, watching as Tik and Tok cut Danny free. "Well, a word to the wise: if you are trying to get away, book an Uber."

"What?" Danny asked as he massaged his freed hands.

"You returned your rented car instead of getting an Uber to the airport. They always say follow the money, but in this case, we followed your rental car."

Danny gulped. "Oh," he said as Tik and Tok hoisted him up.

The Owl walked to the door.

"Mr. Guffini," Danny said as Tik pushed him forward.

"Yes?" The Owl said.

"What would have happened to me if I *had* stayed and been honest . . . about spending all your money?" Danny asked.

"Instead of trying to escape?"

"Yes."

"It would be the same result as now, of course." The Owl smiled. "A trip to the woods. That'll stop you taking the piss . . . permanently."

TWENTY-SEVEN

Jimmy Webb believed he had done the cops a favor coming in, but now they were taking the mickey. He had been waiting here for almost an hour. Where exactly were they?

The door of the interview room suddenly swung open. Detective Ryan and Detective Yang walked in.

"How's the coffee?" Ryan asked, pointing at the empty paper cup on Jimmy's table as he sat down.

"Tasted like piss," Jimmy said and stopped as an ugly thought occurred to him. "No one pissed in it, did they?"

Detective Ryan shook his head. "Of course not, and I'm sorry about that. I've been trying to get them to make better coffee."

Jimmy grunted. "Yeah, well, I've been here forever. And this place isn't exactly Shangri La," Jimmy said, waving his hand around the windowless, soulless room. "You know, thinking about design is hard, but—"

"Not thinking about it can be disastrous," Detective Ryan interrupted.

"Very good," Jimmy said. "You're an educated man."

Ryan nodded. "It's something I once read. And you? Where did you hear that?"

"In an interior design course I took."

Just like his mother, Detective Ryan thought. The world was a small place.

"You wanted to become an interior designer?" Detective Yang asked, settling into her chair.

"Yeah. Wanted to . . . still want to . . . It's a job I'd kill for."

Detective Yang glanced across at Ryan. "Kill for" was an interesting choice of words under the circumstances.

"But you're not working in that field currently?" Ryan asked.

"No. I don't have the contacts and can't get a job . . . .. Look, can we get on with this?" Jimmy said, tapping his fingers impatiently on the desk.

Good, he's ready, Ryan thought. The detective liked to keep interviewees waiting. After eating a sandwich, Zoe and he had spent the last half hour studying Jimmy through the one-way mirror, watching as he became increasingly agitated. Finally, Detective Ryan had decided it was time to go in.

Ryan pressed a button on a panel embedded in the desk. "Interview with Jimmy Webb," he said, glancing at his watch. "Commencing at 10:15 p.m., Wednesday, September sixth. Present are the interviewee Jimmy Webb, Detective Ryan, and Detective Yang."

Ryan paused. "Before we begin, a few housekeeping notes. First, can I call you Jimmy? Is that okay?"

"You can call me what you like if it gets me out of here faster," Jimmy said.

"Good. Also, you'll see a small camera there," Ryan said, indicating a device set high up in the corner, pointing over the detective's shoulder at Jimmy. "The video is to be used with the audio recording." The detective paused. "And just to clarify, you have the right to silence."

"Me, silent? You've got the wrong man for that." Jimmy stroked the side of his handsome, unshaven face. "But I *would* prefer better lighting," he joked.

Ryan peered at Jimmy. Despite this outward nonchalance, the detective knew he was nervous.

"Jimmy, you work as a receptionist at The Palms Hotel, correct?" Detective Ryan asked.

"Worked . . . past tense."

"Oh. So . . . you were let go?"

"Let's just say it was mutual." Jimmy stopped. "Can you tell me what this is about?"

"You don't know?" Detective Ryan asked.

"Nope."

"So, if you didn't know why we wanted to speak to you, why did you run?"

"Because you're cops," Jimmy said.

"You could tell?" Detective Yang looked doubtful.

"Dressed like that?" Jimmy scoffed. "Put it this way, you didn't look like you were on a date."

"People don't usually run from the police unless they have something to hide," Detective Ryan said, steering the interview away from Jimmy's wardrobe critique.

Jimmy scratched the side of his neck nervously. "Look, if I had something to hide, as you put it, why did I come in voluntarily?"

"That's a stretch," Detective Yang said, ignoring the look Ryan gave her. Just because he was the lead detective didn't mean he was the only one allowed to talk. "You came with us because you had no choice."

"Yeah. Yeah. Whatever. But I'm here now, and neither of you have told me why." Jimmy stopped as a thought occurred to him. "Did *he* send you? Is that why I'm here?"

"Who's *he*?" Ryan asked.

Jimmy peered at the detective. If this was a trap, he wasn't about to fall into it. He shrugged. "Could be just about anyone. I have a habit of pissing people off," Jimmy said, slumping back in his chair.

Ryan studied the man. If he wasn't careful, Jimmy would ask for a lawyer any moment now.

"Tell us about Gary Young and the twenty thousand dollars," Detective Ryan said.

Jimmy leaned forward, sneering. "That bastard tell you he gave me that? Well, he's lying. He wouldn't give me a cent."

"But you've extorted money from him before, Jimmy. Am I right?" Ryan said. It was a guess, but an educated one.

"He *gave* me that money. I didn't *extort* anything," Jimmy said.

Bingo.

"You were lovers?" Detective Yang asked.

"Wow. You two are really on the ball." Jimmy rolled his eyes. "And that money he gave me was to tide me over. You try living on a hotel receptionist's wage."

"How much?" Detective Ryan asked.

Jimmy hesitated. Then: "Around a hundred thousand."

"That's a lot of money. Why would he do that?" Detective Ryan asked.

"We weren't just lovers, we were *in* love," Jimmy said.

"But he wouldn't give you twenty thousand more," Ryan said.

"What? You can't prove that," Jimmy said defiantly.

"You were overheard arguing."

"Who by?" Jimmy asked, surprised.

"We can't tell you that," Detective Yang said.

Jimmy sat silently for a moment, then was struck by a thought. "It was Steve and that new security guard, Alex Riva, right? Gary was always complaining about them smoking under his window." He shook his head in disgust. "Fuckers," he spat.

"Gary Young accused you of being a grifter, and you were furious. Your little racket was coming to an end," Detective Ryan said.

Jimmy said nothing.

"That's why you killed him."

Jimmy raised his hand. "Whoa! *What* did you just say?"

Nothing.

"He's dead?" Jimmy was shocked.

"He was murdered on Saturday night," Detective Ryan said.

"For real?"

Ryan nodded.

"Murdered?" Jimmy repeated and paled. "Fuck."

More Silence. Then: "Where?"

"His body was found in a hut in the national park," Detective Ryan said.

"Next to The Palms?"

"Yes."

Jimmy shook his head in disbelief. "That's where we were supposed to spend the weekend. Gary told his wife he was going to a conference."

"Supposed to? You didn't spend time with him there?" Ryan asked.

Jimmy shook his head. "I got the shits when he wouldn't help me out." He looked from Ryan to Yang, pleading his case. "The money was peanuts to him. He was worth a fortune!"

"So, if you didn't kill him, who did?" Ryan asked.

Jimmy shrugged. "No idea. That's your job. . . . Look, Gary could be a real asshole." He paused before continuing in a subdued voice. "But I don't know anyone wanting to do that."

Ryan said nothing. He continued to stare at Jimmy.

"Where *were* you on the night that Gary was killed if you weren't at the cabin?"

Jimmy sat up, defiant. "If you still think I killed him, you're barking up the wrong tree." He smiled. "I have a rock-solid alibi."

TWENTY-EIGHT

"ARE YOU SAYING THAT JIMMY WEBB was with you all Saturday and Sunday?" Detective Ryan asked the handsome barman sitting opposite.

"Yes," Vinnie Malone said emphatically.

Ryan reached into his pocket, took out his cell, and pressed the screen to reveal the picture of Jimmy Webb and Gary Young. "And this is Jimmy Webb?" the detective asked, pointing at Jimmy.

"Yes," the man confirmed.

"And he's your longtime boyfriend?"

"Yes."

"But when I showed you this earlier tonight, you said that you didn't know if he'd been in Baxter's," Ryan said.

"Yeah, I'm sorry about that," Vinnie replied sheepishly.

Detective Ryan shook his head. "Lying to a cop is a criminal offense, Vinnie. Punishable by up to a year in prison."

The man paled as Ryan continued, pleased to have the bartender on the back foot.

Detective Ryan had left Zoe with Jimmy Webb while he checked out his alibi—that he'd been with one of the Baxter's bartenders over the weekend and, therefore, couldn't have killed Gary Young.

Detective Ryan and Vinnie had retreated to a small office behind the bar to talk.

"So, why *did* you lie?" Ryan asked.

"I was just trying to protect Jimmy."

"From what?"

"You know what," Vinnie said.

Ryan leaned over the desk, pushing his face close to Vinnie's. "No, I don't, so why don't you tell me?"

"Look, I warned him he was being stupid, but Jimmy, being Jimmy, went ahead anyway." He smiled. "It's what I love about him. His determin—"

"Vinnie, I'm not going to ask again. What were you trying to protect him from?" the detective interrupted.

"He told me he would get some money off Gary."

"You knew about Gary Young?"

"Yeah." He shrugged.

"And did he? Get more money from Gary, I mean."

"Nah. Told him to fuck off."

"Jimmy told you that?" Ryan asked.

"Not as such. No. But I just knew."

The detective stared at him. He "just knew," too, that Vinnie was telling the truth, just as he had known that Jimmy Webb wasn't lying, either. Detective Ryan's gut told him. Jimmy had not killed Gary Young.

"Can I go now, Detective? I've still got a couple of hours left of my shift, and they'll be spitting chips if I don't go back out there soon."

Ryan nodded. "Okay."

The men rose and walked to the door.

"One more question, though, Vinnie," the detective said.

The bartender stopped.

"Weren't you upset about your boyfriend having an affair with another man?" Ryan asked.

"Shit, Detective, you are *so* last century," Vinnie said.

Detective Ryan watched as the barman left. There was nothing more to do—only to call Zoe, tell her to release Jimmy, and go home.

Exhausted, Ryan decided to do the same.

TIK AND TOK WERE TIRED, TOO—TIRED of Australia and Pietro Guffini.

Initially, they had embraced all the "lucky country" had to offer.

However, the dream had soured. They didn't exactly hate Australia; they just missed Italy—its food, its people, and *la dolce vita*.

Moreover, the twins had never worked for just one man before. Although The Owl had bent over backward to help the brothers settle in, he was, in Tok's words, *una scopata impegnativa* (a demanding fuck).

But more problematic than anything else was the bizarre realization that they'd had enough of killing for a living. The twins hesitated at first to talk about it. But, as they say, better out than in. And one day, both admitted they were starting to feel sorry for some of their victims. Not all of them, of course, only a few, like Manny the Chin, who had a great sense of humor and made the twins chuckle. And Good Fortune Willie! The brothers had dispatched him quickly and efficiently but then had had regrets. In their opinion, Willie was a good guy who didn't deserve what he got. And now, Danny Ivey—which was why they had driven up to the Sydney Heads with his corpse instead of burying it in the woods, per their boss's orders.

The twins had watched Danny playing poker and admired his bravado. True, he had tried to run off without paying back his debt to The Owl, but it was a relatively small sum, and other punishments better fit the crime.

So, the brothers decided they couldn't just leave Danny's body in the woods to be eaten away by creepy crawlies. He needed a decent burial.

"Uno, due, tre," the twins chorused before releasing the corpse.

"Uno in piu," Tik said as the body disappeared into the angry foaming waves below.

"Si," Tok agreed.

They'd do The Owl one more favor. Then that would be that. It was time to go.

TWENTY-NINE

Eᴀʀʟʏ ᴛʜᴇ ғᴏʟʟᴏᴡɪɴɢ ᴅᴀʏ, Mᴄ𝐊ᴇɴᴢɪᴇ Sᴀᴋᴇʀ climbed into the back of the Uber, dropping her black Prada purse onto the seat and reaching for the safety strap.

"McKenzie? Creek Road, Church Point?" the driver asked.

"Yeah," McKenzie confirmed, clicking the belt into its holder.

The driver accelerated out of Circular Quay, glancing up at the rearview mirror to check out the well-dressed woman. "Had a good night?" he asked, smiling.

"Yeah, it's been fabulous," McKenzie said, brushing strands of her long brown hair out of her eyes before pulling down her brightly colored silk dress.

Although McKenzie Saker was in her early fifties, the full-figured woman knew she could still attract her fair share of male attention.

"And you? How's your day . . . I mean, your night . . . been?" McKenzie queried.

"Too many drunks." The driver stopped as he saw the woman frown. "I didn't mean . . ." he began.

"It's all right. No offense taken." She stared at the back of the man's bald head. "And you're right. I may have drunk a little too much, but you've got to let yourself go sometimes, right?"

"Sure," the driver said as he drove onto the bridge. "I guess you've been on one of those harbor cruises?"

"Yeah," McKenzie said.

"So? Were you celebrating something?"

McKenzie sighed. It was time to shut this down.

"No, not really," she replied before resting her head against the window. "You don't mind if I nap, do you?" It was a rhetorical question, and the driver took the hint.

"Oh, right. No problem," he said, staring straight ahead.

McKenzie put her hand to her head. That last double gin and tonic had been the final straw. Before she arrived home, she needed to sober up. If Luke saw her like this, he would be unimpressed, to say the least.

But what the heck? It had been a good night, a celebration that Haley, McKenzie's BF, had suggested.

"A celebration for what?" McKenzie had asked.

"Just life, darling," Hayley had said.

McKenzie knew that was a white lie. Hayley, and Mary and Sue, her two other best friends, had arranged the event knowing Luke and McKenzie were struggling. They never saw each other now. He was always working in the day and spending nights at the casino.

McKenzie closed her eyes and dozed off, only waking as the Uber drove up her driveway and parked.

She reached across to pick up her bag. "Have a good rest of the day," she said before exiting the car and climbing the brick and slate stairs to the front door to enter the house.

The Uber slowly did a U-turn before heading back down the long driveway. From behind, the driver suddenly heard a distant shout.

Glancing back, he saw the woman he had just dropped off waving her hands at the open front door, frantically signaling for him to stop.

The driver waited for the woman to arrive before cracking open his window.

"What's up?" he asked.

"It's my husband . . .." McKenzie said, gasping for breath. "I think he's dead."

"ARE YOU SURE?" SUPERINTENDENT DUDLEY ASKED as Detective Ryan sat down next to Detective Yang.

"Yes. Jimmy Webb did not kill Gary Young," Ryan said.

"That's disappointing," the superintendent said, leaning forward. "You know why I brought you into homicide, Ryan?"

"Yes, sir, you made that clear. Because the squad's conviction rate was low."

"And sir, with due respect . . ." Detective Yang began.

The superintendent waved his hands. "Detective."

"Yes, sir?" Yang said.

"Let Ryan do the talking." Dudley stopped. "The conviction rate isn't just low, it's abysmal, so I was hoping you'd have made progress by now. But apparently, you've achieved nothing."

Ryan knew that when the superintendent was in this kind of mood, there was little that he could say or do that would appease him—nothing, that was, except finding Gary Young's murderer. Unfortunately, this was unlikely to happen while they sat in his office.

"Sir, we discovered that Gary Young recruited a private investigator to confirm his suspicion that his wife was having an affair. The PI took photos of Mrs. Young over the same weekend that Mr. Young was killed. So, he can alibi Abi Young *and* her tennis coach lover," Detective Ryan said.

"Fantastic. So, you have definitely confirmed that another possible suspect *didn't* do it," Superintendent Dudley said sarcastically. "What about if the wife hired someone to do the killing? Have you considered that possibility?"

"Yes, we have explored that avenue, sir," Ryan said.

"And?"

"A search of both hers and the tennis coach Mr. McMillan's phone records failed to uncover anything suspicious. Similarly, there weren't any unusual withdrawals from their bank accounts. On top of that, I believed her when she said she thought her husband was at a conference in Melbourne that weekend." He said the last part carefully, realizing that his instincts couldn't be called conclusive evidence.

Dudley's eyes narrowed. He turned to Zoe. "You agree with that assessment, Yang?"

"Yes, sir," Zoe said.

"So, any more suspects?"

"Not at the moment, but we're still waiting for the forensic report on the shoe print and the rope traces," Detective Ryan said.

"Forensics haven't done that yet?" Dudley asked.

"They're short-staffed and a little behind," Ryan explained.

"Well, move them along, will you?"

"We'll do our best," Detective Ryan said.

"I suggest you aim higher than that," the superintendent said, looking straight at Ryan. He paused, considering his next words. "You do know you're not well-liked here?"

"I'm aware there is some resentment in the squad," Detective Ryan said.

"And the same applies to you, Detective Yang. They think you're a DEI hire."

Yang bristled at the suggestion she'd been brought in to satisfy some departmental diversity quota.

"Sir, I am grateful for the opportunity I've been given," Detective Yang said diplomatically.

"That's good, because my neck is on the line." Dudley paused. "I'm relying on you two to solve this case."

"These investigations take time," Ryan said.

"Which I don't have!" Superintendent Dudley bellowed.

There was a knock on the door.

"Enter."

The door opened, and Detective Terry Burke appeared.

"Sir, there's been a development—another death. Luke Saker, a partner in the Faith Company," Burke said, addressing his boss directly and ignoring the two detectives.

"Homicide?" Dudley asked.

"Not confirmed as yet," Terry Burke said.

"So, what are you two still doing here?" the superintendent said, looking pointedly at Yang and Ryan.

The pair stood up and made a hasty retreat past Detective Burke and out of the office.

Burke stayed where he was.

"Something else, Detective?" Dudley asked.

"Actually, yes. I was wondering if I could have a word?" Burke said.

"Go ahead." Superintendent Dudley gestured for Detective Burke to take a seat.

"I just want to say how happy we all are about your promotion, sir," Detective Burke said.

Dudley glared at the detective. "That's what you wanted to tell me in private, Burke?"

"No, sir. I just needed to make that clear."

"Good. Mission accomplished, then. Now stop blowing smoke up my butt and tell me what you really came in to talk about."

Burke took a deep breath. "It's Ryan and Yang, sir. . . . It's just . . ." The detective hesitated.

"You don't like them?" Dudley said.

"With respect, liking them has nothing to do with it."

"Good, because that would be very unprofessional."

"Agreed, sir." Detective Burke paused for a long moment. "We feel . . ." he began.

"We?" Superintendent Dudley interrupted.

"The squad."

"Oh, so now you're speaking on behalf of *everyone*?"

"I'm just saying there's a general consensus that introducing Yang and Ryan into homicide may be counterproductive. I understand they aren't making much progress on this case, which now appears to involve two deaths. So perhaps it would be best if . . ."

"If they were reassigned. Maybe to another department?" Dudley cut him off.

"Precisely, sir."

Dudley twisted in his chair and peered out the window at the busy city streets below. After a few moments, he spun back around and stood up.

"You know what I think, Terry. I think this reeks of isms."

"Isms?" Burke repeated, confused.

"Racism and sexism!" Dudley roared.

Burke shook his head vigorously. "No, sir. Not at all!"

"Good. Because I won't stand for it!"

"Yes, sir. I know that."

"And I suppose you think *you'd* be better suited to head this investigation?"

"Me . . . or another member of the squad," Detective Burke said quietly, clearly having lost some of his earlier confidence.

"I see," Dudley mused. "You *are* aware that homicide's conviction rate is woefully inadequate and has been for some time?" Dudley hissed.

"I don't think that's quite . . ." Burke tried to protest, but Dudley cut him off.

"Well, I'll let you in on a little secret." Dudley put his hands on the desk and leaned forward. "I don't give a rat's ass *what* you think. Ryan and Yang were brought in here to shake things up! And if you're not happy about that, maybe *you* should think about transferring to another department."

Burke nodded, his jaw set. Realizing that the meeting had ended, he pushed back his chair and stood.

"Fair enough," he said and headed for the door.

Dudley watched him leave. He had a feeling that it wasn't the last he would hear on the subject.

THIRTY

LUKE SAKER'S BODY WAS SPRAWLED OUT on the living room floor. Pathologist Noah Bellman was crouched by his side, finishing his on-site examination. Detective Ryan descended the stairs, which, it appeared, Luke had fallen down. He watched Noah for a moment, hands in pockets.

"Accident or foul play?" he asked the pathologist.

"Could easily have been an accident," Noah replied. "He's drinking a soda." The pathologist pointed to the can of Diet Coke lying a short distance from the body. "Not watching where he's going, and BAM! Takes a tumble and breaks his neck."

Ryan nodded thoughtfully as he considered this theory. "Bit of a coincidence, though. Three days after his business partner is murdered."

Noah gave him a wry smile. "You're the detective."

Ryan crouched down beside the pathologist to take a closer look.

"Time of death?" Detective Ryan asked.

Noah sighed. "I've told you . . ."

Ryan interrupted, having heard Noah's protests a dozen times before. "Roughly."

"A few hours ago. But don't hold me to that."

Ryan pointed down at a pool of liquid a few feet from Luke Saker's head.

"Diet Coke?" Ryan asked.

"I assume, but we'll take a sample." He gestured to Sophie Flores, wearing full forensics protective gear, as Ryan turned in her direction. She bent to pick up the Coke can and dropped it into a ziplock bag.

"So, how long before I get the results?" the detective asked.

"Soon," was all the forensic assistant would commit to.

"Ryan." The detective looked around as Detective Yang walked over. "The wife's pretty shaken up. Are you ready to see her?"

"Lead the way," he said and followed her across the room. She slid open the double glass doors to the terrace.

McKenzie Saker sat at an ornate, cast-iron patio table. She didn't look well. Her eyes were bloodshot, her face tear-stained and pasty white despite the heavy makeup. A man dressed in an open-necked shirt and jeans stood close by. They both watched as the detectives walked over.

"Detective Ryan, this is McKenzie Saker, the late Mr. Saker's wife," Detective Yang said. "And Frank Pavlov's the Uber driver who brought her home earlier," she said, pointing to the standing man. "Mr. Pavlov picked Mrs. Saker up at Circular Quay and dropped her off in the drive. Before he could return to the road, Mrs. Saker rushed out of the house, screaming for help."

Yang looked to the Uber driver for confirmation, and he stepped forward.

"It was me who called the police," the driver offered.

"I see." Ryan paused. "Do you know Mrs. Saker?"

"No, we've never met before," Frank Pavlov said. He stepped closer to Detective Ryan. "Any chance I can go now? I've already told the other detective everything I know."

Detective Ryan turned. "Detective Yang, you have this man's contact details?"

Zoe nodded.

"Okay. Detective Yang will show you out."

As they left, Ryan sat down opposite McKenzie Saker. "This shouldn't take long. I just need you to answer a few questions."

"Couldn't we do this later?" she responded tearily.

"We prefer to question witnesses as soon as possible. I know this is a terrible time for you, but . . ."

"I'm not a witness. I'm Luke's wife," McKenzie said, turning to stare out at the immaculately coiffured lawn.

"Of course," Detective Ryan replied quietly. "And I'm sorry for your loss."

"Thank you."

The terrace door slid open, and Zoe returned. Ryan waited for his partner to sit down next to him.

"Roughly what time did you catch the Uber at Circular Quay?" he asked.

"Around six-thirty this morning."

"Why were you at the quay at that time?" Ryan said.

"I had just come off a boat." She looked across at Detective Yang. "It was one of those ladies-only cruises. I was there with my girlfriends. It was a great night." McKenzie started to cry. "I rarely stay out that late . . . ." She dabbed her swollen eyes with a tissue.

"And what happened when you entered the house?"

"I shouted for him when I came in. I knew he'd be up. When he didn't answer, I went into the living room. That's when I saw him."

"At the bottom of those stairs?" Ryan said, pointing through the glass doors into the living room.

"Yes. He was dead," McKenzie said.

"You knew that?" Ryan asked.

"He wasn't breathing and had no pulse." She noted the looks of surprise from the detectives. "I was a nurse before I married," she explained.

"When *was* that?" Detective Ryan asked.

"When I married?"

Ryan nodded.

"Twenty years ago." McKenzie stopped. "Please . . . I don't think I can answer any more questions."

"Just a few more," Ryan cajoled.

"It really will help us," Detective Yang added sympathetically.

"So, was he about to go to work this morning?" Ryan asked.

"I'm not sure. He didn't go into the office every day."

"But he was up early and in a suit?" Ryan said.

"Yes, but . . ." She shrugged. "They could be yesterday's clothes. I don't think he slept here last night," McKenzie said.

Ryan nodded. He'd already checked around the house and seen that none of the beds appeared to have been slept in.

"Really," the detective said. "Where do you think he was?"

"I think he was at the casino," McKenzie said, her eyes welling with tears at the thought.

"The one in town? The Sun?"

"Yes."

"And was that a regular occurrence?"

McKenzie looked across at Detective Yang and then back at Detective Ryan before replying.

"It's a problem my husband has.. . ." She paused. "Had."

"With gambling?"

McKenzie looked at her hands, slowly turning the wedding band on her ring finger.

"Yes," she replied quietly.

THIRTY-ONE

DETECTIVE RYAN PEERED AT A MONITOR in the security room of the Sun Casino. The dead man, Luke Saker, was one of a group sitting at the roulette table.

"Seen enough?" a voice said.

The detective looked around at a black-suited man with a face like a crumpled handkerchief—casino manager Jake Easton.

"When did Luke Saker leave?" Detective Ryan asked.

"Around five this morning," Easton replied.

"How much did he lose last night?"

Easton hesitated. Whenever the police came calling, he trod a delicate line—supplying some help but not too much, just enough to keep the police on side.

"You know I can't tell you that, Detective."

"A lot? A little? Help me out here."

"Let's just say he wasn't a happy camper when he left," Easton said.

"He was a regular? And a big spender?" Detective Ryan asked.

Easton hesitated. "Yeah, he liked to splash the cash." He paused. "So, we're done?"

"Yep," Ryan said, standing. "Thanks for your time."

"Always a pleasure, Detective," Easton said. "Shall we?"

The two men walked past the bank of monitors to the door. Easton opened it. "After you."

The detective stepped out onto a metal stairwell landing.

"By the way, Ryan, congratulations on the Homicide Squad promotion," Easton said, joining him.

"Thanks," Ryan responded. The detective had no idea how Easton knew about his move from the Organized Crime Unit to homicide, but in the casino manager's world, finding out who was doing what in the police was vital.

"The glamor unit." Easton grinned, following Ryan down the stairs.

"So they say."

"I'm not surprised. I've always had you tagged as a guy going places," the manager said, reaching the bottom of the stairs. "Next, a superintendent, I'm guessing."

Ryan glanced over at Easton. Casino managers and detectives had one skill in common. Both were good at reading people, but in this case, Easton was only partly right. Ryan had initially joined the police determined to rise through the ranks. But once he became a detective, he realized he'd found what he sought.

"So, what exactly happened to Luke Saker? He looked okay when he walked out of here," Easton said. "Alive, at least," he added wryly.

"You know I can't tell you that." Ryan frowned.

"Now look who's being all coy," Easton said. "Saker's dead, though, right?"

The detective said nothing.

"Ryan, homicide guys don't investigate the living."

The detective still said nothing.

"Please. Luke Saker was worth a lot to us."

"How much?" Ryan asked.

Easton pulled a face.

"Tit for tat?" the detective said.

Easton sighed. "More than a couple of mil this year."

Ryan whistled. "That much?"

"Yeah."

"And how much did he lose?" the detective asked.

"Again, I can't tell you that. Even if I knew, which I don't. Not offhand, anyway."

That was a lie. Ryan knew the casino manager could supply the answer to that question immediately. High rollers like Luke Saker were protected and nurtured by the casino; every dime they won or lost was meticulously noted. They were nicknamed whales because if you caught one, you could feed on it for weeks. Some were so wealthy they thought nothing of gambling what the average person might make in a year, but Ryan was pretty sure that wouldn't have been the case for Luke Saker. True, he was a partner in the Faith Company, and he did have a lovely house in an expensive location . . . but could he afford to gamble millions?

"Come on. Your turn," Easton prompted, typing in numbers on the touchpad on the steel exit door.

Ryan considered the question. He knew he needed to keep Jake Easton happy, so he had to offer him something.

"He was found dead a few hours ago at his house," Ryan said.

"Oh," the manager said, pulling the door open. The sounds of the casino floor rushed in. "How?"

"Fell down some stairs," Detective Ryan said, stepping out. "Well, thanks for your help."

"It was good to see you again, Detective. And keep me in the loop on that Saker thing."

"Will do," Ryan said, knowing that would never happen.

"Good," Easton said before closing the heavy steel door behind him.

DETECTIVE RYAN LOOKED AROUND. THERE WAS a feel . . . a *look* to a casino floor that was always the same. There were no clocks, no windows, nothing to remind you of the world outside . . . just hushed conversations, the clicking of gaming wheels, the bells and whistles of the slots, and the jangle of coins as gold and silver uniformed waitresses carrying metal trays filled with glasses and bottles glided past the gamblers. The players were a mixed bunch—some expensively dressed in designer suits and haute couture dresses, and others more casual—shorts and lurid T-shirts. The casino didn't mind. It had no real dress code, only a money code. If you had it, you were welcome. If not, why were you there?

Ryan's feet sank into the plush red and blue swirl-patterned carpet as he walked to the central stairway. The detective had emerged onto the first floor, the level below where whales like Luke Saker spent most of their time. Downstairs, on the ground floor, the casino's less affluent gamblers fed cash into clusters of one-armed bandits or lost their money at the numerous blackjack and roulette tables.

A poker tournament was currently being staged on this central floor. The area was crammed with tables full of a ragtag mix of men and a few women players.

The gambling bug had never infected Detective Ryan; for him, life was enough of a gamble—a fact that had been driven home when he had seen his mother at the hospital. Ryan shivered as he remembered that Mumta would be getting her test results any day now.

A hand slammed down on the detective's shoulder, and Ryan turned to face a thick-necked, square-faced man wearing round grandpa glasses. He was dressed in a crumpled black suit, a blue shirt, its top button open, and a red and white striped tie pushed up close. The man was framed by two giant goons, look-alikes with pug noses, squinty pig eyes, and black hair razor cut to a stubble. One wore a red Hawaiian shirt and black shorts, the other a blue Hawaiian shirt and white shorts. Both men's feet were encased in large black workman boots.

"Ryan," the man with glasses said, "fancy seeing you here."

The detective reached up to carefully remove The Owl's hand from his suit jacket. Behind, the big men stiffened.

The Owl saw the movement. "Easy," he said to them. "Detective Ryan is one of us."

"One of us? I don't think so, Guffini," Ryan said.

The Owl shrugged. "Please yourself. But just a note . . . it's Mr. Guffini to you."

Ryan said nothing. There was no way the detective would ever call the crime boss "mister."

"Now let me introduce you to the brothers," The Owl said. "He pointed to the man to his left. "That's Tik . . . and his twin brother, Tok. Tik and Tok. Get it?" The Owl said. "Thought of that myself." He frowned. "But you've met them before, right?"

"No, never," said Ryan.

"Oh, no, of course not. You've moved to pastures new. The Homicide

Squad is taking up all your time now, is it?" The Owl said.

Ryan stared at Guffini. Everyone seemed to know of the detective's transfer from organized crime to homicide, including the head of one of Australia's most prominent crime syndicates.

"I've got to go," Ryan said, moving away.

"Now that's disappointing," The Owl said, following. "I thought we could have a drink and a bit of catch-up. Me to find out how the new job is going, and you to quiz me on my new interest."

"New interest?" Ryan said, stopping. "What's that?"

"Poker." The Owl indicated the tables. "There's a big tournament at the moment, and I'm sponsoring a few players."

"Poker, huh? So, you've given up your life of crime, then, Guffini?" He said, deliberately omitting the honorific.

Guffini paused but decided to let Ryan's lack of respect slide—for the moment, anyway. His smile was slightly menacing as he addressed the question.

"I've never had a 'life of crime'. As you well know, I'm the CEO of an international finance company."

Before Ryan could reply, a loud bell rang, and the poker players began to stand. The tournament was taking a short break.

"I won't keep you from your work, then," Detective Ryan said, heading down the stairs, Guffini watching as he disappeared from view.

THIRTY-TWO

A S HE ARRIVED ON THE GROUND floor, Detective Ryan felt another tap on his shoulder. "For Christ's sake, Guffini . . ." he said and spun around to face a blond-haired, blue-eyed woman.

"No, not him," she said, beaming.

It took Ryan a moment before he recognized her. "Heidi? Heidi Miller?" the detective said, staring.

"In the flesh." She grinned. "And look at you, Ramesh . . . still as handsome as ever."

Ryan blushed bright red. Heidi remained the only woman capable of making him do that. "What are you doing here?" the detective stammered, instantly regretting the question. It was not how you were meant to greet a woman you hadn't seen for nearly two decades.

"I'm playing in the poker tournament," Heidi said and paused. "Look, have you got time for a catch-up?"

Ryan nodded. "Yes, sure . . . that would be good," he said, hoping Heidi couldn't hear the sound of his beating heart.

"Follow me," she said.

The pair wove their way through the rows of jangling slot machines to reach a curtain of shimmering thread. Pushing through, they walked across the low-lit room and sat at the bar.

The barman approached.

"What would you like?" he asked.

"I'll have a gin and tonic, and I'm guessing you'll want a Coke, Ramesh, seeing as you're on duty?"

Ryan nodded, surprised. How did she know what he did for a living?

"You're wondering how I guessed you were a cop?" Heidi said as Fred, the bartender, left to get the drinks.

"Yes," Ryan admitted.

"Two things." She paused, keeping him in suspense for a moment before throwing a look at the gun holster peeking out of his jacket. He followed her gaze and smiled awkwardly as he realized.

"Ah." He adjusted his jacket to conceal the weapon.

Heidi leaned over to touch Ryan's lapel. "The clothes, though, are a little confusing. You're a pretty natty dresser for a policeman. But then again, even at university, you were always a bit of a fashionista."

"Fashionista?" Ryan laughed. "No, I was never that. I just liked good clothes." He paused. "And the second thing?"

"That was the clincher . . . I asked one of the waitresses." Heidi's eyes had a mischievous sparkle. "Apparently, you're quite well known here."

Ryan went to speak. Heidi put up her hand. "Before you ask, it's not that I didn't recognize you, but a girl has to be absolutely certain."

It appeared to Ryan that Heidi had not changed one bit since the last time he'd seen her. Maybe an extra laugh line or two, but that just seemed to make her more attractive, if anything.

"So, you said you're playing in the poker tournament?"

"Yeah."

"There you go," the bartender said as he put their drinks down. He waited as she took a sip of the gin and tonic.

"Good?" he asked.

"You can't really do much wrong with a G and T, can you, Fred?" Heidi said.

The bartender smiled. "You'd be surprised. Next time, though, maybe you could give me more of a challenge. I'd love that."

He placed the bill folder next to the drink. "Shall I put this on your room?"

Ryan raised his hand. "No, I'll pay."

"Nonsense, Ramesh. All my expenses are covered here . . . 482."

The bartender nodded and left.

Heidi swiveled around to face her old friend. "So, where were we?"

"I believe that man was flirting with you," Ryan said, raising an eyebrow in mock fashion.

Heidi smiled playfully. "He was?" She paused. "Jealous, are you, Ramesh?"

"Of course," Ryan said, attempting some flirting of his own.

"Heidi."

She turned to see someone heading her way.

"Oh, hi," Heidi said.

It was the man who had buttonholed her in the bar the other day.

"I just came to thank you for your advice." Dave Jupiter smiled.

"Well, I didn't really . . ." Heidi began.

"Yes, you did," he interrupted. "You put me on the right path. So, thank you."

"No problem."

"Sorry to disturb you." Jupiter glanced over at Ryan before exiting.

Ryan watched the man go. "Another admirer?"

"He's no one . . . .. Just a guy who wanted to pick my brains about getting poker sponsorship."

"Oh," Ryan said, taking a sip of the Coke. "So, poker? Can we talk about that?"

"Sure."

"I thought you were going to be an actress?"

Heidi picked up her drink and took a sip. "You remembered?"

"Seemed a pretty exotic ambition at the time," he explained. "So, what happened?"

"After university, I did take an acting course and got a few roles, but nothing big, and certainly nothing that paid well. Eventually, I realized that acting wouldn't work financially, so I took a real estate course."

"What are you doing here if you're in real estate?" Ryan asked.

"Just like a cop . . . all questions." Heidi grinned.

Ryan raised his hand. "Sorry. It's a bad habit."

Heidi smiled. "I don't mind. I've got lots to ask you, too." She paused. "I went out briefly with a guy who was a professional poker player. He taught me about the game. Before long, I was beating him. That's when I decided to take up poker professionally."

Heidi leaned back, her eyes sparkling bright as she stared at the detective. "So, what about you?"

"Not much to tell." He shrugged. "I joined the force when I left college and went from being a uniformed policeman to a detective, which is what I am now."

"And it's working out for you?" Heidi asked.

"Yeah. I love the job." Ryan paused. "What about you and poker?"

"The same. I think I've found my niche."

They both took sips from their drinks.

Silence. Then: "How is Mumta?"

"You remember my mother?"

"Of course."

Ryan was surprised. Heidi and Mumta had only met a handful of times.

"I know. It was eons ago," Heidi said as if reading his mind. "But your mother's very memorable."

"She liked you, you know . . . a lot." Ryan grinned. "Thought we should have been an item."

Heidi smiled. "Really?"

"Yeah, but you had . . ." He clicked his fingers as if searching for the name. He wasn't. He remembered Goran Maric well, a charismatic Serbian; he and Heidi had been considered the perfect pair.

"Goran," Heidi said.

"Yeah, that's him."

"I haven't seen him in years. Though I did hear he married a model and now has a couple of kids." Heidi sighed. "Life, eh? So many twists and turns." She stopped. "I daresay you're married, too . . . with children?"

Ryan shook his head. "Nope. Of course, I've had girlfriends, but no one's ever been 'the one.'" He thought about adding: *Except for you, of course*, but he stopped himself. How stupid would that have been?

Heidi glanced at her watch and sighed. "Break over, I'm afraid. I have to get back." She stood up. "This really was a wonderful surprise . . . . Look, I'm here for a few days. Maybe we could meet up again? I finish around nine." She reached into her pocket and handed him a card. "Call me?"

Ryan's phone rang.

"Sure," the detective said, giving her a small smile.

She pecked the detective on his cheek as his cell rang again. "Bye for now, but hopefully not for long. Not twenty years, anyway."

The phone rang a third time.

"Answer it, please," Heidi said, walking.

His cell rang yet again.

Distracted, Ryan clicked on the phone. "Yes?"

"I've got an update for you," Detective Yang said.

THIRTY-THREE

THERE WAS ALWAYS A TIME IN a case when nothing seemed to be coming together; the leads the detectives had pursued searching for Gary Young's murderer had come to zero. As for Luke Saker, the cops still didn't know exactly how he'd died. So, after Detective Yang confirmed McKenzie Saker's alibi—that she was on a boat in the harbor last night—Ryan decided they needed to speak to Simon Faith again. Two people dying in the space of a few days, both partners in the same company, seemed to be more than coincidental.

"Detective Ryan and Detective Yang," Yvonne announced, entering her boss's office.

"Take a seat, please, detectives," Simon said, wearing a serious expression. He indicated the chairs on the other side of his desk.

Yvonne handed her boss a newspaper as the detectives sat.

"Today's," she said.

Simon glanced at the paper as the PA left. Then he turned his attention back to the cops. "So, Detectives, you're here about Luke?" His face was grim.

Detective Ryan stared at him, surprised.

"His wife contacted me a few hours ago. Terrible. First Gary and then Luke." He paused. "She said it was an accident. He fell down the stairs." He looked from one detective to the other. "Is that what *you* think happened?"

Neither cop answered. Then: "We'll get on to Luke Saker in a minute,"

Ryan said. He studied the man in front of him for a moment before continuing. "Is there anyone you can think of who might have wanted to kill Gary Young, Mr. Faith?" Detective Ryan asked.

Simon Faith shook his head. "No. Gary had no business enemies that I knew of."

"And what about in his personal life?" Ryan asked.

"No idea. I rarely saw Gary outside the office."

"So, you didn't know he was having an affair?" Ryan queried.

There was silence as Faith decided how to answer the question. "One of the security men might have mentioned something about it." Simon stopped. "I'm assuming you've checked it out?"

"His lover has an airtight alibi," Detective Yang informed him.

"Oh."

"What about Luke Saker?" Detective Ryan asked. "Did you know about his gambling?"

The hotel boss peered at the detective. "Sorry, I'm confused. What?"

"Did you know about Luke's casino visits?"

"What has this got to do with anything?"

"Please answer the question, Mr. Faith."

Silence. "Yes, I knew."

"So, were you aware of the extent of Luke's losses at the casino?"

"Yes."

"And that wasn't a problem for you?" Detective Ryan said.

"Why would it be?" Simon asked.

"Well, I assume each of your partners had a stake in the company."

"Correct. When we set it up, Gary, Luke, and I all put in money."

"Equal amounts?" Ryan asked.

"No. I put the most in, so I had the majority stake."

"Even so, I imagine Luke's share is worth much more now than when he first invested."

"Yes," Simon confirmed.

"So, would the company have been impacted if Luke asked for his stake back to pay off his gambling debts?"

Simon stared at Detective Ryan. "Impacted? You used the word 'impacted.'" He paused. "You think I had something to do with Luke's death?"

"Did I say that, Detective?" Ryan said, looking over at Zoe Yang.

"No, you didn't," Yang confirmed. "Detective Ryan was simply wondering what would happen to the company if either of your partners had decided to take their money out."

"I think you're suggesting much more. You're implying that would be a motivation for someone to kill them. Someone like me, for instance?"

"Not at all, Mr. Faith," Ryan said, somewhat disingenuously. "I'm surprised that you would jump to that conclusion."

Simon suddenly looked worried as he considered his options. "Do I need a lawyer?" he asked.

"We can't advise you on that, but as far as we're concerned, this is just an informal chat. Introducing a lawyer would take it to a new level," Detective Ryan said.

Simon thought about that. "Okay. No lawyer . . . for the time being. But just so we're clear, if either of my partners had opted to end their association with me and the company, it wouldn't have been a problem. When I set up the organization, I needed their help, but now the banks are falling over each other to offer finance." He stopped. "In fact, Luke, Gary, and I were recently reexamining the details should any of us ever want to cash out our stakes."

"Did Luke want out?" Ryan said.

"As I understand it, and as you have confirmed, he had considerable gambling losses. I knew he was in a bind, and in business, you always have to think ahead, so that was a possibility."

Simon stood up. "Detectives, you may have noticed all the work around the hotel . . . the new security system, painting, artwork, and sculptures. We are giving The Palms a radical new look for its official reopening, and consequently I am exceptionally busy, so if you don't mind." He stopped and shouted, "Yvonne!"

Moments later, the door opened, and the PA stepped in.

"Mr. Faith?"

"Yvonne, could you show the detectives out, please?"

Detective Ryan and Detective Yang stood up.

"Thank you for your assistance, Mr. Faith," Ryan said. "Don't hesitate to contact us if you think of anything that might be important."

THIRTY-FOUR

AFTER THE DETECTIVES HAD LEFT, SIMON picked up the newspaper, flicked through to page six, and began to read. Finishing, he angrily crumpled it up and threw it into the garbage bin at the side of his desk.

"Fuck!" he yelled. "Fuck, fuck, fuck!"

Moments later, the office door opened.

"Did you need something, Mr. Faith?" Yvonne asked, peering anxiously at her boss.

"No, Yvonne," Simon snapped, trying to calm down.

"Okay," she said, turning to leave.

"Yvonne?"

The PA swiveled back uncertainly.

"Did you read the article?" Simon said.

Yvonne shook her head. "No," she said.

"Good," Simon huffed.

The PA again tried to leave.

"Yvonne. When you read it, and I have no doubt you will, you have to know it's a load of garbage, full of lies and innuendos."

"Yes, Mr. Faith," Yvonne said. She reached for the door handle. Should she say something to appease her boss? He was agitated, and unless he settled down, he would make her day even more miserable than it was already.

"Mr. Faith?" Yvonne said, turning back.

"Yes?"

"I don't think many people are going to read that," she said, pointing at the paper. "I mean, no one reads newspapers anymore, do they?"

Simon thought about that. "Yes, you're probably right." He stopped. "But they can still see the article on the Internet, can't they?"

"I guess. But it's only one man's opinion, isn't it?" Yvonne said.

Simon stared at his PA. She had lied. She *had* read the piece.

"That one man's name is Mike Burford, and he's a real son of a bitch!" Simon exclaimed. "But yes, you're right. Thank you, Yvonne, you can go."

As the door closed behind the PA, Simon stood up and walked to the window. He peered out. He had chosen the large corner office because it afforded a magnificent view of the golf course and out over the national park beyond. Soon, the Faith Company would add two more tower blocks to the complex—and that was just the start. There was so much more to come. But how would his partners' deaths affect those plans?

Simon stroked his chin as he thought about Gary Young and Luke Saker. He and his two partners had all been willing to do whatever it took to get rich quickly. They had worked together at the start; Gary had been the details man, Luke the legal and sales and marketing, and Simon, the leader. Together, they called themselves the Three Musketeers.

As time passed, Simon's desire to succeed at any cost never dimmed, but, as the others had gotten richer, they had lost their edge. They had become self-satisfied and lazy. In truth, their deaths now would be a blessing . . . he could run the company as he had always wanted to, with no naysayers to drag him down. Of course, that wasn't something Simon would ever admit to anyone.

Why did he feel that his world was spinning out of control today? Simon thought about that. What if Luke's death wasn't accidental? What if he *had* been murdered? But who would possibly do that? And why?

The CEO walked back to his desk and sat down. On hearing the news of Gary's death, Luke had suggested they knew one person who could have done it. He had been skeptical back then, but now Luke, too, had died. Simon thought some more. It couldn't be him, could it?

Two of them were dead now, and he had thought about quitting . . . but only for a moment. No, they had to stick to the plan. It had always been all or none.

He spooned up the gray flakes of ammonium nitrate from the fertilizer bag. Adjusting the red metal canister with one hand, the man tipped the chemical into it with the other. Finishing, he glanced at the plastic oil-filled jerry can on the floor. He would add the oil to the canister tomorrow.

He reached across to examine a small, gray aluminum tube, closed at one end. The blasting cap had already been loaded with a detonating charge; one gram of eighty percent mercury fulminate and twenty percent potassium chlorate mix.

He would attach a small timer to the charge tomorrow, too, before closing off the other end of the tube. Once ignited, the mix would burn the oil first, increasing the amount of hot gas and heating the fertilizer.

Then . . . BOOM.

THIRTY-FIVE

Detective Ryan's cell rang. Taking one hand off the steering wheel, the cop reached into his pocket, took out his phone, and tapped the green icon. "Yes," he said.

"It's Zoe."

"Hi. How'd the house-hunting go?" Ryan asked.

"I put in an offer on one unit, but I reckon there were at least seventy-five other applicants," she said, sounding a little defeated.

After the hotel visit, Zoe had left early to check out new rental accommodations. Staying with her aunt was only ever going to be a temporary fix.

"Anyway, changing the subject . . . we have to go to pathology tomorrow morning. Noah said Luke Saker's autopsy results will be back by then," Zoe continued.

"He rang *you*?"

"You *did* say you wanted to use me as a point of contact," Zoe said, hearing the annoyance in Ryan's voice.

"Yes, I did, didn't I?" the detective admitted.

"Ten o'clock tomorrow, then?"

"Okay."

Ryan ended the call as he pulled into a space opposite his Potts Point apartment. The detective exited the car, crossed the street, and pushed open the metal-barred front gate of his art deco block. It creaked as it scraped over the concrete. The gate was old and stubborn, but for

Ryan, something was reassuring about its reluctance to do what it was meant to.

Closing the gate, the detective walked to the lobby and climbed the stone stairs to his third-floor flat. He turned the key in the lock, pushed the door open, and flicked the living room light as his cell rang again. He answered without checking the number.

"Forget something?" Ryan asked, throwing his briefcase onto the couch.

"This is your mother, Ramesh."

"Oh, sorry, Mom . . . are you okay?" the detective said quickly.

"Of course, I'm fine," Mumta said. "Why wouldn't I be?"

"Because it's late," Ramesh said.

"So?"

"So, you're always in bed by nine," Ramesh said as he flopped into an armchair.

"Maybe I've decided to change my routine . . . live dangerously. Did you consider *that*, Detective?" Mumta said with a mischievous tone.

"Is this to be a permanent change?"

"It's a trial," Mumta said and yawned. "So, how's your day been?"

"Fine." He paused. "This isn't about the hospital, is it?"

"That's the first thing that comes to mind, Ramesh? Not that I might want to talk to my only son . . . my *childless* son."

"Childless? Mom, we've discussed this."

"I'm guessing that you still haven't found anyone?"

"You only saw me yesterday, and the answer is still no."

There was a pause. "You telling porkies, Ramesh?"

"What?"

"I'm your mother, Ramesh. I can tell."

Amazing, he thought. How did she do that?

"Where do you think you got your detective genes from, Ramesh?" his mother said as if reading his mind. "It certainly wasn't from your father, God rest his soul." She stopped. "Who is she, then?"

Ramesh scratched his head. He didn't know what to say. Perhaps telling the truth was the best way forward.

"I'm not *seeing* anyone, as such."

"But?" his mother prodded.

"Do you remember a woman called Heidi Miller?" Ryan asked.

"Heidi Miller?" There was a pause. "Your beautiful friend from college? The woman who wanted to be an actress?"

"Yes," Ramesh said, shocked. "You remembered?"

"I may be old, but I'm not that old. I liked Heidi. Her boyfriend was a complete waste of space, though. You would have been a much better catch for her."

"I had a girlfriend at the time, Mom."

"Yes." Mumta snapped her fingers. "Chrissie or Cynthia or Cindy . . ."

"Claudine."

"That's right. Another in the long line of totally unsuitable women you've dated."

"I don't think that's fair," Ryan said.

"Oh no, says the man who was once seriously considering going out with a serial killer. Imagine if you'd had children with that one. She could have given birth to a brood of murderers." Mumta stopped. "Now, tell me about Heidi."

Ramesh hesitated. He knew his mother wouldn't stop pestering him if he didn't give her something.

"I met her in the casino today," he said finally.

"Oh. You haven't taken up gambling now, have you?"

"No. I was there for work."

"A case?"

"Yes, Mom, a case."

Silence.

"Mom, you still there?"

"I was thinking. Why was Heidi at the casino?"

"She's a professional poker player."

"She's given up being an actress?"

"That was years ago, Mom."

Silence. Ryan could almost hear his mother's brain whirring.

"A poker player? Does she make a good living doing that?" Mumta asked.

"Yes. I think so."

There was another long pause. "Where's the boyfriend?"

"Long since gone."

"Is she single then . . . like you?"

"Yes."

"Good."

"Good?" Ryan repeated, surprised. He'd never have imagined that "poker player" was on his mother's list of suitable girlfriends.

"Mom? Didn't you hear me? She's a professional poker player."

"Who is making money? Yes, I know. It's not ideal, but neither is being a thirty-eight-year-old single detective. It depresses me to say it, but you're not much of a catch, you know. Now, if you'd been a lawyer or a doctor, we're talking an entirely different game." She paused. "When are you seeing her again?"

"I . . . don't know."

"You haven't asked her out?" Mumta sounded disappointed. "Well, you must," she insisted.

"Why's that?"

"Because you liked her."

"That was a long time ago, Mom."

"Don't give me that, Ramesh. I could tell when you said her name just now that you still like her."

His mother was supremely intuitive.

"Even if I wanted to, Mom, I'm just too busy."

Mumta released her breath, exasperated. "Too busy? That's a lousy excuse. You mean you can't be bothered going after the woman who could be the love of your life? The one who could give me grandchildren. That one?"

"Mom, don't you think you've jumped a few stages there?"

"Not at all. I expect you to ask her out in the next few days."

Mumta waited.

Silence.

"Ramesh?"

"Yeah, okay . . . whatever."

"Good. Keep me updated."

The detective shook his head. There was no way in hell he was going to do that.

"Well, goodnight then, Mom, and thanks for calling." Ramesh went to switch off the phone.

"No, wait. I've got something to tell you. I've just got an appointment with the hospital about the results. Friday morning."

Ryan felt a sinking in the pit of his stomach.

"Okay, well, I'll go with you."

"There's no need. . . ." There was a note of uncertainty. "But if you insist . . ."

"I do."

"Okay. It'll be nice to see you again, anyway. You can tell me how you got on with Heidi." She yawned. "Now I'm off to bed. You know I'm not entirely convinced this new routine suits."

"Goodnight, Mom."

As Ryan clicked off the phone, there was a knock on the door. He got up, opened it, and did a double take.

Heidi Miller stood on the landing looking sensational. Her long blond hair spilled over her shoulders onto a yellow dress that appeared to have been sprayed on. It showed every curve of her body and finished a country mile above her knees, showcasing long, sinewy legs.

"Heidi?" Ryan tried to disguise his delight. "How did you know where I live?"

"You're not the only detective around here." Heidi smiled. "So, aren't you going to invite me in?"

"Yes, of course," Ryan said, pushing the door open.

Heidi took a step forward and slipped past him. The detective followed and closed the door.

"This is nice," Heidi said, looking around. "One bedroom?'

"Yes. There," he said, pointing.

Heidi dropped her clutch on the couch and walked across to the bedroom. She stared through the open door.

"So . . . what are you doing here?" Ryan asked, genuinely nonplussed.

"This is nice, too," Heidi said, ignoring the question.

"I would have made the bed if I had known I'd have visitors," Ryan said, stepping up behind her.

Heidi walked to the bed and sat, her skirt riding even higher as she did.

"Why didn't you come and see me tonight?"

"I . . . I was thinking about it."

"That's what I figured. But I know you, Ramesh. A girl could grow old waiting." She tapped the bed. "Come on, sit down."

Ryan did as he was told.

Heidi turned to stare into his eyes. "You know I would have dropped Goran like a hotcake if you had made just *one* move . . . just one."

"You would have? But I thought—"

"You thought wrong," Heidi interrupted. "I was waiting for you to do something. Of course, times have changed. Now, women don't wait anymore. We go out and get what we want."

Heidi put her arm around Ryan's back, edging toward him. "Tonight, sitting alone in my hotel room, I thought, why not?" She brought her lips close to his. "Why not, Ramesh?"

THIRTY-SIX

I T HAD BEEN A CLEAR, STAR-FILLED night, and so, when morning arrived, the few wisps of clouds that traced across the sky had quickly burned off. It was going to be another gorgeous day. But as Maude Adams, president of the Leeton Regis Strata Association, stared out of her Potts Point apartment window, she had more pressing things on her mind than the weather—*one* important thing, actually. Where was Detective Ramesh Ryan?

Maude had hoped to spy the detective returning from his regular morning exercise. Then, she could have "accidentally" bumped into him, but he didn't seem to have taken a run. No matter. She decided she couldn't delay this anymore. It had to be done.

Maude left her unit and climbed the stairs to the detective's apartment, feeling a twinge in her hip as she did. Arthritis! There was nothing she could do about that, though—the curse of old age.

Reaching the detective's door, Maude hesitated. She had been a battler all her life, willing to take on anyone and anything, but policemen still unnerved her. She didn't know why, but she always felt guilty around them.

Brushing her apprehension aside, Maude knocked hard on the detective's door.

Footsteps. The door opened.

"Maude," Ryan said, peering out. The woman looked wilder than usual, her spiky, dyed orange hair poking left and right.

"Where were you?" Maude asked.

"Sorry?" Ryan said, taken aback.

"The strata meeting last night?" Maude said. She stared at him. What was wrong with the man? He looked like he'd just gotten up, his shirt only partially buttoned, his trouser belt undone. And what was up with his hair, all matted and snarled? Usually, every strand was brushed neatly into place.

"The strata meeting about the rats?" she said.

"Oh, of course," Ryan said as Heidi came into view. She wore a man's white shirt, showing off her impressively long shapely legs.

"Coffee?" she asked.

"Yes, sure," Ryan said, turning. "The coffee is . . ."

"I'll find it," Heidi said, heading for the kitchen.

Ryan turned back. "Sorry, what were you saying about rats, Maude?"

"We had a meeting last night about them. You were invited."

"I apologize. I meant to be there, but I was busy."

Maude glared at him. "Even though I had you down as a definite?"

"I only said that I would try to make it."

She paused. Then: "Well, I'm not going to give you a blow by blow, just the highlights. There was a lot of argument. Some didn't even seem to mind the rats."

"Amazing," Ryan said.

"Milk and sugar?" Heidi said as she reappeared behind the detective.

"Just milk," Ryan said, smiling at her.

Maude coughed.

Ryan turned. "Sorry. Heidi, this is Maude, chairperson of the strata association."

"President will do, thank you very much. I don't go for all that woke nonsense." She held out her hand to Heidi. "Maude Adams."

"Hi, Maude, Heidi Miller," Heidi said, shaking her hand. "Ramesh, why don't you ask Maude in?"

Maude raised her hand. "No need, thank you. This won't take long."

"Well, it's nice to meet you anyway. I'll finish making the coffee," Heidi said to Ryan before returning to the kitchen.

Maude watched her go. "Others favored introducing cats," she said after a moment.

"What?" Ryan asked.

"At the meeting," Maude said.

"Yes, of course. The meeting."

"There was a push for ferals," Maude continued. "There were, of course, a couple of problems there. First, no one knew where to find a pack of strays. Second, feral cats may or may not kill the rodents, and even if they did, we'd be left with large numbers of felines who, in the absence of rats, may turn to decimating the local lizard and bird populations. We couldn't have that, could we?"

"No. We couldn't," the detective confirmed. "So?"

"So, we all agreed on one solution."

"That being?"

"Poison," Maude said. "That should fix them."

SIMON FAITH DIDN'T FEEL WELL. He gulped down water and swallowed two Tylenol tablets. Hopefully, they would help.

He had hardly slept, tossing and turning all night and arriving at the hotel office early, but had felt too ill to start work immediately. Instead, while waiting for the pills to take effect, he continued to mull over his partners' deaths.

Simon had never felt empathy for anyone, so although he had been in business with the men for over twenty years, he felt no sadness or loss at their demise. He did, however, feel one emotion—fury. Why had this happened now?On the eve of the hotel's reopening! Then again, he had to give it to him. The man was smart. He knew when to apply maximum pressure.

The CEO gulped down more water and thought about what to do next. He had always kept a rigid workday routine: urgent phone calls first up, and then onto the computer. He inspected the hotel in the morning and afternoon, sandwiching it with a light lunch in the restaurant. He was home by around eight o'clock to watch an hour or so of TV. Then it was time for bed. Weekends were the same, except for Saturday and Sunday golf games. Occasionally, he was forced to break the routine, but only for important work events.

The hotel boss was convinced that sticking to the same daily plan was one reason for his business success. Now, however, a giant spanner had been thrown in the works.

Simon sat up in his chair. His ability to think outside the box was his not-so-secret weapon and was recognized as a major asset. His late partners, though, had always been nuts and bolts men. They had relied on him to develop creative ideas for taking the business to ever-dizzying heights.

Now, the very audacity of his new thought took Simon's breath away. It was daring. It was novel. It was an actual eureka moment.

He would appease the murderer. Yes, he could do that—as for the cops, he needed them off his back, not rifling through his business affairs . . . but that would be easy. Distraction. That was the name of the game.

"Yvonne!" Faith yelled.

The office door opened.

"Yes, Mr. Faith."

"What happens to the garbage?"

"The garbage?"

"Yes, the stuff I throw away in there," Simon said, pointing to the metal bin beside his desk.

"It's emptied every night by the cleaners, Mr. Faith."

"So, it's gone?"

"Yeah."

"Damn . . . .. Okay, I want you to get me another copy of yesterday's paper."

"Now?"

"Yes, right now. And can you also get Steve Prince up here?"

"Will do," Yvonne said and hesitated. "Anything else?"

"Yes." Simon searched in his pocket and produced a business card. He waved it in the air with one hand and signaled the PA over with the other. "I want you to ring the cops who came here yesterday. Tell them that I need to speak to them urgently."

Yvonne took the card and stared at it.

Simon glared. "What are you waiting for? Snap, snap."

"Yes, Mr. Faith," Yvonne said, turning.

"Snap, Snap," she repeated under her breath. He really was the rudest, most obnoxious man she had ever worked for.

THIRTY-SEVEN

NOAH BELLMAN HAD ARRIVED TEN MINUTES late for their ten o'clock mortuary meeting, explaining to Detective Yang that his vehicle wouldn't start.

"Where's Ryan?" he said as he looked around.

"He's not here yet," Detective Yang said.

"That's odd. I've never known him to be late," Noah said.

Moments later, the door opened, and a flustered Detective Ryan barreled in. "Sorry, everyone. Problem with my car."

"Looks like today is not a good day for vehicles," the pathologist said. "My car broke down, too. Anyway, shall we begin?"

Not waiting for an answer, Noah walked over to the metal table in the center of the room and pulled the cover off Luke Saker's body.

Detective Ryan and Detective Yang stepped forward to peer down at the corpse.

A large, deep, Y-shaped incision had been made from shoulder to shoulder, meeting at the breastbone and extending down to the pubic bone.

"So, the headline news is Luke Saker was poisoned," Noah announced.

"What type of poison exactly, Noah?" Detective Ryan asked, seemingly unsurprised.

Noah picked up a small brown glass bottle with a white cap and a black rubber nozzle. He held up the container of colorless liquid. "This type. Thallium," he said.

"Rat poison," Ryan said, taking the bottle and examining the fluid.

"Exactly," the pathologist agreed. "Otherwise known as the 'poisoner's poison.'"

"What does it do to you?" Detective Yang asked.

"Causes peripheral nerve damage, gastrointestinal problems, visual impairment, skin lesions, confusion, and hair loss."

"But Luke Saker has a good head of hair," Detective Yang said, gazing at the body. "And I don't see any skin lesions."

"Yes, because hair loss, along with most of those other symptoms, occurs with chronic exposure over time. Whoever did this to Saker wasn't prepared to wait."

"You're saying the toxicology report showed high levels?" Ryan asked.

"Extremely high," Noah confirmed.

"But I thought thallium was banned in Australia," Detective Yang said.

Noah looked from Zoe to Ryan. "You've got a good one here, Ryan. Quite right, Yang. After the Thallium Craze of the 1950s, when a number of women dispatched unwanted husbands with relative ease, unrestricted access to thallium was prohibited. You can't kill vermin with it anymore, but you can, surprisingly, still use it as a homeopathic remedy." He rolled his eyes as he said it, clearly not a believer.

Ryan bent down and stared at Luke Saker's head. "It wasn't the poison that killed him."

The pathologist smiled. "You're right again, Ryan. No, it wasn't the thallium."

"I'm sorry? Didn't you just say it was the poison that caused Luke Saker's death?" Detective Yang said, confused.

"I said he'd been poisoned, yes. But before it could kill him, he became disoriented and fell down the stairs, breaking his neck. *That's* what killed him."

"But homicide nonetheless," Detective Yang said.

"Exactly. Whoever poisoned this man had every intention of killing him," Noah said. "Though they may not have planned on it panning out quite the way it did."

The door behind them opened, and a woman in a white lab coat with a manila folder stuffed under her arm hurried in. "Morning," Sophie Flores said.

"Hi, Sophie," Noah said. "You've met Detective Ryan, but have you met his partner, Detective Yang?"

The woman walked over and shook Yang's hand. "Sophie Flores. Forensics."

"Zoe Yang. I saw you at the hut, but we weren't formally introduced."

"Well, detective, it's good to see another woman breaking the glass ceiling. These guys like to keep the work to themselves," Sophie said, gesturing around.

"Sophie's a feminist," Noah said to no one in particular.

"Not so much a feminist in this instance, Noah, more a realist. Now, are you about wrapped up?"

"Yep," said Noah. "Unless there's something else you need from me, detectives?"

"Just a hard copy of the autopsy report," Ryan said.

"That's in my office. You can pick it up there. I'll also email you."

"That would be good," Ryan said.

"And I've put the two forensic reports on Gary Young and Luke Saker for pickup and will also send you copies," Sophie said. "But I can give you the main bullet points now, if you like."

Ryan nodded. "Go ahead."

"Has Noah explained the thallium and its involvement in Luke Saker's death?"

"Yes," Detective Ryan confirmed.

"Well, we also found traces of the poison in the Coke can found by the body and in the spilled cola next to him. Thallium is tasteless, odorless, and water-soluble, so the drinker wouldn't notice it mixed with Coca-Cola. We also checked the two other unopened cans of cola in the refrigerator at the house. They both contained large amounts of thallium, too. It appears someone had jimmied the tab and injected the poison into the tins before resealing them," Sophie said.

"You can do that?" Detective Yang asked.

"Most certainly. Pretty easily actually," Sophie said.

"Those extra cans were backup?" Detective Ryan asked.

"Yes. The killer was taking no chances."

"Did you find any prints on the Coke cans?" Ryan asked.

"Just those of the deceased," Sophie said.

Ryan nodded. "What have you got for me on Gary Young's death?"

"Whoever killed him did a thorough job of cleaning up evidence and destroying any DNA traces with bleach. We did, however, narrow down the source of the cleaner. There are two main types of bleach—chlorine and oxygen. This is a chlorine bleach, sodium hypochlorite diluted in water."

"Could you identify the brand?" Ryan asked.

"Yes. From the chemical mix, we're certain White King Premium Bleach was used," Sophie said.

"That narrows it down, then," Detective Yang noted wryly.

"Yes. White King is, unfortunately, the most popular brand of bleach in Australia. Millions of bottles sold yearly."

"What about the duct tape on the chair, then?" Detective Ryan asked.

"Same problem. We examined the tape's variability, construction, and composition and determined it was Gorilla Tape."

"Another popular brand," Detective Yang sighed.

"True," Sophie agreed. "But we do know something about the perp from their tape of choice. They did their homework and went for the most expensive brand."

"Meaning?" Detective Ryan asked.

"Again, thorough. And not prepared to scrimp. Gorilla Tape usually rates number one in any list of the best tapes because it has incredible holding power and durability. And because it's so strong, you need to use less of it."

"You sound like an infomercial." Zoe smiled

"What about the shoe print outside the hut?" Ryan asked.

"There, we *do* have something. It's from a size eleven shoe, so, assuming it was the perp, Gary Young's murderer could be somewhere between five eleven and six foot two, which means the killer is more likely to be a man than a woman. And assuming the print does belong to him, statistically, he is more likely to be a Caucasian rather than an African or an Asian. In Australia, those ethnic groups tend to be shorter."

"Anything else from the print?" Ryan said.

"There's good and bad news there. Good news is we have identified the brand of shoe from the tread pattern found outside the cabin. The bad news is, it's a fake Nike Air Force One sneaker, making its origins harder to trace."

Sophie took the file from under her arm, opened it, and pulled out an A4 sheet. "I brought you this because it's easier to explain with a picture."

The detectives peered at the photo. It showed the white soles of two sneakers side by side.

"These are both Nike Air Force One soles?" Detective Ryan asked.

"Yep," Sophie said. "But one is authentic, and the other is a fake."

Ryan examined the picture, nodding. "The stars of the one on the left are crisper and arranged differently." He pointed to the Nike logo. "That one has a trademark *r* above the letter *e* and below the letter *n*. The one on the right has the logo and a slightly different font."

"Spot on, Detective Ryan. We think the perp was wearing a fake Nike based on the shoe print we found. This narrows down the field, and I'd say that if you were to find a suspect and he had a pair of fake Nikes, it's probably him."

"That's it?" said Ryan, satisfied with what he'd heard.

"That's all I've got, Detectives. And I know that's not much to go on. However, forensics can only offer what science allows. No more . . . no less," Sophie said, snapping the file closed as Ryan's cell rang.

The detective tapped the screen. "Yes?"

He listened for a moment. "We'll be right over, Yvonne."

THIRTY-EIGHT

Detective Ryan stopped at the closed hotel driveway gates protected by a ragtag band of uniformed security guards. After a few moments, the gates pulled open, and Ryan drove through, stopping beside the hotel's head of security, Steve Prince.

"Morning, Steve. What's with the extra security? You anticipating trouble?" Detective Ryan asked.

"I'm sure Mr. Faith will fill you in. I assume you've come to see him."

"Yes," Ryan said.

"You're expected?"

"Invited, actually," Detective Yang interjected before Ryan could reply.

"I'll let his PA know you're here." The security guard gave the detectives a thin smile as he stepped back. Ryan watched in his rearview mirror as the man raised his walkie-talkie to call through their approach.

Detective Ryan drove on and parked at the hotel entrance. The two detectives got out and headed for the lobby.

"Detectives." Yvonne smiled warmly as they entered the hotel. She walked over. "Good morning. I'll take you up to Mr. Faith's office."

The detectives followed the PA to the bank of elevators.

"What exactly is this all about, Yvonne?" Detective Ryan said as the PA pressed the lift button.

"All I know is that it has to do with the deaths of Mr. Faith's business partners. He wants to speak to you urgently, and he could only do it face to face," she said, pausing. "What happened to Mr. Saker was dreadful. Falling down those stairs . . . and coming so soon after Mr. Young's death, too." She shook her head and confided, "This is not what I was expecting when I took this job."

"Of course not," Detective Yang sympathized. "How well did you know the partners?"

"I didn't see much of Mr. Young, but Mr. Saker seemed nice. He always said thank you."

"Thank you?" Detective Ryan asked.

"For looking after him," Yvonne said as the elevator arrived.

Detective Ryan stared at the PA. She blushed and shook her head. "No . . . nothing like that. Mr. Saker's wife hated him drinking soda. He asked me to buy him two packs of cola weekly. He was very particular. Only Diet Coke, which he mostly drank here, at work. I kept it for him in the fridge."

"Which fridge?" Detective Ryan asked as the elevator door opened.

"The one in the restaurant kitchen."

"Can you take us there?"

THE PA PULLED OPEN THE DOOR of the big, shiny, stainless steel commercial refrigerator. Four cans of a ten-pack of Diet Coke sat on the fridge's bottom shelf.

"These them?" Detective Ryan asked, peering in but not touching them.

"Yes. I bought two cartons for him every week."

After gloving up and briefly looking them over, Ryan assigned Detective Yang to return the Coke cans to forensics for examination. Then Ryan and the PA rode the elevator to Simon Faith's office.

"SIT DOWN, PLEASE, DETECTIVE," THE HOTEL boss said as Yvonne and Detective Ryan entered his office.

"Coffee, tea . . . something stronger?" Simon continued, motioning at the bottles lined up on a side table by the window.

"No. Nothing for me, thank you."

"Okay, Yvonne, that'll be all then," the CEO said, dismissing his PA.

The boss stood up. "You don't mind if I do, do you, Detective?" Simon asked.

"Go right ahead."

"Thank you for coming so quickly," he said, walking over to the drinks. "I don't usually indulge midday, but as you can imagine, I've been devastated by Gary and Luke's deaths." As he spoke, he lifted one of the bottles, unscrewed the top, and poured the mahogany-colored liquid into a crystal glass.

"It's to be expected," agreed Detective Ryan. "I am surprised, though, you haven't taken some time off."

"What would you have me do? I'm divorced, have no children . . . not even a dog," he said, sipping the drink. "Sad, right? That's what you're thinking?"

The detective peered at the CEO. "Not at all." He paused. "Your work is your life, then, I take it?"

"Correct, Detective," Simon said, returning to his seat, glass in hand. "This hotel . . . this development . . . means everything to me. I mourn my two partners by working harder. That's the only way I know to overcome grief." He stopped. "Now, let's get down to brass tacks. Let me tell you why I needed to speak to you so urgently."

Ryan raised his hand. "Before you begin, can I ask about Luke's Coca-Cola?"

"What?"

"Yvonne tells me Luke's wife hated him drinking cola. She wouldn't have it in the house," Ryan said.

"McKenzie's a very opinionated woman. She believes in everything being organic. Diet Coke doesn't fit the bill."

"And Luke was happy to go along with that?" the detective asked.

"Luke is . . ." He paused. "*Was* a tough businessman, but he had one fatal weakness. He allowed himself to be henpecked."

"It may have been a weakness, but it wasn't the one that killed him," Detective Ryan said, looking squarely at Simon.

"I'm sorry. I don't follow," the man said, confused.

"It appears that Luke's addiction to Diet Coke is the thing that has led to his death."

"What the hell are you talking about?"

"Luke was poisoned, Mr. Faith," Ryan said, watching the CEO's shocked reaction. "The poison was in the Coke, and I believe whoever killed Luke also killed Gary Young." He paused, allowing Simon to absorb the information. "And the only thing I can see linking the two murders is that both were partners in the Faith Company."

Simon nodded slowly, his face ashen. "That's why I wanted to see you. I think I know who could have been involved."

Simon picked up the newspaper from the desk. He offered it to Detective Ryan. "Our local rag, the *Church Point Gazette*, yesterday's edition. Take a look at page six."

Ryan leafed through to the opinion page. He started to read.

"That's why I have my security men on the gates," Simon continued.

"You're expecting trouble?" Ryan asked, looking up.

"Yes. From the man who wrote that article. Mike Burford."

THIRTY-NINE

THE HEAVYSET BEARDED MAN FELL BACK from the dining room table, collapsing onto the parqueted floor. Seeing this, the others leapt up: a young man, a middle-aged woman, and a middle-aged man. All were dressed in Edwardian costume.

The young man bent down and checked the bearded man's pulse.

"Is he . . . ?" the woman asked.

"Tell us," the middle-aged man said, his face taut.

"Yes," the young man said quietly. "He's dead."

Behind, a dark-haired woman wearing maid's attire entered. Seeing the corpse, she released a high-pitched scream.

Mike Burford clapped his hands over his ears. "Mary, do you have to do that every time?"

"I'm just trying to get into character," the maid, Mary Porter, said.

"Yeah, well, we could do without it at this point. It's giving me a headache," Mike said.

"I like it," the young man asserted.

Mike glared at him. "Are you the director now, Edgar?"

"It's just my opinion."

"Well, keep it to yourself."

"Can I get up now? The floor is *really* hard," the bearded man, Joe Grossman, said, rising.

"Stay," Mike ordered.

"But . . ."

"Wait until I say get up," Mike ordered.

"Well, if you insist," Joe muttered, dropping back as the dining room door opened. A young red-haired woman entered with Detective Ryan in tow. Like Mike, Harper Park wore contemporary clothes—big, black Doc Marten boots, ripped jeans, and a blue sweatshirt with the words *I believe. Don't you?* stenciled on it.

Mike looked around, irritated. "Harper, I thought I said no interruptions."

"I know Mike, but the detective was insistent."

"Detective?" Burford smiled. "Well, it's about time . . .. Okay, Harper, thank you."

Ryan walked over to Mike as Harper Park left.

"You are Mike Burford?" Detective Ryan asked.

"Yes . . .. And *you*, Detective, are late, even though I informed your agency of the start time and that this was a *dress* rehearsal. And you have chosen to turn up out of costume." Mike forced himself to take a deep breath. "But never mind. At least you're here."

He swiveled back around to address the others. "This is our new policeman, who has bravely stepped into the breach following Phil Evans's medical emergency."

Mike pointed. "Detective, meet Mary Porter . . . she's playing the maid."

The young woman smiled.

"Edgar Roosevelt is our intrepid doctor."

"Delighted," the young man said.

"Jane Cheltenham," the middle-aged woman trilled.

"And last but not least, I'm Joe Grossman," the dead man said from the floor.

"Detective Ryan," the detective said.

"Detective Ryan?" Mary Porter queried, addressing Mike. "So, he'll be called Detective Ryan from now on? How come he can change his character's name and I can't? I mean, Felicity Fluffer? What kind of a name is that? It sounds like a porn star."

"I don't see the problem with that," Joe Grossman offered. "Maybe it was your character's profession before she took up waitressing. That would certainly be believable."

"The Me Too movement passed you by, did it Joe?" Mary Porter asked.

Mike headed over to the table. "Joe, apologize to Mary."

"Sorry, Mary. . . . It was just a joke."

"Well, it wasn't funny," Mary said.

There had clearly been a misunderstanding, and Detective Ryan attempted to jump in.

"I'm sorry, but I think . . ."

"Quiet." Mike spoke over him, glancing at Ryan as he did so. "Your name is Detective Reagan, not Ryan. And to bring you up to speed, that man"—he pointed to Joe —"has just been poisoned."

"Mr. Burford, you have me confused," Detective Ryan tried again, but the director wasn't listening.

"Yes, of course, in a moment. First, I need to rehearse this scene again," Mike said.

"Mr. Burford, I think we've got our wires crossed." Ryan produced his ID.

Mike glanced at the card and then spun back around. "Our recruit has gone to the trouble of making up a fake policeman's ID, though it's not entirely accurate. There was, of course, no Homicide Squad in Britain in 1907."

Detective Ryan leaned into Mike. "I don't know how I can make this any clearer. I am a *real* detective, and I need to speak to you. Do you understand?"

Mike stared at the detective. Finally, the penny dropped. "You mean . . ." The color left his face.

"I'm not an actor," Ryan said quietly. "Can we talk somewhere private, please?"

"Right." Mike clapped his hands. "Everyone. Something has just come up. While I take a short break, I want you to run the lines. Make sure you're off book."

He looked back at Ryan. "Follow me, Detective."

FORTY

MIKE BURFORD CAREFULLY PUT THE CUPS down on the kitchen table. "That one's yours, white and no sugar," Mike said, indicating the mug nearest to Detective Ryan. "Unfortunately, I'm still addicted to *sucre*."

He said *sucre* with a French accent and picked up the other mug. Ryan resisted the urge to roll his eyes as Mike pointed to a blue and green sketch of a Sherlock Holmes–type figure printed on the mug. The words *Murder Mystery Theater* appeared underneath. "We had these ordered after a highly successful season last year."

Detective Ryan took a sip of the coffee.

"How is it?" Mike said, watching.

"Good," Detective Ryan said, surprised. The coffee was almost up to his standard.

Mike took a gulp from his cup. "Not bad," he concurred. "I grind the beans myself, you know."

"Ethiopian?" Detective Ryan asked.

"Yes. From the Yirgacheffe region." He paused. "How did you know?"

"I'm a bit of a coffee snob myself."

"Right. Look, I'm sorry about the misunderstanding upstairs. In my defense, I've never met a policeman who wears work clothes quite as sharp as yours."

Detective Ryan leaned forward. "Mr. Burford . . ."

"Please, call me Mike."

"Okay, Mike. How long have you been directing here?" Detective Ryan asked, putting his mug down.

"Since the Murder Mystery Theater first started eleven years ago."

"You like doing it?" Ryan asked.

"I love it, and people seem to enjoy seeing the productions. We've successfully raised funds for the Bay House's upkeep."

"That's important to you?"

"Yes, of course. I think it's essential to retain our heritage and ensure capitalists don't destroy everything beautiful in this world," Mike said, his voice hardening.

"Capitalists? Like the Faith Company, you mean?"

Silence as Mike stared at Ryan. "So . . . you mentioned that you're here about the article I wrote?"

Detective Ryan reached inside his jacket and pulled out a folded newspaper. "Please take a look at page six," the detective said, handing it over.

Mike glanced at the paper's front page. "No need. I know the one you're referring to."

"It's all about the Faith Company?"

"Yes."

"Which is one of the principal targets of the Conservation Foundation. A group that you lead."

"Correct. And, in case you're wondering, any protests we take part in are always carried out in full accordance with the law."

"Does your group intend to protest at the official reopening of The Palms Hotel, then?"

Mike glared at the detective and stood up. "He sent you, didn't he? Simon Faith?"

"What do you mean, sent me?" Detective Ryan asked.

"Oh, come on, Detective. I know he has friends on the force. I've met enough of them over the years." Mike shook his head in disgust. "You're here to intimidate me, so we don't wreck his precious hotel reopening."

"Please, sit down," Detective Ryan said.

Mike hesitated. "I won't be bullied."

"Please sit."

Mike shrugged. "All right." He resumed his seat.

"Where were you last weekend?" Ryan asked.

"What? Why?"

"Just answer the question, please."

Mike stared at the detective. "Oh, now I get it. I've heard the rumors—about someone connected with The Palms Hotel being killed—and Simon Faith thinks *I* had something to do with it." He paused. "Am I right?"

"We're checking out all leads. So, where were you?"

Mike shrugged. "I flew up to the Gold Coast to see my mother."

"And she will confirm that?" Ryan said.

"Of course."

"And yesterday?"

"I was here early, rehearsing. And there are seven actors upstairs who can verify that." Mike shook his head. "It's amazing the sway the rich and powerful have, even when it comes to the law."

"Mr. Faith holds no sway with me, I assure you," Ryan said.

"Oh, yeah?" Mike looked skeptical.

"Yes." The detective pointed at the paper. "That article, though, is very provocative."

"It's just an opinion piece. I've written a dozen others. And it was thoroughly vetted by the lawyers. It's part of the campaign to inform the public about what the company is up to *now*. To try to prevent any . . . excesses."

"And how successful has this campaign been?"

Mike sighed. "Seeing as the Faith Company is reopening their newly expanded and refurbished hotel and has also put in plans to build housing that will threaten the very future of the national park, I would say not very. But we will keep at it, despite whatever Simon Faith does to try and stop us."

Mike paused. "You know his company originally claimed they just wanted to build a small recreational facility? And now look where we are. The sad thing is this all could have been halted years ago. We got *this* close." Mike separated his fingers by a few inches.

There was a knock on the door. Harper Park entered with a young, mustached man wearing a black top hat, a gray three-piece suit, and shiny black leather boots.

"Mike, Teddy Alexander's here."

"Sorry I'm late, I've come to play Detective Reagan." Teddy smiled.

Mike offered the man his hand. "Nice to meet you, Teddy. I see you're dressed to impress. Excellent . . . Harper, please take Teddy upstairs while I finish down here."

The director and the cop waited for the pair to leave.

"So, Detective Ryan, do you have any more questions for me? I do need to get back to the rehearsal," Mike asked.

"Just one. Can you think of anyone in your protest group who hates Simon Faith and his company enough to use violence against them?"

"There is someone." Mike was silent for a moment as he considered what he was about to say. "Irwin Cooper."

Behind him, the kitchen door opened.

FORTY-ONE

"**N**OT INTERRUPTING, AM I?" JOE GROSSMAN said, entering the kitchen.

"What are you doing down here, Joe?" Mike asked.

"There's not many lines to run when you're dead, Mike. I've just come to make a cup of coffee," Joe replied.

"Now is not convenient," Mike said. "The detective and I are talking."

"Well, on that subject, I couldn't help but overhear your mention of Irwin Cooper," Joe said.

"Overhear" was a euphemism. Joe had spent the last few minutes outside listening to the conversation.

"Cooper's quite crazy, you know," he continued.

"Correct. And dangerous," Mike added.

"I'm not sure about that, Mike. But he's certainly become more erratic since he ran Justice for Nature." He paused. "Were you in that group back then?"

"Just a very junior member, Joe," Mike said. He turned to Ryan. "Look, don't get me wrong, Detective, I'm not saying Cooper would actually do anything, but . . ."

"You think he has a grudge against the Faith Company?" Ryan asked.

"Oh, definitely," Mike confirmed.

Detective Ryan now understood why Simon Faith had presented the idea that Mike Burford could be a suspect. He'd wanted to cause trouble.

The detective doubted that Simon Faith had seriously thought Burford had anything to do with his partners' deaths. Instead, he had hoped the police questioning would scare off the activists and put paid to any demonstrations.

"It all goes back to the crash," Joe said.

"What crash?" Ryan asked.

"An accident, twenty-odd years ago," Joe began. "On returning from a climate change demonstration, the van carrying some protestors skidded on the wet road and plunged over a cliff. Nine people died, though miraculously Irwin Cooper survived. At the time, there was lots of talk of it being the driver's fault. But the coroner decided it was an accident. No one responsible."

"You know, I was at the demonstration that day, Joe," Mike said, breaking in. "I lived around that area, too, so I could have been in that van with them." He shook his head, still amazed by his luck. "But I got a lift into town from a girl I knew. It was my first protest. Twenty years old and a virgin environmentalist." The director looked over at Detective Ryan. "Before you ask, the woman was my first half-serious girlfriend. We split up soon after. Now she's got two kids and a dog and lives in Melbourne."

"And Irwin Cooper?" Ryan asked, trying to get things back on track.

"He was a newlywed, and his wife was killed in the crash. It sent him completely bonkers. Soon after, he lost his job *and* his house."

"And this was twenty years ago?"

"Give or take," Mike confirmed.

"Okay . . . so Cooper has been a little unhinged ever since he lost this wife. But what's his connection to the Faith Company?" the detective asked.

"He's been living in a caravan on Faith Company land for twenty years rent-free . . . and about six weeks ago, they served him with an eviction notice," the director explained.

Detective Ryan put his hand up to his forehead. He was getting a headache.

"And you know this, how?"

"Because Cooper came to us wanting help. We said we'd look into it." Mike shrugged.

"But Irwin didn't want to hear that," Joe added. "He wanted more of a commitment. Started to shout and scream about us all being on the side of 'The Man.' It was madness; he scared the living daylights out of me."

"But did you help him?" Ryan asked.

"Look, I hate Simon Faith and his company . . . we both do," Mike said, looking across at Joe. "But Cooper has been living rent-free on the firm's land for two decades and has only now been given notice. That's a pretty sweet deal."

"Why did they agree to that in the first place? Most big companies wouldn't be so generous," Ryan asked, puzzled.

"The Faith Company initially offered Cooper a site for his caravan because they were getting pilloried in the press over their development plans," Mike said. "It was an easy and cheap way to turn the tables . . . to show they were the nice guys."

"Why didn't the company just move him along once they got the publicity?"

"It wouldn't have been in their interest. First came the golf course, followed by the original hotel, and then the new, bigger, refurbished hotel. Whenever they put in new development plans, they used their agreement with Irwin Cooper to show they were on the side of the angels," Mike said.

"Okay, so why evict him now?" Ryan asked.

"Because their latest tower block development involves using the land where Cooper's caravan is," Mike explained.

"Right . . . but sweet deal or not, this *does* seem like the kind of cause the Conservation Foundation would get behind," Ryan suggested.

"Consider it from our point of view. We're interested in the bigger picture: trying to stop Simon Faith from reopening that hotel and being allowed to build in the national park. We need public support, and hitching ourselves to Irwin Cooper's wagon won't get us that. The man is, as you said, unhinged. That's why I suggested you should investigate him."

"And he's still living in the caravan?" Detective Ryan asked.

"Until he's removed by force, I imagine. Ask at The Palms. I'm sure someone will show you where the van is." Mike pushed his chair back from the table and stood up. "Are we finished here? We really should get back to work."

"Just one more thing." The detective stood and took a business card out of his pocket, handing it to the director. "Could you text me your mother's contact number in Queensland?"

"Yeah, sure," Mike said, pocketing the card and grabbing Joe's arm. "Come on."

"But I haven't had my coffee."

"Joe!" Burford said.

Joe reluctantly followed the director and the detective out into the hallway.

THEY WALKED DOWN THE CORRIDOR.

"So, Detective, will you come see our show?" Joe asked. "There's a twist." His eyes lit up as he said it.

"I know," Detective Ryan said, pushing the front door open.

"You know?" Joe said, curious.

The detective turned. "You're the killer, Joe. You're just pretending to be dead. You've taken a drug that makes it look like you've died. When it wears off, you creep upstairs and kill the doctor, who is your secret lover. With his death, the inheritance reverts to you."

Astonished, Joe Grossman looked over at Mike. "Did you tell him?"

Mike shook his head. "No. You've seen the play before, then, Detective Ryan?" he asked.

"I read the flyer, that's all."

"Then how?"

"I'm a detective, Mike. A real one. It's what I do," Ryan said with a wry smile as he stepped outside.

FORTY-TWO

As HE DROVE BACK TO THE Palms Hotel, Detective Ryan mulled over his meeting with Mike Burford. He had formed a low opinion of the theater director. Doubtless, Burford would be out protesting the reopening of the hotel. There would be press and TV coverage, and he would be front and center, reveling in all the attention. But helping a man to save his home was not sexy enough for him.

The detective eased his foot off the accelerator pedal, reached for his cell, dialed, and waited.

"Hi, Ryan," Zoe Yang answered. "I was just about to call you. Dudley's been asking for updates. I told him we were making progress." Detective Yang paused. "We are making progress, right?"

"Possibly. I'm following up on another lead. And I want you to check out an alibi for a man called Mike Burford. He says he was with his mother on the Gold Coast last weekend. I've just texted you her number."

"Okay." Yang paused. "So, where exactly are you?"

"On my way back to The Palms."

"Oh." The *oh* hung heavy in the air.

"I'll update you later," Ryan said quickly. "Could you also get me a copy of the coroner's report on a crash that happened near Church Point twenty years ago and killed nine people? And I want anything you can find on a man called Irwin Cooper."

"Who's he?"

"The possible lead I mentioned."

"That's it?" Detective Yang asked.

"Yeah."

There was a pause. "So, you'll see this Irwin Cooper guy now?"

"Yes."

"On your own?" Detective Yang asked.

"That's right." Ryan cut the conversation short. "Let me know what you find out."

He rang off. Zoe sounded thoroughly pissed, but he couldn't do anything about that now.

His cell rang again. The detective checked the ID on the screen. It was Heidi.

"Heidi," he said, sounding pleased.

"I'm surprised you answered." Her voice had a cool edge. Ryan was suddenly nervous.

"Why is that?"

"I was under the impression you would call me," Heidi said.

Ryan was caught off guard. It didn't happen often.

"Oh, well, yes . . . I was, I mean, I am, but this case . . . I've just been swamped," he stuttered.

"We're all busy, Ramesh."

There was a pause. "You're right. I'm sorry."

"That's it? I didn't think you'd be one of *those*."

"One of *what*?"

"The wham, bam, thank you, ma'am, type."

"Heidi, that's not who I am! I just . . ." Ryan protested, shocked by the suggestion. He took a breath. "To be completely honest, I didn't want to be a nuisance."

Heidi let out a genuine laugh.

"Okay. Well, I wasn't expecting that." Her voice was warm and encouraging. "Would you like to see me again? I promise I won't think you're a nuisance," Heidi said.

Ryan smiled to himself, pleased with how this was going. "If you're sure," he said with renewed confidence.

"How about tonight, then? Around nine?"

Tonight? Ryan hesitated momentarily, thinking about all the work still left to do on this case. He imagined Dudley's angry expression.

"Ramesh, I will end this call now unless you say something."

"Tonight would be great," the detective said.

"Perfect. Come to the hotel. I'll order room service. We'll talk and do some more catching up."

"Sounds good," Ryan said, turning the wheel and pulling the car off the road. He had reached the hotel. "See you then," the detective said, halting before the closed gates.

"Ramesh?"

"Yes."

"You haven't asked for my room number," Heidi said.

"Four eighty-two," Ryan replied.

"Inspector Poirot strikes again!" She laughed. "I'll see you at nine . . . and don't forget to bring your toothbrush."

The phone clicked off as a security guard approached the car.

Ryan cracked open the window. Alex Riva peered in. "Detective Ryan. Back already?"

"Can you let me through?"

"Who are you here to see?"

"A guy called Irwin Cooper. I was told someone could take me to his caravan."

"Sure. I can do that. But first, we have to check in with the boss."

DETECTIVE RYAN AND ALEX RIVA TOOK the elevator to the pool deck on the top floor, where Simon Faith awaited. On their way, they passed the Wellness Center. The guard explained that only a few chosen employees were allowed to use the facility. He was one of them and even had his own locker.

On arriving poolside, the hotel boss had difficulty recalling anyone named Irwin Cooper.

"Cooper? Nope. Never heard of him," Simon said after a long pause.

"He's the man who lives in the caravan on the edge of the property, Mr. Faith," Alex said.

Silence as Simon thought some more. "The crazy man," he said finally.

"That's the one," Alex confirmed.

"Detective, why would you want to see . . ." Simon paused and looked over at the guard for help.

"Irwin Cooper," Alex said.

"Yeah, Cooper."

"His name came up in my conversation with Mike Burford," Detective Ryan said.

"Oh, yes, Burford, so how—" Simon began but was interrupted by a shout.

"Easy! Easy!"

Distracted, the hotel boss looked around. "One moment, Detective," he said before heading to a group of workmen trying to maneuver a golden sculpture into place.

"Do you think this is the right spot for that, Archie? At the side of the pool?" Simon asked the skinny young man overseeing the activity. Sculptor Archie Watts looked like he hadn't slept for weeks. Dark circles were under his bloodshot eyes, and his long, floppy black hair was lank and greasy.

"Yeah, definitely, Simon," Archie said, nervously running his hands through his unkempt hair.

"I think we need a second opinion," Simon said. "Detective Ryan!" he shouted, waving for the cop to join him. "What do you think about the sculpture's position?" Simon asked on Ryan's arrival.

The detective didn't answer immediately but stared up at the twisted mass of metal and then down at the letters written on the gold plate at its base.

"*C & P*," he said, reading. "What does that mean?"

"Camel and palms. A mix of space, continuity, texture, and proportion to evoke the predominant images of the desert," Archie Watts said. "With the gold reinforcing the color of the desert sky and sand."

"The gold was my idea," Simon said proudly. "What do you think?"

Ryan had an eclectic taste in art, but one of his pet hates was ugly corporate commissions like this one.

"*C & P* certainly has an impact," the detective said diplomatically.

Archie beamed.

"And its position?" Simon asked.

Ryan studied the piece for a moment.

"It seems a little . . . intrusive."

"But people who come to the pool deck will immediately see it," Archie said defensively.

"True. But it blocks the path to the pool." The detective stopped. "Perhaps if you moved it over to the end—"

"It could be discovered!" Archie exclaimed, interrupting. "Of course. Good call."

Archie turned to Simon. "He's quite right. I should have thought of that. If we position it against the far wall, guests will have a sense of *finding* the art themselves. The search will give them a sense of achievement."

Simon considered what was being said. His mantra as a developer had always been, if you've got it, flaunt it. But maybe, in this instance, he would take the detective's advice.

"Good idea," Simon said after a few moments of silence. "Boys, move the sculpture to the far wall."

"Hold the work, guys," Archie shouted and hurried off to scout out a new position for the artwork. In the meantime, Simon indicated for Ryan to take a seat opposite him at a small wooden table. Alex Riva came over to stand close by.

"You've been to see Mike Burford? What happened there?"

"He has an alibi for last weekend."

"Really? Did he tell you he's leading the campaign to protest the hotel's reopening?"

"Yes. He did mention that."

"And it's obvious from the article he wrote that Burford hates me, this company, and everything we're doing," Simon said.

"Yes. But if every person with a grudge were a murderer . . ." Ryan shrugged. The statement hung in the air for a moment. Simon returned a thin smile.

"That's your professional opinion, is it?"

"Yes."

Silence.

"If you eliminate Mike Burford, then you have no suspects," Simon said, sounding to Ryan a little too much like Superintendent Dan Dudley.

"I'm not sure where you got that idea." Detective Ryan looked Simon directly in the eye. "In fact, your knowledge of our investigation is minimal at best."

Simon narrowed his eyes and then snapped his fingers.

"I've got it! Irving Cowper is your new suspect, correct?"

"Cooper, sir. Irwin," Alex corrected.

Detective Ryan remained silent as Simon continued stroking his chin. "What do *you* think, Alex?"

"I don't know, sir. I've never met him," the security guard said.

"But I thought you took the lawyer's papers over?" Simon Faith said.

Ryan glanced at the CEO. He *had* been lying; he knew precisely who Irwin Cooper was.

"Yes, I did take them. Steve Prince and I went together, but Cooper wouldn't open up, so we pushed the papers under the door," Alex Riva said.

"The door of the caravan?" Simon Faith asked.

"Yes, sir."

"He's still living there, then?"

"He's legally got another week, sir," the security guard said.

Simon turned to Ryan. "You see what I'm up against, Detective? It's a wonder we get anything done in this country. There's a law for this and a law for that. A law for everything. But where's the protection for an honest businessman like me?" He paused. "Burford mentioned Cooper's name?"

"Yes," the detective confirmed.

"Mike Burford's a slippery son of a bitch. He wants to distract you by naming someone else." The hotel boss paused. "I'm no policeman, but I trust my instincts. Mike Burford is your man."

"If we draw a blank on his alibi, then we will follow it up," Detective Ryan promised. "Meantime, could someone take me to Mr. Cooper's caravan?"

Simon Faith nodded. "No problem. Alex will do that. But you're wasting your time. It's a dead end."

Ryan curtly nodded before following Alex out of the pool area.

Simon smiled. "Dead end," he said under his breath and chuckled.

FORTY-THREE

The sun was dropping and the sky darkening as Alex Riva drove the golf buggy off the fairway. The electric vehicle bounced up and down on the rough ground as the guard explained to the detective that using the cart was the easiest and quickest way to reach Cooper's caravan, hidden at the far end of the property.

"You know, I think Mr. Faith is right about Cooper not being a murderer," Alex said, pulling the wheel around to avoid a pothole.

"How so? I thought you said you'd never met him," the detective said.

"I haven't. But that's the point. If there had been any trouble with him, we would have known. He's had a pretty good deal, living rent-free on the company's land."

"But now he's been evicted," Ryan said. "He must resent that."

The guard shrugged. "Not necessarily. It's not how I would feel."

"No?' Detective Ryan said.

"I'd know the good times had to end sometime."

Alex pointed as they drove on. "When we reach those trees, we'll have to walk. Unfortunately, this cart doesn't have four-wheel drive."

"Okay," the detective said. "Cooper lives on the edge of the national park?" Detective Ryan asked.

"Yeah, but on Faith Company land."

"Why exactly is he being evicted?" the detective asked.

The security guard shrugged. "Mr. Faith thinks he's in the way of the company's new housing development."

Alex pulled the cart to a halt. "Time to walk," he said.

The men climbed out of the buggy. Ryan followed the security guard.

"This detective business, is it good fun?" Alex said as they walked on through the trees.

"Fun? I don't think that's how I would describe it."

"But you like it."

"Yes, I do."

"That's good. You live longer if you enjoy what you do," Alex said.

"What about you? You like your security guard job?"

"Yeah, so far."

"So far?"

"I've only had this gig for a couple of months. I used to live up north in Queensland, doing different things. Farming, laboring. You name it, I've done it."

"Why'd you come down to Sydney, then?"

"For this job. I saw it advertised and thought, why not? It's well paid, with reasonable hours," Alex said.

Ryan's phone rang. He reached into his pocket, pulled out his cell, and pressed the screen. "Yes, Zoe," he said.

"Mike Burford's alibi checked out. His mom confirmed he was up the Gold Coast all weekend."

It was what Ryan expected.

"When do you think you'll be back?" Detective Yang asked.

"Soon. Why?"

"Dudley wants to see us ASAP."

"Updates?" Detective Ryan said.

"I think it's more like, have we solved the case yet? If not, why not? That sort of thing."

"Great," Ryan said.

"See you later, then," Yang said cheerily.

The phone clicked off, and Ryan jammed it back into his pocket. Looking ahead he could see a small clearing where a shabby blue and white caravan was parked. Branches hung over the rusty roof of the wheelless wagon, and thick grass and weeds clung to its sides.

Ryan heard the clang of a chain. Spinning around, he saw a monstrous snarling, spitting rottweiler, its mouth wide open, sprinting toward him. The guard stepped in front of him before the dog could reach the cop.

"Hey, hey," he shouted. The animal froze midstride, closing its mouth and skidding to a halt. The dog tilted its head up to peer at the guard.

"Behave, Max," a voice said.

Ryan spun around and saw an old man wearing dirty jeans and a sweat-shirt standing at the caravan's open door.

He walked over and stroked the animal. "Max, go."

The dog turned and trotted back where he'd come, disappearing behind the caravan.

"Mr. Cooper? It is Mr. Cooper, isn't it?" Detective Ryan asked.

"Who wants to know?" the man said.

"Detective Ryan, New South Wales homicide."

The old man didn't wait for him to finish. He was looking hard at Alex.

"Nice uniform," he sneered.

Alex didn't reply.

Cooper spat on the ground. "I've still got one more week."

"Yeah. Yeah. I know," the guard said. "That's not why we're here." Alex pointed at the detective. "He wants a word with you."

Cooper glared at the policeman. "What about?"

"Could we talk inside?" Ryan asked.

"No. Go away," he said and walked back to the caravan.

"Just a few minutes of your time, Mr. Cooper," Detective Ryan shouted.

"You got a warrant?" Cooper said, swiveling around as he reached the door.

Detective Ryan said nothing.

"Didn't think so . . . .. Well, I'm not saying anything to anyone, and unless you got one of those warrants, there's no way either of you are com-ing inside. You can piss off." Cooper slammed the caravan door.

"What now?" Alex asked after a moment.

"Guess I'm gonna need a warrant," Detective Ryan said and sighed.

FORTY-FOUR

COPS ARE SOCIAL CREATURES, AND THERE was usually time for chatter, gossip, and some dark humor—not tonight. The Homicide Squad office was eerily quiet on Ryan's return.

The detective headed over to Zoe and took in the board mounted on the wall behind her. It was a link board filled with photos. Some cops loved them, but Detective Ryan hated them. He preferred to keep his cards close to his chest.

"Your idea, Zoe?" Ryan said, pointing at the board.

Detective Yang reddened. "Superintendent Dudley's," she said quietly.

Ryan nodded. Yeah, that figured. Dudley wanted it to prove that the case was progressing at a clip.

A hand rested on his shoulder. "How's it going, Ryan?"

The detective turned to face Terry Burke. "Oh, you know . . . slowly but surely, Terry."

Detective Burke smiled and pointed at the wall. "The board's a good idea. I was wondering when you'd do one." He studied it. "You know if you need any help . . . anything . . . all you gotta do is ask." His tone was condescending.

"Ryan, come!" a voice shouted. "You too, Yang."

Superintendent Dudley stood by his office door, waving the detectives over.

"Good luck," Detective Burke said as the pair headed to Dudley's office.

The superintendent ushered them in. "How's it going, Ryan?" Dudley asked as he closed the door.

"We're getting close," the detective said.

"But no cigar?" the superintendent said, returning to his desk.

"No. Not yet."

Silence.

The detectives waited.

"What's your opinion of Nancy Shams, Ryan?"

"Nancy Shams," the detective repeated, confused about the non sequitur. "The woman with the crime podcast?"

"That's her," Dudley said.

Ryan hesitated. He should give the superintendent the diplomatic answer, that everyone was entitled to do their job, Miss Shams included, blah, blah. But it was late, and he'd had a frustrating day. "I think she's a dangerous amateur who broadcasts misinformation and opinions about investigations she knows little, if anything, about. In other words, she's about as useful as a chocolate teapot."

"Or tits on a bull, as my old man used to say." Dudley roared at his joke. "Anyway, no need to sugarcoat it, Ryan." Dudley smiled. "I appreciate your honesty, but we *do* need to get people like Nancy Shams on our side, right, Yang?"

"I agree, sir," she said. Hearing a sharp intake of breath, she chose not to look at Detective Ryan.

"Okay. Good. Well, until now, your case has flown under the radar. But today, Nancy rang to tell me she was preparing to make a podcast about the murders . . . plural. She said she would not only name the first victim, Gary Young, and describe where and how he was discovered, but also reveal that Luke Saker was poisoned."

"How can she know that, sir? That information has only just been confirmed." Ryan was outraged.

"I've no idea, but that's just the tip of the iceberg."

"Shit," Detective Yang muttered under her breath.

"Shit indeed," Dudley said. "And half an hour ago, I got a frantic call from Simon Faith, the CEO of Faith Company. Nancy has also contacted him, and he's furious. He started to accuse the police . . . you two in particular . . . of leaking the information."

"Why didn't he call me, then?" Detective Ryan said. "Or Zoe?" He turned to his partner. "You didn't get a call, did you?"

Detective Yang shook her head. "Not a word."

"Hardly surprising," Superintendent Dudley said. "You're both first-class detectives, but to a man like Faith, you're just the monkeys, if you'll pardon my French. I, on the other hand, am the organ grinder." Dudley paused. "Anyway, he sounded distraught. Had his hopes pinned on those murders being kept under wraps until after the hotel's reopening."

"And this affects us, how?" Detective Ryan asked.

Frustrated by Ryan's laissez-faire attitude to New South Wales Police politics, Dudley threw him a withering look. "I think I mentioned that the Faith Company is a big supporter of police charities—namely the Eighteen-Footers Club?"

The superintendent let out a slow sigh and walked over to the window. He stared out into the darkness. "I told Faith that Nancy Shams and I are meeting tomorrow. I will offer her an exclusive . . . all the details on the case . . . provided that she only broadcast *after* we've found the killer."

The detectives looked at each other.

"You *do* understand the problem? Nancy won't hold off forever. And I certainly don't want her going ahead with any broadcast before we find the murderer. Otherwise, I'll get a bucketload of shit poured over my head."

"Do you really think Simon Faith would pull his support from a kids' charity?" Detective Yang asked.

"Yes, I do," he said with a grim expression. "But that's not my only problem. I'm here to increase the squad's abysmal conviction rate and improve public perception. The last thing I need is some self-important podcaster advertising that we *still* haven't made progress on this case," Dudley said.

This was why they had been called in, Ryan thought. Superintendent Dudley's promotion to lead the Homicide Squad was a significant feather in his cap. If he was successful, the sky was the limit—but there was a considerable risk involved, too: failure! And even though Teflon Dan was a masterly political operator, he had made enemies on the way up, people who were only too keen to plunge a knife into his back. It explained the atmosphere outside. The squad knew Dudley could be in trouble and were worried about what would happen next.

The superintendent walked back and settled into his chair.

"Detective Yang tells me you need a warrant," he said.

Ryan nodded. "Yes, sir."

"For someone called Irwin Cooper?" Dudley continued. "Who is he exactly?"

Having done the research, Zoe opened her notebook. She looked to Ryan for his approval before beginning.

"Well, he was a teacher years ago . . . a chemistry teacher, actually . . . at The Grove, a prestigious private school in Church Point. He worked there up until his wife was killed in a crash nearly twenty years ago. After that, his life spiraled out of control. He lost his job, his house . . . everything," Detective Yang said.

"And how is he connected to the victims?" Dudley asked.

"We are yet to establish a direct link between Irwin Cooper and Gary Young or Luke Saker. However, Cooper currently lives in a caravan on Faith Company land." She paused, closing her notebook. "And he is about to be evicted."

"Bit of a long bow, if you ask me." Dudley slumped back down in his chair.

"He's been described as 'unhinged,' and from what I can tell, he has nowhere to go once he's evicted. Anyone's capable of murder under the right circumstances," Detective Ryan said.

The superintendent scrubbed a hand across his face. He seemed to have developed bags under his bags, Ryan noted. Finally, Dudley spoke. "Okay. It's more than a bit of a stretch but if you say it's necessary to get Cooper to talk I'll get that arrest warrant for you."

"Thank you, sir." The two detectives spoke in unison.

"That's it. You can both go." Dudley waved them off.

Ryan and Yang walked to the door.

"One more thing," the superintendent said.

They turned.

"If this Cooper proves to be a dead end, like the other 'suspects,'" Dudley said, making air quotes, "I'll have no choice but to bring others in to help you with the investigation. So don't let me down. Understood?"

"Yes, sir," Ryan said.

Superintendent Dudley watched as they left the room, and he sighed heavily again. He had trusted Ramesh Ryan and gambled big time by bringing over Zoe Yang . . . but had he made a colossal mistake?

FORTY-FIVE

*T*HE MAN, LIKE THE SUPERINTENDENT, BELIEVED *he had made a mistake, but not for the same reason. He now realized he had severely underestimated Detective Ryan. How had that happened? As a rule, cops were only good at picking the low-hanging fruit . . . cases that usually had one thing in common: the perpetrators were dumb and made stupid mistakes. But that wasn't so here. The murders had been meticulously planned and professionally carried out, or so he had thought . . . impossible to find the culprits, until the detective came along. Detective Ryan would be back tomorrow with the warrant, and that would be just the start.*

He pulled up the window and felt the cold air brush his face. He had always known what he would do if the police got too close. He didn't want to, but sometimes tough choices had to be made, and they had to be made quickly. He would put his plan into action tonight.

DETECTIVE RYAN PUT THE CELLOPHANE-WRAPPED CHICKEN sandwich beside the two cups of coffee. It didn't look very appetizing, like it had been in a fight with a particularly vicious cat and lost. But beggars couldn't be choosers.

Picking up the tray, he walked across to the cash desk.

"That's not much of a meal, Ryan," the brassy-blond-haired, middle-aged cafeteria cashier said, pointing at the sandwich.

"Don't worry, Sal, I'm getting a home-cooked meal at my mother's house tonight," Detective Ryan said. It was a lie, but he knew it was the simplest way to prevent Sally Wellings from lecturing him on his lifestyle.

"That's all right, then," the cashier said, taking the detective's credit card. "Who's the woman?" she asked, indicating Detective Yang, who sat alone at a table at the back of the empty room, looking pensive. "I've not seen her around."

"Detective Yang," Ryan said.

"First name?"

"Zoe."

The cashier handed Ryan his credit card back.

"She's pretty. Is she new?"

"She came down last week from the Central Coast."

"So, she's . . ."

"My new partner, yes," Ryan said as he picked up the tray. Walking away, he was conscious of Sally's eyes boring into his back. He knew the insatiably curious cashier, a long-term fixture in the police café, had wanted to hear more about Zoe, but that would have to suffice for now.

Reaching Detective Yang, Ryan handed her a cup of coffee before taking his seat. He then unwrapped the sandwich, took a bite, and grimaced. It tasted like roadkill stuffed between two pieces of lightly grilled cardboard.

"Not good?" Yang said, seeing his expression.

"Like you, I should have waited until I got home," Ryan said diplomatically. "Have you got the report?"

Yang lifted her briefcase, clicked it open, pulled out a document, and handed it to Ryan. "It wasn't easy, but luckily, their office keeps good records."

Ryan flicked through the document—the coroner's report on the van crash that had killed Irwin Cooper's wife and eight others years ago.

"I've also emailed it to you," Yang said.

"Good. Did you speak to the coroner?" Ryan asked, looking up.

"He's dead. Died last year."

"A shame. Have you read the report?"

"Skimmed it."

"And?"

"On the face of it, the accident was just that . . . except for one thing."

"What's that?" Ryan asked.

"Something the van driver's wife claimed at the inquest," Zoe said and stopped.

"Go on."

"I'd actually prefer you read the document yourself first."

"You don't want me to be influenced by your opinion?" Ryan smiled.

"Not that you would be, but ..." She shrugged, a little embarrassed.

The detective nodded. Zoe Yang was learning fast. Ryan slipped the report into his briefcase. "I'll read it tonight."

"We're done?" Zoe asked.

"Almost, but I do have one question. Why were you kissing Dudley's butt just now?"

"What are you talking about?" Yang looked askance, then realized. "Is this about the podcaster?"

"I think you and I have enough on our plates without worrying about some tacky, true-crime radio show that no one will listen to."

Zoe raised an eyebrow in surprise as Ryan continued. "And it would have been nice if you could have said that to Dudley instead of reinforcing his paranoid delusion that he's one step away from being demoted."

Detective Yang shook her head with feigned astonishment. "You really are a luddite, you know that?"

"I may well be. But am I wrong?"

"Actually, yes. Millions of people in Australia listen to podcasts every day, and true-crime podcasts are the most popular. I know that, and Dudley knows that. Maybe he's entitled to a little paranoia." Zoe stood up. "Now, if that's all."

"Sit, Detective," Ryan said, then softened. "Please."

Detective Yang stared at him and then slowly sat back down.

Ryan appeared somewhat chastened. "Look, I'm sorry . . . about the 'kissing butt' comment. Clearly, popular culture is not my thing." He took a breath. "But maybe I said it because . . . I don't know . . . I'm getting the sense that we're not on the same page, you and I."

Zoe looked away, avoiding Ryan's stare. After a moment, she turned back. "The thing is, Ryan, I'm thinking about returning to the Central

Coast," she said.

Ryan stared at her. There it was. He knew something was up . . . something Zoe hadn't been telling him.

"You decided this in just a few days down here?"

"More or less."

Ryan stared at Zoe. "Is this because of me?"

"Well. I don't much like that you won't communicate with me."

Detective Ryan went to speak, but Yang raised her hand. "It's not just that, though." She stopped. "I'm giving up a lot to be here. Too much, maybe."

Ryan peered at her. "Something up with Louise?"

"You remembered." Zoe smiled, pleasantly surprised.

"I may be an asshole," Ryan joked. "But there's nothing wrong with my memory."

Zoe nodded with a sad smile. "Louise doesn't want to come to Sydney with me."

"Because of her work?" Ryan asked.

Zoe sighed. "No . . . her work isn't that important to her. And anyway, she could easily find a good job here."

"Well then?" Ryan began.

"She's happy where she is. We have a great life on the coast, and . . ." She shrugged. "Louise is afraid that the job will take over, and she'll never see me."

"Oh," Detective Ryan said. "She's probably right."

"Yeah."

Zoe couldn't help but smile at his honesty. They sat in silence for a moment.

"The thing is, you might never get another chance like this one. Is that something you could live with?"

"I don't know," Zoe admitted. "But it would probably help if I knew where I stood with you."

Ryan frowned. "Don't you know that already?"

"Clearly I wouldn't be asking . . ." Zoe peered at him.

Ryan gave a wry smile. "My mother always said, 'If you want something done well, do it yourself.' I may sometimes take that idea too far."

"You're the senior. The one with the experience. I get that. But how will I learn if you don't give me any responsibility? If you don't trust me?"

"It could be that I have a problem," he joked. Then, becoming more serious, "But I *do* trust you, Zoe. You're the only one in the squad I want to work with."

Detective Yang was pleased. Coming from Ryan it was practically a gushing endorsement. But now she had a decision to make.

"What do you think I should do . . . about Louise, that is?"

FORTY-SIX

As Detective Ryan drove home to Potts Point, he had much to consider. There was the case, of course, and tonight, he would look through the coroner's report. Then, there was the worry about his mother's health . . . and fresh into the mix came Detective Yang's bombshell.

Ryan was more upset than he had shown when Zoe had discussed returning to the Central Coast. Working with someone else, someone like Detective Terry Burke, would be a nightmare. Zoe Yang was an inexperienced detective but with good instincts and a willingness to learn. The Burkes of this world were hacks with no flair or finesse.

In answer to Zoe's question about what she should do about Louise, Ryan could have said that a partner who wouldn't allow you to do something you loved was never right for you. But he had held back; Zoe had to decide for herself.

Whatever the decision, her dilemma had brought up some uncomfortable feelings for Ryan. Despite his mother's disappointment in his marital status, Ryan had never really tried to commit to anyone. He knew the job came first, and he couldn't—*wouldn't*—ask a woman to take second place. Still, it was a lonely life at times, and he wondered if he'd be happy with his choices in another twenty years.

Ryan hummed the tune "All by Myself" as he pulled off William Street. Driving past the Coca-Cola sign, he stopped singing. It was a corny song, the kind of tune that desperate drunks sang in karaoke bars.

The detective pulled up outside his art deco block. He had work to do.

HEIDI MILLER WASN'T THINKING ABOUT WORK. She was pacing her hotel room, thinking about Ramesh Ryan. She peered at the clock next to her bed. It was ten o'clock. Where was he? Had he forgotten?

Heidi slumped back down on the bed. This was all wrong . . . the way she was feeling. She stretched her right hand out and lifted her index finger. Count the reasons. Number one, she hadn't seen Ramesh for years, so he couldn't be that important to her. She raised the middle finger. Number two, she had only met him again a few days ago. And third, and most importantly, didn't he deserve to know the truth about her?

Standing, Heidi again began pacing the room. Maybe it was just lust, the urge to sleep with a handsome man and escape the tension of the poker championship, nothing more. Perhaps then it was best that he hadn't come around tonight. Except, except, except . . . she didn't believe that. "Trust your instincts, Heidi," she said out loud. She trusted those instincts when she played poker, so she reasoned that she should trust them now. You weren't mistaken, she thought. *Both* of you had felt something . . . something real. Something strong.

Heidi stood by her window and peered out at the twinkling night lights of the Harbour Bridge and the boats bobbing up and down in the choppy water of the bay. Sydney was a spectacularly pretty city, the sort of place where she would be happy to settle down with a man she loved and who loved her—but she had chosen her life, so that wasn't an option. And yet . . .

Heidi took her cell out of her pocket. Should she call Ramesh to remind him of their date? She was about to dial and stopped. Was it a date? Was that what Ramesh and she would be having? Something that sounded so light, frivolous, and fun? Is that what this was all about? He was a detective working in the city, and she toured the world playing poker. Their lives were so different. Their *real* lives. Not some fantasy. They really were like that old saying . . . what was it? Ships in the night? Probably best if she never saw him again.

Then her phone rang.

Surprised, Heidi stared at the name in capitals on the screen. RAMESH.

Shit. What to do?

"Yes, Ramesh," she said, answering.

"I'm sorry. I got caught up, but I'd still love to come over." There was a pause. "If that's okay with you?"

Heidi hesitated. Hadn't she just decided that it would never work? So . . .

"Yeah, I'd love that."

"Great," Ryan said.

The call ended and Heidi stared into space. Okay, now you've done it. Now you'll have to tell him the truth . . . the whole truth and nothing but the truth. He had to know.

DOWNSTAIRS, IN THE HOTEL LOBBY, DAVE Jupiter rubbed his eyes. He was tired. He hadn't slept well, kept awake by the cold air blasting out of the air conditioning. He'd thought about getting an early night but, trusting his instincts, decided to stay. He was betting on Detective Ryan turning up.

Jupiter's interest had been sparked when he saw Ryan and the woman, Heidi Miller, together. He knew of the detective's reputation as a dogged investigator, but then again, people weren't always what they seemed.

At first, Jupiter had worried that he might have been made, though, thinking it through, that was unlikely. He knew he had the perfect face for his line of work . . . nondescript, someone no one ever registered or remembered.

The lobby elevator door opened.

Jupiter sat up.

Detective Ryan stepped out.

Jupiter felt a frisson of excitement as he watched the detective walk across to the reception desk. There, he began chatting to one of the receptionists.

Jupiter couldn't hear what was said but saw the receptionist lift the phone and hand the receiver to the detective. After saying a few words, the cop gave back the device and returned to the elevator.

As the lift doors opened, Detective Ryan stepped in. Jupiter hurried across to join him.

The detective pressed the number four button and looked over at Jupiter, recognizing him as the man who'd approached Heidi in the bar.

"Hi."

"Hi," Jupiter responded.

"You're staying here?"

"Yes."

"Floor?" Ryan asked.

"Same," Jupiter confirmed.

The doors closed, and the elevator set off. When it came to a halt, Ryan exited first, turning right. Jupiter went left and walked down the corridor. He stopped in front of a door and, as he pretended to look for his key, glanced over at Ryan. The detective had stopped outside a door. He knocked and waited. The door opened. Heidi Miller. She smiled and motioned the detective in.

FORTY-SEVEN

DETECTIVE RYAN WAS USUALLY KEEN TO face the world head-on and eager to fight the good fight, but not this morning.

The fact that he had woken up next to a beautiful woman should have counted for something, but it didn't. Not after what Heidi had told him last night, something he should have realized but, like a love-sick fool, had missed.

As he drove his car through busy, peak-hour traffic, Ryan pushed these thoughts to the back of his mind. An hour later, he was standing at the entrance of Luke Saker's impressive two-story home.

The door opened, and McKenzie appeared, her face pasty white, her eyes bloodshot.

"Morning, Detective. Come in," she said.

Ryan followed McKenzie down the hallway and into the living room.

"Take a seat, please," the woman said, indicating the sofa. "Can I get you a coffee or a tea?"

Ryan shook his head. "No, thank you, Mrs. Saker."

"McKenzie," the woman corrected.

"McKenzie. You're probably wondering why I'm here."

"You said on the phone that you needed to ask me something. Something to do with my husband." McKenzie glanced over to where Luke's dead body had lain only thirty-six hours earlier.

"Mrs. Saker . . . McKenzie," the detective said, correcting himself, "there's been a change in the direction of the investigation."

"Because Luke was poisoned?" McKenzie said.

"I wasn't aware you'd been informed," Ryan said, surprised.

"Detective Yang told me when I went to arrange collection of my husband's body yesterday." McKenzie sat down opposite the detective. "I don't suppose you know who could have done this?"

"It's too early for any definite conclusions," Ryan said.

"Oh." McKenzie stared at Ryan. "Could I ask you a question, Detective?"

"Go ahead."

"How do you do this?"

"Do what?" Detective Ryan asked.

"Your job. I mean, it's horrifying. Nothing but death . . . and dealing with the kind of people who don't mind tearing other people's lives apart. How do you shut off from all of that?"

Ryan hesitated. "I try to remember that it is exactly those 'other people' that I'm doing this for. People like you and your husband, who deserve justice."

McKenzie thought about what the detective had just said. "Yes, I can see that may help." She paused. "What exactly did you want to know so urgently?"

"Okay. Well, can you tell me how often your husband gambled at the casino?"

McKenzie frowned. "Two or three times a week."

"After work?" Ryan asked.

"Generally."

"And when he came home, were you usually asleep?"

"Why do you want to know that?" McKenzie looked puzzled.

"I just have to fill in a few gaps in the investigation." Detective Ryan smiled reassuringly.

McKenzie sighed. "Okay. Well, yes. I *was* usually in bed by the time he got home."

"Asleep?'

"No, I was awake."

Ryan waited for more.

"I was worried about him, Detective."

"Because?" Ryan said.

McKenzie shook her head. "Because he was a gambling addict and losing money . . . a lot of money."

"And you knew that for certain?" Ryan asked.

McKenzie stared at him. "What are you getting at, Detective?"

"I'm not getting at anything," Ryan said. It was a lie. He needed to hear her answer.

"Luke and I were married a long time. I could tell when he was troubled."

"Over the losses?"

"Yes."

"Did you ask him about it?"

"Of course. But he denied there was a problem." McKenzie paused. "He said gambling was just a hobby. Not something he was addicted to."

"Despite the evidence?" Detective Ryan asked.

"Yes, despite that."

"What did you do?"

"What could I do?" McKenzie asked.

"You could have told him that you knew he had a problem, and he had to do something about it."

"Such as?"

"Gambler's Anonymous?" Ryan replied.

"If you knew Luke . . ." She sighed. "He said it wasn't a problem. That was the end of that."

Ryan nodded thoughtfully. He paused before asking his next question.

"Did you and Luke have a happy marriage?"

"If what you're really asking is, why did I stay with him, then the answer would be because I loved him." She took a deep breath. "But he knew that the gambling upset me."

"And?"

Another long pause.

"He suggested we split."

"Was he serious?" Detective Ryan asked.

McKenzie shrugged. "He only said it the one time."

"And did he usually go straight to bed when he returned from the casino?"

McKenzie peered at the detective. "That's a strange question. No. He normally went to his office upstairs."

"I see," the detective said. "Can you show me?"

"His office?"

Detective Ryan nodded.

"Sure," McKenzie said. "Follow me."

FORTY-EIGHT

Luke Saker's home office was sparsely furnished with just a wooden desk, a Herman Miller chair, and a green fabric two-seater couch. The wood-planked floor was broken by a multicolored Persian rug that filled the space between the desk and the sofa. There were no posters, photos, calendars, paintings . . . nothing on the walls or the desktop.

McKenzie watched Ryan take in the room. "I know what you're thinking, Detective," she said. "It's not very homely, is it?"

"Did your husband work in here?" Ryan asked, looking doubtful.

"Not really. He just used it as a room to zone out in."

"And you think that's what he was doing? After returning from the casino?"

"No. I think he was poring over our finances."

"It must have been hard for you . . . that he didn't confide."

"Yes."

She turned away from him and walked to the window, peering out. "Don't you think the weather seems strange nowadays? One day boiling, the next wet and cloudy. I guess that's down to climate change." She watched as a young mother pushed a pram along the footpath at the front of her house. "Luke was the kind of man who had to work things out for himself. Over the years, I learned to adjust."

The detective watched her for a moment before speaking.

"Would you mind waiting downstairs while I have a bit of a look around?" he asked, treading carefully. "It helps the process . . . not having any distractions."

McKenzie shrugged. "Okay." She walked back to the door. "I'll be in the living room."

Ryan waited for McKenzie to close the door before stepping over to the desk and running his hand over it. Then, bending down, he opened the drawers. They were all empty. Next, the detective looked under the desk, again running his hand across the wood.

Finding nothing, Ryan bent down and rolled the rug back. Where it had lain, thin, barely visible lines marked out a rectangle on the floor.

Detective Ryan took a key from his pocket. He pushed it into one of the lines, and the metal slid in quickly. He ran his hand along the gap and pulled at a short leather tag. The detective drew the key farther across and grabbed another tag. Holding both, the detective carefully lifted the wood to reveal an open rectangular box. The container was crammed full of bundles of high-denomination bills.

DAVE JUPITER PEERED THROUGH BINOCULARS AT the front door of the Sakers' home. He would have loved to follow Detective Ryan into the house and listen to the conversation, but obviously, that was out of the question. Watching from his car was the next best thing.

Jupiter had luck on his side. He had somehow managed to find a parking space opposite the house. It hadn't been easy. The property was in a cul-de-sac, so just stopping at the end of the street would have been a problem. Anyone who tried to turn would have cursed him out. However, there was a space between a tradie's truck and an SUV.

The front door opened, and McKenzie Saker and Ryan appeared. The detective carried two plastic grocery bags. The man and woman said goodbye before Detective Ryan headed for his car.

Jupiter put down the binoculars and picked up a small black camera from the passenger seat. The Canon EOS R10 wasn't the most sophisticated camera on the market, but it was ideal for his purposes.

Jupiter pulled out the device's small screen, pushed down on the video button, and recorded the detective as he opened the trunk and dropped the bags inside. Slamming the trunk shut, Detective Ryan climbed into his vehicle.

Jupiter lowered the camera and slid down in the driver's seat as the detective's Hyundai reversed out of the driveway and onto the street before heading down the hill.

Jupiter sat up. He had decided to follow the detective, and his instincts had proven correct. Now he had a result—he had his man.

FORTY-NINE

A FEW MILES AWAY, SIMON FAITH PARKED outside the Ozjusto Bank. He had already rung Yvonne to say he would be late. He didn't explain why, and his PA hadn't asked. She knew better than to do that. If her boss had wanted to tell her, he would have.

Simon hoped that his trip to the bank would be quick and discreet. He had already rung the manager, Gerald Griffin, to arrange the cash pick up and mentioned that he would appreciate being let in the back door.

Simon was one of the bank's more important customers, regularly depositing substantial sums of money in his account, so the manager was only too happy to oblige the unusual request.

Griffin was waiting at the back door. He led the hotel boss through to a small back room. Leaving Simon there, the bank manager returned a few minutes later with bound blocks of bills.

"There you go," Gerald Griffin said, placing them on the table.

"If you could give me time to count it," Simon said.

"Of course." The manager stepped back from the table and waited.

"In private," Simon added.

Usually, the customer accepted the bank's word that all the money was there, but then again, it was a considerable amount, and Simon had never been the trusting kind.

"Oh, right," Griffin said before exiting the room.

NOT THAT FAR AWAY, DETECTIVE RYAN pulled up next to Detective Yang's car. Both vehicles had just enough room to park in the narrow driveway, but it was a tight squeeze.

The detective exited his car and walked up the gravel drive to the modest bungalow. As he approached, the front door opened, and a brown-haired woman in her midfifties wearing a faded floral dress stepped out.

"Detective Ryan, I assume," the woman said as the cop reached her.

"Yes."

"Anne Clarke. Please, come in."

The woman ushered the detective inside, leading him down the hallway to a small but cozy living room where Detective Yang waited.

"Tea, Detective?" Anne asked as Ryan sat on the sofa beside Yang. The detective hesitated. As a small child in Britain, he had watched adults gulp down gallons of the brew but had never understood the attraction. For him, tea rated a poor second to even the most mediocre cup of coffee.

Seeing Ryan's reluctance, Detective Yang jumped in. "Anne does make a good cuppa," she said encouragingly, raising her mug of tea.

Ryan nodded and smiled. "Well, yes, then, I'd love a cup if it's not too much trouble, Mrs. Clarke."

"It's Anne, and it's no trouble at all," the woman said. "Milk and sugar?"

"Just milk, please," Ryan said.

The detective waited for Anne to leave for the kitchen before turning his attention to Zoe.

"You were right about the coroner's report," Ryan said quietly. "The wife's testimony. It was a good catch."

"Thank you," Zoe said, surprised. She wasn't sure which Detective Ryan she preferred . . . the old offhand one or this new, more conciliatory version.

"By the way, I've got the warrant from Superintendent Dudley. But he did say that he'd had difficulty convincing the judge that you needed it," Yang said, stopping as Anne entered the room.

"Here you go," she said, handing Ryan a mug of tea. He peered dubiously at the orange liquid and took a sip.

"Delicious," the detective lied.

"Yes, there's nothing like a good cuppa to perk you up," Anne declared, sitting in an armchair opposite the two cops. "So, how can I help?"

Ryan glanced over at Zoe. "Did you . . .?" he began.

"Yes, I explained to Anne that we wanted to speak about the crash," Detective Yang confirmed.

Anne nodded. "Can't say I'm surprised. I've been expecting you," she said.

"You have?" Detective Ryan sounded surprised.

"Of course. It makes sense, doesn't it?"

"It does?" Ryan and Zoe exchanged curious glances.

"The deaths. Two Faith Company partners in a few days?" She looked at them both, eyes wide. "So, yes, I knew you'd come," the woman said.

"You know about the deaths?" Ryan asked. "There's only been a little about it in the papers, and we're yet to release any information."

"Yvonne loves to gossip." She grinned.

"Yvonne?" Ryan said.

"Yvonne Gomez. She's Simon Faith's assistant."

"You mean Yvonne Lewis?" Ryan said.

Anne nodded. "Sorry. Yvonne Lewis . . . She's only just divorced Pablo, and I still think of her as Yvonne Gomez."

"Her ex-husband was Spanish?" Detective Yang asked and looked over at Ryan.

"Yeah . . . anyway, I heard all about the deaths from her." She paused. "Yvonne was pretty shaken up."

Detective Ryan leaned forward. "So, let me get this straight. You know about these . . . recent events from Simon Faith's PA."

"Yes," Anne said. "I've known Yvonne since she was a child. Her mom was one of my best friends. She lived just around the corner. Yvonne and I got close when her mom died . . .." Anne stopped. "Cancer," she said, and shook her head. "It comes out of nowhere, you know."

"Yes," Ryan said slowly. For a moment, he seemed to be lost in thought. Detective Yang stepped in.

"So, why do you think the crash had anything to do with those recent deaths, Anne?" she asked.

"I'm not saying it does. It just makes sense that you consider motive when looking for culprits." Anne paused. "I'm a bit of a web sleuth, and I know any decent detective would make the connection. Then, after what I said at the inquest . . .."

"You expected us," Detective Ryan said, interrupting.

"Exactly."

"Right," Ryan said, reaching down and unclipping the catches on his briefcase. He pulled out the coroner's report and flicked through it. Stopping, he began to read: "I know exactly who did it . . .."

"No need for that. I remember word for word what I said."

"Very good," Ryan said, placing the report on the coffee table. "So, you thought the crash had something to do with the Faith Company."

"I thought the van could've been tampered with. Simon Faith was a mechanic before he became a so-called development guru, and the company owned several garages back then," Anne said.

"But you had no proof that the Faith Company was responsible for the crash?" Ryan asked.

"No. I didn't, but it just made sense. They had a motive."

"They did?" Detective Yang said.

"Yes. Because of the Morinas. The family owned a small farm on the land Simon Faith wanted to develop. He and his partners had plans for a golf course and a hotel."

"Which they have completed," Ryan said.

"Yes. But before the crash, it didn't look like any of that would happen. The company had bought up everything around there, except for the Morinas' farm. They wouldn't sell. Then, they died in the accident, and the wife's sister, who lived in Queensland, sold the farm to the Faith Company." Anne paused. "So, you see, the crash wasn't a tragedy for Simon Faith and his cohorts but simply a business opportunity."

"That's a pretty harsh assessment," Detective Yang remarked.

"It's the truth," Anne insisted. "At the time, though, everyone was trying to blame my husband, Tommy, because he was the van driver. But that was rubbish. He had nothing to do with the crash. That was the coroner's conclusion, too. He said it was an accident . . . pure and simple." She paused. "I'm sure the coroner will tell you the same thing if you ask him."

"Unfortunately, Mr. O'Sullivan died a few years ago," Detective Yang said.

Anne stared at her. "Really . . . I didn't know."

"Mr. O'Sullivan *did* reject your accusation regarding the Faith Company, though, didn't he?" Detective Ryan said.

"Yes."

"Do you still believe the Faith Company was responsible for the crash?"

The woman was silent for a moment. "Look, at the end of the day, I was just happy Tommy was cleared. The rest is water under the bridge."

She stood up. "Let me show you something." She walked across to a bookshelf and pulled out a photo album. Returning, Anne sat down and flicked through the book. She stopped on a page and pointed at it.

"This is the last picture I have of my Tommy," Anne said, indicating a thin man in his midthirties in the center of a line of people standing alongside a Transit van. "For him to be accused of causing the crash, well, it made my blood boil."

"Who are the others?" Detective Yang asked.

"Everyone who was in the van that day."

"Which one's Irwin Cooper?" Ryan asked.

She looked up from the album. "You know about Irwin?"

"Yes," Ryan said.

Anne pointed at a geeky-looking man in a suit. "That's him. The poor guy went downhill after his wife was killed."

Ryan reached into his pocket and took out his iPhone. "Do you mind?" he asked.

"Go ahead."

Detective Ryan took a picture of the photo.

"Thank you," he said, stuffing the phone back into his pocket.

"It was a tragic day for most, but one of miracles, too, for some."

"How so?" Detective Yang asked.

"Well, Irwin Cooper and Sasha Morina"—Anne pointed at a skinny kid in an ill-fitting jacket and shorts—"survived the crash. That was a miracle. Having this photo is a bit of a miracle, too. God only knows how they retrieved the camera unharmed from the water."

SIMON FAITH PLACED THE LAST BUNDLE of notes in the case and flipped it closed. As he did, there was a knock, and Gerald Griffin entered. The bank manager looked over at Simon and the Gladstone bag.

"Finished?" he asked.

"Yes, all done," Simon said, standing and grasping the bag's leather handle. "Shall we?"

Together, the manager and hotel boss headed to the back entrance.

"So, Mr. Faith, I hope we've lived up to our motto, Banking You Can Be Proud Of," Gerald Griffin said as he tapped a code into the keypad and pushed open the door.

Simon nodded. "You've been very efficient," he said, smiling.

Returning to his SUV, Simon carefully placed the bag on the floor under the passenger seat and checked his watch. He thought about taking the case home but decided to return to the hotel instead. He couldn't afford the time for that. He had a busy day ahead of him.

FIFTY

D RIVING AWAY FROM ANNE CLARKE'S HOME and heading to The Palms Hotel, Detective Ryan felt confident he had reached a tipping point in the case. Almost everything he needed to know to unravel the mystery of the two men's deaths was out there, within touching distance. He just needed to put all the pieces together and in a way that would convince a jury he was right. That was the hard part, helping others to see what was often so apparent to him. He hoped the photo he had just sent to Elina Bennett in the IT department, with a note to complete the work as a matter of urgency, would help.

Reaching The Palms' driveway, Ryan stopped. The gates were still closed, protected by a phalanx of security guards who stood watching a small group of activists. The activists held homemade banners aloft, protesting the hotel's reopening.

A guard approached the detective's vehicle and signaled Ryan to open his car window.

"ID," the guard said.

Detective Ryan produced his identification, and the man checked it over.

"The car behind is with me, too," Ryan said, indicating Detective Yang's vehicle.

The man glanced at Yang's car before returning the ID to Ryan.

"Okay, Detective, you can both go through."

Moments later, the gates swung open, and the cops headed down the driveway. They parked outside the hotel.

"Did Simon Faith's PA confirm someone would come to take us to Irwin Cooper?" Ryan asked Zoe as she joined him.

Yang nodded, watching a golf buggy head their way. It stopped, and Steve Prince, the head of security, leaned out.

"Detectives, hop in," Steve said.

"We get the head honcho this time, do we?" Ryan joked as Yang and he climbed into the back of the buggy. "I thought you might have been too busy."

"Because of the hotel reopening?" Steve asked.

"And the protestors," Detective Ryan added.

Steve snorted. "Those idiots. They're just a nuisance. A complete waste of time." He released the hand brake and accelerated away. "This is a waste of time, too. There's no way that Irwin Cooper's a killer."

"Why do you say that?" Detective Yang asked.

"Because I've been in security for years, and I just know. That's why."

No one spoke as the buggy drove down the narrow track, passing Alex Riva, who was washing a black Range Rover.

Detective Yang pointed. "That's security work?" she asked.

"Not exactly. Alex volunteered to clean Mr. Faith's car," Steve said. "I would prefer if he didn't. It's not in the job description, and it makes the rest of us look bad." A look of disdain crossed his face. "Scores points with the boss, though."

Detective Ryan stared at the back of the bald man's head. "You don't like Alex much?"

"That's not what I said." He took a breath and smiled. "We all do what we have to, to get on."

After a few minutes, the buggy reached the tree line.

"We walk from here," Steve said, parking the buggy. He jumped out. Ryan and Yang followed.

"I take it you have the warrant?" Steve asked.

Detective Yang produced the document and offered it to the security chief. "Here."

Steve ran his eyes over the paper, grunted, and set off. Detective Yang glanced at Ryan and pulled a face. She didn't like the guard much.

The group reached the clearing. As they approached Cooper's caravan, his rottweiler, Max, suddenly ran out of the bushes, growling and barking. It almost reached them but was stopped by a chain that held the animal back.

"Christ!" Steve held his hands up defensively. "Calm down, buddy," he called out to the dog as he looked around nervously for the owner. "Cooper! Get this creature out of here, can you?" the rattled head of security shouted.

There was no answer.

Detective Ryan slammed his hand hard on the caravan door. "Mr. Cooper, open up. We have a warrant."

Silence.

Detective Yang went to the window and peered through a gap in the curtains.

"I can't see anyone," she said.

Ryan twisted the doorknob. "Mr. Cooper?" He pushed open the unlocked door and peered in. The caravan was empty.

"He's not here," Ryan said, closing up and looking back at the dog. It was still growling at Steve.

"Perhaps if you moved back a few paces, he might calm down," Detective Yang said.

The guard backed off, and the dog responded in kind. Ryan looked to Yang, impressed.

"He was just reacting to a threat," she explained. As she said it, a thought crossed her mind. "Hang on a sec," and she returned to the caravan.

"That dog needs to be put down," Steve muttered.

A couple of minutes later, Zoe returned with a plastic container. She removed the lid and threw the contents so they landed just in front of the dog.

"The universal language of food." Ryan nodded appreciatively.

"He's a guard dog. He was doing what he's been trained to do," Detective Yang said, inching closer to Max. "Rottweilers aren't naturally aggressive."

"I hope someone told *him* that," Steve responded doubtfully.

Zoe crouched down. "Hi, it's nice to meet you."

Max kept one eye on the detective and one eye on the raw steak as he made short work of the offering.

"Where's your owner, hey, boy?" she asked, keeping her voice low and steady. Suddenly, the dog started to bark, catching Zoe off guard. She quickly moved back, but Max didn't advance. He just kept barking. Zoe watched him for a moment before coming to a realization. "There's something wrong," she said. "This dog is distressed."

"Who cares?" Steve said.

Detective Yang ignored him and took another tentative step toward the animal. "What's up?"

The dog barked and ran to the side of the caravan.

"He's trying to tell us something," Yang said.

"Let's have a look," Ryan said, joining Zoe.

"Fine, you do what you want. I'll wait here," Steve said.

Leaving the security guard, the detectives followed the dog, carefully remaining just out of reach while squeezing past overhanging branches to get to the back of the caravan.

Max stopped and stared up into the trees.

Ryan followed the animal's gaze.

"Christ!" he said.

FIFTY-ONE

A FULLY GROWN OAK TREE CAN REACH up to seventy feet high, with a spread of over fifty feet. Although big, the one Detectives Ryan and Yang were peering up at still had a way to go. Nevertheless, its branches were strong enough to hold Irwin Cooper's dead body.

An oiled manila rope had been coiled, knotted, and twisted around tree branches. The other end, fashioned into a noose, gripped tight to the man's neck. He was dressed casually in worn blue jeans, a grubby sweatshirt, and big brown work boots that dangled above the ground.

Detective Yang had mixed emotions on seeing Cooper. She'd only had limited experience of suicide and was both saddened and fascinated in equal measure by the sight.

Detective Ryan, though, was unfazed. He had been a cop long enough to have seen many deaths, including several hangings.

"Zoe, we need assistance here right away," Ryan said.

"On it." Zoe nodded, reaching for her cell phone.

"Don't bother," Detective Ryan said. "Reception here is nonexistent. Go back to the hotel with Steve and make the calls. Wait there until the team shows up."

AFTER ZOE HAD LEFT, RYAN BEGAN carefully checking around the big tree. Some of the thick foliage at the base of the trunk had been crushed, presumably by Cooper, before he climbed it, the coil of heavy rope slung over his shoulder.

Ryan stared up at the soles of the dead man's boots. They were clean. That was no surprise. It had been dry last night, so there was no reason anything would stick to them.

The detective twisted around as a low sigh came from behind. Max lay on the ground about six feet away, restrained from coming any closer by his chain. He was still staring up at his master's body.

"You okay, Max?" Ryan asked.

The dog lowered his large brown eyes and peered at the detective.

"Did you see it?" Ryan asked. The dog ignored the detective and looked back up at his master's body.

Ryan had always been dismissive of owners who treated their animals like people and credited them with human emotions. Now, though, seeing Max, the detective was revising his opinion. The dog seemed genuinely upset . . . sad in a human way about his owner's death.

Ryan stared back up at Cooper's body. The man's hostility could have been because he was a loner and saw no reason to talk to the police—but the detective's gut told him there was more to it than that. Was Cooper capable of murdering two men? Ryan *had* thought it possible, but the man's apparent suicide was casting doubt on that theory.

Ryan glanced again at Cooper and decided to wait for the pathologist before examining the body. He had other work to do before forensics arrived.

RYAN RETRACED HIS STEPS, WALKING PAST Max and back to the clearing. Emerging, the detective peered at the caravan. Shaped like a jelly bean, it had seen better times. Its blue and white paint was peeling, and it lurched to one side. Despite its battered appearance, the detective noticed two new-looking white panels on the caravan roof. Cooper may have been off the grid, but he had ingeniously wired up some form of solar power.

Ryan removed a pair of thin white surgical gloves from his pocket and, slipping them on, opened the caravan door. Stepping inside, he pulled back the drapes and looked around.

A kitchen counter ran along the back wall. Above and below it, there were yellow-painted wooden cupboards. A small stove and a fridge were the only appliances, and a stainless-steel sink had been cut into the faded Formica top. A single bed ran from left to right along the far wall. It was unmade, the sheet and blanket pulled back. A wooden table and chair were pushed against the wall to his left.

The detective started his search in the kitchen area. He walked over to the sink. A dirty cup, a set of used cutlery, and an unwashed bowl with a few thin strands of pasta clinging to its side lay on the counter. A splash of red sauce was visible on the off-white walls above the basin. Ryan touched the spot with his finger—a trace of the sauce attached to his glove. It appeared that Cooper had eaten the spaghetti meal recently. Detective Ryan was well aware of the complexity of human nature, but would a man who was about to commit suicide go to the trouble of cooking a meal first?

Detective Ryan sniffed the air as he moved from the sink to the bed. The caravan had the distinct sweaty smell of someone who wasn't too fussy about his hygiene. The cop bent down and looked under the bed. Several pairs of jeans, T-shirts, sweaters, underwear, and socks filled the space. There was no sign of a wardrobe in the small caravan, so this was obviously where Cooper stored his clothes. It was further proof, too, that the caravan had been home to just one person. If someone else had lived with Cooper, there would have been obvious signs of cohabitation.

Standing, Ryan walked over to the table and chair. Three large blue and green bags of Richgro slow-release lawn fertilizer were stacked behind the seat. An open metal box sat on the desk. Detective Ryan peered into it and saw work tools—metal pliers, a screwdriver, spanners and sockets, a hammer, and a spirit level. The tools were all old but clean, signs that Cooper valued them and looked after them well. He was something Detective Ryan had never been—a handyman.

The detective lifted the toolbox. Underneath was a small trace of red paint. Putting the box down, Ryan ran his fingers over the stain. It was dry but recent—it hadn't had time to soak into the wooden top.

Gardening tools—a rake, a set of pruning shears, a shovel, and a gardening fork—were stacked on the floor on the table's far side. Gardening equipment inside the caravan? The detective thought about that. The tools would have been precious for someone with little money and few possessions, and despite living in a forest, Cooper must have feared they could be stolen. That was why he kept them inside.

From outside came the sound of approaching sirens. The cavalry had arrived.

FROM WHERE HE LAY HIDDEN BY *the trees, the man saw the two marked police cars pull to a halt. Four cops, two from each vehicle, got out. Moments later, a golf buggy appeared and parked next to them. Simultaneously, the caravan door opened, and Detective Ryan came out.*

The man had hoped to see Ryan die alone. Now, with the arrival of the others, things had become more complicated.

He glanced at his watch. What to do? He had to get back soon, or some-one would notice. It was time to go.

FIFTY-TWO

"Afternoon," Simon Faith said as Detective Ryan walked over.

"I'm afraid this area is off-limits to the public," Ryan said, looking at Detective Yang.

She began to protest. "I did try to tell—"

"Keep your shirt on, Detective. Just wanted to confirm Cooper's . . ." Simon searched for the right word. "Demise. For my peace of mind."

"Peace of mind?" Ryan queried.

"Well, yes. With Cooper gone, I can go ahead with the hotel's reopening unhindered," he said.

"Mr. Faith, three people are dead, all associated with you and your hotel in one way or another, and you want to continue as if nothing has happened?"

"Not at all. This has been a tragedy. And harrowing for *all* of us. But it's over now," Simon said. "You've found the killer, and he's dead. I don't see that he should have any more power over us than he's already had."

"Cooper's involvement has not yet been confirmed," Detective Ryan said slowly.

"Oh, come on, Detective. That man's behind all of this, and you tracked him down, so well done."

"You've changed your tune. You said he couldn't possibly be guilty."

"Well, we all make mistakes," Simon said dismissively before glancing at Steve. "Let's go," he said to the security guard.

"Detective Ryan. Detective Yang," a voice said from behind as Steve and his boss climbed back into the golf buggy.

The detectives turned to see three people approaching, all dressed in coveralls and carrying cases and equipment.

"Sorry we're late. We had to leave the vehicles back there," pathologist Noah Bellman said, pointing through the trees. "Now, let me introduce you. This is Walt Matthews, the videographer," he said, pointing to a skinny young man. "And you know Sophie Flores, of course. . . . Now, where's the body?"

"Behind the caravan," Detective Ryan said. "But before we start, how are you with dogs?"

"Dogs?" Noah asked. "You mean canines in general?"

"No, I mean a chained-up rottweiler."

"Fine, I think," Noah said. "How about you?" the pathologist said, turning to the others.

Sophie shrugged. "Okay. As long as the animal remains chained."

"No problem for me, either," Matthews said.

"Right," Detective Ryan said. "Follow me."

BEHIND THE CARAVAN, A CONSTABLE BALANCED on a thick branch and unknotted the rope Irwin Cooper hung from. Below, Sergeant Roger Baldwin steadied the dead man's legs.

"You got him, Sergeant?" Detective Ryan asked, looking over.

Sergeant Baldwin stared at the detective and said nothing. His opinion of Detective Ryan hadn't changed since their first encounter three bodies ago. The man was condescending and full of himself.

"You ready then, Sarge?" the constable shouted as he finished untying the rope and prepared to release it.

"Always, Constable Williams," the sergeant said.

Williams let go of the cable, and Sergeant Baldwin, taking the weight of Cooper's body, lowered the corpse to the ground.

"You can come down now, Jonno," Baldwin shouted. "That's if the detective's okay with it?" he added, glancing across at Ryan.

"Yes, yes, fine," Ryan said, ignoring the cop's tone.

As Constable Jonno Williams climbed down, Detective Ryan stooped beside Noah. He pointed to the straight-line bruise that encircled Cooper's neck.

"What do you think, Noah?" Ryan asked.

"Same as you, I imagine," Noah said, glancing across at the detective.

"Which is?" Detective Yang said, seeing the look between the two men.

Before either man could answer, a dog growled behind them.

Detective Yang twisted around. Max was on his feet, eyeing Sergeant Baldwin and Constable Williams.

"Is someone going to take this animal away?" the sergeant said nervously.

"A dog handler has been called," Detective Yang confirmed.

"Well, he'd better come soon. We can't work with it here," Sergeant Baldwin said, edging past Max, who was straining on the end of his chain.

"I'll leave you to it, then, Noah," Ryan said, standing up.

There was a grunt from the pathologist.

"Come with me, Detective," Ryan said to Zoe as he marched toward the caravan.

A DROP OF SWEAT DRIPPED FROM SIMON'S forehead down his cheek. He wiped it away before replacing the burner phone to his ear. What was going on? He had made it clear, hadn't he? The man who'd answered his call had seemed to understand, though it was difficult to tell. His voice was accented, and his English was limited. "I NEED TO SPEAK TO HIM NOW!" Simon shouted, believing that raising your voice with a foreigner was the best way to get your point across.

"I'll check," the man had said.

As Simon waited, another thought occurred to him, and it wasn't a good thought. Guffini would probably be furious that Simon was trying to contact him, but what choice did he have? The killings had to stop.

"Yes," a voice said at the other end of the phone.

"We need to talk, Mr. Guffini," Simon said. "About the money."

"Go on."

"I'm sorry about it. Really sorry. It was an accountancy error," Simon said.

There was a grunt at the other end. Then: "So?"

"I've only just discovered it. But I'll repay all the money right away."

Silence.

"You still there?" Simon said, aware now that the single drop of sweat had become a torrent.

"You have it all?" The Owl said.

"Yes."

There was silence. "Bring it. Tonight, at nine. The usual place," The Owl said.

"I want to . . ."

There was a click.

The hotel boss walked back to his chair and sat down. By "the usual place," Simon assumed Guffini meant the woodside rendezvous where they had met before.

He reached into his pocket, pulled out his handkerchief, and wiped his face. Then, after replacing the handkerchief, he snapped the phone in half and stuffed it in his pocket.

Had that gone well or poorly? He had no idea.

DETECTIVE RYAN REENTERED THE CARAVAN. DETECTIVE Yang followed.

"So, Ryan, do you mind explaining—" Detective Yang began and then stopped as there was a knock on the door.

She opened it to find a heavyset man in a blue police uniform carrying a catch pole.

"Douglas," the uniformed man said.

"You're the dog person?" Detective Yang asked.

"Yep. Where's the animal?"

"Can you take him to Max, please, Detective Yang?" Ryan said.

"But . . ." Yang began.

"Come back afterward."

Detective Yang stared at Ryan. "He's around the back, Constable Douglas."

Ryan waited for Zoe to leave before he resumed his search of the caravan.

Walking across to the kitchen, Ryan opened one of the two cupboards. It was filled with tinned foods—canned vegetables, beans, peas, tuna, sardines, canned meat, packets of long-life milk, and bottles of beer. The other cupboard was empty except for a half-full bottle of whiskey and two glasses.

Crouching and pulling open the door under the sink, Ryan viewed the white plates, bowls, glasses, mugs, and cups. Cutlery—stainless steel knives, spoons, and forks—was stored in a brown wooden caddy.

A single small, clear jar stood alone to one side. It was half-filled with fine white powder.

The detective picked the jar up and unscrewed the top. He sniffed the powder and reached into his pocket for an evidence bag. Carefully shaking some of the white powder into it, he sealed the bag and put it into his pocket.

Standing, Ryan looked around again. Searching the room was proving depressing. Cooper lived a sad life, and it all had ended even more sadly-- hanging from a tree in the middle of a forest.

Behind him, the door opened, and Detective Yang entered.

"Done?" Detective Ryan asked.

"Yes. Now, can you please explain what's going on? What were Noah and you talking about when you said you were thinking the same thing?"

"What we meant . . ." the detective began as he opened the refrigerator door.

There was a soft click and the sound of ticking.

Ryan peered into the fridge, spun around, and grabbed Zoe forcefully by the arm.

"Run!" he cried, sprinting to the door and dragging the detective with him. A bewildered Zoe had no time but to do as she was told. As they leaped from the caravan, there was a deafening explosion.

FIFTY-THREE

"A BOMB?!" SIMON FAITH WAS INCREDULOUS. "CHRIST! What next?" Steve Prince had just delivered the news. Looking grim, he stood in front of his boss, awaiting instruction. A minute later, there was a knock on the door, and Yvonne entered the office.

"Sorry to interrupt, but Alex Riva . . ."

Alex stepped past the PA. "I wanted to get an update on the explosion."

"Prince, fill him in, will you?" Simon said.

"Irwin Cooper's caravan was blown up and destroyed," Steve said.

"Blown up?" Alex asked, wide-eyed. "How? Gas bottle?"

Steve shook his head. "Bomb, apparently. Bloody lucky no one was hurt. Those two cops nearly didn't make it."

Alex shook his head in disbelief. "That's . . . crazy." He looked to Simon. "Will this affect the hotel reopening?"

"Absolutely not," Simon said. He sounded adamant, but his expression betrayed something of his uncertainty.

"Shit," he said, thinking on it some more. "Shit!" He said again, a little more loudly this time. "Yvonne!" he yelled. A moment later, the PA appeared.

"Draft a press release. Something to the effect that the hotel's reopening has been delayed due to . . . an unforeseen supply-chain problem. Then, email everyone on the guest list. Keep it vague. We'll reschedule the event as soon as the issue has been resolved."

"Yes, sir," Yvonne replied and quickly stepped out of the room, closing the door behind her.

Simon sat at his desk, fuming. He had moved heaven and earth to keep the reopening on track, but with two murders and now a bombing, something had to give. He closed his eyes briefly, forgetting that the security guards were still in his office.

"Mr. Faith?" Alex began.

Simon looked up, surprised. "What the hell are you still doing here? Get back to your jobs! Both of you!"

Steve immediately headed for the door, but the other guard persisted.

"It's just that I've finished detailing your car, but I can't refit the fire extinguisher because the bracket has come loose . . .."

"Then fix it, you moron! Use your bloody initiative! Can't everyone see that I'm in the middle of a giant clusterfuck?!"

"Yes, Mr. Faith. I'll take care of it." Alex followed Steve out of the room, leaving the door ajar.

"SHUT THE DOOR!" Simon roared. The door quietly closed, and Simon put his head in his hands. He sat there for what seemed like an hour. His mind was racing. Things were getting out of hand, and there was something about this latest development that didn't sit right. A bomb? Hadn't he just spoken to Guffini? Told him he had the money? Arranged a meeting for tonight? Why, then, was he now not just killing people but blowing things up, too?

Simon sat back in his chair and thought about that. "Shit," he muttered. What if that detective, Ryan, had been right? What if Cooper had committed the murders in revenge for being forced to leave his home and had planted the bomb to take the cops with him? Perhaps the murders had nothing to do with the gang boss. Maybe Guffini had no clue he'd been skimming money from him. And now he had agreed to hand all that cash back.

THE BOMB SQUAD BOSS, CONSTABLE LES Wright, removed his heavy green helmet and took steady gulps of air before waving for Detective Ryan to join him.

Detective Yang went to follow her partner. "Just Detective Ryan, please," Constable Wright ordered, putting up his hand to stop her.

The constable was a stickler for protocol. He knew that Ryan alone, as the lead detective and the highest-ranking cop, should be the first to be informed of the situation.

"Well?" Detective Ryan asked, arriving.

"I'm satisfied there are no other explosives here," Constable Wright said.

"And the bomb?"

"It seems to have been a pretty crude affair . . . probably homemade, but still effective," the cop said, glancing around at the smoking remains of the caravan.

"What about Cooper's body?"

"The cadaver at the back?" Constable Wright asked.

Ryan nodded.

"It got a little charred, but it's still all there."

"So, can we continue the investigation?"

"Be my guest," Constable Wright said.

"We've got the all-clear," Detective Ryan shouted to the others standing well back.

As everyone began to return, Detective Yang walked over to Detective Ryan. "Ryan . . ." she began.

"One moment," he said. "Sophie." He signaled to the forensics assistant to come over.

"In all the excitement, I almost forgot." The detective reached into his pocket and took out an evidence bag containing the white powder.

"Found this in the caravan before it went up," Ryan said, handing the bag over. "Can you check it out?"

"Will do," Sophie said.

"Well, are you going to fill me in or not?" Detective Yang said as the forensics assistant walked away.

"About what?" Ryan asked as he turned suddenly and headed for his car. Taken by surprise, Zoe was forced to run to catch up.

"About what you and Noah were referring to when looking at Cooper's body."

Detective Ryan paused by his car door, searching for an answer.

"Look, it's nothing." He shrugged. "I'm not a pathologist, so anything *I* think is just conjecture at this point."

Zoe stared at him open-mouthed.

"I really cannot believe you! After all our discussions," she said, shaking her head. "You're still holding out on me. We were both almost killed, and you're still holding out!" She spat the words at Ryan before turning and heading for the path that led back to the hotel.

Ryan watched for a moment before letting out a small sigh. "Shit," he said under his breath.

"Zoe! Wait!" he called out as she reached the edge of the clearing.

Zoe stopped and turned. She looked at him defiantly as she crossed her arms. Her body language was unambiguous, and Ryan knew he would have to swallow his pride.

"Look, you're right . . ." he started, but Zoe wasn't about to make this easy.

"We *talked* about this, and you said things would be different. I told you I was thinking about going back to the Central Coast! I confided in you about my personal life!" For a second, it looked as though she might cry, but she managed to keep it together.

Detective Ryan nodded, looking chastened. "I know," he said. "I just . . . it's hard to change the habit of a lifetime overnight." He looked at her and attempted a small smile. "I have never before worked so hard to keep a partner." He searched for the words. "I know that might be hard to believe."

Zoe took a deep breath. She knew how difficult it was for Ryan to open up.

Zoe offered him a half-smile. "I pity your previous partners then."

"Yes, apparently, I'm not the easiest person to work with," he said wryly.

Detective Yang laughed. "Okay. So how about you put your money where your mouth is?"

Ryan considered this just long enough that Zoe thought he would try to evade the question yet again.

"Cooper didn't commit suicide," Detective Ryan said quietly.

"What?" Zoe paused. "Noah told you that?"

"No. Not as such," Detective Ryan said.

"So . . ." Yang said and stopped. "That look between you. That's what you both realized?"

Detective Ryan nodded. "Hanging compresses the veins, causing small bleeding sites on the lips, mouth, and eyelids. And the face and neck are congested with blood and become dark red."

"Which was exactly what I saw on Cooper's body. So?" Detective Yang said.

"Yes. But it wasn't caused by the rope."

"I don't get it," Yang said, confused.

Ryan explained. "Hanging also *always* leaves an inverted V bruise around the neck. Irwin Cooper didn't have that. His neck had a straight-line bruise, which is a telltale sign of strangulation."

"You're saying that Cooper was strangled and then hung from the tree?" Detective Yang asked.

"Precisely. And whoever did it wanted to disguise the murder as a suicide."

Detective Yang frowned. "Okay, but why?"

"Because—"

"No. Wait. I've got it," Yang said, interrupting. "Someone who knew Cooper was a suspect used him to throw us off the trail. So . . . you think he had nothing to do with the murders?"

Ryan shook his head. "Not at all. I have no doubt Cooper was involved in the killings. I believe the evidence I gave to Sophie will prove that. But the point is, he wasn't the only killer."

"No?" Detective Yang said.

"No. And I have a plan to find out who else was involved. But to make it work, I'll need your help."

FIFTY-FOUR

WHEN SHE HEARD THE SCREAM, YVONNE had just started typing the email about postponing The Palms Hotel's reopening. She knew it would have cost her boss dearly to make that decision, and by the sounds of things, he wasn't easily coming to terms with it. At the sound of something heavy crashing against the adjoining wall, Yvonne spun around, grabbing a ceramic vase of flowers as it threatened to topple off her desk.

After moving the vase to a nearby bookcase, the PA cautiously approached Simon Faith's office door. She could hear breaking glass and more items bouncing off walls. Imagining a scene of total destruction, she decided against getting involved and returned to her desk, where she sat, thinking about her next move.

Yvonne had been warned about her boss's temper tantrums, but this was the first time she had encountered one, and she didn't like it.

Her first instinct was to collect her few belongings and leave, but she decided it would be best to leave at the end of the day. So, as the noise subsided, she returned to her work, completing and sending out the email before making tea.

Cup in hand, the PA knocked tentatively and entered the office. She glanced around the room as she headed over to her boss. The place looked like a tsunami had hit it: papers on the floor, a smashed glass paperweight under the desk, and his precious golf trophy, presented for coming fourth in the New South Wales Amateur Championship, lay face down.

Yvonne carefully placed the cup on the desk. "There you go," she said.

"Thanks," Simon said calmly.

"Shall I . . . ?" Yvonne asked, indicating the mess on the floor.

"Go ahead," her boss said coolly.

The PA began clearing up as Simon sipped the tea.

"I trust that this little . . . *incident* will remain just between us?"

"Of course, Mr. Faith," Yvonne said as she cradled the broken items. "What shall I do with this?"

"Just dump it in the corner. I'll deal with it later."

The PA stood up. "I'll get a dustpan and brush for the glass."

"Don't worry about that; you can get the cleaners in."

Yvonne hesitated. "You sure?"

"Of course."

"Okay," Yvonne said, walking over to the corner. "By the way, Mr. Faith, Steve Prince called about twenty minutes ago—I didn't want to disturb you—but those detectives are coming to see you again."

"Now?"

"Yes. They're on their way."

ALEX RIVA TWISTED THE ALLEN KEY and tightened the nut before placing his hands on either side of the fire extinguisher bracket. He tried to move it, but it wouldn't budge.

Satisfied, Alex stepped out of Simon Faith's Range Rover and, bending down, carefully picked up the red painted extinguisher.

There was the sound of a horn.

The noise surprised Alex, and he almost dropped the cylinder. Twisting around, the guard saw a golf buggy heading toward him.

"Hi," Steve said as he parked the vehicle.

Alex glared at the security chief. "What the fuck did you do that for?"

"I was just making certain you knew we were here," Steve said as he and Detective Ryan and Detective Yang clambered out of the buggy.

Alex grunted and then smiled at the cops. "I hear you guys had a busy morning. Where you off to now?"

"Meeting with the boss," Steve said.

The security chief motioned for the detectives to follow him. The group crossed the underground car park to the elevator.

As Steve pressed the lift button, Detective Ryan's cell pinged. He checked the screen. "The adjusted photo from Elina Bennett," Ryan said, offering the cell to Detective Yang.

She glanced at it. "Good," was all she said as the elevator doors opened.

FIFTY-FIVE

"DETECTIVE RYAN AND DETECTIVE YANG, TO see you," Steve Prince said, entering Simon Faith's office.

The hotel boss smiled. "Come in, please." He indicated two chairs before his desk. "Thank you, Prince."

The security chief turned to exit, but Detective Ryan raised his hand. "I'd prefer it if Steve stayed."

"What? Why?" Simon Faith said.

Before Ryan could answer, there was a knock. Yvonne entered. "Do either of the detectives want tea or coffee?"

"Ah, Yvonne . . . I was just about to ask you to join us." Ryan smiled.

The PA hesitated. "Me?" She looked uncertainly at her boss.

"Are you sure, Detective?" Simon asked, now thoroughly confused.

"Yes." Ryan looked reassuringly at the young woman. "And did you let Alex Riva know that he was needed?"

Before she could answer, Alex appeared in the open doorway. "I've fixed that bracket for the fire extinguisher in your car," the guard said, walking across the office. He placed the keys onto his boss's desk and looked around curiously at the other people in the office. "I assumed that's why I was called."

Simon stared at the two cops, fed up with being kept in the dark. "Okay, enough, Detectives. What's going on? Why is everyone here?"

"All in good time, Mr. Faith. But first, let me explain what's been happening. As you may already have been informed, after we found Irwin Cooper, a bomb exploded, destroying his caravan," Detective Ryan began. "The immediate area has now been searched, and we are satisfied there are no more explosive devices."

"Very good. But you do know that your police vehicles tore up my golf course. I assume I'll be getting compensation?"

"That decision is above my pay grade, Mr. Faith," Detective Ryan said. "Someone at headquarters will deal with it."

"They'd better," Simon said icily.

"Moving along," Detective Ryan said quickly, "We now definitely believe Irwin Cooper was involved in the murder of your partners, Mr. Faith."

"What a load of BS. What reason did he have?" Alex scoffed.

Ryan smiled at the guard. "I'm glad you asked, Alex." He turned to his partner. "Would you like to enlighten the good people, Detective Yang?"

"Well, I think everyone here already knows he had a motive." She looked around the room. "He was old, and he was about to be evicted. Without friends or family to turn to, he would likely have ended up on the streets."

"Oh, spare me." Simon rolled his eyes. "The man lived rent-free for years! He could hardly have expected that to last forever."

"Whether his motive was justifiable or not is beside the point," Ryan asserted.

Steve shrugged. "He was angry. That doesn't mean he did it."

"You're right. Reason alone is not enough. It helps to have evidence," Detective Ryan said.

"If there was evidence, wouldn't it have been blown to smithereens?" Yvonne asked.

"Indeed, it would. Luckily, I managed to gather some *before* the bomb went off."

Ryan had the undivided attention of the whole room, and he paused for effect. The tension was getting to Simon.

"For Christ's sake, Detective! Don't keep us in suspense," he spat.

Ryan smiled and turned to his partner. "Detective Yang . . ." he offered.

Zoe took the baton, a little surprised that Ryan had handed it over. "Detective Ryan found a large supply of a banned substance that was once used to kill rats in Mr. Cooper's caravan—the same poison that was found in Luke Saker's body," she informed them.

"Forensics is currently analyzing it, but I'm confident that a positive result will be returned," Detective Ryan added.

Simon's eyes narrowed.

"What are you talking about? You said Luke fell down the stairs."

"He did," Detective Yang replied. "But only because he'd been poisoned."

"And the killer used Luke's love of Coca-Cola to administer the toxin," Ryan told them.

Shocked, Yvonne put her hand over her mouth. "Oh my God. It was in the Diet Coke."

The room was silent as everyone took in the information.

Steve was the first to speak. "And Mr. Young? You think Cooper killed him as well?"

Ryan nodded. "Cooper had, over twenty years, built up an extensive knowledge of the local fauna. He knew the deadly effects of the plant used on Mr. Young."

"And then Cooper set up the bomb and committed suicide?" Steve asked.

"Not exactly," Detective Ryan said.

"What do you mean?" Alex appeared skeptical. "Wouldn't that make sense?"

Ryan hesitated before dropping his next bombshell. "I believe Irwin Cooper was murdered."

There was a collective gasp in the room.

"Are you certain?" Simon said.

"I'm waiting for the autopsy results, but that is my professional opinion."

"And the bomb?" Alex asked.

"I don't think Cooper was responsible for that, either."

"But that would mean . . ." Simon trailed off as he realized what Ryan was saying.

"It would mean that at least two people were involved," the detective said, finishing the sentence for him. He then turned to the PA. "You were responsible for purchasing the Coca-Cola for Luke, weren't you, Yvonne?"

"Yes," the PA said cautiously.

"Forensics has confirmed that the most recent batch of Coca-Cola collected from the restaurant refrigerator contained rat poison," Detective Ryan said.

The PA reddened. "Really?"

"Anne Clarke is your neighbor and a good friend, too, Yvonne, isn't she?" Ryan asked.

"What? Yes . . . but . . ."

"You would know, then, that she's the wife of Tommy Clarke, the driver of the van involved in a terrible accident twenty years ago," Detective Ryan continued.

"Anne Clarke?" Simon repeated, trying to place the name.

"You know her?" the detective asked.

Simon stroked his chin. "Yes . . . Yes, I do. The mad woman who claimed my company was responsible for the crash?"

"She's not crazy," Yvonne said indignantly.

"She tried to destroy the company! And she's a friend of yours?!" The hotel boss couldn't quite believe what he was hearing.

The PA took a step forward. "Anne is a beautiful human being! She cares about others. She is not a psychopath . . . unlike *some* people here."

"What the hell are you implying," Simon began.

"Okay, that's enough," Detective Ryan said. "Yvonne, Anne Clarke still has strong negative feelings about the Faith Company. Right?"

Yvonne took a deep breath and was aware that all eyes were on her. She stepped back.

"I don't know. Maybe," the PA admitted.

Simon stood up. "Why didn't you tell me you knew that woman when I interviewed you?"

Yvonne glared at her boss. "Why would I? I knew you wouldn't have hired me, and I needed the job. Though working here was the worst decision I've ever made." She pointed at Simon. "You are an insufferable human being, and I haven't enjoyed one single second here!"

Simon walked over to her. "You're fired. Get out. Now!"

"Fuck you," Yvonne said, turning to leave.

"Yvonne, wait," Ryan said, striding over to block the PA's exit. "We'll need you to come with us."

Yvonne stared at him. "What?"

"We need to ask you some questions about your relationship with Irwin Cooper," Detective Ryan said.

"What relationship?!" Yvonne exclaimed, horrified. "I never met the man!"

"We're not so sure about that," Detective Yang said. She walked over to grasp the PA's arm.

"Please. I didn't know him." By this time, she was sounding scared.

Ryan attempted to calm her. "Just a few questions, that's all. You're not being arrested." He smiled reassuringly, and after a moment, Yvonne reluctantly allowed herself to be bundled out of the room by Detective Yang.

Silence, as everyone waited for the door to close. Then Simon spoke: "I would never have guessed it. Cooper and that woman conspired together, Detective?"

"It would appear so," Detective Ryan said. "Didn't it strike you as odd that the killings began soon after she came to work for you, Mr. Faith?"

Simon shrugged. "No, I didn't make the connection."

"And you're saying you can prove a relationship between Cooper and the woman?" Steve asked.

"Yes," Detective Ryan confirmed.

"You have the killers?" Alex said. "Job done."

"Not exactly. There is still one loose end."

"A loose end?" Steve repeated.

"Yes. I think there was a third person involved—a man. And I need your help on that," Detective Ryan said, looking at Alex and Steve. "I want you to round up all the male hotel workers who are six feet tall or over so I can interview them."

"Six-foot-plus men?" Alex queried. "Why?"

"We found a fresh shoe print from a Nike Air Force One, size eleven, close to the hut where Gary Young was murdered. Whoever made that print was likely involved in the murders," Detective Ryan said. "Because of the shoe size, I believe the individual was tall and male."

"Fine. But why do you think he's working for my company?" Simon asked.

"Your employees had access to the restaurant kitchen where the cola was stored. He most likely helped Yvonne Lewis move the soda in and out of the hotel," Detective Ryan said.

"You want to find out if any six-foot-plus workers own Nike AF1s?" Steve asked.

"Yes," Ryan said.

"But aren't Air Force Ones, like, the most popular sneakers in the world?" Alex asked.

"They're certainly up there," the detective said. "But the shoe print we found was unlike the print from a typical pair of Air Force Ones. The sneakers we're looking for are forgeries with a very distinctive tread. I'm guessing the suspect bought them without even knowing he'd been ripped off."

FIFTY-SIX

WHILE DETECTIVE RYAN WAS WRAPPING UP the murder investigation, Dave Jupiter was completing his work.

Like Ryan, Jupiter preferred operating alone, but today, he had company. It was protocol for two officers to be present for any essential meetings, which was why Detective Inspector Larry Cowan was accompanying him on the trip up the Parramatta River.

The senior officer's choice of transport was down to him. DI Cowan loved boats and had decided that the two cops should take the ferry from Circular Quay to their rendezvous.

But while Detective Cowan enjoyed the trip, staring out of the boat's full-length glass windows and watching as mangroves replaced riverbank houses, Dave Jupiter remained tense.

The detective had served for seven years on the Australian Federal Police's Fraud Squad, and the current investigation was his biggest yet. He had spent weeks trying to nail down the case. Then, as sometimes happened, everything suddenly came together. Today was a massive day for him; he would have traveled by camel to this meeting if his boss desired it.

The ferry slowed, swung left, and steered into the pier. The detectives waited impatiently for the boat to dock and the other passengers to leave. Then they disembarked.

Detective Cowan scanned the horizon, his gaze taking him past the

Port Bar Pizzeria and the Riverside Eatery and coming to rest on the Wharf Café.

"There it is," the cop said, pointing at the small, nondescript building perched at the end of the pier.

They set off, and upon reaching the café, they immediately recognized the person they were meeting. The man, built like a prizefighter, looked up from studying a plastic-covered menu as the detectives approached.

"Take a seat, gentlemen," he said, and as Cowan and Jupiter settled, a waitress appeared. She placed menus beside the newcomers. "What would you like to drink?"

"Flat white coffees, all round?" the bald man asked, not waiting for the others to answer.

Detective Jupiter looked across at Detective Cowan. It was a delicate moment. When police from different divisions came together for an official meeting, there was always a bit of to and fro . . . the age-old macho ritual of dick waving.

Larry Cowan was a federal detective who had organized the get-together, so if anyone were to take the lead on choosing drinks, it would usually be his prerogative. However, Superintendent Dan Dudley, although only a state cop, outranked him.

"Sounds good," Detective Cowan said after a pause.

"I would suggest a ham and cheese toastie, too. You can't go wrong with one of those," Dudley said. "Am I right on that, Jolene?" the superintendent asked, addressing the waitress by the name tag on her white blouse.

"Good choice." Jolene smiled.

Detective Cowan hesitated. The superintendent may have been his superior, but this was taking the piss.

"I think . . ." he began.

"It's on the house, of course," Dudley added, knowing Larry Cowan's reputation as a tightwad.

"In that case," DI Cowan acquiesced, "I'll have a ham and cheese toastie as well."

"Me too," Jupiter joined in.

"Very good." Jolene jotted down the order and left.

The police waited until the woman was out of earshot. Then Superintendent Dudley began: "Well, gentlemen, we're all busy people, so can we get straight down to this?"

"Yeah, fine," Detective Cowan began, "but let me reiterate the rules of the game."

"An off-the-record, out-of-office meeting to put cards on tables," Superintendent Dudley said, jumping in.

Detective Cowan peered at the superintendent, unhappy that he had been interrupted. "Exactly," he said finally. "Now, Detective Jupiter here has been my boots on the ground for this investigation, so I'll leave it to him to give you a summary of work to date."

Dave Jupiter leaned forward, keen to begin. "Well . . ."

"Three large flat whites," the waitress said, returning and placing one cup beside Jupiter and the others beside Detective Cowan and Superintendent Dudley.

"And your toasties will be along in a jiffy," the waitress added before leaving.

"Maybe we should wait for the food," Superintendent Dudley said.

Detective Jupiter glanced over at Larry Cowan. "Boss?" he said.

Cowan sighed. "Yeah, let's wait."

They sat in silence until Jolene returned with the toasties.

"Anything else?" the waitress asked, putting down the plates and scooping up menus.

"No . . . nothing," the cops chorused.

"Very good," Jolene said and walked away.

"Okay. Let's try again," Detective Cowan said. "Dave?"

"As you know, Superintendent, I'm involved in a money laundering investigation focusing on two areas, the Faith Company and organized crime, specifically the gang currently led by Pietro Guffini—" Detective Jupiter began.

"The Owl," Superintendent Dudley interrupted.

"Yes, that's how he's known." Detective Jupiter attempted to keep the disdain from his voice. Even in the Sydney underworld, the mob boss's alias was a bit of a joke.

"Now, we believe Guffini's organization and the Faith Company are working together to launder drug money through casinos," Detective Jupiter continued.

Dudley raised his hand. "Before you go on, my squad is currently investigating the murder of two of the Faith Company's partners." Dudley stopped and looked from one policeman to the other. "But I assume you know that already."

"Of course. And there may be a link, right, Dave?" Detective Cowan asked.

Jupiter nodded. "Exactly."

Superintendent Dudley considered the new information. "You're saying that these murders have something to do with money laundering?"

"Perhaps," Detective Jupiter said.

"Hmm. Well, our inquiries are leading us in a different direction," Dudley countered.

"I don't think we can rule out anything. Not at this stage," Detective Cowan said.

Dudley stiffened. Had these feds come to interfere in his murder investigations? If so, they should butt out.

"Is that why we're here?" the superintendent asked.

Detective Jupiter looked from Dudley to DI Cowan. "Look, no one's trying to step on anyone else's toes, are they, Larry?"

"Of course not," DI Cowan said, satisfied that he had gotten under Superintendent Dudley's skin.

"Then, I think you'd better get to the point before I lose my patience." Dudley stirred his coffee and licked the spoon without taking his eyes off Detective Cowan.

Cowan sat forward. "Dave thinks one of your officers is assisting in the laundering of that money. Right, Dave?"

Detective Jupiter nodded. "That's correct."

Dudley stared at the two men. "Are you saying that one of my squad is bent?"

"Yes, sir," Jupiter said. He paused and took a deep breath. "Detective Ramesh Ryan, to be precise."

FIFTY-SEVEN

BACK AT THE HOTEL, DETECTIVE YANG maneuvered Yvonne into Ryan's car. She had thought about telling the PA the truth—that they knew she had nothing to do with the murders but had used her to create a diversion. However, Ryan had been adamant. Tell her nothing—not until the real killer had shown his hand.

Detective Yang explained to Yvonne that they needed to "go over a few details" with her at police headquarters and that she should wait in the car while the detective collected her boss.

Yvonne, a woman with a touching faith in authority, nodded. She could do that.

After watching Detective Yang leave, Yvonne made herself comfortable in the back seat. She hadn't slept well last night, worrying about her job. Anne had been right—she should never have taken the position. There had not been a single day when she'd been happy working for the Faith Company. Simon Faith was a terrible boss—mean, bad-tempered, charmless—the worst.

Yvonne yawned and closed her eyes. Now would be an excellent time to get some shut-eye.

IN THE HOTEL, ON THE TOP floor, Felicity Knowles followed the sign to the pool, passing the entrance to the Wellness Center on her way.

When she arrived poolside, the technician opened a small blue plastic case and took out a test tube. She pushed the tube deep into the water and filled it. Removing the vial, Felicity added five drops of phenol liquid and then measured the pH value while testing for chlorine, calcium hardness, and alkalinity levels in the water.

To hotel boss Simon Faith, Felicity was another bureaucratic lackey tasked with checking up on the myriad regulations the government unfairly placed on entrepreneurial endeavors, but Felicity had a passionate belief in the importance of her work. She knew that if the water in a pool was not treated with the correct range of chemicals, harmful microbes would flourish and cause health problems like gastroenteritis and ear, nose, and throat infections, or worse—and if your guests started to drop like flies, where would you be? Closed, that's where. Hemorrhaging money like there was no tomorrow.

After finishing, Felicity put all her tools back into the case and clipped it shut. Later, she would write a report confirming that the water met all safety requirements.

She stood up and, for the first time, took a good look around. It was something she always did after her work was completed. The pool butted up against the far wall and looked over a golf course and the national forest beyond. A bar area to her left was filled with umbrellas that poked above rows of small tables and comfortable-looking chaise longues.

Felicity squinted at the unusual shape between the pool and the far end of the terrace and headed over to the twisted metal monstrosity. What was this thing? A palm tree, and something was standing under it. Felicity smiled. Now she had it. It was a camel. That was it.

The technician leaned one hand on the sculpture. It moved. Felicity took a step back. That was odd. Had they left the statue freestanding? If so, that would be a breach of regulations. She pushed against the sculpture again, and again it moved.

The young woman bent down. The metal was attached to the wall by two brackets, both screwed into the brickwork. Felicity grasped the first bracket. It moved. Then she tried the other, grabbing and shaking it. Two screws fell to the ground, and the bracket swung down.

Felicity picked up the screws. The intention may have been to secure the sculpture, but the wall they'd used had not been well constructed. The plaster had already crumbled, leaving gaping holes.

This was an accident waiting to happen.

DOWNSTAIRS, DETECTIVE YANG STEPPED OUT OF the elevator. It was time for part two of the plan.

She looked around the hotel lobby and spotted a red box marked FIRE.

Heading over, Yang smashed the box's glass with her elbow and pressed the button. The fire sirens and strobing red lights started up almost immediately.

"Fire! Fire!" Detective Yang shouted. "Get out now!"

Hotel staff in the lobby looked around, confused.

"Go!" Yang repeated and waved her hands toward the entrance. "Now!" she yelled.

Finally, some started for the exit.

FIFTY-EIGHT

COMING OUT OF THE ELEVATOR, STEVE Prince sighted Detective Yang and ran over.

"What's going on?" the security chief said, struggling to make himself heard over the noise of the sirens.

"Fire! We have to get everyone out!" Detective Yang said.

Steve glanced at those hurrying to leave.

"But where's the fire?" he said, looking around for signs. "And have you spoken to Mr. Faith about this yet?"

Detective Yang shook her head and ignored his first question. "No time. Come on. Help me!"

Steve frowned. What should he do? One thing was certain—it would be a career-ender if he didn't get his boss out of a fire-ravaged hotel. He could see the headlines now. *Hotel boss burnt to a crisp. Security chief blamed.*

"There's your boss now," Detective Yang said, pointing.

Steve swiveled around to view Simon Faith walking out of the elevator. The security chief sprinted over to him.

"Mr. Faith," Steve said, putting his arm around the CEO's shoulder. "Come with me."

"For Christ's sake, Prince, I'm not an invalid," Faith said, pushing the guard's arm away and striding over to Detective Yang.

"What's going on, Detective?" Simon demanded.

"I'm evacuating people."

"Because there's a fire," Steve said.

Simon ignored his security chief. "That's not your job, Detective. I have people for that." He paused. "And how do we know there's a fire?"

"A cleaner saw smoke on the . . . second floor," Zoe lied. "She's the one who activated the alarm."

"Where's the woman now?" the CEO demanded.

"Outside somewhere, I guess." The detective tried to convey a sense of urgency. "We can waste time looking for her, or we can get everyone out. It could be a false alarm, but do you really want to take that chance?" Zoe demanded.

Simon hesitated. "Fine," he said after a moment.

"Come with me, Mr. Faith," Steve shouted, reaching for his boss's arm.

"Stay here and just . . . do your job," Simon said, brushing the security chief's hand aside. "I can make it on my own, thank you."

Steve shrugged. He was immune to his boss's bad temper. He watched him leave before turning back to Detective Yang. "What next?"

"You deal with the firemen when they arrive; I'll go check upstairs and make sure everyone is out," Detective Yang instructed, running to the stairwell.

LIKE SIMON FAITH, FELICITY KNOWLES WAS initially unsure whether the fire alarm was just a drill. But, as the sirens continued, she decided that maybe discretion was the better part of valor and headed out.

Reaching the corridor, Felicity saw a man dressed in a hotel security guard uniform step out from the elevators.

The man saw her and hurried over. "You need to go, madam," he said.

"That's what I was about to do, but . . ." she began, her voice trailing off as she looked the guard over. He was about her age and handsome. Very handsome.

Because she was so absorbed with her work, Felicity's social life had always taken a back seat. Beneath her logical and no-nonsense exterior, though, she had a heart primed for romance. Felicity believed that love could rear its beautiful smiling face anywhere, anytime; lo and behold, it just had.

All thoughts of fires, brackets, and loose screws vanished as Felicity peered into the man's sparkling brown eyes. "What's happening?" she asked coyly.

"You have to get out," the man repeated.

"Why?" Felicity asked.

"Because there's a fire," the guard said slowly.

"Sorry, yes, of course," Felicity said and paused, thinking of a way to extricate herself from the hole she had just dug. She didn't want the future love of her life to assume she was a moron.

"Yes, I know that, of course," she said, grinning like an idiot. "What I mean is, could it be a false alarm?"

"In my line of work, it's best to assume that the danger is real until informed otherwise," the guard said.

"And you haven't been informed otherwise?"

"Not yet, no," the man said.

"Oh," Felicity said.

"So?" The guard looked at her askance. Why wasn't this woman moving?

"I'll be off, then," Felicity said, racking her brain for a way to extend the encounter.

"So, should I use the stairs or the elevator?" Felicity asked finally.

"The stairs."

"Right," Felicity said and waited a few more seconds before deciding that she did have to go.

"Good luck," she said, walking away before stopping and spinning back around.

"Excuse me," Felicity shouted at the guard.

"Yes?" he said.

"Do you know when this will all be over?" Felicity asked and smiled, revealing her best feature—a perfect set of glistening white teeth.

"Over?" the man repeated. "No idea. But please go as quickly as you can."

Felicity's smile faltered as she waited for him to say something more . . . something like, "After all this is over, maybe we could meet again?"

But "go" was all he repeated.

"Okay . . . the stairs," Felicity said, and feeling deflated, she pulled open the stairwell door.

FIFTY-NINE

OUTSIDE, THE FIRE TRUCK SKIDDED TO a halt. It had arrived in just seven minutes. The firefighters would have made even better time if TV crews and reporters, there about the murders, hadn't blocked the driveway.

Senior Firefighter Jason O'Neil stared through the windshield. He saw that a crowd had gathered at the marked fire assembly points. That was good.

Jumping down from the truck, the firefighter instructed three of his team to unroll the hoses while two more were to search the hotel to remove any remaining stragglers.

UPSTAIRS, DETECTIVE RAMESH RYAN PEERED THROUGH the shower room door into the locker area. Here, rows of black metal cabinets lined the walls of the empty room.

The detective took a deep breath. Had he miscalculated, or worse still, had he been entirely wrong? Ryan had difficulty coping with that concept. While he accepted that some parts of his life were in shambles—as his mother liked to point out—the detective knew he had skills. He was an expert at solving crimes, and in this arena, rarely, if ever, did he get things wrong. Moreover, the plan he had hatched and explained to Detective Yang should have been foolproof.

Detective Ryan had pointed the finger at Yvonne, identifying her as a coconspirator in the murders of Young and Saker, knowing it was a lie. The

PA was innocent, but the detective had done it to lull the guilty party into a false sense of security.

Ryan believed he knew who this guilty party was, but knowing something and proving it in a court of law were two different things. He had *some* evidence, but Detective Ryan needed to catch the perp red-handed—hence the plan.

The screaming hotel sirens indicated that Zoe had done her part—setting off the fire alarm to clear the building. But Ryan was banking on his instincts that the killer would be the last to leave. The detective knew that since the meeting in Simon Faith's office, the killer would have business to attend to.

Finally, the locker room door opened.

Relieved, Detective Ryan slid back out of sight. The perp would be looking around the room now, ensuring no one else was there. After establishing the coast was clear, it would take him no time to open his locker and retrieve the Nike AF1 sneakers.

Detective Ryan lifted his gun and readied himself to strike.

That's when his cell phone rang.

Detective Ryan swore under his breath. The phone was muted, but since her health scare, his mother's number had been reprogrammed to allow her calls to come through.

He quickly pressed the screen to end the call, but it was too late. Alex Riva dropped the trainers and yanked his Smith & Wesson .38 pistol from its holster.

"Alex, put the gun down. You are under arrest," Detective Ryan yelled as he broke cover.

"Oh, yeah?" the guard said, his weapon trained on the detective. "Come on, then, arrest me!"

Stalemate . . . or it would have been if Detective Zoe Yang hadn't rushed in at that moment, her weapon out. She pointed it at Alex. "Drop the gun!" she shouted.

Alex looked from one detective to the other. He understood immediately what had been going on. He had been an idiot. The cops had used Yvonne as a stalking horse to lure him into believing they had the killers. He should have waited to pick up the shoes but had been panicked by their talk of the identifying soles on the bottom of his fake Nikes.

"Put the weapon down, Riva," Detective Ryan repeated.

Alex Riva fingered his pistol. He was prepared to shoot Ryan or the woman, but accepted he wouldn't have time to deal with both—there might be another a way out. He had watched enough crime documentaries to know that, in reality, police were reluctant to initiate a gunfight.

Alex twisted his body around to look at Detective Yang. Though the weapon was pointed at him, it was swaying slightly. She was the weak link.

The guard stepped closer to the female cop. "Okay. You got me," he said.

Alex saw the woman detective relax just a little. Now, he thought, one more step, and he could overpower her . . . probably. But it was still a gamble.

Then things changed again.

Two firefighters, Jessica Mooney and Brandon Cook, barreled into the room. On their way up, they had passed a young woman who'd told them she had seen a handsome security guard on the pool deck—obviously, the area needed to be evacuated.

"Okay, folks," Cook shouted, "we want you all down . . ." He stopped, taking in the scene for the first time. There were three people, all pointing guns at each other. It was like something from *Reservoir Dogs*.

The hesitation gave Alex all the time he needed. He brought his gun down hard on Detective Yang's hand. Pain shot through the young detective's arm. She released her weapon. As it fell, Alex folded his arm around her neck and jammed his pistol hard against the side of her face.

"Move!" he shouted.

Dragging the reluctant detective through the open door to the corridor, Alex stopped to lock the door behind him. Detective Ryan immediately tried to follow, but the door wouldn't budge. He turned to the stunned firefighters.

"Either of you got an axe?"

SIXTY

Downstairs, firefighter Jason O'Neil, was trying to find out exactly what was happening.

"Everyone's been evacuated," Steve confirmed proudly.

"Good," O'Neil said. "On which floor was the alarm set off?"

"This one," Steve said, pointing to a red box with its front glass panel smashed in.

The firefighter walked over. "Did anyone report smoke or flames in the building?" he asked as he examined the smashed glass.

"A cleaner, apparently," Prince said.

"Where is that person now?" the firefighter asked.

"No idea," the guard admitted.

It was a huge red flag for O'Neil. Whoever had activated the alarm hadn't hung around to offer assistance. In his experience, this was unusual, where the threat of fire was real. Considering that the automated alarm had gone off, he made a judgement call.

"Turn the sirens off," O'Neil said to Steve.

"You sure?"

"Yes. False alarm," O'Neil confirmed.

As the building suddenly went quiet, Ryan was already in the corridor, having been aided by the firefighters, but knew he had no time to lose. As he quickly headed toward the pool area, he thought about how Alex should have been locked up in the back of a paddy wagon by now. Best laid plans, Ryan thought, angry at how things had turned out, but regret was a luxury he couldn't afford. If he was going to be of any help to Zoe, he needed to focus.

Ryan reached the pool deck. Alex, with his arm still around Detective Yang's throat, was standing at the far end, clearly looking for a means of escape. He turned when he heard Ryan's entrance, leaning back against the gold *C & P* sculpture as he raised his gun once again and put it to Zoe's temple.

"Stay where you are!" Alex yelled.

Ryan fingered the trigger of his Glock. Behind him, he heard chatter from a radio. The firefighters had followed the detective to the pool and were now radioing to explain what was happening. He just hoped they had the sense to stay back.

"You've got nowhere to go, Alex. It's over," Detective Ryan called out.

"I don't think so, Ryan. Now, I need you to get me out of here. And we best do that before the cavalry arrives."

"You honestly think I'm going to help you?" Ryan said, reaching into his pocket with his free hand.

"Sure. Or I'll kill her," Alex said, jamming the pistol harder into the side of Detective Yang's face. Zoe winced.

"But you'll be dead, too. Is that really what you want?"

"Life in prison isn't much of an alternative."

Silence as Ryan appeared to be considering his options. "Okay. We'll do this together if you answer one question," he said, pressing his finger on his cell phone screen.

"Shoot," said Alex. "Metaphorically, that is."

"Was it because of the crash?" Ryan asked.

"What?"

"The reason you killed Gary Young and Luke Saker?"

"Duh, yeah . . ."

"But you were just eight years old when the accident happened."

"They killed my mom and dad and fucked up the rest of my life!" Alex cried.

"Who? Young and Saker?" Ryan sounded dubious.

"Come on, Detective, don't play dumb. They were all in it together."

"The Faith Company?"

"Right in one."

"No doubt?" Detective Ryan asked.

"No doubt. They fixed the van's brakes." He stopped. "Okay. Enough talk. It's your turn. Get me out of here . . . NOW!"

THE ARMORED BEARCAT TRUCK'S HEAVY METAL doors swung open to disgorge the New South Wales Tactical Unit—six masked, helmeted men wearing gray camouflage uniforms. They carried an array of weapons: holstered Glock Model 22s, assault rifles fitted with optical sights, and Heckler & Koch UMP submachine guns.

The cops were all muscular and tall, but one, their leader, towered above the rest. He was at least six feet eight inches tall, his shoulders stretching out for an eternity, each of his legs appearing to be hewed from the trunk of a massive tree—Sergeant Tyson "The Crusher" Donovan.

The Crusher signaled for his men to wait as he sprinted to the hotel's front entrance, pushed it open, and entered.

"Who's in charge?" The Crusher shouted to the small knot of men standing in the center of the lobby. They looked at each other, unsure who should answer the giant.

"Well, I'm the CEO," Simon Faith said finally.

The Crusher walked over to the hotel boss. "I don't need you. I need the operational head," he said.

That was a problem. Although Jason O'Neil was in charge of the firefighters, his chain of command was through the fire department. Frank de Basio headed up the ambulancemen, but they didn't get involved with hostage discussions. That left only one man.

"I guess that would be me," Steve said a little uncertainly.

The Crusher peered at the guard. "And who are you exactly?"

"Steve Prince. Head of hotel security."

The Crusher snorted. He despised security guards, regarding them as pompous uniformed idiots. But if needs must. "Right, then . . . where are we on this hostage situation?" he asked.

"It's not good," Steve said.

"SHOOT HIM," DETECTIVE YANG YELLED.

Alex clamped his hand over the young woman's mouth. "Quiet, bitch."

Detective Ryan shook his head. He felt like he was in a B movie with everyone spouting clichéd lines. He looked from the guard to Zoe. His partner's eyes were wide open, but not from fear. Staring directly at him, she was trying to signal something . . . but what?

"What do you want me to do, Alex?" Ryan asked.

"Where's your vehicle?"

"In the car park."

"Good. Put down your gun and give me the keys. Then tell everyone to step away, and your partner and I will go downstairs," Alex said.

"And drive off in my car?" Detective Ryan asked.

"That's the idea."

"Alex . . . even if they allow you to get to the vehicle, they'll just follow you out."

"If they do anything, I'll kill her, okay?" Alex said, jamming his gun once more into Yang's head. Ryan held his hands out, palms up, in a conciliatory gesture.

"Okay. So, let's say you make it out . . . what happens to Detective Yang?"

"When I know I'm safe, I let her go, of course," Alex said.

"Really?"

"I only kill people who deserve it."

"Like Irwin Cooper?" Detective Ryan asked.

"That was your fault. If you hadn't gone snooping around . . . Look, Cooper did what he wanted to do. He got his revenge so he was happy." Alex paused. "Now, can we do this?"

"Sure . . . but like I said . . ." Detective Ryan began.

"You'd better make sure it works, Detective," Alex interrupted. "And first up, tell those two not to do anything stupid," he said, indicating the firefighters.

Detective Ryan twisted around. "Do not attempt to interfere. You got that?"

The firefighters exchanged glances and nodded, neither keen to get shot.

"So, we're all on the same page then, Ryan?" Alex asked.

"Yeah," the detective said, staring at Zoe. Alex still had his hand clamped over her mouth, but she was rolling her eyes at him. What was she trying to signal?

"Okay. Put your gun down and toss over the keys," Alex shouted.

Detective Ryan put the Glock on the ground before reaching for his car keys.

SIXTY-ONE

How well you thought things were going depended on your viewpoint. The hostage situation was either being resolved in a logical and nonviolent way, or a cowardly Homicide Squad detective was freeing a thrice-murdering psychopath.

If the seriousness of the situation hadn't been so apparent, firefighters Mooney and Cook might have felt like they were on the set of a film. Neither of them had ever seen a gun in close proximity, except hanging on the hip of a uniformed policeman, and they'd certainly never seen one actually pointed at someone. At this point, being in a burning building would have been preferable.

They watched as Ryan searched his pockets. Then he raised his hands. "I don't have the keys," the detective called out.

"Do you expect me to believe that?" Alex shouted.

"No, honestly, Detective Yang has them."

Alex was torn. Was this a trick? He stared at Ryan, wild-eyed, the gun shaking slightly as he tried to decide what to do.

"Please, Alex. I'm telling you the truth. Check her pockets," Ryan pleaded.

Alex hesitated and then removed his arm from around Zoe's throat. He began searching her jacket. Detective Yang threw her partner a look.

"Back pocket," she instructed her captor.

Alex moved back slightly and, with his free hand, reached for the keys. As he did so, Zoe spun away. In one coordinated move, she knocked the gun from his hand and gave him an almighty shove. Losing his balance, Alex fell back against the heavy metal sculpture behind him, loosening the screws in the only remaining bracket, which popped out of the parapet and fell to the ground.

Freed from the last brace, *C & P* tipped forward, putting all its weight onto the low wall, which, in turn, began to give way.

Feeling the sculpture move, an already off-balance Alex tried to steady the metal monstrosity, but it was useless. As the last bricks fell to the ground, so too did the gold eyesore and a terrified Alex Riva along with it. Hurtling down from the top floor of the hotel.

DOWNSTAIRS IN THE LOBBY, EVERYONE HEARD Alex Riva's blood-curdling scream.

There was a shocked silence.

"What the fuck was that?" Crusher asked as Jason O'Neil's cell phone rang.

Steve looked a little bewildered. "Sounded like a scream," he said.

O'Neil waved for silence as he listened to his phone. "Right," he said after a moment and hung up.

"Someone's gone off the top. South side." He pointed in the direction of the restaurant as he said it. Crusher signaled to his men.

"This way!"

THE COUNCIL HAD REJECTED SIMON FAITH's original plans for the hotel's Sahara Restaurant, so the CEO was forced to agree to something with a much smaller footprint.

Knowing he couldn't market the restaurant simply on its size, Simon had changed tack and sunk funds into what he would claim was the best-designed hotel restaurant ever.

Although he had not achieved this lofty ambition, there was no denying the restaurant was unusual.

Tall date palms were dotted around the room, their trunks marked with the pruned stubs of old leaf bases and crowned by shining pinnate leaves. They hung over teal-colored fabric umbrellas, wicker tables, and sand-colored chairs. The full-length windows were arranged in a half circle and framed by Doric columns, which were more Greek than Arabic. Above, the restaurant's glass roof was shaped like a pyramid and designed to retract, opening the room to the sky.

Today, the roof had been folded back in anticipation of the six-course banquet Simon Faith had intended to serve at the now-postponed hotel reopening. Only a canvas awning, designed to shade the area partially, remained. The forced delay had been a catastrophe for the hotel boss but a massive stroke of luck for Alex Riva. When he and the gold *C & P* sculpture had plunged headlong over the low parapet, *C & P* had fallen unhindered into the restaurant. Alex, however, had gone through the awning, which somewhat broke his fall.

When Ryan, Yang, and the two firefighters arrived, Alex's eyes were closed and his body was contorted, but the guard still appeared to be breathing.

"Alex?" Ryan asked, leaning over the body. He expected no reply and got none.

"What do you think?" Detective Yang asked as Ryan stood up.

"Well, he's alive and—" Detective Ryan began but was interrupted by a groan. Looking down, the detective saw that Alex's eyes had flicked open. The guard lifted one finger, pointed it at Ryan, and motioned with a twist of his head for the detective to come closer. The cop bent down again.

"I got them all . . . right?" Alex said and smiled. A moment later, his eyes closed, and he again drifted into oblivion.

"Hey!" a voice shouted from behind.

The cops and the firefighters swiveled around to see the giant figure of Tyson Donovan, aka The Crusher, sprinting toward them.

"Is that him?" Crusher asked, coming to a halt and pointing at Alex.

Detective Ryan stared at the newcomer. Although he had never met the Sergeant face to face, he knew of The Crusher's impressive reputation.

"I'm Detective Ryan, the lead detective, and you must be . . ."

"Sergeant Donovan, Tactics and Rescue Unit." He pointed down at Alex Riva. "He doesn't look good."

"Depends on your perspective," Brandon Cook noted, still shaken from the events of the last half hour.

The Crusher gave the firefighter a dismissive look before returning his attention to Detective Ryan. "The only perp?" Crusher asked.

"Yes," said Ryan.

"Certain?" Crusher queried.

"Definitely," the detective confirmed.

"Hostage situation?" Crusher continued.

"Yes. I was the hostage," Detective Yang said.

"Gunpoint?" Crusher queried.

Detective Yang nodded.

"Dealt with, then?" Crusher said, looking around.

"Affirmative," Detective Ryan said, aware that he was now mimicking Sergeant Donovan's infectious staccato speech pattern.

"Good," Crusher said, "but best wait for my squad in the future."

"Will do," Detective Ryan concurred.

"I'll be off, then," the big man said and strode past two medics carrying a gurney.

SIXTY-TWO

SIMON FAITH AND STEVE PRINCE WAITED in the lobby for The Crusher's return. The big man had made it clear that they were not to accompany him upstairs.

"This is an official operational matter, and you are not qualified," Crusher said after Steve objected to being left behind. His tone and look sent shivers down the security chief's back.

After Crusher went upstairs, Steve tried to save face with his boss. "That fucking Donovan's got a cheek. I should be the one checking things out."

"Why didn't you, then?" Simon asked.

Steve hesitated. "Well, I would have, but there are already too many people in there."

"I see," the hotel boss said, not buying Steve's excuse for a moment.

"So, you didn't have any inkling about Riva?" Simon asked.

"No." Steve shrugged. "Why would I?"

"Well, you are my head of security, and, in light of this . . ." Simon stopped and searched for the right word, ". . . this incident . . . maybe somebody should be questioning your fitness for the role."

Steve frowned. That fat, bald asshole honestly expected him to have spotted Alex Riva for what he was? He tried to contain his anger. Steve hated his boss, but he liked his job and wanted to keep it.

"I think you're confusing me with HR. Mental instability is the kind of thing they're supposed to pick up on. They have all those checks, don't they? Like that inkblot thing?"

"The Rorschach test?" Simon said.

"Yes, that's the one," Steve said. "That should have caught him out, surely?"

"Maybe," said Simon begrudgingly. Yes, he was prepared to admit that, and if heads had to roll—and roll, they would—then it was easier to hire a new head of Human Resources. They were a dime a dozen. On the other hand, even a moderately competent head of security, someone like Steve Prince, was more difficult to recruit and keep.

"Do you think they were wrong about Yvonne Lewis? Or were there three people involved?" Steve asked.

"Shit. I forgot about her." Simon shook his head. "Yet another disastrous decision from the HR department."

Steve shrugged. "Anyway, at least everything's under control now."

"Yep, under control," a booming voice repeated from behind.

They turned to see The Crusher emerging from the elevator and barreling over to them.

"You've checked it all out, then?" Simon asked.

"Yes. Homicide has the situation in hand. The perp will be taken to the hospital under police guard. And that means my work here is done."

Without another word, Crusher turned and headed for the door.

There was silence as the security chief and his boss watched the giant leave. Simon turned to Steve and waited.

"What?" Steve asked.

"Is there a reason you're still here?"

The security guard looked confused.

"The crisis is over, you moron. Bring everyone back in."

"Yes, sir," Steve replied with a tight smile.

"If anyone needs me, I'll be at home."

With that, Simon strode off, leaving Steve quietly seething.

SIXTY-THREE

THE COPS EMERGED FROM THE HOTEL and headed for Ryan's car, where Detective Yang had left Yvonne waiting for over an hour. In the distance, they could both see Simon Faith standing at the rear of his Range Rover. They watched as he put a leather carry-all into the passenger seat before driving off. They walked on in silence for a moment.

"That was a nice maneuver you pulled off," Ryan said.

"Thanks." Zoe smiled. It was the first time Ryan had complimented her.

"How did you know the sculpture was unstable?" he asked.

"I saw the bracket was loose. But I didn't know for sure that it wouldn't hold," she admitted.

"You took a big risk. Don't do it again." He smiled.

Zoe smiled back as they reached the car.

YVONNE LOOKED RELIEVED TO SEE THEM.

"You said you'd be back in a few minutes," she said sulkily to Detective Yang through her open window. "You've been away ages, and all these police cars and tanks arrived. What's been going on?"

"Sorry about that, Yvonne," Detective Ryan said as he slid into the driver's seat and started the ignition. "Thank you for waiting. But we won't need to interview you after all."

Detective Yang opened the car door, and Yvonne looked at her incredulously.

"I waited all this time, and now you don't even want to talk to me?" She sounded almost disappointed.

"You've already helped us more than you could ever know," Ryan said from the front seat.

It was clear to the PA that she wouldn't be getting any more from him than that. Still, she didn't move. "Well, the least you can do is drive me home," she suggested hopefully.

The detectives shared a look.

"Yvonne has been extremely cooperative," Zoe offered.

Ryan knew the women had him cornered. "Fine. We'll drop Yvonne off and then head to Alex Riva's apartment. We can pick your car up on the way back."

Detective Yang nodded and closed Yvonne's door before getting into the car beside Ryan.

"Alex Riva. You said Alex Riva. You think he's involved?"

The detectives remained silent.

"Well, clearly something happened for all those emergency services people to have turned up," she persevered. "Plus, I saw the Channel Seven News van. So, what's been going on?"

"I'm afraid you'll have to wait for the evening bulletin." Ryan grinned.

There was a small huff of dissatisfaction from the back seat. "Well, whoever it was involved in those murders, they failed," Yvonne said, almost to herself, as she stared out the window of the moving car.

"I wouldn't call three dead a failure," Detective Yang said. "At least not from the killer's perspective."

"But whoever did it didn't get them all, did they? They were clearly targeting the Faith Company partners, and they missed the most important one."

As he maneuvered the car around a wide bend, Ryan thought this over. He hit the brakes and swung the car into a turnout, throwing up a shower of loose gravel.

"Shit!" He pounded the steering wheel and looked at Zoe. "Alex said something just before he lost consciousness."

"What?" Zoe looked at him, bewildered.

"He said, 'I got them all.'"

The young detective shook her head, still not understanding.

"Don't you see? Simon Faith is still alive, but Alex was . . . content, somehow. I didn't think anything of it, but why would he say 'I got them all' when he'd only gotten two?"

Zoe's eyes widened as she realized what Ryan was suggesting.

"You think he's set some kind of trap for Simon Faith?"

"I'd bet my badge on it. And we know he's got a thing for explosives."

He paused. Then: "Faith's car! He was working on it earlier. Remember Steve Prince said it wasn't part of his job?"

Ryan spun around to speak to the wide-eyed PA in the back seat.

"Yvonne! What's your boss's address?"

"YOU'VE GOT TO BE KIDDING," SIMON Faith muttered as he read the text on his phone. The meeting time and place with The Owl were changing. Now, he was to be picked up at home.

Simon thought about that. Did he really want those guys coming to his house? Was nothing sacred?

The hotel boss sighed. He knew this wouldn't be happening if he hadn't made a colossal mistake. It had now been confirmed that the killings had nothing to do with Pietro Guffini. The crime kingpin hadn't carried them out in retribution for a so-called "accountancy error." Guffini may not even have known about Simon skimming the cash . . . an extra to the agreed fee for laundering the crime boss's takings. Simon slapped his forehead in frustration. What had he done? Nothing much. He'd just gone and told one of the most dangerous men in Australia that he'd "accidentally" been misplacing his money. What a schmuck!

He thought some more. On the other hand, it wasn't entirely his fault. Who would have thought that two morons would go on a killing spree and murder his partners? Simon moistened his lips. Irwin Cooper was a sociopath, of course, and in his opinion, quite capable of murder. Alex Riva, though, was another matter. Simon hadn't seen that coming. He liked the guy. He was a good worker, always doing things above and beyond.

The car hit a bump in the bitumen, and Simon grasped the wheel tightly. One day he would make the council repair this shitty road. He turned up the volume on the radio. Music relaxed him, and he certainly needed that on a day like today.

SIXTY-FOUR

"**P**UT YOUR SEAT BELT ON, YVONNE . . . now!" Detective Ryan shouted. The brusque tone was unexpected, but he was stressed. He was no great shakes as a driver and was now having to put his unimpressive skills to the test.

Detective Yang looked up from her iPhone. "Turn right in four hundred yards," she instructed.

"No, go straight ahead," Yvonne ordered as she clipped her belt.

Detective Yang spun around. "What?"

"Don't follow the directions on Google. It'll take us the long way."

"You sure?" Yang asked.

"I'm certain. I've driven Simon home a few times when he's had too much to drink. I learned the shortcut from him."

"Straight ahead it is, then," Detective Ryan said, speeding past the turnoff.

"Since no one needs me for directions anymore, I'll give Faith another try," Detective Yang said, tapping in the number on her cell. She waited.

"Still no answer," she said after a few moments.

"Take a left. There," Yvonne said suddenly.

The detective spun the car wheel around and accelerated up a gravel road.

Yvonne leaned forward. "There he is," she said, pointing at a vehicle in the distance.

"You sure?" Detective Yang asked.

"I'd know that car anywhere." Yvonne reached for her cell. "My turn to call," she said. "He won't answer unknown numbers, but he knows mine."

She listened for a moment. "Mr. Faith, Yvonne Lewis."

"I thought you were in jail," Simon said, turning down the music.

"Look, I can't explain that now. You need to get out of that car!" The urgency in her voice was unmistakable.

"What?" Simon replied. It seemed that Yvonne was losing the plot.

"Put him on speaker!" Yang ordered the PA, who dutifully complied.

"Simon, it's Detective Yang. You need to pull over immediately and get out of the car!"

"What the … what are you *talking* about?" Simon sounded dumbfounded.

"Because if you don't, you're going to die!" Yvonne yelled from the back seat.

"What?" Simon said.

"STOP THE CAR!" Detective Ryan shouted with as much authority as he could muster.

THE RANGE ROVER SUDDENLY SWERVED ONTO the soft verge and abruptly pulled to a stop as Simon waited for the cop car to catch up.

It sped past and skidded to a halt just in front of the SUV. The detectives jumped out and sprinted to Faith's car.

Ryan pulled open the driver's door. "Get out, Mr. Faith."

Simon didn't move. He wanted answers first. "What's going on?"

"We think there's a bomb in your car," Detective Ryan said.

"You're joking," he said.

"Do I look like I'm joking?" Ryan asked.

The hotel boss stared at the grim-faced detective.

"Get out of the fucking car before we're all killed!" Detective Yang cried, frustrated by his inaction. Simon quickly unbuckled his belt and reached over to the passenger seat to grab his Gladstone case before clambering out.

"Get in the car!" Ryan instructed Simon, pointing at his Hyundai.

Simon did as he was told. Detective Ryan looked over at Yang. "Drive three hundred yards, park, and stop any traffic," he said.

"You're not coming?" Detective Yang asked, confused.

"I need to check something. It'll only take a minute."

Yang hesitated.

Ryan shook his head. "We're wasting time, Zoe, do as I say."

Concerned, Detective Yang nonetheless decided to trust her partner.

"Don't be long," she said. Ryan nodded.

DETECTIVE RYAN WAITED FOR YANG TO reach his vehicle and get in.

So far, so good, he thought as the car drove off and stopped a distance away. Everyone was now out of range of any explosion. Everyone except him.

Detective Ryan walked to the back of the Range Rover and opened the trunk.

Empty.

He lifted the floor space cover and peered in at the spare, running his hands around the tire. Nothing. The wheel was clamped hard to the floor, so there was no space underneath.

Walking back, Ryan opened the driver's door and got in. He looked around. The passenger seat was empty, and there was nothing on the dash. He leaned forward and unclicked the glove compartment. Inside, there was an owner's manual and a plastic folder.

Ryan took the folder out and opened it to find registration and insurance papers, a pen, and a notebook. He flicked through the pad—just blank pages.

The detective closed the glove box. Where else would someone hide a bomb? He looked down at the central console and opened it. There was just a box of tissues and a flashlight. No explosive.

Closing the console, Ryan kneeled and peered under the driver's seat. Nothing.

He moved across to look underneath the passenger seat. Nothing again.

Twisting around, Detective Ryan stared at the back seats. They were empty, too.

Had he been wrong, he wondered? Not about the bomb, perhaps, but Alex Riva could have planted it anywhere—at Simon Faith's house or in his office. His mind was racing. He should call the bomb squad and let them handle it. That's what Zoe would do. That was what any other cop would do.

And yet, he knew there was no way he was going to let Alex outsmart him. His ego wouldn't allow it. Damn! One day it would get him killed, he thought grimly.

Ryan recalled the gathering in Simon Faith's office. Alex had come in talking about a bracket for the fire extinguisher. The memory had barely registered when he twisted around in his seat to scan the rear passenger area. Then he saw it—a red fire extinguisher secured to the back of the front passenger seat.

Ryan jumped out of the Range Rover, opened the back door, and slid in. Leaning forward, he took a good look. The extinguisher was red, the same color as the trace of paint he had found on the desk in Irwin Cooper's caravan.

Detective Ryan peered closely at the device. He could see brush strokes where red paint had been reapplied to the head of the extinguisher. But Cooper had done an excellent job. Anyone just glancing at it would never see that it had been tampered with.

The detective put his ear against the metal. He heard a low ticking. The countdown must have begun with the car's motion when it had been driven out of the car park. It was clearly on a timer, but just how long it had left, Ryan couldn't know. He checked his watch and remembered that when Google Maps had re-routed, the time to the destination had been ten minutes. If Alex had intended the bomb to go off as Simon Faith arrived home, then by Ryan's calculations, he had maybe half a minute until detonation.

SIXTY-FIVE

DETECTIVE RYAN SPRINTED FROM THE RANGE Rover.

His feet smashed down on the gravel.

Twenty . . . forty . . . sixty . . . eighty . . . one hundred yards.

Not far now, and he should be safe.

A deafening bang followed a startlingly bright flash of light.

Ryan felt like Mike Tyson had punched him in the back.

The detective shot through the air and landed face down on the gravel road, his eyes closed, his ears ringing.

Darkness.

Ryan heard someone say something but couldn't make it out.

He blinked his eyes, trying to focus.

Someone gripped his arm, helping him up.

Zoe had her arms around his shoulders, supporting him.

Ryan shook his head, trying to clear his ears, which felt like they were stuffed with cotton wool.

"What did you say?" he asked.

"I said, can you make it to the car?" Zoe said.

"I think so," Ryan said.

Holding tight to Zoe, he took one step forward. And another. Then another. And one more. He straightened. He didn't feel so bad.

"I'm okay," the detective said, freeing himself from Zoe's grip before twisting to look back at the Range Rover.

Flames poked up from the twisted, smoldering wreckage. It was in far worse shape than he was.

Zoe yanked open the car door.

"Sit down," she ordered.

Ryan lowered himself into the passenger seat.

Zoe got in, too.

"You all right, Detective?" Yvonne said from the back seat. The color had drained from her face.

"Yes, I'm good."

Ryan brushed down his collar. "This suit could do with a dry clean, though."

"You think you've got it bad. I'm going to need a new car," Simon said with a weak smile, though he was clearly shaken. His ex-PA, however, didn't appreciate his gallows humor and shot him a filthy look.

From outside came the sound of approaching sirens.

Detective Ryan reached for the door.

"Sit tight, Ryan," Detective Yang said, pushing the driver's door open. "The cavalry is here. I'll deal with them."

Ryan nodded. "Okay."

Zoe was welcome to handle the new arrivals—the uniformed cops who would block off the road, the firefighters who would douse the car down, and the bomb squad who would prod and poke around before coming to the same conclusion as Detective Ryan—that the danger was over.

Ryan opened the passenger door and yelled, "Zoe, can you cancel the ambulance? I won't need it!"

"You sure?" she shouted as a marked police car pulled up opposite her.

"Positive. A couple of scratches. I'm fine," he assured her.

"So, what now?" Yvonne said as Ryan closed the car door.

"We'll organize for a patrol car to take you both home. But don't leave the country," he said with a small smile. "We'll need to talk to you about what happened here."

Yvonne nodded solemnly while Simon was silent. He understandably had a lot on his mind.

Detective Ryan's phone rang.

"Ryan," he said, answering it and listening. "Yes, Superintendent, I've got that . . . immediately . . . right," he said.

SIXTY-SIX

DETECTIVE RYAN'S SILVER HYUNDAI WOUND ITS way along the coastline. Inside, the two police officers didn't speak. Detective Yang discreetly glanced at her partner, who appeared to be lost in thought.

"You okay?" she asked.

"Yeah, fine."

"You sure? No one would blame you if you wanted to take the rest of the day off."

"Not necessary," Ryan responded. He didn't take his eyes off the road ahead.

Zoe considered leaving it at that, but the thought was fleeting.

"It's just . . . you've been very quiet."

"It was stupid not waiting for the bomb squad to search the Range Rover," he said, by way of explanation.

Zoe did a double take. Ramesh Ryan was admitting a mistake.

"Well, I guess after Irwin Cooper's caravan exploded, it may have been prudent to exercise a greater degree of caution . . . .. Then again, I don't think caution has ever been part of your MO."

Ryan allowed himself a small smile. He shot Zoe a quick look.

"Maybe not."

"Anyway, you didn't tell me why Dudley needed to see us so urgently."

"He didn't say. Probably wants to reprimand me for taking an 'unacceptable risk.'"

"Well, if he does, I'll tell him to back off," Zoe said indignantly. "No one else could've put those puzzle pieces together the way you did. Simon Faith would be dead if it wasn't for you."

Ryan raised an eyebrow at his partner's outburst.

"Careful. You wouldn't want me to get a swelled head," he said.

"Credit where credit's due," she replied.

"And just when we're starting to get along, you're going to leave me." Ryan threw her a rueful look. Detective Yang was silent for a moment.

"Actually . . . I've decided to stay."

"You have?" Ryan said, surprised.

"In Gwyneth Paltrow's immortal words, Louise and I are consciously uncoupling."

Ryan nodded, and Zoe thought she could detect a look of relief. Then she had a thought.

"You didn't tell Dudley I was thinking of leaving, did you? Maybe that's why he wants to see us."

"Actually, it's not us, it's me. Dudley said he only wanted to see me. I'll drop you back to your car," Ryan said, pressing his foot hard on the accelerator.

SIXTY-SEVEN

THE PATROL CAR STOPPED, AND SIMON Faith, case in hand, got out. As the vehicle drove off, the hotel boss hurried to the front door, pushing his key into the lock. Finally, he could have a much-needed shower.

Opening the door, Simon stood for a moment in the hallway. It had been an incredible few days. His two partners, men he had known for years, were dead, and if it hadn't been for that cop, Ryan, he'd have joined them. He smiled to himself. He always had been a lucky bastard. Still, the CEO believed you made your own luck, which was why it was his name on the side of the building and not those other two losers.

The funerals would probably take place next week once the coroner had released their bodies. Simon would be delivering eulogies, of course. He would recount how they had worked together, succeeding against all odds, and how their contributions had been so crucial to the success of the Faith Company.

None of that was true, though. Well, maybe the bit about their helping to build the business at the start, but that was only for the money they were prepared to put into the fledgling company. The inspiration, drive, and vision had always come from him.

Simon continued walking and entered the living room. It was a soulless, sterile space filled with expensive furniture and impersonal knick-knacks. That didn't bother him, though. He had bought the vast mansion, with its state-of-the-art kitchen, viewing room, terrace, spa, and outdoor pool, for only one reason—as a prop. It was a way of showing the world how successful he was and would continue to be, despite the murders, the bombings, and being forced to postpone the hotel's reopening.

Nothing could nor would stop Simon's rise and rise.

The ding-dong of the front doorbell brought Simon out of his reverie. Who could that be?

He considered ignoring them. He had a lot to do before his meeting with Guffini.

The bell chimed again. Simon sighed. He guessed he'd better answer it. Still clutching his case, Simon headed to the foyer.

SIXTY-EIGHT

DETECTIVE RYAN TAPPED ON SUPERINTENDENT DAN Dudley's office door.

"Come," Dudley said.

Ryan entered.

"You wanted to see me, sir?"

"Congratulations on your work today, Ryan. Very impressive," the superintendent said, getting up from his desk.

Dudley gestured to a vacant chair opposite two suited men sprawled out on the couch at the back of the room. "Take a seat, and let me introduce you, Ryan," he said.

"I know these gentlemen already, sir," Ryan said, sitting. He indicated the smaller of the two. "Detective Cowan from the Fraud Squad has quite a reputation," he said. "And, of course, I know Detective Jupiter. He's been following me for the best part of a week."

Ryan turned his gaze to Superintendent Dudley. "Detective Jupiter needs to brush up on his surveillance skills, sir. He sticks out like a turd in a fruit bowl."

"Oh, yeah?" Jupiter said. "Well, smart ass, you may have made me, but not before I saw you loading bags of money into the trunk of your car."

Ryan stared at him. "Oh, that," he said after a moment.

"Yes . . . *that*," Jupiter said aggressively.

Detective Cowan placed a restraining hand on Jupiter's arm. "Easy, Dave."

Detective Jupiter turned to Cowan. "Can we just cut to the chase and arrest this crooked bastard?"

"Arrest me?" Detective Ryan said, incredulous.

"Ryan, the Fraud Squad has been investigating the laundering of money by the Faith Company on behalf of Pietro Guffini," Superintendent Dudley said.

"You mean the cash Faith's partner Luke Saker was washing in the Sun Casino before passing it on?" Detective Ryan asked.

"Exactly, Ryan," Detective Jupiter said. "But you forgot to mention your part in that."

The cop stood up. "Detective Ryan, I am arresting you on the charge of larceny. Please hand over your badge and gun."

Ryan didn't move. He looked unfazed.

"Come on, Ryan, you heard him," Cowan said, also standing. "Put everything on the desk."

Detective Ryan still made no move.

"Please, Ryan. Let's not make this any more difficult than it is already," Superintendent Dudley said.

Ryan got up. "You're signing off on this bullshit, then, sir?"

"From what I've seen and heard, there does seem to be strong evidence of your involvement," Superintendent Dudley admitted.

"The evidence is irrefutable. I have photos of you piling cash into the trunk of your car, the money Luke Saker stored at his house," Jupiter said. "Now, your gun."

Detective Ryan stared at Jupiter. "Very well," he said, walking to the superintendent's desk. He unholstered his weapon and placed it on the polished wooden top.

"Your ID and badge, too," Detective Jupiter said as there was a knock on the door.

"Sir," Detective Yang said, entering. "A word?"

"This isn't a good time, Yang," Superintendent Dudley said.

"Sorry, sir, but Detective Ryan mentioned earlier that you may need me to corroborate some information."

"Information?" the superintendent queried.

"Relevant to the proceedings," Detective Yang said, walking over to join her partner. "A short time ago, I accompanied Detective Ryan to the evidence room to deposit a hundred thousand dollars."

She stopped, produced her cell, and pressed the photo tag.

"That's the signed receipt," she said, offering the phone for Superintendent Dudley to view.

Dudley stared at the screen for a moment. "Do you mind if I show this to the others?"

"No, go right ahead."

The superintendent handed the phone to Detective Jupiter. Detective Cowan joined his colleague. They both stared at the receipt.

"It's for the money I collected from Luke Saker's house and deposited as evidence a short time ago," Detective Ryan said.

"This doesn't prove anything," Detective Jupiter said, handing the phone back to Superintendent Dudley. "It's garbage. Ryan is as guilty as sin. He picked that money up this morning. He must have gotten wind that I was about to arrest him, so he handed it in, using his partner as a witness."

Dudley thought for a moment. "You say he's had this money since this morning, Detective Jupiter?" He paused. "Is that correct, Detective Ryan?"

"Yes, sir."

Jupiter smiled. "He should have put it in hours ago, not when he realized we were onto him."

"What have you been doing today, Detective Ryan? Please refresh my memory," Superintendent Dudley asked, feigning ignorance.

"Detective Yang and I have been involved in two bombing incidents and a hostage situation, sir," Ryan said.

"So, not much time to return to headquarters to deposit the money, then?" Dudley said.

"No, sir. That's correct," Detective Ryan confirmed. "Once the crisis ended, I returned to hand in the evidence. After that, I intended to tell you and the Fraud Squad what I knew about the laundered cash."

Detective Jupiter began to say something. Superintendent Dudley held up his hand. "And what is that exactly?" he asked.

"That Simon Faith used his partner, Luke Saker, to help launder Guffini's dirty cash in the Sun Casino. Of course, Saker lost some money but also won a lot back. And, unlike the cash he used for the betting, this new money was clean. Saker stored the winnings at home and took them to Simon Faith weekly. Faith would then remove his cut and pass the rest on to Guffini. The scheme was a win-win for them all," Ryan said.

"Detective Ryan explained this to me earlier, sir," Detective Yang said. "He was aware that a detective from the Fraud Squad had been following him and may have leaped to the wrong conclusion."

"As I said, I intended to clear everything up on my return," Ryan explained.

"And as you noted, sir, both of us were pretty busy before that," Yang added.

"Busy?" Dudley grinned. "That's an understatement."

He looked across at the Fraud Squad detectives. "I think that clears up everything, don't you, gentlemen?"

"It still doesn't explain why he spent time at the casino in the company of a certain Miss Heidi Miller," Jupiter persevered.

"Heidi Miller? Who's she exactly?" Superintendent Dudley asked. "No one has mentioned her to me yet."

"A friend I bumped into the other day during my investigation into the murdered man, Luke Saker. I knew her when I was at university. She's competing in the world poker tournament at the casino," Detective Ryan said.

"A friend?" Jupiter appeared dubious. "Oh, yeah?"

"What are you implying, Detective? I don't think Ryan's personal life has anything to do with any of us, does it?" Dudley interjected.

"Sometimes it does. What about Heidi Miller's connection to Guffini, sir?" Jupiter demanded.

"She knows Pietro Guffini?" Dudley rubbed his hand across his face wearily.

"Heidi Miller is one of several players that Guffini sponsors. He pays for their tournament expenses. I've checked, and this has nothing to do with any of his illegal activities. Taking poker winnings is a legitimate source of income for him, one he uses to polish his businessman's image. I can vouch that Heidi is unaware of the other areas Guffini is involved in and intends to pay off his investment as soon as possible," Ryan explained.

"I see," the superintendent said. "And will you be seeing Ms. Miller again?"

"No. Although I'm confident that she has nothing to do with anything illegal, I realize the optics are not good for me as a working detective," Ryan said. "Anyway, Heidi is leaving Australia as soon as the tournament ends."

"Good." Superintendent Dudley turned to address the Fraud Squad detectives. "This all looks cut and dried to me," he said.

Neither Fraud Squad detective said anything for a long moment. Finally, Detective Cowan turned to his subordinate. "Dave, bearing this new information in mind, I think Detective Ryan should take his gun and badge back."

Everyone turned to stare at Detective Jupiter.

"Fine," Jupiter reluctantly agreed.

"Well, that's good of you both to be so magnanimous," Superintendent Dudley said, watching Ryan retrieve his weapon and ID.

He paused. "I assume everything's been cleared up now, to everyone's satisfaction?"

There were nods and murmurs of agreement.

"That's settled, then," Dudley said. He looked at the Fraud Squad detectives. "Where do you go from here?"

"We're picking up Simon Faith later," Detective Cowan said. "We've enough to get him on a money laundering charge, but the big fish is Pietro Guffini."

"You're going to offer Faith a plea bargain?" Superintendent Dudley asked.

"Yep, and he's going to squeal like a pig. I'll bet my house on it," Detective Jupiter said.

"Excellent. We'll all be delighted to put Guffini behind bars, so good police work all around." Superintendent Dudley stopped. "Now, if there's nothing else, I think this meeting is at an end."

SIXTY-NINE

"Meeting," the big man said to Simon Faith as he opened the front door.

"Yes, but—" Simon stuttered, caught off guard by the unexpected appearance of the henchman.

"Signore Guffini . . . waiting," the giant interrupted. Grasping Simon's arm, he guided him toward the waiting SUV.

Simon tried, unsuccessfully, to free himself from the giant's grip. "One moment. Why hasn't your boss stuck to the original plan?"

"*Non me lo ha detto. Ci ha appena chiesto di prenderti,*" the man replied in Italian.

"English . . . English," Simon pleaded. The colossus ignored him and, opening the front passenger door, pushed Simon into the car. The car's suspension groaned as the giant settled in the back seat.

The driver, another huge man, glanced across at Simon Faith.

"Tik," he said in heavily accented English. Then he pointed to the man in the back. "Tok."

Now, this Simon understood. These two were the infamous Tik and Tok, Guffini's new capos. The hotel boss had never met them but knew they had helped The Owl cement his position as the new crime boss, taking over from the late Oscar Bruno.

The driver, Tik, jabbed his elbow hard into Simon Faith's side. "Belt," he said.

"Okay!" the hotel boss protested, putting the Gladstone bag onto the floor and pulling down the seat belt.

The vehicle took off.

"Where are we going, Tik?" Simon asked.

"No speak English," Tik replied.

"No English," Tok echoed from the back.

Great, thought Simon. How would he get these two onside if they didn't speak the same language?

Then he had an idea.

The hotel boss leaned forward, picked up the bag, and opened it so the driver could see its contents—tightly packed wads of hundred-dollar bills.

"The money," Simon offered.

Tik, the driver, glanced across and smiled.

Good, he understood that, Simon thought.

The hotel boss closed the case and returned it to the floor.

The Brothers Grim remained silent.

Maybe it was time to try again.

"So, will Mr. Guffini be meeting us?" Simon asked.

"No speak English," Tik repeated.

Simon nodded. Yes, he got that the first time. He turned to stare out the car window. They were driving down a road that cut through eucalyptus trees. Where exactly were they going?

Silence.

Then, he had an idea of how to find out.

Simon reached into his pocket. Behind, Tok tensed and leaned forward, slamming his hands hard down onto the CEO's shoulders. Simon swiveled around and opened his jacket slowly.

"Phone . . ." he said, speaking loudly and pointing to the pocket.

Tok smiled and released his hands.

Simon took out his cell, opened his phone contacts, and found the number for The Grocery Man. It was Simon's code name for Guffini. He pressed the screen and waited.

"The number you have dialed has not been recognized," an automated voice said.

Simon wasn't surprised. Guffini must be using a new burner.

Time to try again. "Got number? Your boss?" Simon asked.

Neither of the men said anything. A dead end.

Then Simon had another thought. Holding the phone up, he selected the iPhone Translate app and opened it. He had used the app on trips overseas, and bar a few minor glitches, it had worked well. The hotel boss scrolled through the languages and, reaching Italian, tapped on it. Then, he hit the microphone symbol.

"Where are we meeting?" Simon asked, pointing the cell at the driver and pressing the audio button.

"*Dove ci incontriamo?*" the machine said.

Tik smiled.

Yes, Simon thought, he understood that.

Changing the language to English, the hotel boss pointed the phone at Tik. "Your turn," he said.

"*Proprio in fondo alla strada,*" Tik said.

"Just down the road," the translator voiced.

"How long?" Simon asked.

"*Per quanto?*" came the translation.

"*Presto,*" Tik said.

"Soon," the machine translated as the SUV swung off the road onto a narrow, bumpy track that ran through the trees.

Silence.

The car drove on for about a minute and then slowed to a stop.

"Are we here?" Simon said into the phone.

"*Siamo qui?*" the machine translated.

Tik leaned across, twisted the phone to face him, and spoke. "*Si, hai raggiunto la tua fine.*"

Simon leaned over to press the English translation button.

"Yes, you have reached your end," the mechanical voice translated.

That didn't make complete sense, thought Simon. Maybe it was the big man's accent that confused the translator.

"What does that mean?" Simon said into the device.

"*Cosa vuol dire?*" the automated voice said as Tik yanked the phone from the hotel boss's hand. Simultaneously, Tok leaned forward and wrapped a thin silk scarf around the hotel boss's neck.

"Bye-bye," Tik said as Tok yanked the garotte tight.

Simon twisted and kicked his legs out, desperately trying to free himself, but it was useless. Tok was far too strong.

Simon turned bright red. His eyeballs looked ready to pop out of their sockets. Tok held fast until the man's body went limp.

Tik leaned across, opened the door, and casually pushed Simon's body out of the vehicle. Behind, Tok dialed his phone and waited.

"Is it done?" a voice asked.

"Yes, boss," Tok replied in English.

"And the money?"

"All here, boss."

"Good. Make sure he's never found," The Owl said, ending the call.

Tok put down the phone.

Tik looked across at his brother. *"L'ultimo* (Last one)," he said.

"Si, ci liberiamo di questo stronzo e poi torniamo a casa (Yeah, we get rid of this asshole and then we go home)," Tok replied.

SEVENTY

AN OVERWEIGHT WOMAN IN HER LATE forties, sporting jet-black cropped hair and wearing a bold patterned dress, met Detective Ryan and Detective Yang at the front entrance of the apartment block. She introduced herself as Edwina Jones, the property manager.

Detective Yang offered the manager the search warrant Superintendent Dudley had arranged for them.

Edwina scanned the document. "Everything seems to be in order," she said self-importantly, though it was clear to the detectives that she didn't know what she was looking at. "Follow me, please," she said, heading to Alex Riva's apartment.

Alex had been lucky to find a unit near The Palms Hotel. Just ten minutes away, it was in a nondescript, redbrick, low-rise block from the 1970s.

The property manager and the cops rode the elevator to the third floor. As they ascended, Ryan and Yang slipped on gloves while Edwina peppered the cops with questions: "What exactly has Alex done? Will he return to the apartment? If he doesn't, what will happen to his belongings?"

Detective Ryan parried all the woman's questions, supplying that their search was part of a general police investigation and that no one would be allowed to visit the property until the investigation ended.

Exiting the elevator, Edwina led the cops down the hallway to a green door numbered twenty-one.

"Did Alex have many visitors?" Detective Ryan asked as Edwina pushed the key into the lock.

"I didn't see any." She stopped. "Not that I keep an eye on all the tenants all the time, but . . ."

Edwina stopped as she pushed open the door. The smell of bleach wafted out. She took a step back. "My goodness, that's strong."

"Thank you. We can take it from here," Detective Ryan said, holding out his hand. "We'll return the key when we're done."

"Yes, of course," she said, handing it over.

The detectives stepped into the room.

"Before I go . . ." Edwina said.

The detectives turned.

"I was just thinking . . . Alex worked as a security guard at that hotel." She paused. "The Palms. And I heard there was a bit of trouble there this afternoon."

"Heard?" Ryan asked.

"It was all over the news. Anyway, I'm sure it's nothing, but . . ." Edwina halted and waited. Getting no response, she continued, "But I don't suppose you being here and Alex working at The Palms has anything to do with anything."

Detective Ryan held the manager's gaze. "As I explained, this is an ongoing police investigation, Edwina, so we're not at liberty to release any information."

"Yes . . . yes, of course," she said quickly. "Well, I'll be off, then. If you need anything else, you know where to find me." She turned to go.

"Actually?" Detective Ryan said.

The manager spun around. "Yes."

"Did Alex furnish the place himself?" Ryan asked.

"Yes. The apartment was rented unfurnished."

"Okay, well, thank you," Detective Ryan said.

Reluctantly, Edwina turned to walk back to the elevator.

Detective Yang closed the door firmly as Ryan looked around the open-plan living room, which appeared to have been decorated almost entirely by Ikea. A TV sat on an otherwise empty long brown wood-veneered cabinet. The kitchen countertop ran along the back wall, broken by a fridge, oven, sink, and white cupboards. A microwave sat on the counter, and above it, more white cabinets.

Detective Yang began searching the kitchen area as Ryan headed to the shelving on the other side of the room. He picked up one of the books, Arthur Conan Doyle's *The Adventures of Sherlock Holmes*, and flicked through the well-worn pages.

"He didn't use the kitchen much," Detective Yang said from across the room. "These pots and pans look pristine." She bent down to the sink cabinet and pulled out a plastic bottle of White King bleach. "There are three more where that came from. Alex may not have been a cook, but he was a dedicated cleaner," Detective Yang said.

She closed the cabinet door and walked over to join Detective Ryan. He had put the Sherlock Holmes novel back and was studying another tome.

Yang peered over his shoulder at the book's cover. "*The Monkey's Raincoat*," she read.

"Another one of Alex's collection of detective stories. This one's by Robert Crais . . . the first of a series about a wise-assed private investigator."

"Wise-assed, huh? Now, where do I know a detective like that?" Detective Yang asked, smiling.

THE COPS SEARCHED THE SMALL APARTMENT for the next half hour. In the bedroom, they found Alex's few clothes. He was no snappy dresser. Two pairs of jeans, three plaid shirts, a gray sweater, and K-Mart underwear were in the only closet.

"He doesn't seem to have any photos of his mom, dad, or aunt anywhere," Yang said, looking around.

"Nor any photos of friends. Alex is a loner."

"Except for Irwin Cooper," Detective Yang said.

"Cooper wasn't a friend. He was just someone Alex hooked up with to help carry out his plan," Ryan said as his phone rang.

"Detective Ryan," he answered and listened. "Thank you. We'll be right over," Ryan said, ending the call.

"That was the hospital. Alex Riva is now conscious."

SEVENTY-ONE

B Y ANY LOGIC, ALEX RIVA SHOULD have been dead. But there he was—wide awake and surprisingly chipper.

"You got anything to report about Simon Faith?" he asked, peering up at the two detectives standing over him at the side of his hospital bed.

"Like what?" Detective Ryan asked.

"I just wondered if anything unexpected happened to him since our last meeting?"

"Unexpected?" Ryan repeated.

"You know what I mean," Alex said.

Detective Ryan looked over at Detective Yang. "Any idea what Alex is talking about?"

Detective Yang shook her head. "Not a clue."

"Okay, play that game," Alex said, wheezing. He raised his hand to his mouth as he hacked and croaked. Finally, the coughing fit over, Alex slumped back on the pillow and closed his eyes.

Doctor Jian Chen had told the detectives that they could go ahead with the interview but that, despite appearances, the patient was frail and could lapse into unconsciousness at any time.

"Alex . . . you all right?" Detective Yang asked anxiously.

Riva flicked open his eyes. "Boo," he said. Startled, Detective Yang pulled back.

"All right, Alex, you've had your fun," Detective Ryan said. "Now we've got a few questions for you."

"Tell me what happened to Simon Faith," Alex said.

"Answer my questions, then we'll talk about that," Ryan said.

They stared at each other. Alex blinked first. "I have your word?"

"Yes."

"Okay, ask away," Alex said.

Detective Ryan looked over at Detective Yang, who tapped *record* on her cell and placed it on the bedside table. "Interview with Alex Riva commenced at New Haven Hospital on December 8, 2024, at 18:45. Detective Ryan and Detective Yang are present."

"All right, let's start with Gary Young's murder. Were you and Irwin Cooper responsible for his death?" Ryan said.

"Oh, I thought you'd ask me how I'm feeling," Alex said, grinning. "Not too bad, considering. The doctors said it was a miracle I survived . . .. Something to do with my incredible powers of recovery."

Detective Ryan said nothing.

"Not interested?" Alex said. "Look, if you're going to ask me about anything else, anything criminal, shouldn't I have my lawyer present?"

Detective Ryan sighed. If Alex insisted on a barrister, then it would be pointless to continue the interview.

"It is, of course, your right to have your lawyer present, but that will take time, and in any case, I can't imagine that you could incriminate yourself any further than you already have. But . . ." Ryan shrugged. "It's up to you."

"Also, our little quid pro quo arrangement will be rendered null and void," Yang reminded him.

Alex took a moment to consider his options.

"It might look bad for me, but you've got nothing solid," he mused. "It's all circumstantial—even the standoff on the roof. I mean, you pointed a gun at me. I was afraid for my life."

"And your confession?" Ryan asked.

"What confession? It's just your word against mine."

"Is that right?" Ryan said as he pulled his cell phone from his pocket. "I'm now going to play a recording made on my phone when we were at The Palms Hotel pool," the detective said. He tapped the screen.

"*Was it because of the crash?*"

"*What?*"

"*The reason you killed Gary Young and Luke Saker.*"

"*Duh, yeah . . .*"

"*But you were just eight years old when the accident happened.*"

"*They killed my mom and dad and fucked up the rest of my life.*"

"*Who? Young and Saker?*"

"*Come on, Detective, don't play dumb. They were all in it together.*"

"*The Faith Company?*"

"*Right in one.*"

Detective Ryan clicked off the phone. "You're going to prison, Alex, but helping us could reduce your sentence." The detective paused. "Why don't you start by filling us in on a few details?"

Silence. Alex let out a low sigh. "What do you want to know?" he asked.

"Let's begin with Gary Young's death. Your partner, Irwin Cooper, and you—"

"Not my partner," Alex said quietly.

"What?" Detective Ryan said. "Are you saying that Irwin Cooper wasn't involved?"

"He was involved, but we weren't partners. He was just the dogsbody. He needed me to work everything out."

Bingo, Ryan thought. Alex's belief that he was the smartest man in the room would be his Achilles' heel.

"So, you were the brains of the operation?" Detective Ryan asked.

"Of course. Cooper just did the technical stuff. He helped make the bombs and put the poison into the Coke, but he was not the planner. And he wasn't there when I murdered Gary Young."

"You said you believed that Gary Young was involved in the death of your parents?" Detective Ryan said.

"Not just him."

"No. All three . . . Young, Saker, and Faith?" the detective asked.

"Yes," Alex said and yawned.

"What I'm curious about is why you chose to torture Gary Young. Did he have more of a hand than the others?"

Alex was shaking his head. "I wasn't torturing him, though I can see how you might think that. I just wanted answers."

Ryan was still confused.

"You believed they were all involved . . . ." Ryan frowned, thinking. After a moment, it came to him. "But you just didn't know exactly *how*."

Riva smiled.

"I'd already given Young the poison when I realized it was the perfect opportunity to get all the facts. But he was stubborn. Didn't want to admit to anything. He finally came through when I told him I'd give him the antidote if he'd just come clean."

"Antidote?" Yang asked, surprised.

"There was no antidote." Alex chuckled. "But he didn't know that."

Ryan and Yang exchanged discreet looks. Alex's lack of compassion for his victim was chilling.

"And what did Gary Young tell you?" Ryan asked.

"What I already knew—that my parents refused to sell them the farm. That without that property, all their development plans would have to be scrapped."

"What else did Young say?"

Alex smiled. "He told me that the Faith Company owned garages before it went into development and that Simon Faith was a talented mechanic."

"Simon Faith tampered with the van?" Ryan asked.

"Right. The three partners knew about the protest, and they knew my parents and I were going into the city with the group. They knew, too, that Tommy Clarke, the driver, always parked the Transit van outside his house. So, the night before the protest, Simon Faith loosened the brake lines."

"So the brake fluid would leak out?" Detective Ryan asked.

Alex shook his head. "No."

"What, then?" the detective asked.

"They didn't want the fluid leaking out on the journey down. They just wanted to loosen the nuts. They had calculated that the best place for the brakes to fail would be on the way back as the van went down that steep hill. If Simon Faith had released the fluid that night, the brakes would have failed too soon. The crash had to happen on the return journey."

"So, how did they make sure of that?" Detective Ryan asked.

"You don't know? You haven't figured it out yet?" Alex said, looking at the detectives.

"No," said Detective Ryan. He glanced at his partner.

"No idea," Detective Yang said.

Alex looked from one detective to the other. "I suppose I should have expected that." He smiled bitterly. "It's simple. It was raining heavily the day of the protest, so no one was taking much notice when Simon Faith went under the parked van and finished releasing the loosened brake line. He had done all the calculations. He knew that by the time the van reached the top of the big hill on the return journey, all the brake fluid would be gone." Alex smiled sadly. "And the rest, as they say, is history."

"Incredible," said Detective Yang.

"And Gary Young told you all this?" Ryan asked.

"Yes. But I'd already worked it out. He just confirmed it," Alex said.

"So, even though Simon Faith was the one responsible for the crash . . ." Ryan began.

Alex held his hands up in protest, cutting Ryan off.

"I know what you're going to say, but it doesn't matter who actually did the deed. They were all involved. All a party to it, and they all deserved to die."

Alex slumped back on the bed, resting his head heavily on the pillow. He closed his eyes.

Detective Yang reached for the cell to turn it off, but Detective Ryan shook his head and leaned into Riva. "You waited a long time to kill them, Alex. How come?"

Alex opened his eyes. "What?"

"The accident happened twenty years ago. You're twenty-eight now. What took you so long?"

Alex pushed himself up. "Opportunity knocked, I guess. When I heard about the hotel reopening and knew they were looking for more security guards, I decided the time was right."

"And you persuaded Irwin Cooper to join you?" Ryan said.

"He didn't need to be persuaded once I told him what had caused the van to crash. His wife was killed as well, you know," Alex said emphatically.

"So, he helped you, and then you murdered him?"

"That was your fault," Alex said. "I knew Cooper wasn't strong. I knew you'd get him to talk."

"And the bomb in the caravan? You planted that after you staged his suicide?"

"You were getting too close. I needed the time to deal with Faith." He paused. "Speaking of Simon Faith . . . we had a deal, you and I."

Ryan nodded slowly. "He's alive, Alex. He got out before the vehicle blew up."

Alex fell back onto the bed. "Fuck!" he yelled as the hospital door opened and a white-coated doctor strode in.

"I'm sorry, Detectives, but that will have to be all for today," Doctor Chen said.

Ryan nodded. "Turn off the recorder, Detective Yang."

"The interview ended at 18:50," she said before switching off the iPhone and putting it in her jacket pocket.

Detective Ryan nodded to Detective Yang. "Let's go."

"Ryan!" Alex shouted as the detectives reached the door.

Detective Ryan turned.

"How did you know?" Alex asked.

"Mr. Riva, you really should get some rest," Doctor Chen warned.

"Tell me," Alex said, ignoring the medic. "You owe me that."

Detective Ryan walked back. "That it wasn't just Cooper involved?"

Alex nodded.

"You told me you'd just delivered the eviction notice to Irwin Cooper and that it was the only time you went to his caravan. But the dog—Max—knew you. He quieted down the moment he saw you. That was because you'd been there several times before."

"That's good," Alex said, impressed. "But you still didn't know for certain that I was involved?"

"Not beyond a reasonable doubt, no," the detective admitted.

Ryan reached for his cell and pressed the screen, lowering it for Alex to view. He pointed to two photos. One was a copy of the picture Anne Clarke had shown them of the protestors standing by the van. The other was the same photo, but it had been enhanced.

"Before and after," Detective Ryan said. "That's you as an eight-year-old

. . ." Ryan pointed to one photo and then to the other. "And that's you *after* the techs ran aging software on the child's face."

Alex stared at it. The altered face in the picture bore a spooky resemblance to the murderer. "Yeah . . . it does look like me. Not exactly, but close."

"Right. And Anne Clarke also told us the boy's name, Sasha. When I was a kid, we had a Russian neighbor who was a Sasha. He told me once that it was short for Alexander. Alex," Ryan said pointedly. "Anne also told me that the child's parents were Spanish, so the child had two last names, his father's *and* his mother's . . . Morina Riva. So that's you. Alex, or Sasha . . . Morina Riva."

SEVENTY-TWO

LEAVING THE HOSPITAL, DETECTIVE RYAN AND Detective Yang went their separate ways. Zoe returned home, promising to type up the interview early tomorrow morning. Meantime, Ryan set off for his rendezvous at the Sun Casino. It was to be his last call of the night.

Arriving and heading for the underground casino car park, the detective suddenly braked and pulled to the side of the road. Jumping out, he ran toward the front entrance.

"Heidi!" the detective shouted at the woman wheeling a suitcase out of the building.

Looking around, Heidi Miller stopped and waited for Ryan to reach her.

"You're leaving?" Detective Ryan asked.

Heidi reddened. "Yes."

"But I told you I was on my way over."

Heidi looked around, making sure no one was close. "Haven't you got into enough trouble already because of me, Ramesh?"

"I thought . . ."

Heidi leaned into him. "What did you tell them?"

"Who?"

"Your people. Your boss. Superintendent Dudley, isn't it?"

"I said that Guffini was your sponsor and that that part of his business was legal."

Heidi let out a wry laugh. "Sure. And they said, 'Well, that's all right then.'"

"No, not exactly," Ryan admitted.

"I thought not," Heid said, looking around as a car drew up opposite.

"That's my Uber, Ramesh," Heidi said, looking across at the vehicle. She walked over and tapped the trunk. As it clicked open, Ramesh took the case and lifted it in.

As he turned, Heidi pulled the detective to her and kissed him passionately before finally pulling away.

"I've got to go, Ramesh," she said.

"You sure?"

"No . . .." Her smile was bittersweet. "But there's no alternative."

The detective went to speak, but Heidi raised her hand. "I play poker for a living. It's the life I've chosen. And you chose to be a detective. We're like oil and water. We don't mix." She paused. "I've going to a poker tournament in Rome, and then to one in Las Vegas, and then who knows? And you? Where will you be?" It was a question Heidi answered herself. "You'll be here, Ramesh, catching criminals like Pietro Guffini."

The detective stared at her. "Will you come back?"

"Teaming up with Guffini was the worst decision of my life. I was desperate for a backer and didn't think things through. . . . But will I return? Yes, maybe. But only after I've paid him back."

"So, there's hope?"

"There's always hope." Heidi stopped. "Okay, I've got to go." She kissed Ramesh again, briefly this time, before pulling open the car door. "Keep well. And say hello to your mother," she said as she climbed into the vehicle.

The car took off.

Ryan kept watching until it disappeared around the bend.

SEVENTY-THREE

RYAN HARDLY SLEPT A WINK. NOT because of Heidi, though. He'd accepted her decision and her reasons for it. Ever since Heidi had come clean about their "chance" meeting, they'd both known that a serious relationship would never be possible.

It was one of the few times in his life when Ryan had failed to heed his instincts. Running into Heidi in the middle of a murder investigation, right after a meeting with Guffini, should have rung alarm bells. But seeing her again knocked every bit of common sense out of him. Luckily for him, she told him the truth—that Guffini, having discovered their connection, had asked Heidi to rekindle the romance, hoping he could exploit the relationship.

But Heidi flipped the script. Instead of supplying the crime boss with information about the Homicide Squad, she told Ryan about The Owl's money laundering activities and the link between him and the Faith Company.

So, Heidi wasn't responsible for Ryan's lousy night. His dreams had been filled with thoughts of death and dying—not his own, though, but his mother's.

And when he picked her up in the morning, she immediately knew something was wrong.

"Ramesh, you look awful!" his mother exclaimed as she climbed into his car.

He ignored the comment. "What's in that?" he asked, pointing at the carrier bag she placed at her feet.

"Groceries. When this is all over, I will cook you a meal." She stopped. "I assume you've taken the day off."

"Yes, Mom," he said. "Now, put your seatbelt on, please."

His mother pulled the belt over her shoulder and clipped it in as Ryan pulled into the road.

"So, where's Harry? Is he meeting us at the hospital?" Ryan asked.

Mumta snorted. "That dog. What is it about men? Middle-aged, and they still behave like children!"

Ramesh glanced at her. "I take it you're not seeing him anymore?"

"Of course not. One meal, that's all we had, and he was lucky to get that. He turned out to be a real . . ." She paused. "Player. That's the kindest word I can think of. He had pages on Tinder, RSVP, and Plenty of Fish."

Ryan shook his head in disbelief. His mother didn't just know how to use a computer, she had searched the Internet for dating sites that Harry King was still on. It was a revelation.

Mumta saw her son's expression. "I know," she said. "You're like the rest of them, believing all our brain cells die when we reach sixty. You thought I wouldn't check up on the dog?"

"It's not that . . .." Ryan began.

"Nonsense! Now, keep your eyes on the road. Do you want to kill me before we even reach the hospital?"

Mumta insisted Ramesh wait in the hospital cafeteria rather than "hanging around outside the doctor's office like grim death."

After his mother left, Ramesh bought a coffee and nervously waited. Time seemed to stand still, so he was relieved when his phone rang—anything to distract him.

"Ryan, I'm sorry to bother you on your day off, but you did tell Yang that you would take calls today," Superintendent Dan Dudley said.

"Yes, no problem," Ryan replied.

"Good. Look, compliments again on breaking the Young/Saker murder case. With the interview and all the evidence you put together, the trial should be a slam dunk. There's little doubt Alex Riva will spend the rest of his life behind bars."

"Thank you, sir," Detective Ryan said and waited. The superintendent wouldn't be calling simply to repeat his congratulations. Something was up.

"And on the other thing." Dudley paused.

Here it was. "The other thing, sir?" Ryan asked.

"The Fraud Squad . . . I followed up with Cowan and Jupiter."

"Really," Detective Ryan said, surprised.

"Don't sound so shocked, Ryan. No one messes with one of mine without dealing with me."

"Yes. Right, sir." Detective Ryan was dubious.

"Don't say it like that, Ryan. Maybe I wasn't clear yesterday, but I didn't for one second give credence to anything they said about you."

"I know that, sir," the detective said. Part of him wanted to believe what his boss had just said, but he suspected Dudley would have joined the baying pack if there had been even a sliver of real proof of his involvement in anything illegal. That wasn't surprising. Bent cops were despised by one and all in the force.

"Anyway, the point is, I knew that once they arrested Simon Faith, there would be more proof that you were innocent," Dudley continued.

"More proof?" Ryan repeated.

"That's not to say that the explanation supplied by Detective Yang and you wasn't sufficient," Superintendent Dudley qualified.

"Right, sir."

"As you know, Simon Faith was to be turned so that he would testify against Pietro Guffini."

"Yes, sir."

"Well, there was no sign of him when they went to his house. He'd flown the coop, presumably after somehow getting wind of his imminent arrest."

"You think someone tipped him off?" Detective Ryan asked.

"Seems the most likely explanation, I'm sorry to say."

"There is one other possibility," the detective said.

"Go on."

"Perhaps Guffini killed Simon Faith to prevent him from spilling his guts." As he said it, Ryan saw his mother enter the café.

"You could be right, Ryan. You could be right," Dudley mused.

"Sir, I'm sorry, but I've got to go." He ended the call just as Mumta reached him.

"Well, Mom?" Ramesh asked anxiously, scanning her face for clues.

SEVENTY-FOUR

"IT'S MY RESTING BITCH FACE," MUMTA reasoned. "That's what the youth say, isn't it?"

"I don't think you've got that kind of face," Ryan said diplomatically.

Mumta ignored him, concentrating instead on stirring the chicken, onions, and spices that filled the pan.

"So, you're saying you didn't do it on purpose?" Ryan asked.

"What?" Mumta appeared distracted.

"Look like the end of the world was nigh, back at the hospital?"

"Of course not."

"But you weren't smiling. You looked shocked."

"We went through this on the way home, Ramesh. I told you I was trying to remember whether I had brought the turmeric. I knew I'd be in serious trouble if I had forgotten that. There's no way you would have that spice here. Now, let me get on with the cooking."

"But you still haven't told me exactly what the doctor said."

"I have. I told you he confirmed I was fine."

"It was a false alarm?" Ryan asked.

"Yes."

"Which the biopsy showed?"

"Yes."

Finally! Ryan put his arms around his mother, pulled her toward him, and hugged her tight. "Thank God." Finding murderers was chicken feed compared to the thought of his mother having cancer.

Mumta pulled away and returned to stirring. "So, enough about me. I want to hear more about you."

"Well, we've just solved the case and found the murderers. There were two of them, and—" Ryan began.

"Yes, fine," Mumta interrupted. "You can tell me more about all that later. What I want to hear about is you and Heidi."

Ryan took a deep breath. "There is no me and Heidi. We decided to go our separate ways."

Mumta stared at her son.

"Don't look at me like that, Mom. These things happen."

Silence. "Yes, I suppose. Though I'm sure it didn't help, you being a detective."

More silence. "So now, after Heidi, have you anyone else on the horizon?"

"We only split up yesterday," Ryan said.

"It's never too soon to get back on the horse," Mumta said.

"And there's plenty more fish in the sea," she continued. "Which, by the way, is the name of one of the sites I've signed up for. Perhaps you should, too?"

Ryan shuddered. He couldn't imagine anything worse than looking for a girlfriend on a dating app.

"Well?" Mumta said when her son didn't answer.

"Yes, fine, Mom. I'll do that," Ryan answered, saying what he knew his mother wanted to hear.

Satisfied, Mumta peered into the mixture bubbling on the hob. "This'll be ready in a few more minutes."

"It smells delicious," Ryan said, looking over his mother's shoulder.

"Well, it'll taste even better," she said. "Now, get me some bowls, will you?"

Ryan reached into the overhead cupboard and pulled out two white dishes. As he put them on the counter, there was a knock on the front door.

"Sorry to disturb you," Strata President Maude Adams said as Detective Ryan opened the door. "I saw you arrive and just had to tell you the good news. The thing is . . ." Maude stopped and pointed over his shoulder. "Is that your mother, Detective?"

Ryan turned. Mumta had just walked into the living room.

"Hello," Maude said, waving.

"Oh, hello," Mumta said, coming over. "Mumta Ryan, Ramesh's mother."

"Lovely to meet you, Mrs. Ryan," Maude said. "And that's a pretty . . . ah . . . piece of material you're wearing."

"It's called a sari," Mumta said.

"Well, whatever it is, it looks beautiful on you." Maude paused. "I'm the strata president, Maude Adams, Mrs. Ryan."

"Oh, right. Nice to meet you," Mumta said before turning and walking to the couch.

Maude leaned into Ryan. "It's a pleasure to meet someone keen to advertise their roots."

Ramesh forced a smile.

"I'm all for bringing more cultural color and diversity to Australia. You know . . . overseas influences." Maude paused. "Like yourself, Detective Ryan."

"I'm Australian, Maude," Ramesh said.

"Really? I thought because . . ." She stopped. "Of course, you must be . . . you being a police—"

"You said you had good news?" Ryan interrupted.

"Yes. About the rats."

"What about them?"

"Poisoned . . . every last one of them." She clapped her hands. "All gone. *Vamonos.*" Maude paused. "That's how you'd say it in your mother's language, right?"

"No, that's Spanish. And she would say they're all gone, just like you, because she speaks English."

"Oh, well, whatever. The point is we are free of the pestilence. Good news, huh?"

"Yes. Indeed." Ryan paused, pointedly waiting.

"Well, I'd best be off," Maude said, taking the hint. She looked over at Mumta. "Bye, Mrs. Ryan. Lovely to meet you."

"Likewise," came the reply from the sofa.

Ryan closed the door and headed across to his mother. "The curry should be cooked by now, right?"

Mumta stood up. "Yes. Let's go see."

IN THE KITCHEN, MUMTA SPOONED UP the bubbling liquid and tasted it. "It's good," she confirmed, picking up a bowl and scooping the curry into the dish. "Did I hear that awful woman say something about rats?"

"Yes, we've had a plague of them."

"A plague," Mumta repeated. "So, let me get this straight, Ramesh. Not only does it look like I'll be waiting for a grandchild for some time, but you have also just bought a property overrun with vermin?" Mumta said, offering her son the bowl.

"That's about right, Mom," Ramesh said, trying the curry. "But on the plus side, I have unlimited access to some of the best Indian food in Sydney. So, my life's not all bad, is it?"

Mumta tried unsuccessfully to keep the pleased look from her face.

"Ramesh Ryan, you are a shameless flatterer," she said coyly.

Ramesh kissed his mother softly on her cheek.

"Nothing but the truth, Mom. Nothing but the truth."

The Peralta Brothers

CLIVE FLEURY IS AN AWARD-WINNING WRITER of novels and screen-plays, including most recently the murder mystery *Off Season*, which was the first in the Detective Ryan Mystery series. He is also a TV/Film writer, director, and producer who has worked for major broadcasters and studios on a wide variety of successful drama and documentary projects, in the US, the UK, Europe, Australia, and the Middle East. He has written and directed four feature films, one of which, "Big City Blues," starred Giancarlo Esposito, the late Burt Reynolds, and Balthazar Getty. His most recent film, "Sons of Summer," is a surfing movie set on the Gold Coast of Australia and stars Temuera Morrison and Isabel Lucas. Clive currently spends his time between Miami, Florida, and Sydney, Australia.